**THE THRILLING STORY OF
COURAGEOUS MEN AND PASSIONATE
WOMEN — AND THEIR GLORIOUS
DESTINY ON THE TEXAS FRONTIER!**

CHARLES JUSTISS — He went west with his family
to the raw, untouched country of Texas where herds
of maverick longhorn roamed free — and fame and
fortune waited for men of courage and vision.

ANGELA JUSTISS — Behind her dark-haired
beauty was a rock-hard determination and fearless
devotion to her husband and their children as they
battled for survival against scorching summers, winter blizzards, and the savage raids of bloodthirsty
Indians.

TOGETHER, with a few close relatives and friends,
they would form the largest cattle operation in Palo
Pinto County, symbolizing the fulfillment of their
dreams and hard-won ideals in the glorious new
land!

TEXAS BRAZOS: CADDO CREEK

**SADDLE UP FOR ADVENTURE
WITH G. CLIFTON WISLER'S
TEXAS BRAZOS!**
A SAGA AS BIG AND BOLD AS TEXAS ITSELF,
FROM THE NUMBER-ONE PUBLISHER
OF WESTERN EXCITEMENT

#1: TEXAS BRAZOS (1969, $3.95)
In the Spring of 1870, Charlie Justiss and his family follow
their dreams into an untamed and glorious new land — battling the worst of man and nature to forge the raw beginnings of what is destined to become the largest cattle
operation in West Texas.

#2: FORTUNE BEND (2069, $3.95)
The epic adventure continues! Progress comes to the raw
West Texas outpost of Palo Pinto, threatening the Justiss
family's blossoming cattle empire. But Charlie Justiss is
willing to fight to the death to defend his dreams in the
wide open terrain of America's frontier!

#3: PALO PINTO (2164, $3.95)
The small Texas town of Palo Pinto has grown by leaps and
bounds since the Justiss family first settled there a decade
earlier. For beautiful women like Emiline Justiss, the ad-
vent of civilization promises fancy new houses and proper
courting. But for strong men like Bret Pruett, it means new
laws to be upheld — with a shotgun if necessary!

#4: CADDO CREEK
During the worst drought in memory, a bitter range war
erupts between the farmers and cattlemen of Palo Pinto
for the Brazos River's dwindling water supply. Peace must
come again to the territory, or everything the settlers had
fought and died for would be lost forever!

*Available wherever paperbacks are sold, or order direct from the
Publisher. Send cover price plus 50¢ per copy for mailing and
handling to Zebra Books, Dept. 2257, 475 Park Avenue South,
New York, N.Y. 10016. Residents of New York, New Jersey and
Pennsylvania must include sales tax. DO NOT SEND CASH.*

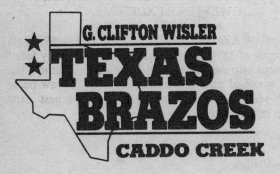

G. CLIFTON WISLER

TEXAS BRAZOS

CADDO CREEK

ZEBRA BOOKS
KENSINGTON PUBLISHING CORP.

ZEBRA BOOKS

are published by

Kensington Publishing Corp.
475 Park Avenue South
New York, NY 10016

Copyright © 1988 by G. Clifton Wisler

All rights reserved. No part of this book may be repro-
duced in any form or by any means without the prior
written consent of the Publisher, excepting brief quotes
used in reviews.

First printing: January 1988

Printed in the United States of America

for David Eiland,
who has known adversity
and found courage

PALO PINTO COUNTY C.1881

Prologue

The Brazos River etches its way into the heart of Texas. From its beginnings in the springs of the caprock country in the far west, the stream stretches nine hundred winding miles before emptying into the Gulf of Mexico.

The history of the Brazos is the story of Texas. The ancient tribes who made their camps along its banks called it Giver of Life. The Spanish who first traversed the wild, seemingly endless grasslands named it *Brazos de Dios,* the Arms of God, for according to legend, only the river's life-giving waters saved the early settlers from death in a time of terrible drought. When the young American dreamer Stephen Austin sought a home for his colony, he chose the hilly country above the Brazos. San Felipe, his first town, sprang up along the banks of the river.

Following independence, Texans began moving north and west up the Brazos's often turbulent waters. By the 1850s Waco was flourishing, and cotton plantations lined the lower half of the river. Even so, the upper Brazos remained a hostile country, left to marauding Comanches and rattlesnakes.

The Civil War found but a few hundred settlers in Palo Pinto County, and many of those abandoned their dog-run cabins and cornfields following fierce Comanche raids in '64. War's close saw the upper Brazos little changed from the time the first hawk had circled the Castle Cliffs. Poverty and desperation soon changed that, though.

By 1870 many Texans who'd struggled to restore their state to its prewar prosperity had abandoned hope. Federal troops still occupied the state, and the government was often more responsive to military garrisons and Washington politicians than to the needs or wants of the people. Taxes soared, and those lacking the income to meet the tax collector's bill lost their land and their home.

But where despair spreads its dark shawl, hope often begins to flicker. For on the desolate stretches of prairie to the west roamed thousands of raw-boned, lumbering longhorn cattle, and by 1868 determined men had rounded up herds of the cantankerous creatures and driven them to markets in Missouri and Kansas. The lure of cattle fortunes and vast lands drew new, iron-willed men to the upper Brazos. They outlasted the Indians and endured the harsh climate. The long trails to Abilene and Dodge City forged them into the strongest of breeds.

Spring 1881 fell upon a land much changed. The Ft. Worth and Western Railroad, barely a year old, was bringing emigrants eager to share a brightening future. Lawbooks and courthouses supplanted the Colt and the Winchester as rulers of the range. Churches and schools brought the steadying influences of wives and families, and in many places chased saloons and brothels from the huddle of wooden buildings that made up the handful of towns along the frontier. Civilization was arriving. Some greeted it with open arms. Others mourned the passing of the old, unfettered ways. One man merely noted the changing world as he observed the gray now sprinkled liberally in his hair.

"It seems the world's grown old," Charlie Justiss grumbled.

Perhaps it was that sense of an era fast slipping away that prompted Charlie to set off westward across the rocky plain toward the Clear Fork of the Brazos. He sat his tall black Arabian stallion as if he were still leading his regiment into battle in the wilderness. Major Charlie Justiss, Fourth Texas Infantry, they'd called him then. The whole regiment had shrunk to scarcely a hundred men when General Lee had set aside his sword at Appomattox. And Charlie had turned homeward to begin a new battle.

That bright May morning he rode between his two youngest sons. To his left rode Joe. At fifteen, the dark-haired youngster had turned lean and hard. Though still prone to pranks, Joe could put his shoulder to a task when it was necessary, and boys in the growing town of Palo Pinto had come to look to him as a leader. More and more young Joe put Charlie in mind of himself in an earlier day.

Chris, on the other hand, was as wild as his unkempt straw-colored hair. Not quite fourteen nor five and a half feet tall, the boy was forever vexing his mother by embarking on adventures during school hours or tormenting the neighbors with this scheme or that. If he wasn't peeking at the bathing Cooke girls, he was likely loosening the wheels on old Granny Grider's buggy or gluing little Ingrid Frost's pigtails to her school bench. The whole town must have breathed a sigh of relief when Charlie rode off with Chris in tow.

"Papa, did you and Uncle Bowie really hunt buffalo out this way once?" Chris asked as Charlie turned his horse off the Albany road northwest toward Fort Griffin.

"Once," Charlie said, pausing to stare at the broken hills and tall grassland. "This was Comanche country back then."

"I can barely remember the Indians," Joe said. "I recall you taking us up to the cliffs when the burying scaffolds were still there."

"I wanted you to see that," Charlie said, wiping beads of sweat from his forehead as he looked north toward where the Brazos even now churned through the west Texas countryside. "A man needs to know the past, *his* past. There's value in that."

"It's why you took us to Fort Worth with the cattle," Chris added. "I wish we could do that again. I like the trail, and I miss the ranch. Nowadays we're all cooped up in town!"

"Not so much as you should be," Charlie complained. "You've got a fine way of drifting off to the river, I understand."

"Well, a Texan can't pass all his growing days staring at Vicki's schoolbooks. He's got to have

12

space to breathe."

"You'd do better to mind your sister and do your lessons, son," Charlie warned.

"Marty says—"

"Marty Steele's a fine cowboy," Charlie said, "but he's not apt to be anything else. That's fine for Marty, as it is for any man that's set on the notion, but you're not yet shaving, Chris Justiss, and I'd have it so you can make your own mind up on what you want for a life. Wes Tyler rides the range, too, but he's settled, has a wife and a family. Being a loner's a hard life."

"Marty does fine by it."

"Maybe, but I don't know it's ever done much for Marty," Charlie said, sadly shaking his head. "Anyway, when you're older, you will do the deciding. For now, your mama and I'll call it as we see fit. Hear me?"

"Yes, sir," Chris mumbled.

Joe, who was obviously enjoying his brother's discomfort, said nothing. Charlie Justiss, aside from being county judge and the largest landowner for fifty miles, was well known to rule his house with a firm hand.

It was well past noon when the three riders topped a small hill and came upon the deserted remains of Fort Griffin Town. Better know as the Flat, the little settlement of picket houses and clapboard sheds had once boasted a dozen saloons, outfitting shops for buffalo hunters, and hospitality houses for the nearby soldiers and everyone from drifting cowboys

13

to professional gamblers. Now only skeleton frameworks remained, and a wild hog or two rooted amidst the refuse left behind.

"This was the Flat," Charlie told the boys.

Their eyes stared in disbelief. The place was legend, for many a tale of the Flat had been spun by veteran cowboys and older brothers. So little remained!

"There are the soldiers," Joe suddenly cried, pointing out a small troop of cavalrymen descending from a hill to the northwest.

"It's really true, Papa," Chris said, sighing. "The cavalry's leaving Fort Griffin."

"No Indians left to fight," Charlie explained. "Frontier's grown tame. Truth is, they probably kept the post active a half-dozen years after it was needed."

"Probably," Joe agreed.

"Still, I hate to see it happen," Charlie confessed. "And I'm hanged if I'll let Henry Eppler leave the Brazos without at least one old friend around to see him off."

"Papa?" Joe asked, surprised at the sudden anger filling his father's voice.

"Marty says we're well rid of those Yanks," Chris declared. "Those bluecoats never were much to speak of."

"They saved your hide when you were still cutting teeth," Charlie responded. "Henry Eppler's as good a man as you'll meet, and he stood side by side with us when some Yanks would just as soon've turned the whole Comanche nation loose on Texas. He got us our first mustang contract, and we'd never paid our taxes if he hadn't recommended we supply beef to Fort Griffin. He's grown gray on the frontier, and he's had little thanks for it from the Army. They've left him a captain in a backwater fort these past five years, and now they're determined to retire him. Well, I'd have him know he's got friends!"

Charlie drew his horse to a halt as the narrow column of horsemen made its way down the hill from the abandoned fort. The boys remained silent. When the soldiers came closer, it was clear to see most were happy to leave behind the stark stone barracks that stood atop the treeless hillside. In summer soldiers called the place Fort Hell, and in winter blizzards would sweep through the place with a vengeance, near freezing anything or anybody in their path.

"Where'll they go?" Joe asked.

"Another fort," Charlie answered. "Those with time still to serve."

"And the captain?" Chris asked, pointing to the solitary officer riding alongside a wagon. Two blond-haired boys slightly younger than Chris stared out the open bed. A petite woman drove the wagon with a firm hand.

"Let's go see," Charlie said, leading Chris and Joe across the intervening ground.

Captain Henry Eppler bore the scars of fifteen years' service on the frontier. His forehead was etched with the worries of command, and his hair showed traces of silver, though in fact the captain was but thirty-six years old. Riding beside his wife,

Catherine, and their two boys Josiah and William, the veteran cavalryman appeared younger, lighter in the saddle. Charlie Justiss couldn't help seeing shades of the youthful lieutenant he'd met near Palo Pinto eleven long, hard years before.

"Well, look who's come to bid us farewell," the captain declared when Charlie and the boys rode up.

"Seemed fitting somebody should be here," Charlie answered. "There's a lot of history in old Fort Griffin, and I hate the notion of its closing being witnessed by rooting hogs and turkey buzzards."

"Thank you for that," Captain Eppler said, nodding sadly as he glanced back at the fort. "Some suggested we leave at dusk, what with the heat and all, but I wouldn't have it. There's not but our one company, but I still thought we should parade. Maybe only ghosts can see, but we're little more than ghosts ourselves these days, eh, Charlie?"

"I wouldn't order a headstone just yet. We've got these boys to see raised, and that's likely to take years of work."

"Oh, they're coming along," the captain said, grinning at his sons. "It may be a bit of a trial for them, living a normal life for once, but they'll soon grow accustomed to having a father home for dinner."

"I will, at least," Catherine Eppler announced. "As for Josiah and Will, they've never known a loose rein, have you, boys?"

The two sandy-haired youngsters shook their heads as if on command, and Charlie smiled.

"So, what will you do?" Charlie asked. "I suppose you'll see the men to their new post."

16

"No, just to Albany," Captain Eppler explained. "I'm a citizen again. Official orders came last week. Truth is, I thought maybe I'd head for Palo Pinto. I heard a man could make a living running horses if he knew his business."

"And if he didn't mind raising a few cows on the side," Charlie said, cheering at the thought of the captain as a neighbor. "There are two or three places up for sale."

"Papa, the Fletcher Place," Joe said excitedly. "It's right on the road, close to town, and there's good grass. There's fair water most of the year, too."

"Sounds good," the captain said. "Provided the price is within our means."

"Mrs. Fletcher's a widow of late," Charlie explained. "She's gone to her sister in Austin, and the daughter's grown and married. Ross's handling the sale, and I'd say the asking price would be more than reasonable. There's cheaper land down south, but the Fletcher place has maybe twenty acres cleared for corn, a good corral, and a house."

"What manner of house?" Mrs. Eppler asked.

"Not much of one," Chris said, laughing. "Spiders and lizards all over the place. Chased a skunk out of the kitchen just last Friday."

"Roof needs some work," Charlie said, scowling at Chris. "Nothing a man with a few shingles couldn't tend. You'll want to add a room for the boys. It's rough, but it'll get you through a Brazos winter."

"Then, it will survive anything," Mrs. Eppler declared. "It's bound to be an improvement over Fort Griffin. What's more, the boys will be close to town.

17

There's a school in Palo Pinto as I recall."

"My daughter's school," Charlie said proudly. "I send Joe and Chris there. Sometimes they even stay through the day's last lesson."

Chris turned his head aside in embarrassment, and the Eppler boys laughed.

"You boys will like that school just fine," Captain Eppler declared. "I've seen Mrs. Pruett. She's as pretty as a peach, and only half as old as that old hag of a sergeant's wife at Griffin."

"Watch her, though," Chris warned. "She swings a switch good as anybody you ever saw. I got the marks to prove it."

Charlie laughed, but Chris's sour look drew respectful nods from the other youngsters.

"Then, it seems that's settled," Captain Eppler said, extending a hand to Charlie. "I'll meet with Ross and sign the papers. Meanwhile, we can stay in the hotel."

"Nonsense," Charlie replied. "You'll be our guest in town. That old house wants company, and it will give the boys a chance to get acquainted. Besides, Georgia Staves asks three dollars a room now at the hotel!"

"It only costs two bits to sleep at the livery," Joe said, "and you can even take a bath in the trough if you like. No charge."

"We'll keep that in mind," the captain said, grinning at his wife. "Meanwhile, I thank you for your hospitality. I'll be making my farewells to the men now. We'll be along toward evening."

"I'll have Angela wait supper."

Charlie then waved Chris and Joe along, and the

18

Epplers were left to say their good-byes to the soldiers and others heading south. Charlie recalled parting company with the twenty scarecrow survivors of the long trek home from Virginia. It was best he leave Henry Eppler to himself for a time. Later there'd be a change to talk, to plan, to chart the future.

"Wasn't it around here that you fought old Stands Tall, Papa?" Chris asked.

Charlie gave a final glance to Fort Griffin, stared grimly at the ruins of the Flat that would, like the ancient scaffolds atop the Castle Cliffs, decay and be swept away by the winds of time.

"Just east of here," Charlie said, pointing at a nearby hill. "We were . . ."

The tale was an old one, and Charlie had told it often. Just then it warmed him to share the past with his sons, for they were the future. Perhaps they would carry with them the legacy of their father, would remember the struggles and the pain. Charlie hoped so.

I. The Newcomers

Chapter One

Caddo Creek marked the Flying J Ranch's western boundary. It had been that way from the moment Charlie Justiss first reached Palo Pinto County. The ranch had spread eastward to the Jacksboro road, and new acreage had been added south of the railway tracks, but the land to the west had long remained deserted, a final vestige of open range stretching on into Stephens County.

That had recently changed. As Charlie made his monthly ride along the ranch's perimeter with his son Billy, he spotted signs of activity on the far side of the creek. Range crews were busily rounding up unbranded longhorns. Smoke from a cook camp marred an otherwise clear horizon.

"I suppose it's time we had neighbors out that way," Charlie said as he nudged his horse into the shallows of the creek. "Lord knows we've got them everywhere else."

Billy followed his father into the creek. No sooner had they reached the far bank than a pair of riders galloped up. One, a tall rangy fellow, waved a pistol at Charlie and called to halt.

"Hold on there," Charlie shouted, holding his arms out to show he carried no weapon. "We mean you no harm."

"This is Kemp land!" the stranger yelled. "We don't abide trespassers."

"We're your neighbors!" Billy cried. "We've only come to meet you."

"Neighbors?" the rider asked. "Well, I don't know about that. Where we come from, there are just two reasons for crossin' onto another man's land, and neither one gets you much of a welcome."

"Well, things are different here in Palo Pinto," Charlie declared. "I'm Charlie Justiss, and this is my son Billy. Our place begins just the other side of Caddo Creek there."

"Oh?"

"I'm the county judge now, so Billy runs the ranch. I don't believe I caught your name."

"Kermit Kemp," the rider responded without lowering the pistol. "My pa owns this land, and you're trespassing."

"Trespassing?" Billy cried. "Why, we were fighting Comanches here before you even thought about moving in."

"We've got title now," a voice boomed out from a stand of junipers. Charlie turned that way in time to see a large man emerge on horseback from the trees.

"You'd be Kemp," Charlie said, nodding.

"Isaac Kemp, though nowadays everyone calls me Ike. I wasn't expecting company. Usually folks wait for an invite before they cross another's land."

Charlie paused a moment. Before responding, he studied his new neighbor. Kemp was broad-shouldered, with a neck thick like a mule's. He weighed well over 250 pounds, and his dark brow and grim face were a marked contrast to the easy smiles worn by most of the county's ranchers. All in all, Kemp appeared to belong in one of Bowie Justiss's rail gangs more than atop a horse supervising summer roundup.

"Hereabouts, it's considered unfriendly not to welcome newcomers," Charlie finally explained. "Besides, I don't get out this way too often. My work keeps me in town most of the time."

"Oh?" Kemp asked. "Do a lot of judgin', do you?"

"Not much trial work," Charlie replied. "But with every train dropping off another dozen emigrants, it seems there's no end to the titles and surveys to record."

"I filed my papers in Stephens County. We've only got ourselves a slice of acres over here in Palo Pinto."

"Well, we're neighbors even so, and if I can be of service, call on me."

"You can," Kemp said, gazing coldly into Charlie's eyes. "You can get off my land. And stay off. I don't like visitors as a general rule, and I've heard enough about you, Justiss, to know I don't care for you. You milked the range dry of longhorns, and now you'd shut off the open range to others by backin' a bunch of hog farmers! Get clear. Next time, Kermit's apt to use that Colt."

"There's no call for such talk," Billy objected.

Kermit Kemp answered by firing a shot that tore a limb from a nearby live oak. The cowboys on the hillside laughed as Billy struggled to control his horse. Charlie only stared coldly at the Kemps and fought to control his anger.

"I wish you well," Charlie called as he led the way back into Caddo Creek. "A man without neighbors has need of good fortune."

"Papa, I don't like this one bit," Billy said after they had ridden a mile southwest toward the line cabin. "I didn't like that one with the pistol even before he fired it."

"It's best we alert Wes, have him keep a rider along the creek for a time. It wouldn't be the first time rustlers moved in on us."

"No, sir," Billy agreed. "Want me to send word to Bret as well?"

"No," Charlie said, shaking his head. "Could be they're just being cautious. Ranching has been a hazardous trade down south the past few years. Might be they've got reason to be jumpy. I don't want to start a feud."

"All right, but I think maybe I'd like to wire Lafe Freeman. I hear he and Malachi Johnson were through here a week back. I wouldn't mind having 'em close-by in case there's trouble."

"Wire 'em," Charlie said, urging his horse into a slow trot. Freeman and Johnson had passed half a decade in the cavalry, and the ex-buffalo soldiers had proved more than able to protect the Ft. Worth and Western rail camps from outlaws. It was Lafe, after all, who killed the notorious Raymond Polk.

"I could send word to Austin, too," Billy suggested. "Find out where this Kemp came from, where he's been before."

"That would be his business, son," Charlie said, halting his horse long enough to stare back across the creek. "So far he's brought us no sorrow, and prying into his past is only going to stir up trouble. Let it rest. We've got other matters to deal with."

Charlie spoke no more about his meeting with Ike Kemp. It clearly troubled him to have such a tight-mouthed neighbor, but after all, he'd endured Comanches and rustlers in his time. He could tolerate Ike Kemp. And in time, perhaps Kemp would soften.

Indeed, when next Charlie happened upon his new neighbor, Kemp appeared a changed man. Charlie was taking his usual afternoon stroll around town when he came face to face with Kemp down at Art Stanley's mercantile.

"Charlie, this is your new neighbor," Art announced as he took a moment away from supervising the loading of a supply wagon to bring the two men together. "Ike Kemp, here's Charlie Justiss. He's one of the real legends in Palo Pinto."

"No, Art here's the legend," Charlie objected. "He was here when men still dressed in buckskins, and the only neighbors anybody had were bare-chested and shot arrows at you."

"Yeah?" Kemp asked. "I never knew Caddos to be particular fierce."

27

"Comanches," Art whispered. "Charlie's bunch and the U.S. Cavalry nabbed the last bunch of 'em not more'n ten years ago."

"And the creek's name?" Kemp asked.

"Left from the old days. Back in '59 they had a reservation to the west. Lots of the creeks up there have tribe names. Indians are long gone now, but the names stuck. Ioni, Keechi . . ."

"Times do change," Kemp grumbled.

"People do most of it," Art explained. "Wasn't so long ago you could buy a drink of whiskey in Palo Pinto. Look at us now, dry as August on the Llano. As for names, some of these new folks movin' in've started renamin' hills and streams. A couple of 'em even stuck their names to bends of the Brazos."

"Guess it's only natural," Charlie said, shaking his head. "I called the stream running through Wolf Hollow Justiss Creek. My brother christened the new town on the railroad Justiss Junction."

"Some men brand cattle," Kemp said icily. "Others want to carve their names on the world itself."

"They just want to be remembered," Art said. "Oldtimers like me and Joe Nance who were here from the beginning have little to show for it. No town bears our name. Once there was Stanley's Crossing and Stanley's Trading Post. Well, there's a bridge over the river now, and I sold the trading post when I built the new store here in town."

"The only sure way to be remembered is to have family," Kemp declared. "You can scratch names on maps till Christmas, but somebody else can come along tomorrow and change them."

"Just look what's come of the Flat!" Art cried.

"In two summers there won't be a plank left to the place."

"It happens," Charlie said, sighing. "There are no buffalo to hunt."

"Nor trails to set longhorns to," Kemp added.

"You drove cattle, did you?" Charlie asked.

"From '66 on. Up the Chisholm and later on the Western trail to Dodge. No fences then, but plenty of other problems. I got my whole outfit shot up in the Cimarron country one year. Even," Kemp said, swallowing hard, "a brother. It's bitter hard, losin' family."

"Yes," Charlie agreed. "Joe Dunlap, across the Brazos, lost a boy north of the Cimarron. That was bad country, prone to outlaws. I don't miss that part of the trail."

"I do miss Dodge, though," Kemp said, grinning for the first time. "Had some wild times there. It's where I met my wife."

"You're married, then?" Art asked.

"Fifteen years. My Abigail gave me five children, though the youngest, little Meg, passed on her first winter."

"Perhaps she'd like to join the ladies' sewing circle," Charlie said. "They—"

"She died two winters back," Kemp said, scowling. "I was off seein' to my brother's business. Farmers down south started fencin' off the water. My boys did what they could, but those farmers brought in Ben Taplock. He rode in one night when everybody was sleepin'. When I got back, I found out they'd taken my eldest, Shaw, and his bit of a brother, Dawes, and strung 'em up in their own barn. Poor

Abby was half-dead of grief, and a February snow proved too much for her."

"That's hard news to find waiting for you," Charlie mumbled.

"Told myself then and there I'd tend to my own needs from then on," Kemp growled. "First thing I did was find Taplock, see he met his end the same way as my boys. Then I rode through those farmers like a whirlwind. No one's found a profit in standin' in my way since!"

Kemp's eyes blazed, and Charlie backed up a step. Art was equally shaken. The veins in Kemp's forehead protruded, and his hands shook with rage.

"We've had no such trouble here," Charlie said sourly. "Not in a long while. There are lots of farms in Palo Pinto County, and ranches as well. We abide each other."

"Sure you do," Kemp muttered as he turned back toward his supply wagons. "You got to watch those plows, though. Elsewise they'll keep creepin' west till they've cut the range into furrows and buried every cow between here and Mexico."

A great uneasiness had settled over Charlie Justiss. He'd glimpsed a kind of madness in Ike Kemp's eyes, a certain variety thought left behind on Virginia battlefields. For four years Charlie had struggled to keep his command alive despite the best efforts of crazed, wild-eyed officers to lead charges up cannon-swept slopes against well-entrenched bluecoat riflemen.

Charlie didn't often share his thoughts, especially

when memories of war and death swept over him. That night, though, when he awoke shuddering, Angela couldn't help but notice.

"What is it?" she asked as she shook him awake. "What's come over you, Charlie?"

"Nothing," he growled, blinking away shadowy figures from his eyes.

"Tell me."

"Just a nightmare. Go along to sleep. I'll be all right."

"Charlie, I've seen it before. It won't go away of its own accord. I'm your wife, you know. You can tell me."

"It's gone."

"Charlie!"

She pulled him close and stared into his eyes. The first traces of dawn sifted into the room, illuminating her charcoal hair, detailing her delicate features.

"I thought I'd put it behind me."

"What?"

"The war. It was so long ago, but I was suddenly back there again, trying to rally the men, when this young colonel hardly old enough to shave sent us back into that cornfield. The whole brigade was chewed up by then, but there that colonel stood, waving his sword, hollering how we Texans could save General Lee's army, hold the left, and keep the Yanks from Sharpsburg. I'd already lost the best part of my whole company, Angela. And that loon of a colonel thought his gold braid entitled him to kill off the rest!"

Charlie sank into his bed and tried to stop his hands from trembling. Angela ran her palms across

31

his chest, and for a moment, he grew quiet.

"What happened then?" she whispered.

"You remember Matt Halpert? He was scarce older than Joe. Well, Matt lifted the flag and raced after that fool colonel. The rest of the boys followed, and I watched the Yanks plumb shoot 'em to pieces. Matt was still holding onto the flag two hours later when I found him. We had to pry his fingers loose."

"And the colonel?"

"Got himself promoted. Didn't get so much as a scratch. I lost twenty good men, though, and by nightfall, the Yanks owned that cornfield anyway."

"What brought all this on?"

"I suppose it was something I heard today. Or saw. This Kemp fellow. He's got that colonel's eyes, and it worries me some. It's hard to know what to expect from a man like that. I can't help worrying. His boy pulled a pistol on Billy. Here I thought we'd got 'em raised and safe. Now it seems there's just more to worry about."

"Oh?"

"It seems just yesterday I was rocking Chris on my knee. Now he's grown tall, is making grown sounds and working on whiskers. In another year we'll be sending Joe off to A & M College. Where's the time gone, Angela?"

"You're feeling the years again," Angela said, taking his shoulders in her soft hands and squeezing the weariness from him. "I can always tell. You start talking about the past, and then you turn to the future. You'd have us all believe you're at death's door when the truth is that you'll outlive the river."

"Nobody'll do that. It's the one thing that never changes."

"Nonsense. It changes every hour, every day. It's either flooding the valley or drying to a trickle. In winter you can ford where summer's quicksands will swallow your wagon. Nothing stays the same for very long."

"Except us," he whispered.

"Yes," she echoed.

But as May gave way to June, it truly seemed everything else was turning overnight. Spring was the season of change, but summer usually brought about a resumption of routine. Cowboys worked stock, and farmers thinned corn plants. Boys swam away the midafternoon heat, and girls tied their hair with bright ribbon and hoped for a Sunday caller.

With new settlers flooding the county, rarely did a week go by when there wasn' a barn to be raised or a cabin built. For as long as Charlie could remember, every able-bodied man for miles had always gathered to help. Some ranch would provide a steer, and old Doc Singer would see it barbecued. Women would cook up greens and potatoes, bake pies or perhaps a cobbler. Barnraising was heavy labor in the best of times, but in summer, the toil wore at a man like the southwestern wind. Only the thought of a feast and a bit of dancing when the work was done kept anyone at his hammer.

That June, Charlie took particular pleasure in seeing Henry Eppler's barn take shape. The captain was more than just an old friend. It occurred to

Charlie more than once that if two old enemies could forge a bond of friendship, then anything was possible. Together they'd seen the land tamed, the Comanches vanquished. They'd dealt with outlaws and raised their families.

"I hadn't realized Chris had gotten so tall," Catherine Eppler remarked to Charlie. "Has he been working at the ranch? If his hair wasn't so yellow-blond, I'd swear he was an Indian. He's pure tanned brown."

"He's been cutting his classroom time short, I fear," Charlie said, gazing at the leathery lad who was helping Josiah Eppler nail planks in place. "It's Texas does it to 'em, I guess. Come spring, she calls to a boy to shed his shirt and take to the range. His brothers were much the same, all save Ross, but Chris is a regular scalawag. He could worm the gizzard out of a chicken, and make the fool bird glad for parting with it."

"He's a good heart, though, Charlie. He's been a wondrous good friend to Josiah and Will. Chris won't abide their being bullied, and though he's got two whole years' growing on Josiah and three on Will, he seems to enjoy their company."

"That's good. His brother Joe's got the eye for Priscilla Comstock and's left Chris to himself of late. Then, too, Chris has always been around older brothers. Does him good to be top hog for a change. Just watch out he doesn't have the lads off into mischief. As I said, he's a scamp."

"Weren't we all at fourteen? I just thank heaven I finally have boys to watch, not little soldiers on drill."

34

Charlie watched Catherine's face glow, and he grinned. A woman's life was never easy on the frontier, but being married to the army called for great sacrifices. He recalled the long years away from Angela, from Victoria and the boys. Every night he felt the heartache.

"Are you goin' to sit there sippin' lemonade and talkin' to the pretty ladies or help build a barn?" Marty Steele suddenly called. Charlie excused himself and joined Marty and a half-dozen cowboys who were framing the barn's west wall.

"Can't do without my help, eh?" Charlie asked as he set a plank in place.

"Don't want you off gatherin' moss, Charlie," Marty quipped. "As for help, why not trot out and ask that crew comin' down the road?"

Charlie gazed to his right. There, leading a line of six riders down the road toward Albany, was Ike Kemp. Charlie turned the plank over to Toby Hart, then walked to the road.

"Hello there!" Charlie called. "Come to lend a hand, Ike?"

Kemp gazed at the skeleton of the barn, then spit down at the road.

"Don't believe a man should ask for help," Kemp growled. "If a job's more'n he can complete with his own hands, then it's best left undone. As for me, I tend my own business and leave others to do the same."

"Everyone joins in a barnraising," Charlie explained. "Come on. You'll get to meet the folks. Later on we'll get you a barn of your own built."

"Didn't you hear me!" Kemp raged, rearing his

35

horse high onto its back legs. "Get away from me and leave me be. I wouldn't soil my hands by helpin' any blamed farmer! You tell 'em to give me a wide berth if they're wise. Do so yourself!"

Kemp raced off westward, and his startled companions hurried after him. Charlie turned and walked back to the barn.

"Who was that?" Henry Eppler asked.

"Ike Kemp. My new neighbor to the west. Strange one."

"Kemp, you say?" the captain said, scratching his head. "I don't think the name's familiar, but the face sure as thunder is. I've seen him before."

"It's the eyes. Puts me in mind of a dozen crazy fools wearing general's sashes."

"No, it's more than that, Charlie. You do as he says. Give him room. I don't think I met him in church. I believe first thing Monday I'll pay Bret a visit in his office. Could be there's a poster or two out on that man."

"He said he rode down some farmers in south Texas."

"I've never been fifty miles south of Palo Pinto, Charlie. It was elsewhere, the Flat maybe. Don't worry. It'll come to me. Meanwhile, watch out. One thing I know for sure. Wherever it was, trouble went with that face."

Chapter Two

Ike Kemp's face appeared on no wanted poster, and inquiries sent to Austin and elsewhere turned up not a hint of wrongdoing associated with Charlie's new neighbor. Kemp, meanwhile, continued to keep his own counsel, and Charlie decided to follow suit. After all, so long as the banks of Caddo Creek remained peaceful, it mattered little that Kemp fumed and stormed about farmers and fences and the ruination of the range.

In truth, the only one in Palo Pinto to lend ears to Ike Kemp was old Joe Nance.

"Haven't I been saying the same thing for close to ten years?" Nance cried. "If folks had heeded my advice, Palo Pinto would be a different place indeed."

Different, yes, Charlie thought. Better? Probably not.

In June, the stream of farmers embarking at

Justiss Junction intensified as never before. Daily, pairs of families arrived to break the soil. Most secured title to land watered by the twin forks of Palo Pinto Creek west of Justiss Junction and sandwiched between the Albany road on the north and the railroad on the south. That stretch had not long before been open range, and oldtimers like Marty Steele complained bitterly as fences outlined small farms of two hundred to six hundred acres.

"Thank God for the mountains," Marty declared. The rugged rock-strewn slopes of the Palo Pinto Mountains seemed to bar further settlement. Of course, only a generous man would have deemed them real mountains. The whole range was little more than a broken ridge, with gaps suitable for wagon roads here and there. Ioni and Caddo Creeks cut across the western range in the spring, but usually by mid-July, water was scarce. Corn wasn't easily grown without ample water.

North of the Brazos, settlement clung to the Jacksboro road. A handful of farms, Joe Dunlap's place, and Luis Morales's horse ranch at Fortune Bend . . . that was about it.

"You ought to buy up what public land's left, Papa," Charlie's son Ross advised. "Especially that range west of the mountains. It's fair pasture, and you know how prices are soaring."

"We've got thousands of acres along Rock Creek already. The stock we raise and sell down there hardly pays the crew and the taxes, Ross," Charlie grumbled. "There are only so many beeves to contract each year, and we've acres enough already for them."

"You wait and see, Papa. Somebody's going to buy up that land. It could be another Ike Kemp, too. I don't care for his temperament. There are certainly better neighbors to have."

"Maybe, but we put up with the Comanches."

"We had those rustlers at Fortune Bend, too," Ross reminded his father. "They brought nothing but trouble. Sure you won't reconsider?"

"No, leave the range be, Ross. For now anyway. Maybe when Joe and Chris are older, they'll need acreage of their own. For now it will likely remain public range. It's late for planting already, so I can't see any farmer settling there."

Charlie was rarely so wrong. The second week of June, a boy perhaps thirteen years old appeared at his office in the new stone courthouse.

"I come to buy land," the boy announced.

Charlie couldn't help grinning. The child wasn't five feet tall, and he was as thin as a peach twig. Under a mop of light blond hair, though, two deeply serious blue eyes blazed.

"Taking up ranching, are you?" Charlie asked, motioning the boy closer. "I don't think I've seen you before. You belong to one of the farmers down south?"

The boy's forehead wrinkled a moment as he absorbed the words.

"No, no. I come to talk for Papa. He comes. We buy land here. Herr Stuffel said to come here."

"Oh," Charlie said, nodding his head. Otto Stuffel had brought seven families to Palo Pinto County from northern Germany back in the spring. The boy resembled the Stuffel lads—seemingly too pale and frail for Texas. But the Stuffels had tanned under the summer sun, had filled out their gaunt faces, and Charlie knew the little newcomer would do as well.

"I say it wrong?" the boy asked as Charlie grinned and shook his head.

"No, just fine, son. Your father doesn't speak English, I guess."

"Not so good as I," the boy boasted. "Not my brothers and sisters. I study hard with my friend Tom Simpson on ship."

"That's fine," Charlie said, rising and stepping toward the center of the office. "I'm Charlie Justiss, county judge. My son Ross looks after the land office two days a week, but he's off in Jacksboro just now, filing a writ." The boy wrinkled his forehead, and Charlie bent over and rested a heavy hand on one shoulder. "We'll take good care of your papa, you and I. What's your name?"

"Viktor Weidling," the boy said, pronouncing the words with a distinct German accent.

"Well, Viktor, let's find your father."

Charlie shoveled the boy out into the lobby of the courthouse. Viktor immediately rushed to the doorway and led a tall, thin man in his middle thirties forward. A smallish, round-faced woman followed, leading a smaller boy by the hand. Afterward scampered a pair of flaxen-haired girls and a boy who was obviously Viktor's elder brother.

"Hello," Charlie greeted each of them in turn. "Welcome to Palo Pinto."

"Ve buy land here," the man said, immediately producing a map and a leather pouch containing banknotes. Charlie took the map and frowned.

There were two X's scratched below the Albany road on either side of Caddo Creek.

"Oh, not there," Charlie argued. "There's no water. It's barren country."

The father turned to Viktor, and the boy babbled something in German. The father replied, and Viktor addressed Charlie.

"Yes, it must be there," the boy explained. "Farm must be beside road. We will find water."

"You don't know this country," Charlie argued. "In August your crops will wither and die. The river's too far distant, and the land's poor at best. It's a mistake."

"No," Weidling said, handing the money pouch to Charlie. "Must be here. Stuffel hast been . . . farm. Is good place."

"For cows. Not for corn."

"We buy," Weidling said, passing into Charlie's hands the money, then a handful of official-looking papers.

"This is for two farms," Charlie said as he carefully read the deed applications. The land had already been surveyed, and two farms of six hundred acres each marked out. "Who are the Schneiders?" Charlie asked.

"They come . . ." Weidling began, then stopped. He whispered something to Viktor, and the boy smiled.

"Tomorrow," Viktor declared. "They come tomorrow."

"You know them?"

"They come mit us on ship," Weidling answered. "From Hamburg."

41

"I see," Charlie said. He then led the Weidlings into his office and began counting out the price of the land. He wished Ross had been there to handle the business. Ross had a way of dealing with papers and forgetting about them. Charlie couldn't help suspecting he was dooming the Germans to failure by letting them purchase such hard land.

He filled in the blank places on the forms, then counted out the purchase price and returned the balance of the banknotes to Weidling.

"I'll see the deed's recorded," Charlie promised. "I wish you luck. You're apt to need it."

Viktor extended a hand, and Charlie shook it warmly. He then found himself shaking hands with everyone else in the family. When they left, Charlie felt a heaviness in his heart, for he knew they faced great difficulties. Even so, he felt a bit envious. They sang their way to the street and climbed into a supply-laden wagon. It took Charlie back to the day he and Angela and the youngsters had arrived in Palo Pinto, broke and exhausted, pilgrims in a strange new land.

"Good luck to you," Charlie whispered as the wagon rumbled westward. "Pray for a rainy July."

July remained two weeks in the future, though, and there were other trials facing the Weidlings and Schneiders. East of the mountains, most emigrants battled insects and rattlesnakes, rocky soil and noonday heat. West of Caddo Creek a greater menace lurked — Ike Kemp.

It hadn't occurred to Charlie that Kemp would trouble himself with a pair of German farmers. After all, most ranchers were readying stock for

42

shipment on the railcars. Again, Charlie was gravely mistaken. Two days after registering the deeds at the courthouse, Viktor Weidling and twelve-year-old Josiah Eppler galloped into town on the back of one of the captain's horses.

"Judge, Sheriff, come quick!" Josiah shouted. "There's trouble!"

Charlie was halfway down the courthouse steps when Bret Pruett and his deputy, Alex Tuttle, charged out of the jailhouse. The three men met the boys in the street.

"Tell us what's happened," Bret said.

Josiah turned to his young companion, and Viktor fought to catch his breath.

"Was bandits," Viktor gasped. "They come to our farm, tie ropes around my brother Rolf and Papa. They shoot guns. I run to get help."

"You did just fine, Viktor," Charlie said, helping the sobbing youngster off the horse. "You bring him from your place, Josiah?"

"Yes, sir," Josiah answered crisply. "Pa headed west, said he'd pick up Wes Tyler at the line cabin. I was to go get the sheriff."

"Well, it's likely that loon Kemp," Bret grumbled, turning toward the livery. "Care to go along, Charlie?"

"I think I'd better. Maybe I can talk some sense into somebody."

"Could be," Bret mumbled, "but I wouldn't bank on it."

By the time Charlie and the others arrived at

Caddo Creek, a lively confrontation was already in progress. Henry Eppler, Wes Tyler, Toby Hart, young Jordy Banks, O. T. Fuller and Marlin Silsbee stood on one side, angrily demanding the departure of Kemp, his two sons, and a pair of cowboys. Kemp, on the other hand, gestured wildly and commanded his boys to continue uprooting fenceposts. Weidling and his boy Rolf remained tied to a pair of junipers.

"Papa!" little Viktor Weidling cried when he saw his father struggling against his bonds. The boy leaped from the back of Josiah's horse and raced right past a glaring Ike Kemp.

"Stop him!" Kemp shouted, and one of the Kemp hands drew a pistol. Bret Pruett pulled his pistol and fired a warning shot into the ground. The Kemp hand discarded his own gun and raised his hands.

"What right have you to interfere in my business?" Kemp demanded to know. "You fools'd let them fence in every acre in the county!"

"It's their land, Mr. Kemp," Bret explained, lowering his pistol. He continued to keep a careful watch on the cowboys, though.

"Farmers!" Kemp muttered. "What do any of them know of this land? It's buffalo grass, and it's meant for longhorns! I won't see it fenced!"

"You'll obey the law or find yourself locked in my jail," Bret declared. "Now get clear and leave these folks be. They've done nothing."

"They're here," Kemp said, staring icily as Viktor Weidling freed his father. "Bunch of foreigners. I've seen it before, how they fence in a man, grab his range, and choke off his stock. It's fine for you to say leave 'em be, Sheriff! You've got steady work in

44

town. And you, Justiss! You've got miles of river to water your stock. Me, I need these acres for my cows."

"You could've bought the land," Eppler said. "You didn't."

"You best stay out of this, Yank!" Kemp shouted. "I've a long memory for faces."

"So do I," Eppler answered. "I've seen yours somewhere, and sooner or later I'll place it."

"A man meddles in my affairs can sure as hell get himself shot," Kemp warned. "You'd be smart to watch your barn. June's a bad month for fires."

"That's enough!" Bret shouted. "You threaten one more person, Kemp, you'll pass the night in my jail. It's a real fine place, with new steel bars and all. Hot enough to fry an egg on the floor around noon."

"Sheriff, I don't make threats," Kemp said, laughing. He turned and grinned at his sons, then waved them toward their horses. "Strange things happen after dark around here, or so they tell me. Comanche ghosts dancin' in the moonlight or some such. Anything's liable to happen."

The Kemp boys laughed, and their father hooted like an owl, then flashed a fiery glance at the Weidlings.

"You hear me good, farmer. Smart folk stay out of my path. Be a shame to have somethin' happen to one of them boys of yours."

Viktor shouted a torrent of German phrases back, but Kemp just turned away and led his companions back down the Albany road.

"Fool farmers can't even speak the language," he called to Bret. "Want to lock somebody up? Jail

45

them for ignorance."

Once Kemp and his men dropped over the western horizon, Charlie rode to where Viktor was helping his father untie Rolf's hands.

"I thought you'd be busy clearing land," Charlie said, frowning. "Don't know fencing was too good an idea, Mr. Weidling."

"I am called Eric," Weidling said, nodding gratefully toward Charlie and the others. "You know my kindern, Rolf, Viktor."

The boys glanced up, and Charlie gave them a smile.

"Cows were everywhere, Judge," Viktor explained, pointing toward the muddy creek. The bank was torn by longhorn hooves.

"Otto Stuffel brought to us a man," Weidling said as he freed Rolf from the juniper. "J. C. Parnell. Stuffel says this man fought for his farm when the cows —"

"Trampled his corn," Viktor finished. "Herr Parnell gave us wire to fence our land. He says this will keep out the cows."

"It will," Charlie agreed, "but it's sure to stir trouble. You might have spoken to somebody first. Whose cattle were they?"

The Weidlings exchanged a few words in German, then shrugged their shoulders. Finally Rolf drew a *K* in the sand, then topped it with a crown. Charlie'd seen such a brand on Kemp's horse.

"Figures," Bret said, scowling. "Kemp's been using this range for his own stock. This isn't trouble that's going away."

"I know," Charlie agreed. "Maybe Tut ought to

46

keep watch a couple of nights."

"I could keep watch out here," Toby offered.

"With roundup coming?" Wes asked. "We've already got a man riding the creek. Maybe once we ship the beeves to market, but for now . . ."

"Wes, look at 'em," Toby pleaded. "We can't just turn our heads away and pretend they're not there. Mr. Justiss?"

Toby was just a hair over twenty now, and there was still more boy to his shoulders than man. He'd grown up on the frontier, though, and he had a way of cutting to the heart of a matter.

Charlie frowned and walked away. He then felt a hand tug on his arm. He turned to discover Viktor Weidling gazing up with solemn eyes.

The Weidlings had listened silently all the while. Viktor and his father now spoke quietly. Finally Eric Weidling spoke.

"It is not for you to decide," he said, rubbing his swollen wrists and staring hatefully toward the distant west. "They make war on us. We will fight."

"Fight?" Charlie asked. "You're new to this country. And these boys haven't grown their first whiskers. Do you have guns?"

"I have rifle," Weidling said.

"Wes, do we still have that case of Winchesters up at your cabin?" Charlie asked. Wes nodded. "Mr. Weidling, I'm going to have some rifles brought out to you. A man will show you how to load and fire. But if you have trouble, you get young Viktor here, or somebody, headed up the creek. My ranch has a line camp up that way."

"Wait for help," Bret advised. "Fellows like this

Kemp need to have the odds in their favor. Keep the young ones under cover. Return fire, but stay put."

"Ja," Weidling said, drawing his sons to his side. "You will send rifles to Schneider?"

"Yes," Charlie promised.

"We'll let word get around that we're keeping an eye out for you folks, too," Bret added. "Maybe that will keep Kemp and his boys at bay."

"We'll keep our eyes open as well," Henry Eppler pledged, giving Josiah a pat on the shoulder.

Weidling tried to look hopeful, but the ordeal of being tied to a tree seemed to have taken a toll on the farmer.

"Thank you, sirs," Viktor said, and his father added his own thanks. Young Rolf only gazed sullenly across the creek.

"I believe it's time we got back to town," Charlie declared. Wes waved for his men to return to the ranch, too.

"I think Tut and I'll stay and have a look around," Bret said. "Thanks for your help."

"Wish I could feel it wouldn't be needed again," Charlie grumbled. "Coming along, Henry?"

Eppler waved Josiah forward and turned his own horse back toward home. The three riders then trotted up the Albany road toward Palo Pinto.

Chapter Three

Charlie Justiss worried about the Weidlings and their neighbors, the Schneiders, but June was a busy time for ranches, and he soon found other cares to occupy his mind. Ross had managed to contract five thousand head of cattle to a Kansas City buyer at top price, and between arranging transport for the cattle on the Ft. Worth and Western, cutting out the cattle from the various Flying J herds, and organizing the short drive to the railhead at Justiss Junction, everyone on the ranch was kept busy.

Long ago Charlie had turned the day-to-day ranch operations over to his son Billy. The large Hereford herd grazing on the south range was overseen by Marty Steele and a small crew. Charlie's son Ryan managed the south range operations and also helped run the orphanage on Buck Creek founded by his young wife, Rachel.

Angela lamented the fact that the family never gathered anymore. It didn't figure to get better. Daughter Victoria was teaching at Palo Pinto's little schoolhouse most of the year and looking after her husband, Bret, and four youngsters all the time. Ross manned the county land office, did the ranch accounts, and practiced law. His delicate wife, Eliza, was expecting a child in July, and that kept the two of them close to home most days.

Even Joe and Chris were out of the house. The two boys, together with their cousin Clay and a young friend, Bart Davis, were working the roundup. Once it was finished, the four would pass the summer at Fortune Bend helping Luis Morales work horses. They'd done it the summer before as well, and Luis was eager to have the help. As for the boys, Charlie suspected they would have worked for nothing so long as Luis gave them leave to sleep under the stars and race the wind on horseback every afternoon.

"I know it does those scamps good to put their hands to a full day's work," Angela commented one night as she and Charlie sat alone at the dinner table, "but this big house is too quiet. It needs children about."

"Well, you could always invite Rachel to bring the orphans over. She has close to a hundred again."

"I thought most of them had been taken in by farm families."

"Most were," Charlie said, laughing to himself as he recalled how the pitiful little wretches had softened the hearts of half the county's womenfolk. "You know Rachel, though. She'll get a letter from this town or that, and the next thing you know, the train will drop some poor urchin off at Buck Creek. They've built a regular train platform there now."

"I thought maybe the grandchildren might care to stay with us for a time. Vicki could do with a bit of rest, and—"

"You could do a fair job of spoiling 'em, eh?"

"I don't spoil them, Charlie Justiss! That's your doing. You think Hope's got to have a new ribbon every time you see her, and even little Tom knows his grandpapa's pocket always has a stick of candy or two for him."

"I'm guilty," Charlie confessed.

"So, will you ride out to have a look at the branding?" Angela asked. "You always do."

"I did promise Bowie I'd visit Clay. Emiline frets about that boy, you know. I thought I'd help with the drive, too. We're shorthanded, and there are so many steers to get to the railhead this time."

"And besides, you miss the range."

"Well, it would give me a chance to visit a bit with Billy. Between his duties at the ranch and those rides he takes to see the Cassidy girl, he's never around."

"Oh, he's around Colleen," Angela said, laughing. "To be truthful, the boys buzz 'round her like a bee. Billy's first in line, though. Could be we'll have another wedding to host."

"It's time. I never figured Billy for the old maid of the outfit."

"He's scarce gray. Anyway, I expect them to announce their intentions once Colleen turns eighteen. Her father's set against her marrying at an earlier age."

"I was much the same where Vicki was concerned," Charlie said, remembering. "You seem particularly well-informed, though."

51

"Have you forgotten that Mary Cassidy and I're sewing the new curtains for the schoolhouse?"

Charlie laughed loudly. Angela was spinning her web, and Billy had best watch out.

Charlie did ride out to look in on the roundup. By now most of the yearlings were branded with the winged-J branding iron, and most of the bull calves were gelded. Cutting steers out for a trail herd was a whole different matter, though. Marty's herd on the south range would select a thousand Herefords. The rest of the cattle would come from a mixed breed Billy was running along Caddo Creek and the more refined Herefords grazing the main pasture between Ioni and Bluff creeks.

To help with the extra work, Ryan had dispatched a dozen boys from the orphanage who were fair hands with a rope and able to sit all day in the saddle. With Joe, Chris, Clay, and the tiny Bart Davis along, the Flying J outfit resembled a nursery scene.

"Papa, can't we find any full-grown cowboys anymore?" Billy cried. "Not that I was any older when I first headed up the trail to Kansas, but I never looked that young! At least I could put both toes in the stirrups. That young Bart's got a heart as big as a watermelon, but in truth, some crow's likely to mistake him for a worm and gobble him up some morning."

"Maybe Doc ought to feed the boy an extra slice of beef," Charlie suggested.

"Doc Singer stuffs 'em all, Papa. Especially Bart

and the orphans. Those kids just run off the extra food, I'm afraid. They do liven up the nights, though, what with their pretty singing and their pranks. Truth is, they put Chris to shame, and that takes some doing."

"Yes," Charlie agreed.

There was more to roundup than pranks, though. Most of the day was spent separating steers from cows and calves, then keeping them apart. With such a large herd to assemble, Billy marked a number of cows for inclusion. He and Wes took care not to take a cow from its unweened calf, and that was another challenge.

Toward late afternoon Charlie paused long enough to watch young Jordy Banks climb atop a cantankerous bull and hang on for dear life. But though the beast flung its head one way, its rump another, and angrily snorted around a hillside, Jordy didn't let go. Only when the other cowboys clapped and hooted their approval did Jordy leap to the ground.

"A fine ride, son," Wes declared. "You hung on real well."

"Had to," Jordy said, grinning from one ear to the other. If I hadn't, I'd been part of the dust. That old bull was mighty mean, you know."

There was no laughter when Charlie and Billy headed west to Caddo Creek, though. There'd been more than a little bad blood between the Flying J cowboys and Ike Kemp's Crown K outfit, particularly after the episode at the Weidlings' farm. Riders patroled the creek on both banks every night, and rather than share campfires or exchange a bit of tobacco or some coffee, the hands traded insults or

53

accusations.

The Flying J bunch was especially provoked by the fact that they'd turned over thirty-five Crown K strays to the Kemps. For their part, Kemp's boys failed to chase a single Flying J animal across the creek.

"Wolves must have gotten any strays that came our way," Kermit Kemp shouted to Wes. "Happens that way sometimes."

Wes wasted no time in telling the Kemp boy who he suspected was the wolf along Caddo Creek.

"Prove it!" Kermit yelled.

Afterward Charlie sat down with Billy, Wes and young Toby Hart to discuss the Kemp trouble.

"I've been keepin' an eye open, Charlie," Wes declared. "I send Toby over to have a look each mornin'. We keep a guard ridin' all night, though it's been hard lately with all the stock to ready for market."

"And what about day after tomorrow when we drive the animals to market?"

"We'll find a way," Wes promised.

"Have you thought about—"

"Papa, please," Billy interrupted. "I know how you feel about this, but you have to trust Wes and me to handle it. It's my place. If you issue orders, the men don't know who to obey. I know you mean well, but . . ."

"I ought to leave it to you, son," Charlie said, grinning. You're right. It's the old soldier in me, I suppose. I'm too used to commanding."

"Well, don't quit thinking things over, Papa. You just need to tell me so I can act. The men need to

54

hear their orders from me, though."

"Agreed."

"So, suppose we can find Hector Suarez and talk him into playing his guitar?" Billy asked.

"I'd guess so," Charlie replied. The two then set off to locate Hector and get the music started. By nightfall Spanish ballads drifted across the rocky hills, and Charlie found himself recalling a hundred nights camped with his companions in those very same hills.

"You stayin' the night, oldtimer?" Doc Singer, who had a good ten years on Charlie, asked.

"Well, I thought to," Charlie admitted. "Angela will pretend anger, but I noticed she made sure I packed my blankets."

"She's a keeper all right."

So Charlie spread his blankets alongside Chris. The boy had a particularly devilish grin on his face, and Charlie expected trouble. Moments later Bart Davis jumped to his feet and cried out, "Rattler! Help! A rattler's got my toe!"

The three orphans who were sharing the camp danced out of their blankets and screamed to high heaven. Chris and Joe were beside themselves laughing. Charlie got everyone calmed down, then freed the terrified Bart's big toe from a string of rattles. The boy stood frozen in his nightshirt, as red as a tomato.

"Don't let it bother you, son," Charlie said. "Chris once had half the girls in the schoolhouse jumping about on account of the same trick. Only that time he tied the rattles to a girl's pigtails."

The orphans howled in laughter, and Bart grinned

55

away the last of his embarrassment.

The following morning Charlie made a final tour of the camps. He shared a few thoughts with veteran cowboys and greeted newcomers. Then he swung south along Caddo Creek to where it met the Albany road.

He wasn't the only rider on the road. Ike Kemp was there as well. Kermit and the younger son, Solomon, were along. The three were busy taunting young Rolf Weidling and the Schneiders' pretty daughter Marianne.

"You'll get no older livin' 'round here, boy!" Kermit warned. "One night we'll creep in on you and slice off your nose. As for you, dearie, soon as we tend your pa, we'll come callin' on you."

Marianne shrank back in horror, and Rolf stepped in front. Solomon Kemp drew out a bullwhip and cracked it loudly in Rolf's direction.

"Help us, please," Marianne pleaded, turning toward Charlie's approaching horse. Rolf remained as before, stonefaced, unyielding. The whip cracked again, and this time the wicked tip tore into the boy's shoulder.

"Care for another?" Solomon asked.

"I don't think so," Charlie called, drawing a pistol and shooting the whip from young Kemp's hand. Instantly Kermit reached for his pistol, but Charlie fired a warning shot which sent Kermit's horse bucking.

"So, it's you again," Ike Kemp growled as he spit. "You got a particular fondness for interferin' in my business, don't you, Justiss? First you bring the sheriff out to stop me pullin' down a fence. Then you post riders on the creek. Now you shoot bullets at my boys. A day of reckoning's bound to come for us. I promise you that."

"Ready right now?" Charlie asked, his face growing dark and cold. "I imagine one of you might even get off a shot before I kill you. Sure would make life easier on young Rolf here."

"Let me take him, Pa," Solomon pleaded. "I can. I know it."

"You know nothin'," Kemp yelled at his son. "I've seen men with eyes like those before. He's deadly sure he can do what he says, and there's no profit in findin' out for certain. It's time to head home."

"Wise idea," Charlie told them.

"This isn't over, though," Kemp promised. "We'll be meetin' again, and next time you're apt to be at a disadvantage. That's liable to get you killed, Judge. You think on that!"

After seeing the children safely inside their homes, Charlie returned to Palo Pinto. Aside from reporting the trouble to Bret Pruett, Charlie kept quiet about Kemp's threats. If word got out to J. C. Parnell and the other farmers, or to Wes and Billy, for that matter, open war might break up. With five thousand cattle to drive to the railhead, the Flying J outfit had enough to worry about.

Charlie couldn't hide his concern from Angela, though.

"I don't care for that Kemp," she declared. "And I don't like the idea of Joe and Chris out there with him riding around waving guns in the air. I'll feel better when they're across the river with Luis."

"The boys're with the main outfit across Justiss Creek, probably safer than we are."

"That's a comfort."

"Kemp may be crazed, but I can't see him and his boys riding into Palo Pinto, blazing away like Raymond Polk's raiders."

"Has Bret found out anything about him? I thought he wired Austin."

"He did. No one knew anything about Ike Kemp. His face hasn't appeared on any wanted posters. Could be he's just what he says — a rancher who's had a bad time of late. He came up with a fair-sized sum to buy all that land west of Caddo Creek."

"Road agents acquire money."

"I'd almost feel better if I thought he was a rustler or a stage bandit. I don't know, Angela. There's something in that man's eyes. If you'd seen him on the road today, threatening that Weidling boy . . . I can't help sensing there's trouble brewing, and I feel so helpless to stop it!"

"It seems to me the time when it was your job to worry about everything that happens in Palo Pinto County is long past. Let Bret and Tut tend to this. Those farmers can fend for themselves the same way we did."

"I can't help it. That little Viktor Weidling is so like Billy. Do you remember how we felt when that snake bit him on the trail?"

"I remember," she said, clasping his hand. "But you can't be everyone's father, Charlie. Lord knows you and Rachel are a pair. She takes to heart every barefooted urchin in Texas, and you feel responsible for each new family who arrives at the depot down in Justiss Junction. The Weidlings have come halfway around the world, Charlie. They faced hardships before. They will again."

Charlie nodded his agreement, but in truth, the German farmers were rarely far from his thoughts. The next day as he rode back to the Flying J to help drive the cattle down the narrow market roads to Justiss Junction, he paused to speak with Henry Eppler.

The former cavalry captain and his young sons were working stock not far from the Albany road. Charlie gave the boys a wave, then nudged his horse toward their father.

"Thought we'd best move our cows back to the south a bit," the captain said as Charlie drew his horse to a halt. "Wouldn't want our animals thinking they had to follow their cousins to the railroad station."

"No," Charlie agreed. "Might be a good day to work out that way. We're liable to raise a bit of dust."

"Oh, we've seen dust," Eppler said, laughing. "No one who's lived at Griffin shies from a bit of sand in his hair."

Charlie tried to find a grin to match his old friend's jest, but all he managed to say was, "I suppose not."

"What's on your mind, Charlie? I know you well enough to say you didn't come up this hill to gab about cows."

"Ike Kemp paid another visit to the Weidling place yesterday," Charlie grumbled.

"I wouldn't fret too much over that. From what I've seen, Kemp is more bluster than bull. If he'd wanted to, he could've mounted up his men and ridden through there like Phil Sheridan. I figure he means to scare those people off. If he wanted to kill 'em, he'd done it by now."

"I guess that's true, but it doesn't make me rest a bit easier."

"Well, I'll keep my eyes and ears open," Eppler promised.

"I'd appreciate that," Charlie declared. "Pass the word, too, eh?"

"Sure," the captain agreed.

Chapter Four

Trailing cattle had never been one of Charlie Justiss's favorite endeavors. Riding alongside a few thousand plodding, troublesome steers down a dusty trail in the midafternoon heat of a Texas summer was about as miserable a way to pass the time as any yet discovered. And yet it took him back to the old days when they'd turned their herd northward toward Dodge City, to weeks of danger and discomfort that sharpened a man's nerves, brought a keen edge to his mind.

Now Charlie rode more to observe Joe and Chris, to share a taste of what the past had been like. The boys, together with their cousin Clay and young Bart Davis, darted in and out of the dust, urging the stock along with ropes' ends or singing out some old trail song picked up from Hector Suarez or Wes Tyler.

Yes, drives are for youngsters, Charlie told himself. But even oldtimers enjoyed the distraction from that other world of worries and weighty concerns.

"Ever think you'd see this many steers on the move again, Papa?" Billy asked when the two of them watched Wes Tyler and the youngsters turn the herd southward toward Justiss Junction.

"When you get to be my age, you quit being surprised about anything," Charlie said, laughing. "I never thought I'd see the day Ryan would be playing papa to a hundred youngsters, and I sure never believed the time would come when the longhorn would give way to these splotched hornless beasts we're driving to market."

"Well, I can't say I'm sorry about either one. Ry's good with those boys, has 'em riding and roping and learning the craft. As for longhorns, how can you miss those ornery critters! These Herefords yield better beef, and more of it. And they don't stick horns through horses or men."

"Longhorns saved us from starving when we first came here," Charlie reminded his son. "They built the ranch."

"No, you did that, Papa," Billy said proudly. "And now we're doing better than ever."

Maybe that was what bothered Charlie. In the old days, with Comanches and floods to occupy his attention, he felt useful. Now it seemed he mainly ruled on petty disputes or wrote letters to Austin. He took pride in the roads scratched through the brush and rocks of Palo Pinto County, in the bridges over the Brazos and its countless creeks, but there was something about putting a shoulder to a task that gave a man a feeling of accomplishment. All through the war, Charlie had insisted on pitching in when the men dug earthworks or repaired railroad track. Even now he chased stray steers himself instead of sending one of the young cowboys out with a rope.

It built a bond between Charlie and his men. It just wasn't possible to respect a man who spent all his time giving orders or overseeing work. Sometimes a boss had to bare his shoulders and dig into the work. Sweat on a brow stood a rancher in good stead with his crew. And if the time came when danger threatened, an outfit responded to a boss they respected.

Of course, Charlie knew it was Billy's crew now. Some of the younger cowboys looked on Charlie as a distant uncle—or aging grandfather. It rankled him some, for he wasn't quite fifty. That sounded a little younger each winter, too.

"Shoot, we're all of us older," Wes noted. "I got four little ones with Alice back at the cabin. Me, Wes Tyler, with a houseful of family. Figure that, Charlie!"

"I'm glad of it," Charlie told his friend. "Somehow the youngsters make all the fighting and suffering and dying worthwhile. You can't help seeing a better day written in their eyes. It's why I was so glad Rachel brought the orphans here. There's room to grow, and horizons to reach."

"Think there will be when Jeff's of age?"

"There's always room somewhere," Charlie declared. "A man only has to find himself a hill to climb, then look."

"I guess so," Wes said, grinning.

Justiss Junction was never designed to handle five thousand of anything at one time, much less the long dusty stream of bawling steers that the Flying J cowboys drove toward the cattle pens on the east side of town. As if funneling the herd down the narrow market roads to the junction hadn't been enough of a challenge, now the crew had to cut out bunches of fifty at a time to run through the maze of chutes that led toward twenty waiting cattle cars.

"Watch yourselves, boys!" Wes called to the orphan boys riding along the western fringe of the herd. "Steers have a way of gettin' uneasy 'bout now."

Charlie made his way to where a pair of sandy-headed teenagers were patrolling uneasily.

"Give 'em a bit of leeway, son," Charlie told the first youngster. "Just keep their heads turned toward the pens. It's natural they're a little nervous in such tight quarters."

"They're nervous?" the boy asked, taking off his broad-brimmed hat and sweeping back a damp mop of hair from his forehead. "I'm the one who's shakin' himself half to death."

"Well, it's fine to be worrisome," Charlie said, riding up beside the young cowboy. "Thing is, you can't let those steers know it. They'll turn on you quick as lightning."

"Yes, sir," the boy said, managing a grin. "I do

believe I'd almost rather be back holding spikes on the railroad, though."

Charlie frowned as the spindle-legged boy lifted a rope's end. The middle and ring fingers were gone from his right hand, a permanent reminder of the day a sledgehammer slammed down on a young hand holding a spike in place. Three quarters of the orphans at Buck Creek had likewise lost appendages, but they never seemed to back away from anything. Charlie knew the youngster would be all right.

And so he was. Once the twenty cars were loaded, a snorting locomotive hauled them off toward the waiting slaughterhouse in Kansas City. Shortly another train arrived, and the loading process resumed. In all, close to three thousand head were shipped directly to market. Another thousand were nudged into the cattle pens to await the next train. Marty had the last thousand prowling the south range.

After feed was spread for the stock, Billy called the crew together.

"You've done a fair day's work," Billy told them. "I've got a bonus for each of you here in my pocket. What's more, there's a bath waiting for you at Tatnall's, and the rest is up to you. I'll expect you back at the ranch by morning, though."

The cowboys cheered and tossed their hats in the air.

Charlie then collected Chris and Joe, Bart and Clay.

"As for you four, I'll be by to take you home toward dusk. I want to ride out and check on the south range, and I figure I'll have dinner with Ryan and Rachel. That ought to give you time for a good soak and a bit of merrymaking. Don't go getting too venturesome, though. Justiss Junction's got a hundred eyes, and I've got a wife back home who's apt to skin anyone alive who gets too sinful, eh, Chris? Joe?"

"Ah, Uncle Charlie," Clay complained. "Joe and I're fifteen now. Don't you think—"

"Clay, what do you suppose your mama'd say if she found out you were up to no good?" Charlie asked. "You figure you'd see sixteen?"

Clay looked at his dusty boots and groaned. Charlie laughed and went to find his horse. The boys were left to consider their plight and likely plan some fitting prank.

Charlie found Marty Steele bedding down a thousand head a mile south of the junction. Marty's crew consisted of Bob Lee Wiley and Tomas Alejandro, a pair of young though veteran Flying J hands, and some twenty of Buck Creek's older orphans. Marty looked a little like a reluctant mama hen, instructing the boys to do this or that. The youngsters responded eagerly, but the southern roundup had obviously taken a toll on Marty.

"You'll never talk me into bossin' another roundup, Charlie Justiss!" Marty growled when Charlie appeared. "Especially with these babes. Why, a quarter of 'em are saddle-sore."

"Ryan said he'd send you the ones best suited to range work."

"He sent Wes the oldest ones. These . . . children, well, they still wet their britches at night, I'll wager."

Charlie laughed loudly. Then he grew serious.

66

"Just remember how it was when you first got to the regiment up in Virginia, Marty. These kids have been on their own a long time. This is new to them, but they'll catch on. Ryan's got a better knack of showing boys how to handle a horse than anyone I've known. Some of these youngsters are near fifteen or sixteen. They have to learn a trade soon, else they'll turn to stealing or worse."

"I know," Marty grumbled. "I guess Ry's got himself a handful back at that orphan's house now, too, what with just the younger ones left. I guess it's just missin' the Kansas trail's got me down. That an' these Herefords. They've not got the sass our old longhorns had."

"You're getting old, Marty. This remembering's an old man's game."

"Well, the years do creep along. You goin' to join us for chow tonight? This young Craddock kid knows his way around a cook fire."

"I thought I'd see if I could wrangle a meal out of Rachel."

"Well, you'd best be along then. They eat early. Don't forget, there's still close to sixty or so of those tadpoles up there. Watch they don't snatch your boots, Charlie. They're a wild crew."

"I'll keep that in mind," Charlie said, laughing.

The Buck Creek Ranch, as the orphans preferred to call their residence, was only a few miles to the east. Even a stranger could find the place easily. All he had to do was listen. Sixty boys, even at their quietest, made more noise than a troop of cavalry.

67

Charlie simply followed the sound.

He found Ryan with a dozen or so scruffy boys down at the creek. The oldest ones appeared no more than nine, and Charlie guessed it was their turn to scrub off a week's mischief. Ryan tossed cakes of lye soap to the bare youngsters, who immediately began bombarding each other with the whitish blocks.

"That's not what they're for," Ryan complained. "Put 'em to use where they do some good. Scrub yourselves so Rachel can tell. You don't pass muster, she'll bring you down here and finish the job herself. None too gently, either."

One of the older boys immediately verified the tale, and even the littlest ones set to work rubbing away the dust and grime from their undernourished frames.

"Marty was complaining of working the cattle with a young crew," Charlie said, joining his son on the creekbank. "I do believe you've got the real challenge."

"Yeah," Ryan agreed. "Most of these kids just came to us. Summer's always the worst time, Rachel says. Folks seem to think they can fend for themselves and send them on their way. One or two are only seven or eight."

"I see she's turned your heart to them."

"Can't help myself, Papa. The new ones cry themselves to sleep for a week. Then they start coming out to the house for a bit of Rachel's nursing. When she's got more than she can handle, she sends them to me. Next thing you know, I'm spinning some old tale of yours, and they practically move in with you."

"You weren't so different when you were that age," Charlie said, planting a hand on Ryan's shoulder. "You were sort of an orphan, too, what with me off to the war."

"I guess that's why I take them to heart, too. There's nobody else. And the older ones, Papa, they're something. Little boys of ten or twelve with their hands mangled, legs and backs bent from carrying water buckets twice their weight . . . and never a complaint when the work's hard and the weather's hot."

"They'll make good men."

"Those who've survived."

"I know," Charlie said, staring at the soapy boys in the creek. "You feel like a father to the lot of them, don't you?"

Ryan nodded, and Charlie grinned.

"It's good to put your hand to a worthwhile task, Ry. And when you've a good woman at your side, you've found gold, son."

"I know," Ryan said, smiling.

"So, Mr. Ryan, aren't you goin' to wash?" a youngster cried.

"Let's get him!" another shouted.

Suddenly an army of boys charged Ryan. They managed to wrestle him to the ground and get his clothes off before dragging him howling into the creek. Charlie made the mistake of laughing too hard, and the urchins then swept back to the bank, captured the former major, and likewise dragged him to the water.

"Hold on, boys!" Charlie called. "Let me shed my

clothes first."

The orphans relaxed their hold a moment, but when Charlie eased back from the bank, they resumed their charge. Near fifty or not, Charlie managed to drag five or six in with him. Then, soggy but refreshed, he shed the rest of his clothes and joined in the bath.

After seeing himself, the boys, and his father scrubbed, dried, and dressed, Ryan led the way back to the orphanage proper. Three bunkhouses sheltered the hundred or so boys sometimes residing at Buck Creek. Nearby, a single plank house served Ryan and Rachel.

"Somethin' smells good," one of the orphans declared as they all drank in the aroma of a bubbling stew pot.

"Papa, you will stay to dinner, won't you?" Ryan asked as he waved the boys along to the middle bunkhouse, the one containing the large dining room and kitchen.

"Thought you weren't going to ask," Charlie replied. "Wouldn't miss it."

And indeed, dinner proved the highlight of his day. Rachel had prepared a wonderful stew of beef roasts, carrots, celery, potatoes, and any odd green plucked from the spring garden or dug from the surrounding hillsides. It was a treat for Charlie to gaze at the sixty-odd smiling faces. More than ever, he was glad Angela had suggested setting aside the land for the orphanage.

"You all know we have a guest," Rachel announced once dinner was concluded. "Who is this?"

"Mr. Charlie," most of them answered. "Grandpapa," some of the younger ones added.

Charlie couldn't help laughing. More than once it had occurred to him that he was probably the whole county's grandfather nowadays. He didn't half mind the notion, and when he gathered the children around the steps two hours later and spun the old tale of how he'd fought Stands Tall, the fierce Comanche, he felt a head or two leaning against his side. Others clasped his weathered hands with their own as they shared the dangers of that bygone day.

"It's getting late," Rachel declared when the tale ended with Stands Tall's final charge. "Time for prayers and bed."

"Ahhh," the boys complained. But when she pretended anger, they scampered off to their bunks.

"Thank you," she said, giving Charlie a warm embrace. "Ry does what he can, but it takes a grandpa's touch to tell a story."

"Oh, I imagine he does just fine," Charlie said as he returned the embrace. "You both do, for that matter."

"Will you stay the night, Papa?" she asked.

"No, I've got four wild young cowboys in town to lasso and head home," Charlie explained. "Angela will expect us."

"Come again . . . soon."

"I will," Charlie promised. "It does a man's heart good to be around so many young faces."

"Does them good to know people care," Rachel added. "God bless you."

"And you all," Charlie said, gesturing at Rachel

and her brood.

After spending a few minutes with Ryan to discuss business and to get a list of the orphanage's needs, Charlie mounted his horse and headed back toward Justiss Junction. He paused but once — just above Marty's camp to listen to Bob Lee Wiley's guitar and the sweet, untrained voices of the young crew singing trail songs of places they had never seen and people they had never known. Charlie filled with sudden melancholy, and he urged his horse into a gallop. In a quarter hour he was at Justiss Junction.

"I suppose it's time for us to head home, huh?" Chris asked when Charlie located the four youngsters on the steps to the hotel.

"Appears so," Charlie said. "Sun's been dead a while now, and I imagine your mama's growing anxious."

Joe nodded and waved his companions toward their waiting horses. In less than five minutes, the boys were mounted and following Charlie northward down the darkened market road toward Palo Pinto.

"So, it's off to Fortune Bend with you four, eh?" Charlie asked.

"Yeah," Chris replied. "Two and a half months of racing ponies and breaking mustangs."

The others whooped their enthusiasm, and Charlie laughed.

"Just remember to sound a little like you'll miss your mama," Charlie told his sons. "And, Clay, I'll bet a letter home would be appreciated."

"Yes, sir," Clay answered.

"So, what are you waiting for?" Charlie asked, rearing his horse into the air and waving them along.

"Race you home!"

The boys shouted their response and howled as they slapped their animals into action. In no time they'd be back in Palo Pinto, and Charlie felt suddenly eager to do just that.

Chapter Five

They arrived in Palo Pinto late. A lantern outside the hotel and a few lamps burning here and there were the sole signs of life. Now that the saloons and gaming houses had been closed down by new ordinances, the town seemed dead by nine o'clock, and it was later than that by the time Charlie and the boys unsaddled their horses and brushed the weary animals' coats. The ponies were given bags of oats, and Charlie led his human companions down the street to the house.

Angela greeted him at the door.

"Long day?" she asked.

"Long week," Chris said as he hugged his mother.

Charlie nodded, then nudged Joe toward Angela. The older boy gave her a polite kiss, as did Clay.

"How are you, ma'am?" little Bart asked. Angela kissed them all, then conducted them along to the kitchen to find a bit of food fit for hungry young trailhands.

Charlie had little interest in eating. Rachel's stew would suffice. The dip in the creek had done only a superficial job of washing off the day's sweat and fatigue, and he'd added another layer of both on the ride north from Justiss Junction.

"Well?" Angela asked, grinning. "The tub's waiting, and I've got a hot kettle on the stove."

Charlie smiled and stepped past the ravenous boys to where the wooden tub stood. He emptied the kettle of hot water into the tub of water, then began removing his clothes. In a flash he was settling into the swirling warmth of the bath.

"Old bones getting to you, eh, Papa?" Chris joked.

"I think I hear 'em cracking," Joe added.

"Who got his horse to town first, huh?" Charlie asked. "As for these old weary bones of mine, they've earned their rest."

The boys grinned and went on with their eating. Angela had a time getting a fresh platter of food to the table before the previous one was emptied.

"Doesn't old Doc Singer feed the crew anymore?" she asked. "Charlie, you'd best check to see. I don't believe there's a bit of flesh left on these boys' bones."

She raised Chris's shirt and ran her fingers along his ribs. Chris inhaled, and it seemed there was little more than a skeleton sitting in a chair.

"You ought to look at Bart," Clay advised. "If there's more than sixty pounds to him, he's fattened up on your beef, Aunt Angela. A good nor'easter'd blow him to Mexico."

"Oh, you're not so much yourself, Clay Justiss," Bart barked.

Angela leaned over and pinched Bart's arm.

"It's true," she gasped in make-believe horror. "I'll

have to pack you an extra big lunch tomorrow, Bart. Wouldn't want you to starve."

Bart beamed, and the others grumbled. Charlie couldn't help laughing.

When the boys were finally satisfied, Angela left them the kitchen. Charlie climbed out of the tub moments later and let the boys have their turn. As the oldest, Joe, went first. Charlie couldn't help noticing the dark-haired boy seemed to grow daily now. His tanned shoulders had broadened, and a trace of whiskers had sprouted on his upper lip.

We'll soon be sending another one off into the world, Charlie thought. It both saddened and pleased him.

Charlie rubbed the moisture out of his skin and the soreness out of his muscles with a soft cotton towel. Joe was soaping his skin and singing an old trail song. Chris and Clay laughed at the bawdy lyric, and Charlie hoped it was soft enough that Angela wouldn't hear and order an impassioned scrubbing of Joe's mouth. Little Bart Davis moved his chair over beside Charlie and stared at a jagged red scar that cut across his thigh.

"Yank saber," Charlie explained. "Happened at Sharpsburg, September of '62. Makes a dandy of a scar, though in truth the wound wasn't much. The Yank came off the worse for it. I shot him in the head."

"You and Clay's papa both fought in the war, didn't you?" Bart asked.

"That war and others," Charlie said, sighing as he tossed the towel aside and slipped into the clothes Angela had laid on the table. "We had some hard

76

times."

"I'll bet you're glad they're over."

"Yes, glad," Charlie confessed. "Glad you boys haven't faced some of the nightmares I've seen."

"My folks died just after that war," Bart explained. "Wasn't bullets or anything. They caught a fever. My uncle looked after me for a time, but then, well, he had to go away."

"Oh?"

"Clay's papa looks after me now," Bart said proudly. "He says pretty soon I'll be a man worth knowing."

"If you ever reach five feet," Clay joked.

"It's not the size of a boy or a man that makes him worth knowing," Charlie declared. "It's what's inside. I've known men six and a half feet tall to wail like a baby when danger came around. I've seen boys no older than you four grit their teeth and do what was required to keep their families safe."

"Ryan got hatcheted by Indians when he was no older'n me," Joe said. "Billy got shot by rustlers."

"We almost did," Chris said, frowning. Charlie knew Chris was thinking of the day raiders had hit the horse corral at the Flying J. "Papa saved us, though," the boy declared proudly.

"That's all long past now," Charlie said, shaking away the memory as he dried his hair. "With luck, you youngsters will pass out your years in peace, give or take a contankerous mustang."

"Yeah," Joe said, grinning at the thought.

Joe and Chris were scrubbed and in bed in half an

hour. Clay remained with Charlie in the kitchen, waiting for Bart to finish his bath. The pale, pitifully thin boy seemed to shrink in the water, and Charlie hoped a summer of fresh air and Teresa Morales's cooking would fill the boy out some.

"I guess I could sit in here all night," Bart said finally. Seconds later the sound of hurried footsteps on the porch and a frantic knocking at the back door brought Charlie to his feet.

"Who's there?" Charlie called. Bart hopped out of the tub and wrapped a huge towel around his narrow waist. Clay stepped to where a shotgun rested on a gunrack and drew down the weapon. Charlie walked past them both and opened the door. Will Eppler stumbled inside and leaned his exhausted eleven-year-old head against Charlie's side.

"Mr. Justiss, you've . . . got to . . . come quick," the boy stammered. "There's been trouble."

"Trouble?" Charlie asked, taking the shotgun from Clay and replacing it on the rack. Instead Charlie took a Winchester rifle. "What kind of trouble?" he asked.

"Don't know," the boy cried, dropping to his knees. "Toby Hart rode in, said Pa was needed and somebody ought to get you and the sheriff."

"You've seen Bret?"

"No, sir," Will admitted. "I came straight here. There's no one at the jailhouse, and I don't know where the sheriff lives."

"I know," Clay said.

"Go fetch him," Charlie instructed. "Now sit down, Will, and get your wits back. What did Toby say?"

78

"Not much," Will explained as he fought to catch his breath. "Somebody shot up the Weidling place. Vik ran up the creek to get help, but there wasn't much of anybody there."

"All down at the junction with the herd," Charlie muttered. "So Toby and your papa went up to see what was going up?"

"Yes, sir," Will said, getting his color back. "I grabbed a horse and raced it to town. I figure it could be real bad. We heard shots."

Charlie nodded, then loaded the rifle. By the time Bret arrived, Charlie had fastened on a gunbelt and pistol.

"Where to?" Bret asked, nodding at the rifle.

"Caddo Creek," Charlie said. "Weidling place."

"Kemp!" Bret growled. "I'll grab Tut. No point to taking anybody else. It's dark, and we'd only shoot each other."

"Hold on," little Will called. "I'll show you the way."

"You stay put, son," Charlie said, giving the boy a gentle pat on the shoulder. "You did your job. Get some rest. Have Mrs. Justiss put you up for the night. I'll tell your papa."

"I couldn't," Will complained. "Pa went out there, and I —"

"Then get a bit of food and something to drink. Have Joe bring you out in an hour."

"We could bring him," Clay offered. "Bart and me."

Bart nodded, and Charlie shrugged his shoulders.

"Just see you stop at the Eppler place," Charlie ordered. "If you don't, I'll beat the daylights out of the three of your hides. Understand?"

"Yes, sir," the three boys replied.

Charlie then set off with Bret to find Alex Tuttle. Ten minutes later the three of them were riding westward down the Albany road.

"They planned it awfully well," Tut said as they approached the Eppler place. "I was off at the Cooke place, trying to trace some loon who shot up the chicken coop. That put me as far from the Weidlings as possible."

"I was up at Fortune Bend with Luis most of the evening," Bret added.

"And Wes had near everybody from the Flying J driving our herd to the junction," Charlie said, spitting. "Perfect time to visit those farmers. If Kemp's behind this, I'll see him hanged."

"Behind what?" Bret asked. "We don't know anything's been done yet."

Charlie knew. Something eating at his insides warned there'd been killing. Why else would anybody lure Tut from town? No, this was well-planned. Eric Weidling wouldn't send his wisp of a boy flying down Caddo Creek if a tumbleweed blew through the farmyard.

They found young Jordy Banks waiting at the Eppler farm.

"Wes and the rest went along ahead," Jordy told Charlie. "Miz Eppler said young Will went to fetch you, so Wes told me to wait."

"Who's Wes got with him?" Charlie asked.

"Mr. Justiss, Mr. Billy, I mean," the young cowboy said, blinking away fatigue. "O. T. Fuller, and three of those new boys. Barret Jenkins, Lew Old-ham, and Tucker Speers. Tuck's a fair shot with a rifle, too."

"We'd better catch 'em," Bret said, leading the way onward.

"Coming, Jordy?" Charlie asked

The cowboy hopped upon a horse and in a flash was ahead of them all.

"This is a little like old times," Bret said as he led the way slowly, cautiously across the narrow bridge over Caddo Creek. "Takes me back to the times we hunted down Rame Polk."

"I hope we're not up against another Polk," Tut said, sighing. "He near killed us both, Bret."

"I know," Bret whispered as he stopped his horse. Just ahead something moved through the brush. Charlie readied his rifle, but a familiar voice eased his nerves.

"That you, Charlie?" Wes Tyler called.

"Me, Bret, and Tut," Charlie answered. "Young Banks, too."

"Better he should stay there and watch the road," Wes advised. "We've had trouble."

"So I heard," Charlie said, slipping off the side of his horse. Bret and Tut did likewise. The three left Jordy to patrol the road, then tied their mounts to an oak tree and walked slowly to where Wes waited.

"The Weidling kid came to the house," Wes said, trembling. "I wasn't there."

Charlie grew uneasy. Whole wars didn't rattle

Wes.

"Go on," Charlie said.

"Toby fetched the captain. By the time I got here, it was all over."

"What's happened?" Bret asked.

Wes didn't explain. Instead he led the way to the Weidling house. On the porch sat little Viktor, head in hands. The boy's sobs haunted the night. Nearby lay two figures draped in blankets. By the size of the bodies, Charlie guessed they were the boy's folks.

"The other youngsters?" Charlie asked.

"Don't know," Wes answered. "Captain Eppler and Toby are off with the others havin' a look. I don't see how anybody got away, though, Charlie. Look at that house."

Only now did Charlie examine the wall of the Weidling house. Even in the dim light afforded by a lantern, it was plain to see shotgun and rifle bullets had torn the place to splinters.

"Barn's close to as bad," Wes muttered. "Takes a special brand to do this sort of thing. You know when they finished, they rode right past our place, yelled threats at Alice, and left. They might have done the same thing there. Hell, Charlie, my kids were there asleep! I'll see somebody pays for this."

"That's my job," Bret declared. "Looks like there are plenty of tracks. Tut and I'll have a look."

"You know where they'll lead," Wes said, pointing westward. "Wasn't Kemp just up here the other day threatenin' everybody in sight? This has his mark, Charlie."

"And if we prove it, he'll hang," Bret promised. "Threats are one thing, though. It took a special

82

kind of madness to do this."

Charlie nodded. He then sat beside Viktor and pulled the boy to his side.

"Son, I know this has been a nightmare," Charlie whispered, "but your little sisters and your brothers are nowhere to be found. Did your papa have a place for them to hide? Did you maybe get them to safety before heading for the line cabin?"

Viktor only shuddered and whimpered in German.

"You've got to speak to me in English, Viktor," Charlie whispered. "Tell me where to look."

"By creek," Viktor mumbled, shaking like a leaf. "Many rocks are there. Tall rocks. I leave Jakob there. Rolf . . . Rolf take the others . . ."

"All right, son," Charlie said, gripping the boy's shoulders. "I'll go have a look."

Charlie rose to his feet and set off toward the creek. Viktor raced after him and clutched his hand.

"I show you," Viktor said, swallowing his tears and leading the way. They crept through heavy brush and a tangle of willows and briars before reaching the shallow creek. Viktor then called out, and moments later a terrified boy of five crept out from a narrow crevice in a nearby boulder.

"Viktor!" the child screamed, throwing his arms around his brother and holding on as if life depended upon it. Viktor hugged his brother tightly, then stared blankly into Charlie's eyes.

"Jakob, my brother," Viktor explained. "Come, we go find my sisters."

There was no need. By the time Viktor retraced their steps to the house, Martin Schneider was there, his solemn eyes drinking in the nightmare scene.

"I come when I hear shooting," Schneider explained. "I find Anna and little Emma in the tall grass. I take them home, then come back with my rifle. They have gone then, these . . . these swine."

"I know," Charlie said, frowning as he felt Viktor lean against him. "Best thing to do now is head along home. Are the girls welcome to stay the night?"

"Welcome?" Schneider asked, pointing to the bodies on the porch. "How would they not be welcome? We are friends, Eric and I. To see him killed! I will pray God to strike down those who did that."

"No, that'll be my pleasure," Wes said, grinding his teeth.

"Charlie, why don't you head on home yourself," Bret suggested. "I know you've got a houseful just now, but those two seem to have taken to you. Think you've got room for a couple more?"

"In that big house of ours?" Charlie asked as he lifted little Jakob off the ground and held him in one arm. "We've got space for a small army. I do wish we'd find the other boy. There was an older one."

"We have!" Henry Eppler called from the far side of the barn. Charlie hoped to see Rolf Weidler scamper to his brothers' sides, but instead Toby Hart and the captain carried a pale figure on a blanket.

"Rolf!" Viktor cried, dashing to his brother's side. *"Nein!"* he screamed as he stared into Rolf's closed eyes. *"Nein!"*

"He's not dead," Toby said, helping Eppler set Rolf gently on the earth. "Someone shot a bullet

84

through his arm, and he's bled some. He'll be all right in a week or so."

"Looks like another guest for you, Charlie," Bret said, frowning. "Before you leave, I'd like to ask him some questions. He's like as not the only one who saw anything."

"Ask him tomorrow," Charlie said. "He won't make any sense now. See if you can trace the tracks. I'll bet they crossed the Brazos and left their trail there."

"Why bother?" Wes growled. "We know where they came from!"

"Not for certain," Bret declared, "and we can't act on our suspicions alone."

Wes turned to Charlie, who frowned and nodded.

"He's right," Charlie echoed. "We'll need proof. The thing about killers is that they always provide some. We'll find it, and we'll hunt 'em down like the wolves they are."

Viktor returned to Charlie's side and gazed up into the tall, silvery-haired rancher's sad eyes.

"I promise you, son," Charlie whispered. "We'll punish them."

The boy only stared blankly and trembled.

Chapter Six

Eric and Karin Weidling were laid side by side in the churchyard of the Methodist church the next afternoon. The Schneiders brought the teary-eyed girls to town for the burial, and Angela held little Jakob's hand. Rolf remained in bed, as pale as death from loss of blood. Viktor, seemingly a decade older, stood stiff and solemn beside Charlie.

After verses were read and a hymn was sung, Martin Schneider drew Charlie aside.

"They come next to my farm, yes?" the wiry German asked.

"No," Charlie answered. "Wes will have men watching. If it was Kemp's outfit, they'll have a hard time raiding anybody again."

"Who else could it be?" Wes asked as he joined the meeting. "Bret and Tut are out there trackin' 'em right now. Won't be long before we settle accounts."

Charlie wasn't so sure, and he said as much.

"There is other business to talk about," Schneider

said then. "What will happen to the *kindern,* the children?"

"Rolf is going to stay in my house till he's well," Charlie declared. "After that, we'll talk. He's too young to work that farm and tend his family alone. Later, though, he's bound to want the place. For now, it's not wise any of those youngsters should live out there with raiders about."

"I wish the girls to stay with me," Schneider said, taking off his ill-shaped felt hat and scratching behind one ear. "I have mostly boys, and Marianne is like sister to Anna and Emma."

"What of the boys?"

"Rolf is tall and strong. A farm can always use more hands."

"And Viktor?"

"I have already four *kindern*. Rolf can help, and there is no other place the girls should go. Maybe another farm can take Jakob and Viktor?"

"I don't like splitting up family," Charlie grumbled.

"Five? No one can take so many."

Charlie nodded. "I do think we should talk to them, though," he told Schneider.

"*Ja.* Someone will take Jakob. He is small, and there are always men who would have a son. He will make a good farmer. Viktor, I must tell you, is not so good a worker. Even in Germany he keeps his nose in books. He will never be happy on a farm."

"Well, he's welcome to stay with me for the time being. Jakob, too. Later, we'll see who opens a door to them. We also have a place down south a way for orphans. They'd be welcome there, too."

"Good," Schneider said. Charlie could tell it grieved the farmer not to take all the Weidlings in himself. There was a practical side to those Germans, though, and it kept them from overextending their pocketbooks or their hearts.

Charlie told Viktor and Rolf the news over a generous lunch Angela prepared partly as a welcome for the Weidling boys and partly as a farewell meal for Joe, Chris, Clay, and Bart.

"I will not leave my brothers," Rolf vowed.

"Not for a time, anyway," Angela told them. "You'll need at least a week's rest. Besides, I'll want the company. I never could abide a house that didn't have youngsters scampering about."

Viktor said little. He passed his afternoon reading stories to little Jakob from one of the books in Charlie's library. Later, though, Viktor asked Charlie about the raiders.

"The sheriff's tracking them," Charlie explained. "We'll know more later."

"You will kill them?"

"We'll bring them to trial if we can. Then they'll hang."

Charlie wished he had words to erase the boy's bitterness, but he supposed there were none. Bret and Tut returned to town an hour before supper, exhausted from a fruitless search. As Charlie had feared, the raiders had masked their trail by riding through the Brazos.

"We spoke with the Kemps," Bret grumbled. "If they had a hand in it, they sure were smooth. Ike seemed downright surprised. He even offered to send his boys with us to search the river."

"Clever."

"That, or he's telling the truth," Bret said. "Charlie, I just don't know. If it's somebody else, though, we ought to spread the word. No one's likely to be safe."

"If it wasn't Kemp, why hit the Weidling place?" Charlie asked. "Who do it when we were off trailing our herd to market?"

"Well, the inside of the house was torn apart. Maybe they were looking for money."

Charlie found it hard to believe. A mounted party would surely find better pickings than a German emigrant family. Why not hit the bank or the Flying J?

No answers presented themselves. Bret questioned Rolf once the boy was better, but Rolf knew nothing. A bullet had come out of the darkness and pierced his arm. Pain and fear had blinded him thereafter.

Either Bret or Tut was out riding the county every night the balance of June. Charlie had Wes patrol Caddo Creek as well, and Luis kept a wary eye out for trouble as he and his young outfit scoured the northern half of the county for wild mustangs. Not a hint of the raiders was to be found, though.

As for the Weidling boys, in early July Rolf finally agreed to go to the Schneider place. The Weidlings' crops needed tending, and Rolf missed his sisters. Viktor and Jakob remained with Angela and Charlie.

"Don't you think they're doing well?" Angela asked. "Viktor's bright. He reads English like a scholar, and little Jakob is like an extra grandchild."

"Exactly," Charlie told her. "He needs younger

parents, and Viktor would do better to be around other boys and girls."

"Chris and Joe will be back in the fall."

"For what, a year or two? Don't you think it would be better to take them to Rachel and Ryan?"

"No," Angela said, stomping her foot. "I'll talk to Vicki, though. She and Bret could take in Jakob. For that matter, Viktor would probably be welcome, too."

"That's a lot of family for two people as busy as Bret and Vicki."

"Viktor's such a help, though. He's really a man hiding in that little body. I just can't let them go to Buck Creek and get lost in that swarm of urchins."

"You know it's not that way, Angela. Rachel mothers them all, and they look after each other. Viktor might prove a big help with the lessons, too."

"Well, they're certainly going nowhere this summer. I won't have an empty house when there are those in need of a bed."

Charlie grinned and kissed her forehead. He was half inclined to adopt the boys and leave them to her nurture.

In July, Charlie and Angela became grandparents again. Ross's wife, Eliza, brought a boy, Edward, into the world, and Angela relished her chance to rock the baby and pamper him as was the right of all grandmothers. Occupied as she was with little Edward, Angela nevertheless disproved Charlie's notion of delivering Viktor and Jakob to Buck Creek.

"They're family, too, now, Charlie," she declared.

90

"You know Viktor worships you, and little Jakob wouldn't sleep without a story from you."

Charlie sighed and surrendered. It was all true. He'd taken them to heart as well.

July and August were hot as always. There was never enough rain to keep the creeks full or the stock content, and 1881 was particularly hard on the new farms that didn't bound some creek or rest along the banks of the Brazos. Otto Stuffel and other enterprising newcomers loaded barrels in wagons and drove them to the river. The farmers then watered their corn plants by hand.

Others dug small channels from a neighbor's farm to let the life-giving water trickle to their fields. By summer's end, many of the creeks themselves were dry, though, and daily the wagons shuttled water to parched fields.

No raiders disturbed the late summer tranquility. As for Ike Kemp, the rancher had enough concern keeping his stock watered. The fiery-eyed rancher kept his own counsel, and except for monthly trips to Art Stanley's mercantile for supplies, neither Kemp nor his sons ventured from the Crown K.

Charlie might have forgotten about the raiders had not years of experience warned no plague ever went away of its own accord. Bret and Tut cut down on their nightly rides, but Wes kept up the watch on Caddo Creek. And Charlie himself reminded his neighbors to stay on guard.

In September, Chris and Joe returned home taller and tanned as brown as leather. Chris's hair had turned almost white from the August sun, and Joe sounded more and more like a man.

The boys were not at all displeased to discover the Weidling youngsters still at the house. Chris especially delighted in entertaining Viktor and Jakob with tales of mustanging on the open plain. The four boys got on magically, and even Charlie decided it was best to leave them be for now.

September also brought a resumption of Vicki's school duties. Chris and Joe grumbled about the confines of a classroom after a summer of roaming free across the county, but Viktor seemed downright eager. Angela sighed when Jakob accompanied his brother, especially since her granddaughter Hope also began lessons that year.

"Well, you'll have J.P. and Tom to look after," Charlie said, referring to Vicki and Bret's two youngest boys. At three and four, the scampering children were an even match for a score of grandmothers.

For his part, Charlie and his son Ross were busy with the county's tax rolls. Neither enjoyed collecting revenues, but Charlie had discovered the best time was just after harvest when farmers had funds and the ranchers had shipped beef to market. With the flood of new population that had swept over Palo Pinto since the previous year, though, twenty or thirty new bills had to be prepared and handed over to Bret Pruett and Alex Tuttle for delivery to the landholders.

After spending the better part of a week locked up

in his office, amending the tax rolls and updating the land office records, Charlie was in desperate need of a holiday. Whenever he found the walls closing in, he saddled a horse and rode out toward the ranch.

Actually he had another purpose in mind as well. Vicki complained quite loudly how Chris and Joe had resumed their bad habits, slipping away from the school at noon recess to swim away the afternoon. Of late they were also coaxing the Eppler boys and even some of the emigrant farmboys to go along. Bret, upon returning from delivering tax notices, had twice chased the reluctant schoolboys from a branch of Wolf Creek.

Today it was Charlie's turn. He found it hard to fault the boys for choosing the refreshing waters of Wolf Creek over the confines of a schoolroom, but lessons were important, too, and miscreants wanted punishment. The courthouse was in need of a new coat of paint, and Joe and Chris had become experienced painters. Previously they'd added a fresh layer to the church and the new schoolhouse after first sneaking out to watch some ladies in a traveling brothel bathe in the Brazos and later visiting the women on a day Celia Cooke chose to spy on the camp.

Charlie stopped at the school long enough to check on his boys' presence.

"They're off again, Papa," Vicki said, shaking her head. "This time they've talked a half-dozen others into going along. Even Viktor," she grumbled.

"Well, I'm not sure I disapprove where he's concerned," Charlie said, ducking away from Vicki's halfhearted slap. "He's got his nose buried in a book too often. If that boy gets any paler, someone's sure to mistake him for a ghost."

"You'll see they're reprimanded this time?" she asked. "Papa, they're my own brothers. If they get away with this, every boy in the county will slip off with them."

"Are they neglecting their lessons?" Charlie asked.

"You know Chris is my best reader, and Joe's got a head for figures. They're the oldest, and I need their help with the young ones. Even Ryan helped, and Lord knows he was a scamp if ever there was one."

"Joe's off to college next year," Charlie mumbled. "I guess it's time he grew serious. As for Chris, I don't know. That one's got the devil in his britches."

"Papa, it's time they got a good thrashing."

"I imagine we can oblige," Charlie said, scowling. "And the courthouse does want painting."

He crossed the Albany road and threaded his way through the hills toward Wolf Creek. He passed a few cows here and there, but the range east of the creek had been near emptied of stock by the big shipment to Kansas City in June. Charlie paused to help a bawling calf free himself from a gopher hole, then rode along the creek.

Chris was jumping off a low oak branch into a deep pool when Charlie rode up. Joe and the others were cheering their leader onward. Suddenly the boys grew mum and turned toward the judge with sheepish grins.

"Howdy, Papa," Joe said, lowering himself into the stream. "Wasn't expecting you to be about."

"I'll bet not," Charlie said, hands on his hips. "Thought you had a couple of hours of school yet."

"Vicki let us off early," Chris cried as he hugged the branch. "Thought we'd bring everybody up here for a swim."

"Strange she didn't mention that to me," Charlie told them. "I think she did mention something about a thrashing, though. And I've noticed the courthouse could use some paint."

"Oh, no," Joe grumbled, slapping the water. "Not again."

"That's what I was thinking," Charlie said, putting on a convincing frown. "It's bad enough you two sneak off when you ought to be helping the young ones with their lessons. Now you bring Viktor up here. And you Eppler boys! Your papa will have words for you, no doubt. Who else is there? Bailey Cooke? And is that you, Alek Schneider?"

The farmboys did their best to shrink from view, but it was too late. They all grew a shade paler.

"Now I think you'd best locate your clothes and get headed back to town," Charlie told them. "Tomorrow, when you finish your lessons, I'll expect you at the courthouse ready to paint."

"Me?" Viktor cried, pointing a thumb into his bony white chest. "I only come this one time, Mr. Justiss."

"One time too many," Charlie declared. "Now let's get to it, boys."

The guilty youngsters trudged to the bank and collected their clothes. As they dressed, Charlie started to head north. Before he could travel ten feet, though, the unmistakable sounds of gunfire broke the silence.

"Papa?" Joe asked, pulling on his pants and racing to his father's side.

"You boys stay right here," Charlie called. "Right here! Until I find what's happened, I don't want you going anywhere."

Charlie then slapped his horse into a gallop and vanished into the sea of buffalo grass and scrub mesquite beyond Wolf Creek.

He rode maybe a quarter mile before slowing. The shooting had stopped, and it worried him. Gunfire at least gave evidence that a battle was taking place. A brief outburst hinted of ambush or worse.

As he neared Wolf Gap, Charlie came upon a riderless horse. The tack was unfamiliar, but the brand was the winged J of the Flying J Ranch, *his* ranch. He muttered a curse and followed the animal's tracks back to where a solitary figure lay slumped over a boulder.

It was O. T. Fuller. Charlie touched the fallen cowboy's arm, then eased him to the ground. Fuller's chest was torn apart by three shots. He'd died quickly. His gun remained in its holster.

Just across Wolf Creek other tracks headed south. Twenty or thirty head of cattle had been driven in that direction by a half dozen or so horsemen. One rider had crossed the creek and galloped off ahead.

"Billy never sends a man off by himself," Charlie mumbled. The fleeing rider must have been Fuller's partner.

Charlie never hesitated. He slapped his horse into

a gallop once again and splashed through the shallows of the creek. Shortly he was back at the pool.

"Chris, Joe, boys?" he called. "You about?"

Joe peeked out from behind a boulder and waved his father over. Panic spread across Joe's frightened face, and he motioned for quiet. Charlie could hear the sounds of cattle splashing through the creek upstream. The rustlers couldn't be far away. He turned his horse and started to pursue.

"Papa, no," Chris cried as he raced to his father and grabbed the horse's bridle. "There are five or six of them."

Charlie tried to shake loose, but Chris's grip was firm.

"They shot Fuller," Charlie explained. "You can't let killers get away."

"Papa, there are too many," Chris objected. "Besides, we've got Jordy over here, and he needs help."

Charlie surrendered. He couldn't very well leave a wounded cowboy to bleed to death. Grumbling, Charlie let Chris lead the way to where young Jordy Banks lay bleeding.

"Take his horse and see if you can find Billy," Charlie told Joe. "Tell him what's happened. Those thieves will have to cross the Albany road, and they're bound to leave a good trail. I want 'em caught."

"Yes, sir," Joe agreed, mounting Jordy's horse and galloping off toward the gap.

"Jordy, what happened?" Charlie asked.

"I don't know what to say," the young man answered. "O.T. and I were movin' a bunch of cows up the creek. Then somebody opened up on us. He was dead 'fore I knew it, so I got on my horse and headed out of there. They shot me as I got to the creek."

Charlie examined the wound. A single bullet had torn a hole in Jordy's side. Josiah Eppler had washed and bandaged the wound, but it continued to bleed.

"It's not too bad," Josiah declared. "I've seen lots worse at the post hospital at Fort Richardson. The bullet went clear through."

Charlie nodded. Bullets could do a lot of damage to a man's insides, though, and Jordy looked to be in a bad way.

"You figure we can get him to your papa's place, Josiah?" Charlie asked.

"Just a few miles," the boy replied. "I'll bind the wound tighter. That ought to stop the bleeding."

"You know a lot about this," Charlie said, surprised at the twelve-year-old's skill.

"Nothing much to do at a fort," Josiah explained. "I spent most of my time at the hospital."

"He pulls teeth, too," Will pointed out.

"Does he?" Charlie asked, trying to grin. "He's handy to have around."

Charlie helped Josiah tighten the bindings and get Jordy mounted.

"I should wait on Joe," Chris said when Charlie waved for the others to follow.

"I will stay also," Viktor added.

"Then, you'd better take this," Charlie said, pulling a Winchester out of his saddle scabbard. "Don't you fire unless you have to, Chris."

"I won't," the boy promised.

98

Charlie nodded, then headed off southward. He kept his eyes peeled for signs of trouble. None came, and he was able to get young Jordy to the Eppler place in a little less than an hour.

"Glory, what's happened?" Catherine Eppler cried when Charlie led the bleeding cowboy and the gaggle of youngsters toward the house.

"Trouble," Charlie said. "Somebody best head to town and fetch Doc Garnett."

"I will," Bailey Cooke volunteered. "Can I borrow a horse, Miz Eppler?"

"In the barn," she said as Charlie eased Jordy down from the horse. "Hurry, Bailey."

"Yes, ma'am," the boy said, racing to the barn. Bailey didn't bother to saddle the animal. He just hopped up and galloped down the road to town.

Henry Eppler arrived shortly after Bailey Cooke returned with the doctor. The captain's shirt was torn by briars, and his face was black from powder smoke.

"Had trouble?" Charlie asked.

"Raiders made off with twenty or thirty head of my stock," Eppler answered. "I shot one of them. Looks like you had a run-in with 'em, too."

Charlie followed the captain's eyes to his sleeve. Blood splotches stained Charlie's shirt and vest.

"They killed O. T. Fuller," Charlie explained. "And Jordy Banks took a bullet through his side. Doc Garnett's with him now."

"Bad?"

"Bad enough. He's young, though."

"I've known youngsters to get themselves killed out here," Eppler said, frowning. "My boys all right?"

"Josiah did a fair piece of doctoring. They're fine."

"I don't much like this, Charlie. A couple of those riders looked to know what they were doing. We could wind up with a war on our hands."

"No," Charlie vowed. "Going south they'll leave a clear trail. We'll settle with them shortly."

Billy Justiss and some fifteen hands from the Flying J rode into the Eppler farmyard toward dusk. Charlie was glad to see Joe and Chris again. Little Viktor Weidling rode along behind Hector Suarez.

"They hit the Epplers, too," Charlie declared as the boys hopped off the horses. "Hector, why don't you see if you can scare up their trail. Take a good man with you. Everybody else best rest up a bit. Toward nightfall we'll go after 'em."

"In the dark?" Billy asked.

"This is our country," Charlie said. "We know the terrain. Darkness is on our side."

Billy appeared doubtful. Only four or five of the cowboys were as old as twenty. Some of the younger ones' eyes betrayed the fear they held in their hearts.

Better we go in the darkness, Charlie thought. Those raiders can't know we're just a band of children.

"See your horses get some grain and water," Billy commanded. "Hector, who do you want?"

"Let me have the Speers boy," Hector said, pointing to Tucker Speers, the fifteen-year-old orphan from Buck Creek who'd fast become a demon on horseback.

"Take care," Charlie urged.

Hector nodded, then charged off southward, followed by young Speers. Charlie then assigned three or four cowboys to see the farmboys safely home. Chris, Joe, and Viktor remained.

Catherine Eppler fed her two dozen unexpected guests a fine supper. The cowboys then gathered around a small campfire and sang mournful trail songs. A weary Doc Garnett waved Charlie over to the back door of the house and frowned.

"I did what I could, Charlie," the doctor explained. "Never could get the bleeding stopped, and the boy just passed on. Didn't say a word, just looked up at me like I let him down somehow. Then he was gone."

"Happens," Charlie said, biting his lip to keep from boiling over with anger. "Damn! I'm so tired of laying the young ones to rest! Someone's going to pay for this! I promise you that."

"I'll send a wagon for the body. We'll do the burying in the morning. He have family?"

"A sister down south somewhere. Georgia Staves knows her. We can send a telegram."

"I'm afraid I'm leaving you the tough part. You've got five boys in there who don't know. I fear they'll take it bitter hard."

"They should," Charlie said, frowning. "It's hard news."

Charlie collected the youngsters and led them out past the barn.

"I know you boys were partial to Jordy," Charlie began.

"He taught me to play my mouth organ," Will Eppler said, grinning. "It's bad, isn't it?"

"Worse," Charlie admitted. "I'm afraid Jordy's gone. He just bled himself to death."

"I tried to stop it," Josiah said, coughing away tears.

"I know," Charlie said, drawing the five of them to him.

"Was the ones killed Mama and Papa," Viktor said, staring bitterly westward. "You said they would hang."

"I said they'd pay," Charlie replied. "They will. We'll go get them tonight."

"Papa, Jordy was scarce older'n me," Joe said, somehow not believing such a thing as death possible. "How can it be?"

"Life is hard sometimes," Charlie told them. "And death is sudden. It's difficult to understand how it can strike like lightning and take away people we care for. It does, though. You see, if we could live forever, life wouldn't mean much. It's knowing that tomorrow it could be over that makes each moment all the more precious."

"Did Jordy hurt much?" Chris asked.

"Some, son. I won't lie to you about that. But I'd guess that knowing he had friends around made it easier. And tomorrow when we lay him in the ground, I suspect he'll be able to hear our prayers."

"Think so?" Joe asked.

"I do."

"I want to go with you tonight," Joe said. "If I'm old enough to lose a friend, I'm old enough to go after his killers."

"Me also," Viktor cried.

"No," Charlie said firmly. "This isn't a job for a bunch of youngsters. Truth is, I plan to leave a third of Billy's men behind. I'm hopeful of taking the raiders in to trial. If it's a fight they want, though, it won't take many of us to bring their end."

Charlie then gave each of the youngsters a nod and a touch on the shoulder before turning back toward the house. He knew they wouldn't rest easy until the rustlers were swept from the range. Neither would Charlie Justiss.

Chapter Seven

As night settled in around the weary cowboys, Bret Pruett and Alex Tuttle appeared.

"Doc Garnett told us," Bret explained. "So, I guess we'll do some killing."

"Likely," Charlie confessed.

"First, though, I want a chance to bring them in for trial. Charlie, I know they've done wrong, but I'd also like to find out if they were the ones who did in the Weidlings."

Charlie nodded his understanding. He and Billy then began sifting through the men, selecting those who would ride after the raiders. The chosen ten then busied themselves loading rifles and readying pistols for the battle to come.

"Mr. Justiss," young Barret Jenkins complained, "Jordy Banks was my friend. He pulled me out of a tough spot back in June, and I feel I should go."

Charlie eyed the young cowboy and shook his head.

"How old are you, son?" Charlie asked.

"Near fifteen," the youngster answered.

"I won't have my own boys ride tonight," Charlie said. "I sure won't take another man's son."

"I'm nobody's son," Jenkins responded. "I never knew my pa, and I scarce recall a ma or anybody else. I lost two fingers working the rail camps, and an alligator took a toe when I was seven. There's nobody to cry over me, Mr. Justiss. And I can't help thinkin' I'm duty bound to go."

"You're not," Charlie answered. "First of all, you haven't done this sort of thing before. It's dangerous, not just for you but for everybody else that's along. A man can get shot by a friend as well as a foe. I need steel-nerved men tonight."

"Try me," Jenkins urged.

"Second, I've got to bury a boy not old enough to shave regular tomorrow morning. You, son, why, you're not close to full-grown yet. Give yourself time. Don't hurry death. It comes fast enough on its own."

"I'm not afraid, Mr. Justiss."

"I am," Charlie confessed. "You said you have no pa. Well, as long as you ride for us, I'm your pa. If you won't value your hide, I will. There's work ahead of you here, building a ranch and a county. Palo Pinto's going to need good men. It's going to need you. You stay here and watch the road. Could be there are other raiders about."

Jenkins looked deeply into Charlie's eyes. The boy silently pleaded to come along, Charlie's heart was closed to the matter, though, and he wouldn't be swayed.

Two other hands also objected to staying behind,

but Charlie dealt with them likewise. It was bad enough to take Toby Hart and Tony Alwyn along. Both were but twenty. Tucker Speers was with Hector, too, and the Tuck, as the men called him, was Joe's age. Charlie'd take no other babes along.

Henry Eppler was another matter. When the ex-cavalryman stepped out with loaded carbine, Charlie welcomed him.

"Been a long time since we rode after Comanches, eh?" the captain asked.

"A time," Charlie agreed.

It was young Speers who arrived with word of the raiders. Hector was watching their camp.

"They're not much afraid of us," Speers explained. "They've camped in the open, right alongside a little creek. There's rocks above 'em on three sides, and they're burnin' fires tall enough to see for half a mile."

"They're dead," Billy declared. "Like shootin' ducks on a pond."

"Only you just wait and let me talk to 'em first," Bret insisted. "Everybody hear that?"

The others muttered angrily, but in the end, all seemed willing to give Bret his chance to speak to the killers.

All that lay ahead, though. First Charlie motioned for the men to mount up. Then, with Tucker Speers leading the way, the riders set off southward.

Charlie couldn't help noticing the chill that soon crept through the air. A swirling mist devoured the ground, and the moon overhead danced in and out

106

of a single cloud. Off in the distance a wolf howled, and an eerie veil seemed to fall across the land.

Young Speers slowed his pace. He grew confused for a moment. Soon, though, a pinprick of light drew the boy's attention, and Charlie knew the outlaws were close.

When the riders joined Hector, they dismounted and tied their horses securely to willow and live oak branches. Hector then described the encampment.

"Hector, it's best you and young Speers circle around and cut them off from the horses," Charlie whispered. "The cattle are down at the creek, fifty or so, and they'll likely run off with the first shots."

"It'd seem so," Bret remarked.

Charlie nodded, then spread the men in a thin line across the hillside. Finally they started toward the raiders' camp.

Down below, the killers sang and joked about their exploits. It galled Charlie, and he had to physically restrain an angry Toby Hart. In the end, a premature rifle shot would only allow some of the raiders to escape. That Charlie would not permit.

Finally the noose began to close around the outlaws. One by one Charlie's companions took position in the rocks around the raider camp. Each marked one of the figures outlined by the blazing campfires. Then Bret Pruett called out in a thunderous voice.

"You're surrounded," Bret hollered. "Raise your hands and keep still. This is Sheriff Pruett of Palo Pinto County. Move and you're dead."

Instantly the outlaws scrambled toward cover. Seconds later the hillside erupted as Winchesters deliv-

107

ered well-aimed shells into the outlaw camp.

"They're all around us!" an outlaw screamed.

"Run for the horses, boys!" another called.

But rifles spit out tongues of fire, and the voices were soon quieted. Between the mist and the darkness, it was hard to spot much more than a shadow of the outlaws. The ring of marksmen made escape near impossible, though, and anyone darting into the open for long was illuminated by the fire.

"Give it up, down there!" Bret shouted. "I'll see you get to trial."

"Come and get us!" a deep voice answered. "We're here for the takin'."

Charlie frowned. He didn't relish the idea of fighting in close quarters, and that certainly seemed inevitable. He wove his way through his companions, picking the more experienced ones for the battle to come.

"When the opportunity presents itself, move in," Charlie whispered to each in turn. "But keep to cover. "There's little to be gained by getting shot to pieces."

Billy was the first to press the assault. Henry Eppler followed, and Bret and Tut wove their way through the rocks shortly thereafter. Charlie himself set aside his rifle and drew his Colt.

Now's the time, he thought as he moved toward the raiders' campfires, taking care to keep away from the circle of light provided by the flames. He picked as his objective a shadowy figure cowering a few feet from the easternmost of the fires.

The shooting became sporadic, for now firing only served to reveal the shooter's position. In the silence that followed, Charlie continued to close on his enemy. The night was fearfully crisp and utterly still now, and it was easy to believe himself cast into another world.

He knew the others were equally uneasy. Maybe it was even worse for them. Charlie had fought before, faced death and dealt it, too. It was a chill, heartless game, one he thought he'd left behind. But life had a way of turning, and only a fool thought he had seen the last trial to be faced.

"Give it up!" Bret called again.

"Go to blazes!" the shadow in front of Charlie answered.

Soon enough, Charlie thought as he readied his pistol. He hesitated, for taking a life was never easy. He remembered young Jordy Banks's ashen face, though. He aimed and fired.

The shadow stumbled toward the fire, clutching his bloody forehead. Then he fell, lifeless, into the dusty ground.

"Cal?" a companion called.

Two figures raced across the clearing, heading toward the creek and possible escape. The first, a burly man dressed in buffalo hides, managed to reach the shelter of a pile of boulders. The second man was less lucky. He was hit by three shots in succession and spun to the ground.

"There's just one left now!" Henry Eppler declared. "He's headed for the creek."

Charlie allowed himself a chance to catch his breath. Hector had the escape route blocked, and others now moved toward the remaining renegade. Charlie made his way among the dead, satisfying himself that none would rise and empty a pistol into an unsuspecting cowboy. When he turned the corpse nearest the fire over, a flash of light drew his attention. He knelt down and drew out a small locket from the outlaw's pocket. Even in the dim firelight he recognized it as belonging to Karin Weidling.

"So," Charlie muttered, "it's the old story, death following death."

Suddenly a pair of shots tore through the night, and Hector called out in alarm, "He's makin' for the wagon!"

Charlie immediately stuffed the locket in his shirt pocket and turned toward his left. A supply wagon stood twenty yards away, with harnessed team ready and waiting.

"You thought you had me, did you?" the burly outlaw yelled. "Not by half."

Charlie heard a whip snap, and then a volley of rifle fire barked. The ground rumbled, and a bright orange flash followed. The wagon and its driver vanished in a violent explosion.

"Good God," Henry Eppler cried as a shower of splinters descended on the encampment.

"Must've hit a powder keg!" Tut yelled.

Charlie huddled beneath the spreading branches of a juniper and waited for the wooden downpour to pass. Dust and smoke hung heavy in the air even then.

"That's the last of 'em," Billy called out. "Anybody hurt?"

"Just one," Hector answered. In the dim afterglow of the burning wagon, Charlie saw Hector helping young Speers along. The boy limped badly, and a great blotch of red spread across one thigh.

"Get the wound bound," Charlie ordered. "Then get him to town."

Hector ripped off his shirt and set about bandaging Tucker Speers's bad leg. Charlie meanwhile drifted to the nearest campfire. Bret and Tut were dragging the corpses of the raiders there.

"I found this," Charlie said, passing the locket to Bret. "It was Karin Weidling's."

"So these fellows had a hand in that, too," Bret grumbled. "Well, they've paid a price."

"You recognize any of them?"

"No," Bret said, frowning. "Strange, too, isn't it? Doesn't figure a bunch of strangers would hit us and the Epplers like this, much less raid the Weidling place."

"You still suspect Kemp?"

"Don't you?" Bret asked.

Chapter Eight

Early that next morning Charlie stood beside the narrow grave cut in the churchyard as Jordy Banks's comrades laid him to rest. Hector Suarez played a mournful tune on his guitar and sang a ballad that spoke of farewells and spoiled youth. The words were Spanish, but Charlie, gazing into Hector's reddening eyes, understood.

I've been here before, Charlie told himself as he gripped Chris's shoulders in his strong fingers. There'd been too many young men buried in that churchyard. It seemed to weigh on every mind that passed by the simple oak coffin. Youngsters like the Eppler boys and little Viktor Weilding were especially moved. Joe and Chris knelt beside the grave and whispered to their dead friend. Then Chris returned and took his father's hand.

"Papa, it's time to leave," the boy whispered. "Hector and the others'll fill in the grave."

"Sure," Charlie mumbled. He then turned and followed the boys back to the house.

It seemed that autumn had come and gone in that very instant. One minute Charlie was standing in the churchyard paying his respects to Jordy Banks. The next a sharp north wind was announcing the arrival of winter.

Although the summer sun tormented Palo Pinto and everyone who lived there with blazing afternoons and torturous drought, Charlie found winter even worse. Gypsy winds blew in storms from the north or west, fierce blizzards knitting blankets of snow or else pelting everything in sight with hailstones the size of hen eggs. The worst storms always blew down from above the Red River, and they were as sudden as they were severe.

"If only Texas would learn to curb her temper," old Ma Dunlap was fond of saying. "She flays us half to death in summer, then sets us in an icehouse all winter!"

December found Charlie in the courthouse, settling a pair of petty quarrels and eager for Ross to tally the tax receipts for the year. It had been a good one for Palo Pinto, and for Charlie, too. He always enjoyed looking back on twelve months well spent, and with the railroad through to El Paso, Rachel's orphanage complete, Ryan's schooling finished and him married to boot, not to mention Ross's little Edward about to share his first Christmas, the Justiss family had about all it could say grace over.

The town itself had changed so much. The stone

113

courthouse gave the community a finished, permanent look about it, and the stream of wagons and riders heading east or west, north or south, brought home the reality that Palo Pinto was now a crossroads, a center of a growing region.

There were the newcomers, too. Besides Otto Stuffel's little German colony, there were three Italian families, a pair from France, even the Giapoulos family from Greece. The railroad and its lure of cheap land brought them west, but the vitality and generosity of their neighbors enabled them to stay.

The orphans at Buck Creek had an impact on the town and its citizens, too. As Christmas neared, the little unfortunates began to receive visitors. Carpenters came to donate an hour or two repairing a leaky roof, and seamstresses fashioned new shirts. A cobbler made shoes, and a farmer brought cornmeal. Each brought his own gift, but more importantly, all opened their hearts and shared a lonely time with those who needed the company.

Little Viktor Weidling and Marianne Schneider wrote a Christmas pageant, and Celia Cooke organized the children into a company of players. Some twenty from the orphanage took part, those who could be spared from their chores, and the play itself was held in the courthouse's courtroom, the only single room big enough to accommodate so many people. Even then, many had to stand.

When the children performed, near every mother in the crowd shone like polished silver. No one was prouder than Angela, for after all, little Viktor had done most of the writing, her grandson Charlie was the youngest shepherd, and tiny Hope was an angel.

114

Chris and Joe served as ushers.

"Was there ever a finer Christmas in all Texas?" Angela asked Charlie afterward. "Weren't the girls and boys fine?"

"Excellent," Charlie admitted, even though Alek Schneider had lost one wing while lowering himself to the floor from a hoist, and Violet Cooke had punched her brother Bryant in the nose when he wouldn't turn over his bowl of gold fast enough.

Viktor was a whirlwind of ideas, and the pageant wasn't his sole notion. Three days before Christmas he talked Bret and Ross into felling a tall cedar and carting it to the courthouse. They then sank it into the ground.

"Now we can have Christmas," Viktor declared. "We have a *tannenbaum*."

Before anyone could blink, the German farmers began arriving in town with wooden stars and brightly-painted figures, strings of dried corn and paper chains. Martin Schneider took out a mouth organ, and soon the children were singing holiday tunes and wishing everyone good cheer.

Even old grouches like Joe Nance got into the act. Nance carved some cowboys and a pair of horsemen for the tree. Some of the ladies in town made red and green candles to illuminate the tree at night. Art Stanley spread out cotton on the ground in place of absent snow. The best touches of all, though, were shiny bits of glass hung in the upper branches, for the sparkling tree seemed to reflect the wonderment in children's smiles. It caught the magic in a grand-

115

mother's sparkling smile and the recollection of old age and hard times.

"It's Christmas," Viktor explained, as if that was all that needed saying.

"These folks know how to celebrate the season," Charlie told Angela when Martin Schneider assembled some thirty of the farmers at the edge of town one night and led a candlelit parade through town. "They know how to bring light to the darkness, how to raise cheer and foster hopes. They'll make good Texans."

"Most of them," Angela agreed. "Those who don't crack when rain doesn't fall or don't get shot over a barbed wire fence or a bottle of whiskey."

Charlie grimaced. He'd hoped both those battles were over once and for all. Angela only laughed, though, and turned to the subject of grandchildren.

As Christmas Eve arrived, Charlie noticed a strange change come over Viktor. He and little Jakob slipped out of the house early, and Charlie followed them around town for a time. The boys finally walked inside the church and sat on the back bench.

Charlie stood in the door for a minute. The Weidling boys whispered to each other. Then Jakob began crying, and Viktor took his little brother and rocked the child on one knee.

"Mind if I join you?" Charlie called to the youngsters.

"*Ja*, Mr. Justiss," Viktor said, nervously easing Jakob back onto the bench. The smaller boy eyed

Charlie uneasily.

"Got worries, son?" Charlie asked.

"Worries?" Viktor asked, staring up into Charlie's face. "No worries."

"Something's troubling you. Jakob, too."

Jakob hugged his brother's side, and Viktor turned away.

"You wouldn't want to be afraid of an old cuss like me," Charlie told them. "I'm mostly used-up old shoe leather, you know, all wrinkled and bent in all the wrong places."

"I am not being afraid," Viktor said, trying to fight a great sadness off his face. "I talk to Jakob of Mama and Papa."

"Oh," Charlie said, paling. "It seems you two've been with us so long, I close to forgot last Christmas you were with your family."

"*Ja,* in Neustadt," Viktor added. "You have . . ."

"Mrs. Justiss and I've been good to you, but it's not the same thing, is it?" Charlie asked. The boys frowned, and Charlie sat down alongside Jakob and gripped the child's tiny hands. "We will have my family over tonight. I'd like you to be there, too, since you've rather become a part of that family. But maybe tomorrow you'd like to visit your mama and papa, then take a ride out the Albany road and have supper with the Schneiders. That more to your liking?"

"We can see Rolf?" Viktor asked.

"Anna and Emma?" Jakob added.

"I'll speak with Martin Schneider. I'm certain he wouldn't mind a bit of extra company."

"You will not miss us?" Viktor asked, leaning

against Charlie's shoulder.

"Well, I imagine we will, but Mrs. Justiss plans on us taking a ride out to Buck Creek to pass the day with the orphans. We'll have lots of company."

"They, too, will have a good Christmas," Viktor declared. His spirits revived, and with them, his brother Jakob's. It warmed Charlie's heart. He rose to his feet, then led the two boys back home.

Scarcely half an hour passed before Vicki, Bret, and their little ones arrived. Billy drove Ross, Eliza, and tiny Edward over shortly thereafter. Ryan and Rachel came only when Joe and Irene Dunlap appeared to spell them at the orphanage. Ma Dunlap had helped bring close to a hundred youngsters into the world, and it did the round-faced midwife a world of good to spend Christmas Eve with the orphan boys.

At the Justiss place, Christmas Eve was a time of eating, singing songs, and exchanging presents. Joe and Chris, as always, pestered everyone with their devilish pranks, but with the sheriff on hand to keep the two scamps in line, the afternoon remained pretty tame.

Charlie took a few moment after lunch to share with Angela little Viktor's worries.

"Well, it's only right those children should at least be together at Christmas. It's a crime splitting them up, Charlie. You should talk to Martin about taking them all in."

"Do you really think you could give them up?"

"No," she confessed. "But I would if it meant they could all be together."

118

"We'll see what happens."

When it came time to exchange gifts, the lion's share of the booty went to the children. Angela had made a buying trip to Dallas, and all the little ones had new clothes and a toy or doll. Little Jakob received a German music box, and Viktor got a prized volume of American history.

"Thank you so much," the boy said, rubbing his teary eyes. "You have done so much."

"Not so much," Angela said as he nestled in beside her.

"Very much," Viktor declared, kissing her forehead.

The other presents were nice, but Charlie found nothing like the same pleasure from watching Billy or Ryan open a package. Even Chris and Joe had lost the ability to see magic in a bit of ribbon and brown paper.

Ryan and Rachel left early, followed shortly by Ross and Eliza. The baby had no affection for cool air, and Angela deemed it wise they should bundle little Edward and put him to bed.

When Vicki and Bret led their little ones away, the house seemed oddly empty. Only moments before, the screams and shouts of daredevil cowboys had filled the air. Now silence swallowed the big house.

"I'd best head out as well," Billy told his father. "Mama said you thought to ask Martin Schneider to host Viktor and Jake. Want me to ask 'em?"

"It's out of your way, son."

"Out of yours, too, Papa. I'll ask, and send you

119

word."

"Good enough."

Christmas morning, Billy arrived early in Palo Pinto. He drove a wagon filled with supplies for the orphanage. Young Rolf Weidling came along with the Schneiders' buckboard. Viktor and Jakob raced to their brother, piled in beside him, and jabbered away in German. Charlie clasped Angela's wrists and tried to warm her heart.

"I can't help myself," she said, sighing. "It's hard to see them so happy to leave."

"They can't help missing their brother and sisters. Now, why don't we get on out to Buck Creek? I'll bet I know some young ones who are eager to see you."

"Yes," she admitted. But though she tried to paint a smile on her face, it wouldn't come. Charlie hoped the orphans would cheer her.

They did. There was nothing like a wave of mop-haired boys in need of a motherly smile or a bit of nurturing. No sooner did the wagon pull up at the front door than the little goblins descended on the visitors.

"Why didn't you bring Viktor and little Jakob?" Ryan asked his father as Rachel ushered the others along to the dining room.

"They've gone to be with the Schneiders," Charlie whispered. "Don't say anything to your mama. She's a bit vexed. It's only natural they should want to be with their sisters and big brother, though."

"If you ask me, Schneider's got plenty of space

120

out there for those kids," Ryan grumbled. "Viktor could prove a big help come spring planting, and how much trouble can Jakob be? Shoot, Papa, all that boy does is click his heels and rush to do as he's asked."

"I know," Charlie said, sighing. "But on the other hand, Schneider's got a houseful himself, and I understand there's another on the way."

"I've got close to seventy," Ryan said, laughing as he waved at the army of boys racing in all directions. "They're not my blood, maybe, but once you're around them a bit, that doesn't seem so important."

Charlie smiled, and Ryan laughed out loud.

"I guess you never figured me for a brood hen, huh, Papa? It's Rachel's work. In truth, though, I don't mind a bit. You ever figure a way to get so many cheap ranchhands?"

Then it was Charlie's turn to laugh.

Christmas at the orphanage was loud, eventful, and totally exhausting. No one, not even Billy, Chris, or Joe, had a moment to himself. As for Charlie, if the boys weren't recruiting him for some diabolical game, they were begging for a story or showing him some carving or drawing. By supper he felt a hundred years old.

"Come on, Grandpapa Charlie," the youngest ones pleaded when he sneaked off to a corner and sank into a cushioned rocker. "We want to show you the creek."

"I walked that creek before you were born," Charlie objected.

"But you haven't seen the geese," a smallish waif named Michael explained. "And there's a mean old raccoon's got a house in that big hollow oak above the swimming hole."

"How 'bout you show *me?*" Billy said, stepping forward. Charlie gazed up at his son with grateful eyes, and the children raced off to the creek with their fresh captive.

Angela passed the better part of the afternoon with Rachel, baking pies and cakes. It took that long to prepare enough for everyone, even with the help of several of the older orphans and some of the neighboring farmwives. Afterward, she and Charlie took a walk through a stand of junipers and remembered.

"In another week it'll be 1882," she whispered.

"Was it only twenty years ago you sent me off to battle?" Charlie asked.

"And a few times since. Palo Pinto's come of age in that time. Ross is a father, and Vicki's got a houseful of family."

"No, it's Ry's got a houseful," Charlie pointed out.

"Yes," she said, laughing at his crazed smile. "Billy will be next. Then Joe."

"He's gotten tall. I never thought it'd happen. He was born with your face, and it didn't seem possible to me that the soft edges would ever sharpen, that he could grow up."

"He talks more and more of cadet school."

"That's Ryan's doing."

"Oh, you've had a hand in it as well," Angela said, laughing to herself. "He speaks of becoming a doc-

122

tor. We have a lawyer already, and an engineer. I suppose we need a doctor in the family."

"I'll wager Rachel's had a hand in that."

"She has a way with boys."

"Men, too," Charlie confessed. "If you'd had her with you when you were fighting the saloons, even Marty would've signed the pledge . . . and thanked you for the chance."

"Think so?"

"I wouldn't be surprised at anything that woman does. She staked down Ry, didn't she?"

"Yes," Angela said, adjusting her shawl to fend off a brisk winter breeze creeping across the hillside. Charlie wrapped an arm around her, and they took refuge behind the shelter of a large slice of sandstone.

"I spoke with Bowie last week at the junction," Charlie said, pausing as he fought to form the rest of the words on his tongue. "Emiline isn't anxious for Clay to leave the academy just yet, though the boy's as old as Joe and eager to enter the university. Clay and Bart Davis have roomed with an older boy who's off to some eastern school. Bowie suggested Chris might join Clay for a year of polishing."

"Polish? Charlie! I smell Emiline Thayer's hand in this brew!"

"Chris will miss Joe. The two of them are thick as thieves, and besides, you know he'll only find new ways of stirring up the other boys and tormenting Vicki."

"And what of us? You send little Viktor off to the Schneiders. Now you'd have me bid my youngest good-bye as well."

"He'd only be in Fort Worth, and he'd visit every weekend. I thought maybe we could travel a bit, see the places you're always reading about. We've earned a rest."

"I don't know what's come over you. You hate traveling to Austin! Where would we go, China? Charlie, don't rob me of my family."

"I could never do that," he said, holding her tightly. "But we should talk to Chris about going to Clay's Fort Worth academy."

"You know what he really wants to do, Charlie Justiss."

"Oh?"

"Go back to living on the ranch. To tell the truth, that might make good sense. Billy might keep him out of trouble, and working on the ranch might cause him to appreciate a different kind of life."

Charlie nodded his agreement, but he wondered if the ranch would survive Chris unharnessed.

"So I suppose you would have me hang onto my job at the courthouse, eh?" he asked.

"Who else could hold everyone together, Charlie? Not Joe Nance!"

"I thought maybe Celia Cooke."

They both laughed at the thought of Celia, wielding a Bible and tongue-lashing some felon.

"Ross is busy being a papa just now. Guess I'm stuck with the job."

"I suppose," she said, leading him finally back toward the dining room.

Following dinner, presents were handed out to the

children, and Charlie sat back and drank in the good cheer. It surprised him what magic a simple gingham shirt could work on the little ones. For the elder boys, Ryan made quite a ceremony out of presenting boots or a leather hat.

As night started to settle in, Charlie urged his family back to the wagon. Chris and Joe dragged themselves to Billy's wagon and flopped in the bed. Billy led his mother along in high fashion. Charlie joined Angela on the front seat and allowed Billy to nudge the team into motion.

They rode through the brisk evening back to town. For a time the sounds of songs and laughter from Buck Creek haunted the air. Later the lamps in farmhouse windows reminded them of how the county's new farms spread out on either side of the junction road.

By the time Billy had the wagon back in town, Viktor and Jakob Weidling had returned as well. Vicki brought the boys over as soon as Charlie lit the lamp in the front room of the house.

"Welcome home, boys," Charlie said, gripping each of the youngsters by the hand. "Have a fine time, did you?"

Jakob nodded shyly, then raced off to locate Angela. Viktor walked over to where his new history rested on a small table and began reading.

"Hungry?" Charlie asked.

"No, we ate roast pig and great mountains of potatoes," Viktor explained.

"I half thought you might stay the night with the

Schneiders."

"It is very . . ." Viktor began, then stopped. He stared up at Charlie a moment, then handed over the book.

"What's this?" Charlie asked. "Don't you like the book?"

"Yes," Viktor said. His fingers quivered as he pushed the book closer to Charlie's hands. "I . . . wish something else."

"Oh?"

"*Ja.*" Viktor spoke in a whisper, as if he were afraid of the words. Charlie drew the thirteen-year-old closer.

"Remember what I said in the church, Viktor," Charlie reminded the boy. "You can ask me anything. Or tell me. What is it? Do you wish to move back to the farm, be with Rolf and the girls?"

"I can't," Viktor said sadly. "There is no room for us there."

"I could gather some men. We could build on a room."

"This is what you wish?"

"What I wish?" Charlie asked. "That doesn't matter near as much as what you wish, Viktor. Mrs. Justiss and I will only be happy if you are."

"I wish Mama and Papa were not dead," Viktor said, shaking violently. "They are."

"I'm afraid so," Charlie said solemnly.

"You have much room, yes?"

"Yes," Charlie said, squeezing the boy's shoulder.

"Then I would ask if you could take . . . Jakob . . . into your family. You could keep the book. That would be my Christmas gift, *ja?*"

126

"You don't want to live with the Schneiders?"

"Herr Schneider asked us. But he does not wish a son. He would not follow me to the church. He would not worry that I eat. I know this. He needs hands to work the farm, like Rolf. Here we are part of a family, Jakob and me."

"You asked about Jakob. What about you, Viktor?"

"I could stay perhaps?"

"Mrs. Justiss would take a switch to me if I said otherwise. Don't you know you've been part of us for months now, son? If you join our family, it would be a gift to us, not to you."

"Then, I may keep the book?"

"Yes," Charlie said, pulling the scruffy youngster close. "Of course, you're getting an old man for a papa. Think you can help me get up the stairs come midwinter?"

Viktor set the book aside and stood up. He held out his arm, and Charlie took it. The serious-faced boy then assisted Charlie to the stairway.

"We will be a family?" Viktor whispered. "Yes?"

"Yes," Charlie said, grinning.

When he reached the bedroom, he found Angela waiting with Jakob at the foot of the bed.

"Well, Jake?" she asked.

Jakob flew to Charlie and wrapped both arms around the weary man's legs.

"They want to stay," she declared. "What do you think?"

"I already told Viktor you'd take a switch to me if I said otherwise. Shoot, who wouldn't take in a bit of a kid like this?" Charlie asked, lifting Jakob onto one shoulder. "Think we can make him into a cowboy?"

"I'd say so," Angela told him. "But only if you get him some sleep. It's been a long day, and morning comes early on the range."

"Yes, ma'am," Charlie said, allowing Jakob to slide down his back to the floor. In five minutes Charlie managed to collect Viktor, too.

"We will be brothers," Viktor boasted to Chris and Joe when the older boys peeked out of their room into the narrow hall.

"Thought we already were," Chris said, shaking his head. "That mean we can prank 'em proper, Papa?"

"Thought it was the younger ones got to do that," Charlie said. "Anyway, it's late, and your mama's declared it time for bed. Adios, boys!"

Joe and Chris retreated inside their room. Viktor took Jakob's hand, and the two younger boys trotted down the hall. Charlie made a slow turn and headed back to Angela. He knew the youngsters would likely be up halfway through morning, but Christmas came but once a year, and it wasn't often a boy joined a family.

II. Drought

Chapter One

Spring arrived with a flourish. The hills and ravines of Palo Pinto County were blanketed with wildflowers. Azure seas of bluebonnets flowed past ridges of yellow dandelions. Elsewhere Indian paintbrushes added splashes of scarlet. Buffalo grass crept across the landscape, and the tall oaks and willows that clung to the banks of the mighty Brazos and its adjacent creeks put on fresh cloaks.

April in west Texas was as fine a season as there was. It brought a fresher step to young feet and revived bones weary of winter. The songs of cardinals and wrens reminded all that the earth was born anew.

For Billy Justiss, though, the colorful hills and singing birds masked trouble. The Brazos usually swelled with April rains. Instead the waters shrank within their August banks. It took twenty feet of rope to bring water from the wells above Bluff Creek, and in places, the creeks and water holes to the west had vanished.

"Be a hard summer," Billy grumbled as he knelt down and touched the flaky soil that should have held several inches of Ioni Creek. Deep cracks appeared in the ground, spelling trouble for the ranch. Those recesses often snagged a steer's leg and sent the animal crashing groundward with a broken limb. Worse, cattle needed feed and water. Grass wouldn't grow without rain, and the streams from which the stock drank would shrink to nothing in the June heat without spring showers to fill their banks.

Palo Pinto County had known drought before. One year floods would sweep half the houses along the river downstream. The next the sun would bake the land and its people so that by August a kind of madness took possession of everyone for miles around. But it had always rained in April. Until now.

Billy plucked a small plant from the dry earth and touched its roots. There was scarcely a trace of moisture. He rose and rubbed the parched plant in his fingers, then frowned heavily. It was possible to fight Indians, to overcome enemies. Hadn't the Justisses done that? Billy's left thigh bore the scar of an outlaw bullet collected at seventeen. At twelve he'd fought back a fever brought on by a rattlesnake bite. But how could a man battle drought? Rain would come when it would come.

He glanced southward, toward the shrinking creeks that watered newly-planted cornfields. The farmers would have a struggle. The Flying J bounded the Brazos, but those farms depended on the shallow waters of a dozen creeks to keep a crop alive through summer. Already the Hollands' well had gone dry.

"Serves 'em right for breakin' this ground," Marty Steele had declared. "It's range for cows, not meant to be fenced and plowed and planted!"

Billy held a like sentiment, but he couldn't find much satisfaction in watching the thin-faced schoolchildren who splashed around in Wolf Creek on their way home from school.

"Hard times make you strong," Billy whispered as he tossed the shriveled plant to the wind. His father was fond of saying that, and Billy always held it to be a great truth. After all, Charlie Justiss had grown tall and hard fighting a war that couldn't be won. Later he'd outlasted the Comanches and overcome carpetbaggers, climate, rustlers, and depression to carve out an empire from the rugged west Texas landscape. The Flying J Ranch was the largest and most prosperous outfit in the country.

And my responsibility, Billy told himself.

Strange it had turned out that way. First Charlie's brother Bowie had sold out his interest and left to build the railroad out from Fort Worth. Then Charlie Justiss himself moved to Palo Pinto to run the county. For a time Billy's older brother Ross managed the ranch, but Ross had always had a nose for the law and an eye for schooling. He'd gone first to Jacksboro and then to Austin to read the law. Then, when he might have returned to the ranch, he'd taken a wife and started a law practice instead.

Clearly, Billy told himself often, Ross had too much sense to be a good cattleman. When their brother Ryan went off to the new agricultural college, Billy took over the Flying J.

Charlie Justiss expected once Ryan was schooled that he and Billy would run the ranch together. Ryan had gone and married Rachel Harmer, though, and the two of them had their hands full with the Buck Creek Orphanage. Ryan also kept an eye on the new south range, but Marty Steele headed the crew, and there wasn't much else to do, really.

So, here I am, Billy thought, taking off his hat and shaking his unruly tangle of blond hair. He didn't look twenty-four years old. His wide brown eyes were a bit too full of devilment still, and he'd never let a beard grow like some of the young hands he hired on. Those who took Billy Justiss lightly made a mistake, though. He was a hair over six foot one, and the hundred and sixty pounds that clung to a thin frame were wound as tight as the spring inside a Colt revolver. His powerful shoulders and ironlike wrists were forged working fourteen hour days. He could toss an eighty-pound calf about like a feed sack, and even now he spelled Doc Singer at the smith's shed.

"One of these days you've got to turn over some of the work to your outfit," Wes Tyler sometimes complained when Billy fashioned shoes for the horses or split cedar limbs for shingles. "Who'd believe this bare-chested horse of a cowboy runs this place?"

Billy only laughed it off. He'd learned from his father how men formed a bond with their boss when the work was shared. No cowboy who ever sweated away a roundup with Billy Justiss waited to be asked to ride along with him when trouble appeared.

Drought, though, that was a different sort of trouble. It couldn't be licked by mounting up a dozen men and riding the range. No, droughts had to be outlasted.

Billy walked to his horse and climbed into the saddle. The speckled gray mustang wasn't the dignified sort of mount his father would have chosen, but the spry stallion suited Billy. He'd chased the horse down as a colt, and Luis Morales had worked just enough of the wildness from the animal to make him manageable.

We're alike, we two, Billy thought as he nudged the horse into motion. Neither of us is exactly fit parlor company, but we're at home out here in the open.

Billy knew the better half of the county thought as much. After all, how often did he get invited to Sunday supper? Other than family gatherings, Sunday services, and visits to Buck Creek, he rarely left the Flying J. It was, Billy supposed, exile by mutual consent, though. He felt boxed in, trapped, at picnics or barn dances. A quiet afternoon ride along the Brazos with Colleen Cassidy was more to his liking.

That particular day, though, he rode instead alongside what remained of Ioni Creek. Once the stream had marked the ranch's eastern boundary. Then the Stokely brothers had sold out, and Charlie Justiss absorbed the old Triple S. Oh, there remained the charred skeleton of the Stokelys' ranchhouse, and two barns were still used as part of line camps. Otherwise, only oldtimers recalled there had ever been a Triple S Ranch.

Oldtimers? Billy laughed at the thought. These days anybody who'd been in Palo Pinto a year ago was an oldtimer. The past few weeks whole wagons of German farmers and their families had rolled into the southern half of the county. He couldn't carry on a conversation with half of them. They knew how to work, though. He'd give them that. Those broad-backed farmers cleared a hundred acres or so of scrub mesquite and gnarled junipers, then plowed furrows for corn.

Billy stared at the feeble creek and frowned. It would do little good, all that work. Corn wouldn't grow without rain, and there'd been none. It was almost summer now. June never made up for an April shortfall.

"Enough talk!" Billy suddenly cried. He then turned his horse sharply and splashed across the creek. Soon he was swinging south along the Albany road, skirting the rugged shoulders of the Palo Pinto Mountains. It was early afternoon, and he'd sent Hector Suarez and a crew down to Wolf Creek to deepen a water hole.

It took Billy a little less than an hour to ride the five or six miles to Wolf Creek. Even then, he was in no great hurry to locate the work crew. He wove his way in and out of the junipers and live oaks on the hillside west of the creek, occasionally chasing a stray steer back down into the pasture. Then he stopped entirely. Down in the creek a half-dozen boys chased each other through the shallows.

Billy grinned. The older two were his own brothers, Joe and Chris, no doubt escaping the confines of their sister Vicki's classroom once again. The young Eppler boys, Josiah and Will, were with them. Closer to the bank stood frail little Viktor and his bit of a brother, Jake. The two had only just been adopted into the Justiss family, and Billy had given his father a hard time about it.

"Don't you think you and Mama are a bit old to take on two more kids?" Billy'd asked. "Besides, I thought you would have had your fill of boys by now."

"Just cowboys," Charlie had replied. "Besides, Viktor's adopted us, and your mama can't seem to get through the day without little Jake's nagging."

Well, Mama's sure to swat Chris and Joe for sneaking Jake down to Wolf Creek, Billy told himself. Then, unable to resist the chance to wreak revenge on his prankster brothers, he swatted his horse into a gallop and charged the swimmers, howling like a Comanche.

"Lord, save us!" Will Eppler cried as he scrambled out of the water and fought to reach his clothes. Viktor froze like a statue. Chris and Joe raced behind a pair of nearby willows. Little Jake followed, then huddled behind his new big brothers.

The only one to remain calm was Josiah Eppler. Josiah merely gave Billy a good-natured wave and continued his swim.

"It's just your brother!" Josiah called to the others. "He was out here last week when we were with the Frost boys."

Joe stalked out into the open, shaking his head and glaring at his older brother. Billy only laughed at the waterlogged almost sixteen-year-old.

"Glad we amused you," Joe said, picking his shirt off the ground. "It's getting so you can't even enjoy a simple swim anymore without being raided by

137

some fool cowboy!"

"Well, can't blame me," Billy said, pretending seriousness. "I thought I'd stumbled on a bunch of outlaws. Who was I to know my own brothers were down here? Seems to me school's got a good hour yet to run."

"Well," Joe said, his face flashing with pink, "Vicki thought we might take off a bit early today."

"That right, Viktor?" Billy asked.

Viktor was still recovering from Billy's wild charge, and he wasn't prepared for the question. He tried to turn away, but Billy reached down and held him in place.

"Well?" he asked Viktor's guilt-ridden face.

"No," the boy admitted.

"I do believe you're losing your touch, Joe," Billy said, laughing. "Used to be nobody ever caught you."

"Must be getting old," Joe said, shaking his head and grinning as he realized nothing would come of the mischief. "You know how hot it gets in that school, Billy. You never took to books yourself."

"I never stole my six-year-old brother either," Billy said, nodding to Jake. " 'Course, I did lead you two astray, I'm ashamed to say."

"More than once," Chris spoke up. "There was that time when you—"

"I wouldn't be spreading too many tales, little brother," Billy warned. "Elsewise, I might accidentally let slip to Mama who I happened upon down at Wolf Creek."

"Wouldn't want you to do that," Chris responded. "No, then you'd have the burden of our death on your conscience."

They all laughed together a moment. Then Chris led the way back to the creek.

"Well, aren't you going to join us?" Joe asked.

"Got to get on about my business," Billy answered. "I do have a ranch to run, you know."

"Since when that ever keep you from swimming?" Chris called.

"Since now, I suppose," Billy explained, shrugging his shoulders. "You scamps leave a little water for the cattle. And don't let Mama find out you were out here."

"Vicki's likely already done that," Joe declared, "but don't worry. I'll figure a good reason why we had to come."

Billy shook his head and left the boys to their swim.

He found Hector and the others a quarter mile to the north. The cowboys were digging into the muddy pond, hoping to deepen the bottom so that more water would collect for the cattle.

"Don't know how much good this will do," Hector said, setting his spade aside and splashing out of the pond. "You know if we don't get rain soon, Wolf Creek will be dry by July."

"I'm hoping we can move most of the stock to the river then."

"Can't move them all, my friend. We have thousands of head. Can't all of them drink from the river. And what will we do if the river goes dry?"

"Survive," Billy said. "Ross is going to Kansas

139

City next week to meet with the buyers. I think he should sell every steer he can."

"We shipped five thousand last year. You wouldn't want to cut into our breeding stock. It would take years to recover our numbers."

"Hector, I'd rather sell them than see them die."

"You think it will be that bad?" Hector asked. "It will be dry, yes, but you don't think —"

"I think I'm glad I'm not a farmer. And I hope we can sell three, maybe four thousand. All this southern acreage will go dry, even if we get some rain. Wolf Creek's low by August anyway. We'd best take a long hard look at that new south range, too. It won't take much for Buck Creek to go dry."

"Have you spoken to your father about this?"

"Soon. What can he say that we don't know?"

"He has good ears in town, Billy."

"And what is there to hear?"

"I have heard talk of damming creeks. Already some farmers are digging ditches off Palo Pinto Creek. We could lose some of our water if those farmers up on Caddo Creek did that. Wolf and Ioni creeks also."

"You know as well as I do that Wolf and Ioni creeks get most of their water off the mountains on our own land. Caddo, well, it's usually dry in summer anyway."

"It could bring hard feelings."

"Yes," Billy agreed, turning nervously toward the west. "I never did feel we got much of an answer about those raiders last year."

"You have never known a water war, eh?" Hector asked. Billy raised his eyelids, and Hector frowned.

"You remember Stone and Hayley, how they raided our cows. That was an easy battle to fight once we knew who we were fighting. When I was a boy down south, we knew a time of drought. My brothers and I sucked cactus to soothe our thirst. We had near our house a small spring. My uncle Romero built an aqueduct to bring water to a small pond. The man who owned the large ranch next to us said this water which flowed from the earth was his, and he sent men to fill barrels . . . on our land. It was a small pond, and there was so little water. Because of it, two of my uncles died."

"It could happen here," Billy acknowledged. "Water is life, and the man who has it will survive. Men have killed to provide for their families. I pray we won't come to that point."

"I also."

"So let's dig deep, Hector. And tomorrow I'll have Wes get some men to deepen the wells."

"You will talk to your father also?"

"Yes," Billy agreed. "And with Marty about the south range."

He did just that. Early the next morning Billy rode into Palo Pinto. He was an unusual sight, wearing his broad-brimmed hat, blue cotton shirt, rawhide vest, and gunbelt with loaded Colt on his right hip. Firearms were forbidden in Palo Pinto, and some of the school-bound farmboys Billy passed no doubt thought him some escaped desperado. He left the pistol with his horse at the livery.

"This is early in the day for you to be in town,

son," Charlie Justiss declared when Billy appeared at the door.

"Yes, sir," Billy admitted as his father showed him inside. "I've got a couple of things to discuss with you, though, and I thought it best to get right at them."

Viktor and Jake gazed uneasily when Billy dropped his hat on the kitchen table and gave his mother a kiss.

"You boys best get along to school now," Angela Justiss said. "See you stay until dismissed, too. Hear me, Jake?"

"Yes, Mama," the little one said. Viktor nodded, then took his younger brother by the hand and raced toward the door.

"Chris and Joe had them off chasing rabbits yesterday," she explained to Billy. Chasing rabbits had long been Angela Justiss's label for wasting time. Billy pretended surprise.

"Well, it was bound to happen," Charlie said, pulling up a chair and sitting across the table from Billy. "It's just impossible to raise honest, law-abiding sons in Palo Pinto County."

Angela scowled, then poured them all a cup of coffee.

"Papa, you ever know an April to be so dry?" Billy asked.

"No," Charlie confessed. "May, yes. April's generally wet."

"People's wells are going dry. Ioni Creek's inside its summer banks."

"Same's true down south. Up along the Trinity, too."

"We had a mild winter, Papa," Billy said, pausing to sip his coffee. "I'll bet we're usually three times wetter come May. I've not been to engineer school, but I know when plant roots are dry. The ground's starting to crack. This will be a hard summer for ranchers."

"And farmers," Angela added. "Corn needs a fair amount of water."

"Otto Stuffel's had some of his neighbors building dams across Palo Pinto Creek," Charlie grumbled. "May help him some, but it's been hard on the folks downstream. Some are near dried out."

"That could happen out our way, too."

"So what do you think we should do about it, son?"

Billy sipped the rest of his coffee, then nervously rolled the cup in his fingers.

"You know I'd talked about buying those two new Hereford bulls," Billy said, gazing out the window toward the nearly deserted street. "I planned to plant feed along Bluff Creek, too, so we'd have some better hay. I think we should forget all that for now."

"And?" Charlie asked.

"I think Ross ought to sell every head he can. We won't have range or water for ten thousand steers this summer. We ought to clear the south range of everything but breed stock."

"Go on."

"Ryan best dig some new wells for the orphans, too. If those farmers dam the creeks, those kids could wind up high and dry."

"Think it will get as bad as that?"

"I think maybe it will. I plan to ride over and have

143

a talk with the Dunlaps. Ma knows more about this country than about anybody."

"You know if we sell heavy again this year, it will take a long time to build the herd back."

"Sure, Papa, but the price appears fair just now, and if it gets as dry as I'm afraid, we could lose stock . . . hundreds of head. I'd rather sell steers than bury 'em."

"I'll tell Ross," Charlie promised. "I plan to ride out to Buck Creek this afternoon, too. I'll talk to Ry. As for Marty, maybe you should speak to him yourself."

"I will," Billy agreed. "Sorry to be so gloomy about all this, Papa, Mama, but I can read sign."

"We all can," Angela said, gripping Billy's hands. "You can ride into town more often as well. I hear you visit the Cassidys often enough."

"Not so often as you'd like, I imagine," Billy said, grinning at her. "I told you before. Colleen and I are just getting acquainted."

"You're taking your time about it," Charlie grumbled. "You got to pluck a peach when it's ripe, son."

"Oh?" Billy asked, turning to his mother. "That right, Mama?"

"Well, it wouldn't hurt to pick it before you're too old to lift your arm," Angela pointed out. "The way you're going, Billy, I'll have grandchildren from little Jake before you even ask Colleen to sit with you at church."

"Well, you know what Marty says," Billy whispered to her. "A stallion's just naturally shy where a rope's concerned."

"Seems to me Marty Steele ought to mind his own

business," Angela griped. "Now get along with you, Billy Justiss. I've got work to tend."

Billy laughed as she shooed him from the kitchen. It did him good to visit, and he promised himself to come more often.

Chapter Two

"I never knew a spring so good for buzzards," Irene Dunlap had told Billy. "Sure as life, summer will be hard."

Billy'd merely nodded. Ma Dunlap was rarely wrong. She'd predicted flood and drought along the Brazos for twenty years. Billy shuddered at the dark despair in her eyes. Whatever she saw ahead would certainly test the soul.

By the time June arrived, the Brazos was already shrinking. The Flying J wells, even deepened ten feet, were going dry. Creeks had stopped flowing, and springs slowed to a trickle. Water was becoming hard to come by.

To make matters worse, summer threatened to be a scorcher. Already the noonday heat was oppressive. Billy winced at the prospect of beginning branding and roundup. Any work done in the afternoon reddened flesh and sent the younger cowboys toppling from the saddle.

"Best save the heavy work for the cool of the

evening," Wes Tyler suggested.

"What cool of the evening?" Billy asked the veteran cowboy.

It was true. Even at midnight the sandstone boulders remained as warm as campfire embers, and as often as not, there wasn't so much as a feather's worth of breeze.

"I feel like a hen somebody's put in the oven to bake," Bob Lee Wiley complained.

"And got overdone," young Barret Jenkins added.

As if matters weren't bad enough, the water holes and creeks that might have offered a refreshing break from the heat were little more than mud wallows. Some of the cowboys rode fifteen miles just to drown their misery beneath the cooling waters of the Brazos.

"How long will that last?" Jared Dunlap asked as he and Billy met midway across the now shallow river. "I've spent my whole life hereabouts, Billy, and I've never known the river near so low."

"I know," Billy said, nodding sadly. It was like losing an old friend, seeing the river shrink away in the summer heat. Worse, August was still a long way off.

Soon there was little time for worrying about the river, though. Ross was off in Kansas City negotiating a cattle contract, and Billy occupied himself organizing the yearly roundup and branding.

The number of yearling calves was down by half. The huge shipment made the previous June had included a thousand cows that might otherwise have borne calves. Even so, there were more than enough yearlings to keep three crews busy. Once the branding and gelding were completed, most of the cows and all the calves were driven west and north toward the deeper waters of Caddo Creek and the Brazos. Wes Tyler then drove the breeding bulls along after their herds.

The remaining animals were counted off by hundreds and collected in four camps of about five hundred head each. It was quite a challenge to keep the steers and cows from straying back onto the distant stretches of range, and extra hands were signed on. Chris and Joe were enlisted, as was spindle-legged Viktor. Billy grinned with surprise as the yellow-haired youngster appeared, a pair of Joe's old suspenders holding up oversized britches, and a straw hat pushed back from a confused forehead.

"What manner of cowboy are you?" Billy asked.

"What do you need?" Viktor replied. "I'm not so good with a rope, but I can ride a little."

Billy shook his head and pointed toward a pair of cow ponies. Barret Jenkins, at sixteen barely three inches taller than Viktor, helped the younger boy saddle the mount. Once atop the horse, though, Viktor was clearly in trouble.

"Help!" the boy cried as his horse raced off. Billy nearly fell down laughing as the other cowboys scrambled to head off the runaway wrangler. Viktor struggled to keep one foot or the other in a stirrup and cried out angrily a torrent of German curses at the rebellious horse. In minutes the entire crew was mounted and chasing after the young cowboy.

What began as a humorous interlude soon turned serious. The horse was unnerved by Viktor's cries and fought every effort to bring its movements under control. Viktor's hands, meanwhile, gripped the reins fiercely.

"Jump free, Vik!" Billy urged, but the youngster closed his eyes and hung on. Finally the pony did a half spin and bucked its small rider into a tangle of pencil cactus.

"Ahhhh!" Viktor yelled as he rolled into the prickly spines. Young Jenkins lassoed the horse, and Billy jumped off his speckled mustang and inspected the damage to his adopted brother.

"I believe you'll live," Billy announced as he probed the fourteen-year-old's arms and legs for signs of breaks. "May wisn you hadn't, though."

Viktor nodded. Every inch of him below the chin seemed to be peppered with cactus spines. They were only an inch long, as thin as needles, but they had a sting like fire. Billy knew Viktor would be a long time remembering his first day as a Brazos cowboy.

After turning Viktor's prickly problem over to Doc Singer's experienced hands, Billy headed south to visit Marty Steele. The pure Herefords roaming the fenced-in south range were of special concern. If the breeding stock couldn't survive along Buck Creek, Billy knew a section of the main ranch would have to be enclosed for their use. He disliked fencing, and so far the only wire he'd allowed lined the ranch's eastern and southern boundaries along the Albany and Jacksboro market roads. To the west, Caddo Creek marked the property line, as did the Brazos to the north.

Marty and the half-dozen regular cowboys who worked the broad southern acreage bolstered their roundup crew by hiring ten of the older Buck Creek boys. In truth, the older orphans rode that south range whenever they had a chance. Some worked the orphanage's own small herd while others picked up the trade. A good hand with a rope who could ride from dawn to dusk was always in demand in Palo Pinto, and boys like Barret Jenkins who worked hard and listened to Ryan Justiss and Marty Steele could earn their own way at fifteen.

Billy often joked with his brother how the orphans learned more than riding and roping from Marty. It rankled Rachel that Marty persisted in carrying a pocket flask. Marty wasn't above invoking a curse or two when working livestock, either. But no one in the county knew more about handling a bunch of cantankerous cattle than Marty Steele.

He was good with the youngsters, too. Marty would rant and scream, but he had a gentle hand when it was most needed, and no one mistook the right way of doing a thing for the wrong.

"I thought Papa made a mistake sending Marty down here," Ryan once admitted. "I figured Wes, what with Alice and the little ones, would be a better choice. Old Charlie knew what he was about, though. Those boys are the sons Marty never had, and he's a kind of substitute father."

Father? To be more truthful, Marty had turned into an old mother hen where those youngsters were concerned. Of course, it wasn't particularly safe to mention that to Marty.

Billy located Marty and a pair of young hands branding calves on a small hillside a mile south of the railroad tracks.

"Well, what brings the top hog down south?" Marty asked.

"Just wanted to take a look around the range," Billy told his old friend. "It's getting pretty dry up north."

"No better here. You boys get along with your work," Marty then told the others. "I'll be showing Mr. Justiss here where the creeks used to flow."

The range between Palo Pinto Creek on the north and Buck Creek on the south and east was normally cut by a half-dozen jagged streams. Now, Billy noted, the creeks themselves were only a shadow of their former selves, and the streams were little better than mudholes.

"Ryan's had the orphans deepening their wells," Marty explained. "The big one back of the house is close to thirty-five feet down now, I'd judge. They won't hold through July the way this sun is baking the ground. We need rain . . . bad."

"You figure Buck Creek will survive, Marty?"

"Maybe for the stock. They'll drink mud. Be hard on the young ones, though, not to mention those fields they've planted."

"Soon as you can, count your steers, then add what cows you don't think can last out the summer. I want to ship every animal we can to Kansas City."

"We'll need to hold back breeding stock."

"I know, but go light on the numbers, Marty. I figure there'll be a lot of dead cattle in this county before the worst is over, and I'd as soon not have any wear the Flying J brand."

"You talk to Ry about sellin' the Buck Creek

151

herd?"

"Papa has. I know it's hard news, but I don't see we have much choice. We could get rain soon, but even so, I figure we'll lose stock unless we thin the herds."

"You could be right. I can tell you right now we probably have a thousand, maybe more to ship. Add in two hundred Buck Creek animals, too."

"I hope Ross can sell them all. Lord, I hate seeing a cow thirst."

"Memories of the Cimarron country?"

"Yeah, but back then we knew the Arkansas lay ahead. All we had to do was keep the steers going. Now, well, the Brazos herself seems to be dying."

"Yeah," Marty grumbled. "And if she does, the rest of us will, too."

Billy returned to the ranch more worried than ever. He couldn't help sensing that a curtain of gloom was descending upon Palo Pinto County. Even word from his father that Ross had contracted four thousand head to the Kansas City slaughterhouse failed to lift his spirits. But with so many cattle to ready for shipment, he soon was too busy to think about dry creeks or cloudless skies.

Roundup was, at best, a trial. In the ravine-scarred hills above the Brazos, only constant vigilance kept even a small collection of steers from wandering. Hiring extra help eased some of the strain on the regular outfit, but often the newcomers

rience, or even common sense in some
ands like Marty Steele, Hector Suarez,
earned a year's salary that one week.
, he was everywhere. When not riding
check on the line camps, he was conferring with
his father about rail cars.

"It's best if we stagger the herd this year," Billy
declared. "Last year we had too many steers to
handle at one time, and we wound up with over a
thousand head to watch along the creek east of the
junction. Why not ship Marty's twelve hundred first,
then bring out a thousand at a time from the main
ranch?"

"Makes sense," Charlie agreed. "I'll arrange it with
Bowie."

Charlie Justiss was as good as his word. He rode
out early to tell Billy cattle cars would be waiting at
Justiss Junction in two days.

"You can load a thousand or so a day, son,"
Charlie explained. "Ross says he can sell another five
hundred, too, if you can find them."

"We could find a thousand," Billy declared. "I
don't know that I wouldn't have a mutiny on my
hands if I told the boys they have another herd to
trail to the junction, though."

"Think we should pass on the offer?"

"No, sir. Let me have a word or two with Jared.
I'll bet the Dunlaps've got close to that many. You
know Joe. Most of the time he drives fifty at a time
to Jacksboro and lets a broker sell them. He's been
doing it for as long as I can recall, but there's always

a chance he'll realize it's 1882. Besides, Jar
ing the reins more and more."

"The changing of the guard," Charlie said, g
ning. "I'll tell Ross we'll find the beeves."

"And I'll have the first batch waiting at the junction in two days."

It wasn't as easy as it sounded. Driving a thousand head was easier than trailing five thousand, but
that was still a lot of bawling steers, and not a one
of them was eager to tramp twenty-five miles to the
railhead. Billy began by taking half his crew from
the main ranch down to help Marty Steele bring his
twelve hundred cattle up from the south range. Two
hundred of those animals bore the BC Buck Creek
brand, and because of that, close to thirty scrawny
riders joined the trail crew.

The loading pens at Justiss Junction were only a
few hours from where Marty had the animals collected, but it was mostly open country scarred by
dry washes and deep ravines. No roads led to town,
and most of the way the Flying J drovers nudged
their cattle along the railroad right-of-way. By the
time they reached Justiss Junction, Billy was exhausted. The young cowboys insisted on racing their
ponies, though, engaging in roping contest and in
general trying their elders' patience.

"Forget what it was like to be young?" Marty
asked as he and Billy sank into the soft grass
beneath a spreading apple tree.

"I was never that young," Billy declared. "I wonder at how Ry keeps up with them."

"He doesn't," Marty said, laughing. "To tell the
truth, nobody does. Except maybe Rachel. She's a

154

marvel, Billy!"

"Ever sorry you didn't marry somebody, Marty?" Billy asked. "I seem to recall there was a gal dealt cards back at the Flat. And that young widow who cooked at the hotel."

"Oh, I think on it sometimes," Marty said, taking out his flask and taking a long sip. "But take that Miz Cooke, or even your mama. They make such a fuss over a man wearin' a collar to church. Why, they hogtied half the town to sign their fool temperance pledges. Women always want to change a man, make him over into something he isn't. I got no patience for that!"

"Wes seems happy."

"Well, he likes bein' settled. Got all those kids to look after, and Alice, she's a fine woman. Even so, I note he carries a Bible when he rides the trail now. Watch those women, Billy. They've got a reformin' streak to 'em."

Billy couldn't help laughing.

Two days later Billy had the outfit bring the first thousand steers from the main ranch. They waited only a day before returning with twelve hundred more. Both drives proved uneventful, if exhausting. Half a week later Jared Dunlap, aided by Chris, Joe, Hector Suarez, and little Viktor, started the five hundred Dunlap steers across the river. Wes's drovers merged six hundred Flying J beeves with the trail herd, and together they started up the narrow valley above Bluff Creek.

Billy had sent men ahead to open a thirty foot gap

155

in the boundary fence so as to allow the restless animals access to the road. When it was time to move the herd itself into the road, though, trouble arose.

Billy had spread word up and down the county as to which days the Flying J would be trailing cattle to Justiss Junction. It was practically impossible for a farmer to get his wagon through a thousand bawling steers, and a single rider fared little better. So Billy was somewhat surprised when Ike Kemp and his boys rode up after Wes had moved the first hundred or so head out into the road.

"Sorry to hold you up, mister," Barret Jenkins explained as the cowboys guided the herd through the gap in the fence and on eastward toward town.

"You won't hold me up," Kemp growled. "Get out of my way!"

Billy was maybe ten yards away when Kermit Kemp pulled young Jenkins off his horse and dropped the boy down amidst the restless cattle. Fortunately Jared Dunlap was closer. In an instant Jared split the nervous steers and rescued Jenkins from the thousands of trampling feet.

"I never in my life saw such a thing!" Jared shouted so that half the county could hear. "Mister, I don't know where you were raised, but a coyote wouldn't knock a boy into the middle of a trail herd."

"You callin' me names?" Kermit asked, his face reddening as he touched the handle of a Colt pistol on his hip.

"I saw what I saw!" Jared shouted.

Billy finally parted the cattle and rode in between

the angry men.

"Do we have trouble?" he asked.

"This fellow near got this boy trampled," Jared explained.

"He got in our way," Kermit snarled.

"I did my best to let folks know we'd be moving our stock today," Billy said, trying to calm the others. "I'm sorry if we missed you."

"I heard," Ike grumbled. "I don't change my plans so some baby-faced neighbor can do as he pleases."

"Oh?" Billy asked sourly. "Around here, we make allowances for our neighbors. We help those who need a barn raised, and we clear the road so a man can get his stock to the railhead. We even," Billy added with a hard stare, "excuse bad manners."

"That aimed at me, sonny?" Ike snapped. "You want to see bad manners? How about we dust your britches with a shotgun?"

"I wouldn't!" Hector Suarez yelled from ten yards to the right. "I've got a Winchester rifle in my hands, mister, and it can purely put a hole through your brain. Why don't you turn around and go back home? We'll be through with this road in an hour or so."

"You really want to see somebody die, huh?" Ike cried. "Well, I'm willin'."

"I'm not," Billy said, waving Jared by and motioning for Hector to hold his fire. "If you're bound to go ahead on, then go! Just keep your guns holstered. I won't have a stampede."

"Now you're bein' sensible," Ike declared. "Let's go, boys."

The Kemps made a point of riding directly by

Jared Dunlap.

"Billy, this is a mistake," Jared grumbled. "I could've taken 'em myself, all three of 'em."

"You forget the last time we trailed cattle together?" Billy asked. "We buried your brother up in Kansas. Papa didn't much like telling your mama. This time it'd be my turn. Thanks for helping young Barret, but this isn't worth somebody getting killed."

"What is?" Jared asked. "I've known men like this Kemp all my life. You let 'em push you once, they think they've got leave to do it from then on. We had the odds with us this time. Next time . . . who knows?"

"I trust there won't be a next time," Billy spoke loudly enough that everyone could hear. "We've got enough of a challenge ahead without stirring up a war with our neighbors."

"Wait and see," Jared urged. "He's a pusher, this Kemp. He'll be back, and there'll be trouble."

"I always found it best to step aside from trouble," Billy replied.

"Sometimes it isn't possible, though," Jared objected. "It won't be this time."

Chapter Three

Once the cattle were safely delivered to Justiss Junction, Billy settled into a normal summer routine, if there was such a thing. After all, the big house was suddenly bursting with new residents. Chris, Joe, and Viktor simply moved their blankets to the back bedrooms. Two days later Charlie brought out little Jake to join them.

"He said it was too quiet in town with his brothers out here," Charlie explained. "Besides, it's time he learned to tell the difference between a horse and a cow."

"Oh, I suppose he knows that already," Billy said, grinning at the boy. "But we might teach him a thing or two about staying in the saddle."

"Just don't send him back to your mama with a broken leg," Charlie warned. "Or anything else, for that matter. Hear?"

"We'll do our best," Billy promised.

"Know you will, son. Let's take a walk down by the creek."

Billy frowned as he followed his father down the hill to Bluff Creek. Taking a walk was Charlie's way of saying trouble was brewing. When they reached the shrunken banks of the creek, Billy turned to his father.

"You brought more than Jake along," Billy mumbled. "How bad is the news?"

"Not good," Charlie confessed. "Cornfields all over the county are parched. There are six dams across Palo Pinto Creek. There are farmers downstream ready to start shooting their neighbors. We've got these Kemps riding around threatening farmers again. I heard about young Jenkins, by the way."

"You'd likely had it out with Kemp then and there. I thought getting the herd to the junction was more important, Papa."

"You were there. It was your command. As for Kemp, he's sure doing his best to wind up crosswise with us. I had Bret check his posters, but there's nothing. I suppose he's just the contrary type. Keep an eye open for him just the same."

"I will. Wes keeps a man watching Caddo Creek."

"Not a bad notion. Billy, I noticed you've moved most of the stock north, toward the river. Are the wells holding up?"

"So far. I figured I'd start sending a crew to the river to fill fresh water barrels, though. What we're getting from the wells is mostly foul."

"That would seem prudent. You're long on hands

now it's summer, aren't you?"

"For now. If this sun keeps up, though, all that could change. You can't work midday when it's as hot as fire."

"I want you to take a good look around the ranch today or tomorrow. The day after, Joe Nance has asked for a meeting of the Palo Pinto Stockraisers Association. I'd like you to be there to represent the Flying J."

"Sure, Papa."

"Billy," Charlie added, gripping his son's broad shoulders, "you've done a fine job out here. Selling all those beeves the last two years leaves us sound as a silver dollar. I expect the drought to hurt. Don't kill yourself trying to keep every calf alive. We'll lose some."

"It's not in me to sit by and watch stock die."

"I know that, son. But don't let it eat you inside out. Take Jake riding. Go fishing with Joe and Chris. I never knew anyone to pull catfish out of that muddy river like you used to do. And find some time to court that Cassidy girl. You aren't getting any younger, Billy. Neither is she."

"No, sir," Billy agreed with a grin.

But with a whole ranch to ride in a day and a half, Billy found no time for Colleen Cassidy or anyone else. He covered the Flying J from Wes Tyler's cabin above Caddo Creek to the dusty Jacksboro road. The sight of the shaggy Herefords lying under the scant shade of the junipers and mesquites

161

brought a shudder down his spine. The calves especially suffered. Twice he happened upon buzzards picking at the bones of dead stock.

When he met with the other ranchers at the hotel, Billy described the scene in detail. His hands trembled, and he spoke with great emotion.

"It's about the same at my place," Joe Nance declared. The white-haired rancher seemed to lose his thoughts for a moment. Then he went on, saying, "I recall one other drought this bad. Back then we had the whole county for pasture, though. Everyone ran longhorns, too, and they were a heartier breed than these hornless wonders you boys keep bringing up. Why, I remember when we—"

"Thank you, Joe," Charlie said, interrupting. Once Joe got a full head of steam up, he could talk for hours. No one had that kind of time to spare.

"Seems to me the real trouble comes from all these fences," Ike Kemp suggested. Charlie frowned. Kemp was invited more as a spectator since only a slice of his holdings were inside the county.

"All these dams aren't helping things, either," Randolph Nance chipped in. "If you choke off the creeks, then the river goes dry. If that happens, no one this side of Waco will survive."

"Some are already leaving," Charlie said, sighing. "Two families rode through town eastward-bound this morning. Their corn's all withered, and they've lost heart. Those of us who've been around a while know seasons have a way of turning. This drought won't last forever. They never do."

"No, they only last long enough to ruin us," Kemp

grumbled. "If the range was still wide open . . ."

"It isn't," Charlie declared. "Won't ever be again. That's a fact. So, friends, what can we do about the present difficulties?"

Little or nothing, Billy thought. It turned out the ranchers couldn't even agree whether there was a drought or not, much less what to do about it. Billy shook his head in disgust and rode homeward. It was always the same story. Anything that was to be accomplished had to be done with his own two hands.

Billy set to work the moment he returned. First, he put Joe and Viktor in charge of seeing the fresh water barrels were кept full. Next he sent Chris out to the line camps with word to keep the stock from wandering too far from the river. A steer might find good grass for a time in the hills, but the animal would die of thirst before returning to the river. Last of all Billy, with Hector's help, began deepening the wells. Hector also built a stone aqueduct from a free-flowing spring to the house.

The work cast away Billy's gloom. There was a comfort to toil, and when he lounged in Bluff Creek, washing away the grime and dirt of the well shaft from his chest, he couldn't help laughing. His brothers joined him a little later, and the clock seemed to turn in reverse. Sure, Chris and Joe were older, taller, and stronger than when they'd jumped from Billy's shoulders into that same creek. But they would always be younger brothers, after all. Viktor and Jake joined in, too, and Billy couldn't help smiling with satisfaction as the boy's pale shoulders began to tan, as the softness gave way to Brazos leather.

Having his brothers at the ranch brought back memories of those early years in Palo Pinto County when the whole family had lived along Bluff Creek. Having young voices and hungry mouths around pleased Eugenia Contreras, too. The old woman whose niece had married Luis Morales had come to the Flying J a year before to cook and clean house. Actually Eugenia did everything from mend shirts to doctor the horses.

"It is well you have children around this house," she told Billy. "A house is hollow with only men around. You should bring a senorita here, Senor Billy. I have a niece, Dulcinea, who is as pretty as an April rose. I tell you, Senor Billy, she would make you a good wife. See how happy Luis has become? You, too, could be the father of many children."

"Oh, I think I'll do my own looking, thanks the same," Billy answered. "But if I run out of females, I'll take your advice."

"Dulcinea cooks like an angel."

"Sure," Billy said, laughing. "Only if I married her, you'd be out of a job. How could I have that on my conscience?"

"Hombres!" the old woman muttered in disgust. "Men!"

In truth, though, Billy had taken quite an interest

164

in Colleen Cassidy. And as his duties at the ranch slackened, he began taking long rides south along Bluff Creek to the Albany road. On the far side of the road, nestled against the eastern ridge of the Palo Pinto Mountains, stood the Cassidy farmhouse. Most days Colleen was more than agreeable to a stroll along the hillside or a ride beside the creek.

Summer brought out the best in Colleen. Her reddish-blond hair and light features took on a rosy tint, and her delicate fingers glowed with warmth when they touched Billy's leathery hands. She'd just turned eighteen, and a new fire seemed to fill her deep blue eyes.

"Ma's asked again if you'd come to Sunday dinner," she told him as they strolled atop the boulder-strewn hillside. "She plans to bake a goose."

"I'll try to come."

"If you don't, maybe I'll be asking another," she said, hiding the grin on her face. "It isn't every day Patrick Cassidy asks a neighbor to share his table."

"Well, I can't have it said I'm not treating my neighbors right," Billy said, scratching his ear. "You're sure young Flynn won't set the dogs on me again?"

"Ah, that was an accident, I'm sure."

"More likely he knows who'll inherit your chores should you leave the farm."

"Leave the farm?" she asked in pretended astonishment. "Why ever would I care to do that?"

"I thought maybe you were interested in helping out Mrs. Parnell with her sewing. She's opened a shop now, and there's a sign in the window offering work."

"Don't tell Pa that," Colleen said, laughing. "He's like to hire me away to her. Nine mouths to feed from the takings of a dry farm asks a lot of the Lord. And me, eighteen now! A proper girl's got herself a husband by now."

"In the market for one, are you?"

"I might be," she said, lifting her eyebrows. "Don't tell me you've not taken an interest, Billy. You come around here as often as a fox in search of a chicken coop."

"Oh, I thought you'd given up on me. After all, I'm well past twenty, ready to wrinkle and grow gray any time now."

"Pa says an older man's more settled in his ways," Colleen declared. "But if he's got his living and a house to boot, he can be a pleasing prospect."

"Twenty-four's not too old, then?"

"Well, I wouldn't add many more months of delay, Billy Justiss. Ma had Sully walking about and another on the way when she was my age."

"After trying to keep up with Jake the past few days, I'm not convinced I'm ready for fatherhood."

"That's why it's all the more important to choose the right woman," Colleen argued. "If you were to take a skinny, frail thing like Molly McDaniel to your heart, you'd find only grief. Me, I've got a tolerant nature, being the eldest girl in a brood of seven."

"I'm from a big family, too."

"Surely I know that. We're never at the ranch or in

town but that some brother or nephew's about."

"That would prove a problem, especially now Ryan's playing papa to all those orphans at Buck Creek."

"I'd wager we could escape their eyes when the time came."

Billy smiled and took her hands. They stared at the late afternoon sun blazing down from overhead, then sighed.

"I'm not the smartest man in Texas," Billy told her. "There's not much softness to my life, and I often smell of cow dung and horsehide. I'll never be a lawyer like my brother Ross or an engineer like Ryan. In truth, I'm not much more than a simple cowboy, earning his keep off the land, tending stock and wrestling with an uncertain future. I don't plan on passing through this life alone, though. Colleen, I nurture the idea that one day you'll be at my side."

"I'd choose the same."

"Then, I'd like you to consider us courting."

"It's not for me to say," she said, tenderly stroking his hands. "Speak to Pa on Sunday. It may seem old-fashioned, but my family is terribly important to me, Billy. I'll abide by their wishes."

"Expect me after services then. And every afternoon until then."

"I will," she said, smiling.

Billy made daily visits to the Cassidy farm. Often he'd bring a handful of wildflowers or a jar of Eugenia's apple butter or honey. He and Colleen

167

would then stroll or ride a couple of hours. Whenever she clasped his hand or leaned her soft cheek against his shoulder, he felt a warmth grow inside.

Freedom has its merits, Billy told himself, but he'd found nothing to rival the tranquility that came of belonging.

On Sunday he rode to the Cassidy farmhouse directly after services. His brothers stayed in town to dine with their parents, and he would hardly be missed.

"Good afternoon, Mr. Cassidy," Billy said when he arrived at the simple picket house. "I trust all is well with you and your family?"

"As well as it can be in the middle of this accursed drought," Cassidy grumbled. "But come along, son. It's not to argue the weather that's brought you here."

Billy entered the small front room. The younger Cassidy boys, Flynn and Brian, sat together on a small wooden bench beside the window. Cornelia, ten, set knives and forks around an oval-shaped table. Young Patrick, seventeen, chatted with his older brother Sullivan. Colleen and her fourteen-year-old sister Mary Eileen helped their mother move kettles about the stove.

"Look who's arrived," Pat Cassidy announced.

The boys glanced up from the bench, and Cornelia smiled shyly. Colleen's mother Eileen wiped her hands on an apron and greeted Billy with a warm hug.

"I thought you might make use of this," Billy said, passing a jar of peach preserves into Mrs. Cassidy's hands. "And these are for you, Colleen," he added, turning toward the stove and producing a pair of scarlet roses.

"Wherever did you find them?" Colleen asked, cradling the flowers in her hands and brightening like the July sun. "I haven't seen roses . . . well, I can't even remember the last time."

Mrs. Cassidy was equally impressed, and Billy smiled. They'd come from his Aunt Emiline's greenhouse in Fort Worth. Ryan had picked them up at the depot and brought them to Palo Pinto the day before.

"I'll put them in a vase," Colleen said. "We'll have them to look at over supper."

Shortly thereafter Mr. Cassidy waved the others to the table. After a brief prayer, great platters of food started around the table. Billy took only meager portions. Little Brian had a gaunt look about his cheeks, and even the normally robust Flynn seemed to be growing thinner.

"You're hardly eating enough to feed a flea," Mrs. Cassidy remarked. "Come, Billy. Colleen's made the stuffing special. Have a bit more."

"No, thank you just the same," Billy said, waving away a platter of cornmeal stuffing. "I'm afraid I ate too generous a breakfast. Usually I've put in a day's labor by noon and have my appetite back. Today, I confess, all I've done is sit on a hard wooden bench and listen to sermonizing."

"Well, you'd sure been welcome to help me with

the stock," Brian said, helping himself to the remaining food. "I wish I could sit about Sunday mornings."

Flynn frowned, and Brian drew a hostile glance from his father. Billy only smiled, and sipped his mint tea.

"You folks have had a hard time, what with so little rain. How's your well holding up?" Billy asked.

"Went dry a week ago," Sully answered. "The springs are still flowing. For now. They don't help the corn much."

"If it doesn't rain soon," Patrick declared, "the garden will be lost."

"It's the same story everywhere," Billy commented. "And not yet July."

"Maybe August will be wet," Mary Eileen said. "I've prayed it will be."

"Yes," Pat Cassidy said somberly. "When I was a boy in Ireland, the potato blight came. Now the rains have ceased. I wonder that my father didn't name me Job for all the suffering life has brought."

"Hold on," Billy urged. "The rains will come in time. We'll lose stock . . . and crops, but as long as we keep faith with the land, we'll survive."

"I've said as much myself," Pat Cassidy pointed out. "Pray and persevere. It's all that's to be done."

After supper, the boys set off to attend to some chores. Colleen and her sisters helped their mother scrub the dishes. Pat Cassidy lit a pipe and led Billy out the back door.

170

"You've devoted a great deal of attention to my daughter of late," Cassidy said, "You ride with her or walk the mountain. As a father, I believe I've a right to know your intentions."

"Yes, sir," Billy agreed. "I'm not an educated man like some in my family, Mr. Cassidy. I don't claim fine words and lofty promises. I know hard work, though, and I keep faith with my responsibilities. It's my intention to marry Colleen, to ask her to share my home and my life and what future life holds for me."

"And just what prospects do your foresee?"

"As you know, I've been managing my family's ranch of late. I have a considerable interest in the ranch and a generous wage to boot. I don't know what plans my younger brothers may have, but the older ones currently have other directions to take. Barring calamity, I expect to pass my old age on the Flying J."

"I've nothing against ranching, Billy, but a man ought to have his own house, his own land. I've known too many landed families to want my daughter's husband to come of them."

"I always thought to build my own house when the time came to raise children," Billy explained. "I've got money to buy land, but I'm needed on the Flying J. A man can't always just seek his own path. Sometimes his life finds him, and that's what's happened to me. No one can run that ranch with as steady a hand as I can. It's not a boast, sir. It's true."

"There are other questions as well," Cassidy con-

171

tinued. "You're a bit older than Colleen."

"I am. I like to think that means I'll be a truer husband. I worried at taking a younger wife, but there aren't many girls of even seventeen about this county without husbands. In truth, Colleen has rare wisdom for her age. Besides, it's hopeless. I love her."

"Then there's the matter of religion. We're baptized Catholics, you see."

"I confess I don't call myself a religious man, Mr. Cassidy. I'm not schooled to say all the proper prayers or to cross myself before eating, but I trust in God. My mother was Catholic, though she's worshipped in the Methodist church twenty-five years now. There were no priests near the farm in Robertson County."

"Nor many here. You'd see the children not raised heathens?"

"How could that be possible?" Billy asked, motioning to the countryside. "How could a child live here, walk this land, seeing growth and wonderment all around, and not believe someone was behind it? God walks here, too, Mr. Cassidy. Only a blind man would fail to see that."

"Even in these hard times?"

"Hard?" Billy asked, lifting his trouser leg to show the ancient scars made by his father's knife. "A rattlesnake near killed me when I first came here. I've been shot, caught fever and near died. What saved me? Hard? It's the struggles that make us strong."

"Not all of us," Cassidy said, frowning as he

172

pointed to a bare-chested Brian. The ribs protruded through the eight-year-old's pale flesh.

"Has he ever tasted a Brazos catfish?" Billy asked. "I plan to take my brothers fishing tomorrow. I'll bet Brian has the touch."

"We've had little luck up to now."

"I know all the right spots," Billy boasted. "Leave it to me. And later on we'll shoot some rabbits, maybe a deer or some ducks. The land provides."

"Yes," Cassidy said, gripping Billy by the shoulders. "I believe you're right. I welcome your attentions to my daughter, sir. And if it's agreeable, I've always had a fondness for September weddings."

Billy grinned, then set off to share the news with Colleen.

Chapter Four

It seemed to Ryan Justiss that it would never rain. The final week of June the sky filled with clouds, and lightning lit the heavens. But though the ground shook and trees lost limbs, there weren't enough raindrops to fill one of Rachel's thimbles.

Life at the little orphanage at Buck Creek had never been particularly easy. If not for the clothing donated by townspeople and farm families and the livestock provided by the Flying J Ranch, the seventy-odd youngsters would never survive. Now, with hard times everywhere, Ryan knew the orphans would have to do more to help themselves.

The boys knew it, too. They worked the two cornfields and tended the chickens and hogs with rare devotion. Others dipped lines into the creek in hopes of snagging a bass or catfish. Ryan marveled at their efforts.

Even so, he read disturbing signs whenever he walked the countryside. The buffalo grass that covered the plain was stiff and brittle. The few cattle that hadn't been sold off would find scant nourishment from such feed. When Ryan herded the boys down to Buck Creek for their Saturday night bath, he discovered the water was little more than waist deep on the youngest.

"Soon we won't have any creek at all," he told Rachel. "What will we do then?"

"Something," she assured him. "We've known worse times, these lads and myself as well."

Ryan tried to find encouragement in her confidence, but he heard her mumbled doubts in the deep of night. She worried, too.

By the close of July, Palo Pinto had gone another thirty days without rain. The ground cracked, and springs ceased to flow. It seemed fortune had turned her head away and left fate to ravage the land and its people.

Ryan was in the throes of despair one morning when he happened upon what was left of the vegetable garden. Thirteen-year-old Jay Belton, one of Rachel's favorites, was supervising a small army of younger boys plucking weeds from the neat rows of carrots and beans. Little Jay, his unruly blond hair flowing over both ears and halfway down his neck, crawled between rows of plants, grabbing weeds in each hand. The fingers of the boy's right hand worked wonders. The left hand, turned so that two missing digits were less obvious, snatched weeds one at a time.

When Rachel first arrived at Buck Creek, nearly every boy there over eleven bore the scars of duty on the railroad. A mangled hand, a crippled foot, a missing arm or leg was a sure sign of the rigors of the railcamps. Many of the railroad orphans were gone now, though. The few girls were taken in by farm families. The stronger boys were welcomed with open arms by farmers, or else signed on as cowboys on area ranches. In the last year other boys had left Buck Creek for jobs at the new stores in Justiss Junction or to be apprenticed to cabinet-makers, carpenters, or masons. There were less than twenty as old as Jay, and only a handful fit for heavy labor.

At first Ryan had complained bitterly that the boys only stayed until they were fit to earn a wage.

"They're ungrateful," he grumbled. "They could help do some of the heavy work that always needs doing."

"You're wrong," Rachel had countered. "They know there's scarce food for extra mouths here, and many of them will help as they are able."

It proved to be true. Letters arrived with a dollar now and then. Sometimes a former Buck Creek boy would bring by a hog or a sack of flour. Others would build shelves for the school Rachel operated in the third bunkhouse. Outgrown clothing continued to arrive even in the darkest days of July.

"They'll have that garden weeded by noon," Jay declared as he tiptoed his way to Ryan's side. "Won't make much difference if we don't get some water to the plants. They'll all die pretty soon. Look."

Jay held a shriveled carrot in the air. The stalk was

176

brown. Only a dark, hard kernel grew where a half-mature carrot should have been.

"We could still get some rain," Ryan said, gazing into the empty sea of blue overhead.

"In August?" the boy asked. "The corn's burnin' up, too."

"If nature won't lend us a hand, maybe we'll just have to find a way to bring some water to the fields ourselves," Ryan declared. "Ever dig a ditch?"

"I've dug plenty of garbage pits back in the rail camps," Jay answered. "Think maybe we can dig our own creek?"

"Maybe. How about rounding up some of the stronger lads? We'll get started right away."

Jay was off in an instant. He returned shortly with three of the older orphans, Todd Tipton, Ren Newton, and Sime Phipps. The boys had been working leather hides into jackets for sale in Palo Pinto. Clearly, saving the garden was more important.

"Show us what to do, Mr. Ryan," Ren said.

Ryan smiled. If heart counted for anything, those youngsters would get through drought or storm or anything else.

He planned three channels flowing from Buck Creek to the garden. Shallow trenches could be dug to carry the water. Small dams of dirt would serve as gates for the life-giving liquid so that the plants wouldn't be drowned. When water was wanted, a spade could simply move the dirt aside, letting the stream flow. When enough water reached the garden, the dam would close the channel.

In no time Ryan and his three man crew set to the task. When Todd or Ren or Sime began to falter, some fresh face appeared to spell the trencher. In the July heat, Ryan and his companions sweated themselves to exhaustion. Boys brought dippers of water around even as they had done to the track workers of the Ft. Worth and Western not so long before.

Ryan had one ditch half dug when his legs gave way. He sank to the ground and dizzily stared in disbelief. In seconds small hands dragged him to the creek and immersed his body in soothing liquid.

"You shouldn't work so long in the sun," Jay scolded him. "We'll finish it up."

Ryan was helped to the shade of a pair of willows. He looked on as the boys completed the trenches. Then, with a loud cheer, the boys opened the dams and let the precious waters of Buck Creek revive the garden.

By nightfall, Ryan had recovered enough to join Rachel for a twilight walk.

"You shouldn't push yourself so," she argued. "Let the boys help."

"They're so small, though," Ryan argued.

"They've worked harder, and they're stronger than they appear. Little Jay close to carried you to the creek, Ren told me. You wouldn't think that lad could lift his own hat."

"You've cast a spell over them. You take these half-starved children with crippled hands and flash a smile, nurse their fevers and help them learn their letters. You kindle hope in them, and they think they can do anything. Rachel, what happens when the corn crop fails, when the vegetables die, when the creek goes dry like the wells have?"

"I don't know for certain, but we won't let even those calamities defeat us. Maybe we'll load ourselves into some wagons and head for the open plains. Perhaps some friend will give us land on a river. I trust those things to take care of themselves. So long as we refuse to surrender, we'll get by."

"I love you so much," he said, holding her tightly. "I just hate to see you disappointed."

"Disappointed?" she asked. "By you? Ry, I've wandered the railroad, friendless, homeless, deserted, and destitute. The Lord found me a place . . . first with the orphans and now with you. I could never be disappointed again. Don't sell yourself short, either. Those ditches of yours might well save the vegetables."

He wished he could believe it.

Early the next morning the spade crew started digging trenches toward the cornfields. Six entire acres of corn had been planted, and irrigating such an expanse required days of backbreaking toil. Each evening Ryan and Rachel would rub ointment on the blistered hands of the trenchers and listen to their muffled whimpers.

"They never complain," Ryan told little Jay. "Why not?"

"Oh, they complain sure enough," the boy said, grinning and nodding his head so that blond hair flew in a dozen directions. "Just not to you."

"I don't understand."

"We know you could be off buildin' some new

179

railroad," Jay explained. "You stay 'cause of Miz Rachel. And on account of us. We need you. Nobody'd ever admit it to you, but we know your papa gave this land, helped get the buildings put up. We'd do anything for Miz Rachel."

"Me, too."

"We know. Just 'cause we don't read and write as good as some doesn't mean we're altogether stupid. We know somethin' else, too. For most of us, this is the best place we could be. It means a lot to know where you sleep at night. It's good to have friends. We're a kind of family here. We get to plant carrots and watch 'em grow."

"It's nice watching you boys grow, too," Ryan said, grinning.

"Well, some grow more than others," Jay admitted, trying to stretch himself beyond his four-and-a-half-foot frame. "I used to pray maybe somebody'd take a likin' to me and adopt me like my friend Thalia. But nobody wants a runt with half his left hand gone."

"I wouldn't say that."

"You mean Miz Rachel."

"Me, too. You're kind of a particular favorite, you know."

" 'Cause she saved me twice, once when my hand got smashed and again when outlaws hit the camp and shot me."

Ryan nodded, though in truth it was more. He couldn't explain how something inside a man responds to a boy so desperately in need. He'd never had his brother Ross's knack for oratory or even Billy's matter-of-fact way of expressing his feelings.

180

He looked for Rachel. She would have put it just right, but she was busy dosing a fever.

"Yeah," Jay said finally, grinning. "I like you, too."

The canals might have saved the plants if the creek had remained deeper. But each day the depth dropped, and with it, the ditches required deepening. The springs slowed to a trickle, and Ryan tried to dig out the dry bottoms of the wells. The results were disappointing.

"The corn's dyin'," Jay declared sadly. "The ditches aren't workin' anymore."

"I know," Ryan replied. "The whole countryside is turning brown. It's a season of death."

And despair, he thought.

He rode out that same afternoon to visit with Marty Steele. The two old friends rode among the remaining Herefords on the south range.

"Wish they were longhorns," Marty grumbled. "A longhorn can find his own water, even if he has to stampede halfway to Kansas. These shaggy cows will just lay down and die. I've decided to send the strongest ones up north to the main range. They can graze along the Brazos. It hasn't gone dry yet."

"And the weak ones?"

"Thought you might like to have a big barbecue, jerk the beef you can't eat. Those boys would have some hides to work."

"I never thought I'd see the day when Marty Steele

gave up!" Ryan exclaimed.

"Just facin' up to things, Ry," Marty explained. "I'd as soon your orphans get these beeves as have the buzzards pick their bones. Can't be easy up there at what's left of Buck Creek. You know they're damming the headwaters."

"What?"

"Farmers to the west have dammed the creek in two or three places. That's part of the reason it's fallen so much lately."

"I guess it's no different than me digging ditches. Still, I feel like my neighbors are dooming my stock."

"They are. I told Charlie we ought to ride up there and blow those dams to El Paso, but he frowned on the notion. Others are a bit more vocal about it, though. A farmer got himself shot up on Palo Pinto Creek tryin' to shut off the stream and shift the channel onto his land. Water's serious business these days."

"Always has been."

It was Rachel's idea to go downstream for water.

"Instead of damming the creek and shutting off our neighbors from the water they need to survive, why don't we head for the river, fill barrels there, and bring them back. The Brazos has plenty of water," she argued. "It's not so far for us to go."

"Barrels won't do it," Ryan told her. "But if we could convert some wagons, make them into giant half barrels, that might work. We've got the planks, and I can get a couple of boys from town to do the

182

caulking."

"Hugh Price will help."

"Sure, and so will the Beale boy. Meanwhile, we'll deepen the trenches once more and pray for rain."

The rain didn't come, though, and the creek dropped to mere inches in places. Ryan followed three circling buzzards west the next day to where a calf lay lifeless near a dry water hole.

"That's the first," Marty said, emerging from out of the nearby trees.

"But not the last," Ryan added.

"Yes, the last," Marty declared. "I'll have the rest of the animals ready for butchering in two days. I won't have my stock die of thirst, Ryan!"

Marty's eyes lit with anger, and Ryan agreed to the desperate action. Killing off your own stock was madness, of course, but those were maddening times.

Chapter Five

A new madness descended upon Palo Pinto County. Desperate men turned to desperate deeds. Neighbors fought over a quart of water taken from a spring. Others argued over dammed creeks or access to streams and rivers. More than once the quiet of a summer night was fractured by the sound of a shotgun blast as law and reason gave way to anger and violence.

Ryan watched in dismay as the waters of Buck Creek receded until the stream was but ankle deep in places. Even worse, the wells rarely provided more than a bucket of water, and that was so fouled with dust or soil that Rachel boiled half of it away in making it fit.

Soon the wagons would be ready for their first trip to the Brazos. Ryan hoped the springs would keep them going till then. No one bathed anymore, and there was rarely enough to soothe one's thirst.

One night as he lay awake in the sweltering August heat, he heard the rumbling hooves of horses. He rose to his feet, pulled on a pair of trousers and set off toward Buck Creek. In the pale moonlight Ryan detected riders, a dozen at least, headed upstream. The clatter of rifles and shotguns mixed with the splash of hooves in the creek.

"What's happening?" Todd Tipton asked, emerging from the door of the far bunkhouse in his nightshirt.

"Don't know," Ryan confessed.

"They're not headed here?" Todd asked, his wary eyes searching out the cause of the disturbance.

"Upstream, by the sound of it. It's best we go along back to bed. It's apt to be a long day tomorrow."

"Yes, sir," Todd agreed, retiring to the bunkhouse.

Ryan found no rest, though, and when the unmistakable *pop pop* of rifle fire punctuated the night, he rose again. He lacked his father's experience as a soldier, but Ryan had ridden after outlaws and patrolled the range often enough to tell that a battle was going on. By the time he reached the barn, though, the firing had stopped. He didn't bother saddling a horse. He did keep an eye on the creek, though.

Less than ten minutes after reaching the banks of Buck Creek, Ryan heard a sharp bang. A dull rumble followed, and soon the creek began to froth.

A two-foot wave rolled down the dry bed, spilling over the bank in places and filling the air with a refreshing spray.

They've blown a dam, Ryan told himself. A second explosion half an hour later warned a second embankment had been blasted. By the time a third dam had been blown, Buck Creek was two feet deep.

By then the bunkhouses had begun to empty. Boys in oversized nightshirts or union drawers gathered to watch the creek bubble anew.

"The creek's come back to life!" little Jay Belton exclaimed, diving into the muddy water. Others followed. Ryan did his best to keep the youngsters clear, but they only pulled him along into the rising waters. The current swept two or three of the smaller ones along, and Ryan gestured wildly in their direction. Todd Tipton and another older boy, Paul Drayton, hurried to the rescue.

Suddenly the boys stopped their cheering. Upstream, riders galloped along the creek, shouting and firing pistols and shotguns off in the air.

"Get to cover!" Ryan screamed. Instantly the soggy half-clad orphans scurried up the bank and sought refuge in the adjacent wood. In the darkness the riders appeared as mere shadows, grotesque shapes whose angry, drunken voices seemed all the more sinister for their anonymity.

"They blew the dams, eh?" Jay whispered, burrowing in under Ryan's elbow. "Now we'll have water again."

"Yes," Ryan said, frowning. For how long no one could be certain. And at what cost?

186

"I'll bet the ditches are full. Maybe the vegetables will live after all," Jay suggested. "But the corn's dead for sure."

"Yes," Ryan mumbled. He wondered if death had also paid a call on the farmers upstream.

"What's happened here?" Rachel suddenly called from the steps of her house. "Where is everyone?"

"Down at the creek!" Jay shouted. "Somebody's blown up the dams."

The boys cheered again, but Rachel only ordered them back to their beds.

"Shed those wet clothes as well," she added. "And see your feet are dry. Morning will come early!"

"Yes'm," the orphans responded in unison as they reluctantly snaked their way back to the bunk-houses.

"Will the creek be all right now?" she asked Ryan as he took her hand.

"No," he grumbled. "It will hold this water a week maybe. Without rain, though, we'll be dry as before soon."

"By then you'll have the wagons finished. A week may prove a blessing."

"Maybe," Ryan said, wondering at what price a week of salvation had been purchased.

Bret Pruett answered that question early the next morning. The sheriff arrived with Alex Tuttle in time for breakfast. Rachel ushered them inside, and two extra bowls of oatmeal were meted out.

"Short on eggs and bacon, huh?" Tut asked.

187

"With seventy mouths to feed, we save our best fare for Sundays," Rachel explained. "Be glad we have water to drink. The dams broke last night. Lately we've been hard pressed to squeeze a pitcher's worth from the springs."

"Those dams didn't just break," Bret pointed out.

"I heard the blasts," Ryan told them. "Before that, there was shooting. Anybody hurt?"

"More than hurt," Bret said grimly. "Taylor Munden's place was the first hit. Munden heard 'em coming, got his rifle, and ran for the creek."

"And?" Ryan asked.

"Somebody shot him in the head," Tut explained. "I guess they must've gone a little crazy after that. We spotted four or five sets of tracks up by Munden's house. Amy and the girls are all right, but Pierce, the oldest, tried to chase 'em off. Ry, they just shot that boy to pieces. Little Lewis took a bullet through one arm. The cabin's a shambles."

"And the other farms?" Rachel asked.

"Guess they knew better," Tut went on to say. "The raiders tossed some dynamite into the Keggett place, blew it to high heaven. Ed, Millie, and the kids got clear ahead of time, though."

"You see anything?" Bret asked.

"Nothing but shadows," Ryan explained. "They rode north toward the river."

"Who'd want to clear this creek of dams besides you?" Tut asked. "There's just the Taney place downstream, right? They've got a half mile bounding the Brazos."

"I can't answer that," Ryan told them. "If you

188

mean to say I had anything to do with it, you're wrong. I'd never purchase even Rachel's welfare by killing a neighbor. You know me better than to think it, Bret."

"I know Marty, too," Bret responded. "You sure those riders headed north?"

"I'm sure," Ryan answered angrily. "As for Marty, he's been up on the north range with Billy for some time now. We cleared the south range of stock a while back."

"I had to ask," Bret said, rising from the table. "I'll find out who's responsible and see them hung."

"Who's responsible?" Ryan asked. "Not who, what! It's this blamed drought. It's turned people into loons."

"Into killers," Tut declared. "Butcherers. You hear anything, see anything, you let us know, Ry."

"I will," Ryan promised. "Meanwhile, you two take care. Whoever it was last night, there were plenty of 'em, and they seemed to know what they were about."

"I'll take that into account," Bret assured his brother-in-law.

At another time Ryan might have accompanied the lawmen in their search for the raiders. He had a keen sense of justice, and it galled him to think of gunmen riding Buck Creek, shooting farmers and blasting their homes. But the creek soon dropped back to its low-water mark, and Ryan concentrated his efforts on making ready the water wagons.

189

He held out high hopes for the oversized barrels on wheels. With a little luck, a single trip to the Brazos might satisfy the orphans' needs for several days. The wagons could also be used to irrigate the gardens and save the vegetables. So when Rachel announced the creek could no longer meet their needs, Ryan gathered the older boys together and began hitching horses to the water wagons.

"Todd, you and Ren take the second wagon," Ryan called out as the teams were harnessed. "Sime, you and Paul take the third."

Ryan mounted the seat of the first wagon himself, then waved for stout Tom Tubbs to join him.

"Can't the rest of us come, too?" Jay implored. "We can have a swim, cool off."

"It's too far to walk," Ryan told the others. "These horses have enough of a load to pull. Besides, are you forgetting all the work that's got to be done?"

"No, sir," the orphans grumbled. Some trudged along to their duties. Others stared up with solemn eyes. Ryan might have given in a year before, but Rachel had taught him the need for firmness. He shook his head and pointed the disappointed youngsters back toward the bunkhouses and the chores that awaited them.

The ride along Buck Creek to where it flowed into the larger Palo Pinto Creek was a little over a mile, and it wasn't all that much farther to the Brazos. Besides crossing what remained of Buck Creek and rumbling across the F W & W tracks, the journey crossed the northwestern boundary of Lawton Taney's thousand-acre farm.

Taney was a relative newcomer to Palo Pinto County. He'd inherited the land from an uncle who had bought the acreage from Bowie Justiss. It was a fine property, hugging both the railroad and the river. Paul Taney had run a herd of longhorns there and raised a good string of cutting horses. His nephew forsook livestock and planted corn.

Ryan always deemed it a mistake. The hills above the Brazos provided good grazing for cattle, but Lawton Taney had never been able to cultivate more than fifty or sixty acres of corn. True, he also sold wood to the railroad, but the land should have yielded a better living to Taney, his wife, and their five youngsters.

"A pure waste," Marty had said more than once. "All that fine pasture and good water going to seed!"

It's his land, though, Ryan told himself. He's welcome to scratch out a living growing corn if that suits him.

Now, though, with the creeks near dry, Ryan couldn't help envying Taney those acres along the Brazos. The river was down, too, but it wouldn't go dry. What's more, there were fish to be had there, and the refreshing swim little Jay longed for could be had without a second thought.

Yes, of all the farmers in Palo Pinto County, Taney was the luckiest, and he didn't know what to do about it!

Unfortunately, Taney did know what to do about three water wagons crossing his property.

"Hold up there!" the grizzled old farmer shouted as Ryan led the way down the embankment toward the Brazos. "What do you think you're doing?"

"Howdy, Mr. Taney," Ryan called, handing Tom the reins and hopping down to talk with the farmer. Taney cradled a double-barreled shotgun in his arms. His eldest boy, Roy, stood five feet away with a similar gun. Ryan turned and nervously motioned for his companions to stay put. Then he approached.

"Stop right there!" Taney growled. "I'll have no trespassers on my land. Get yourself turned around and go home!"

To add emphasis to his words, Taney cocked both hammers and swung his shotgun in Ryan's direction.

"That's uncalled for," Ryan said, staring hard at the farmer. "For as long as I can recall, it's been understood all men have a right to access the river."

"Not understood by me!" Taney barked. "Get!"

Ryan scowled. He set his feet in the sandy soil and folded his hands across his chest.

"I'm unarmed," Ryan pointed out. "I bring you no harm. Those boys and the others back at Buck Creek are in need of water. We come in peace, and we'll go soon as we have what we need."

"Get!" Taney yelled, firing the first barrel of his shotgun into the air, then leveling the second at Ryan.

"Mr. Ryan!" Todd cried.

"Stay where you are, son," Ryan replied, trying to

control his quivering fingers. "Taney, you best go ahead and shoot me if that's what you have in mind. Only know this: Sheriff Pruett will come and haul you off to jail. Then somebody else will bring those wagons in here and fill them. I'll be dead, and you'll be locked up, unable to help your family, and sure to hang. We'll both pay for your poor judgment. And they will," Ryan added, pointed to the hillside where Amy Taney and the younger children had gathered.

"Lawton, please, put the gun away!" Mrs. Taney pleaded. "That's Judge Justiss's boy, Ryan. He only wants the water for those poor orphans at Miz Rachel's."

"They can't have it!" Taney screamed with wild eyes. "It's my water! They can't have it!"

"The Brazos belongs to everyone," Ryan argued. "If you like, we'll cross Palo Pinto Creek and draw the water from upstream."

"Lawton?" his wife asked. "That sounds fair, doesn't it?"

"Does to me, Pa," Roy said, turning to his father. "I know two of those boys."

"No!" Taney shouted. "You can't have my water."

Ryan began to edge his way closer. He kept his eyes on Taney's fingers, then spoke in a quiet, confident voice.

"Mr. Taney, we don't want to take your water," Ryan explained. "Lord, we're not thieves. We just want to cross the creek and take some upstream."

Taney's tense facial muscles began to relax as Ryan spoke of how the river had flowed through that land a thousand years, of how he'd once fought the

Comanches up in the hills to the north. He went on to tell how many of the boys at Buck Creek helped build the railroad. Finally Ryan got to within a few feet of Taney.

"It's my water," the farmer explained. "All my water. You can't have it."

Taney turned the shotgun toward Ryan, but the younger man was too quick. Ryan jumped to one side, then grabbed the barrel and lifted it as Taney fired. The blast knocked them both to the ground. Roy immediately aimed his gun at Ryan, but Amy Taney raced down to intercede.

"Stop it!" she hollered. "Put that shotgun down, Roy! No one's going to die over water! Not here! Not now!"

Taney sat on the ground, clutching his empty shotgun to his chest. He muttered over and over again how no one would take his water. Ryan took the second shotgun, removed the shells, then handed it back to Roy.

"We'll cross the creek, ma'am," Ryan said, letting out a long sigh. "I'm sorry to have brought you trouble."

"It's not you," she replied, turning back to the children. Only now did Ryan see how thin and pale the youngsters were. Roy, though tall, held his trousers up with suspenders.

"Summer's been hard on everyone," Ryan grumbled. "We'll just get the water and head home."

"I wish I had some coffee to offer you," she lamented. "It's all gone. The corn's parched, and we ate our last chicken a week ago. He hasn't always

194

been this way, you know. It's only that he worries."

"I know," Ryan said, nodding. "Next time we come I'll show you folks how we shifted water to our garden. You could do the same for your corn. You have the whole river to use, and—"

"You won't be back!" Taney suddenly shouted. "You come, and I'll shoot."

"Pa, please," Roy said, kneeling beside his father and holding the man's trembling hands.

"You best get your wagons full," Mrs. Taney told Ryan. "As for the other, we'll speak of it another time."

"Yes, ma'am," Ryan answered. He then motioned the wagons toward Palo Pinto Creek.

It took close to three hours to fill the wagons. Ryan then took great care to keep on the north side of Palo Pinto Creek until he was well out of sight of the Taney place. When they reached the orphanage, Ryan left the boys to distribute the water while he led Rachel aside to share the story of their brush with Lawton Taney.

"Imagine those kids," Ryan grumbled. "Near starved in a bountiful land. Their father gone mad!"

"I don't want you returning there," Rachel argued. "He might have shot you all. We'll think of another way."

"There is no other way," Ryan told her. "But we'll stay to the far side of Palo Pinto Creek. The land up that way is still unsettled."

"Maybe we should move there."

"Maybe. I could have Ross find out who holds the title. For now, though, I want to ride into town, tell Bret what's happened. I'll be home for supper."

"Don't hurry your pace," Rachel warned. "The sun's fierce today, and I don't want you sunstruck."

"I'll keep that in mind, Miz Rachel," Ryan said, kissing her forehead. He then left to saddle a horse and head for Palo Pinto.

Chapter Six

Ryan passed on his news and returned to Buck Creek as promised. The water revived the garden and quenched the thirsts of the youngsters. For two or three days spirits soared. A brief cloudburst settled the dust and allowed seventy crazed boys to stand naked and wash away their weariness under the shower of raindrops.

The rain came and went in minutes, though, and the midday sun blazed down once again on a parched and forsaken Palo Pinto County.

"It's as if we're being tormented," Rachel told Ryan. "Just sprinkle a few drops on the poor fools, remind them what it was like to know rain. Then send the sun back to torture the fields and devour their spirits."

Ryan saw despair fill her eyes for the first time. If Rachel gives up, we're lost, he told himself. The others noticed it, too. Even little Jay Belton's antics failed to bring a smile to Rachel's face. The gloomy children stumbled around as if in a daze, and Ryan knew something had to be done.

"We're going back to the river," he told Jay. "Spread the word. Anybody who wants to come along can follow on foot. We'll leave just before dawn so the heat won't tax the little ones. Bring line and hooks, too. Maybe we'll catch our supper."

"It's to be a holiday then?" the boy asked.

"A needed one," Ryan pointed out.

"I don't know about this," Rachel said when he shared the news. "Agreed, they need an adventure, but I didn't like what Lawton Taney did last time you were there."

"Bret rode out and talked to him," Ryan assured her. "We'll cross the creek and stay clear of his land as much as possible. We need the water, Rachel. And I'm far from certain we don't need a diversion every bit as much. Besides, the smell at dinner is getting as bad as the inside of a barn."

She laughed, and a trace of the old smile returned. Ryan held her tightly, then began making preparations for the journey.

Early the following morning the little caravan left Buck Creek. As promised, Ryan crossed Palo Pinto Creek almost immediately and kept to the far bank.

He kept the boys to the trees so as to shield them from the rising sun and keep them from Lawton Taney's view. The wagons had to travel the creekbed, for it was the only path to the Brazos free of ravines and trees.

The long trip to the river proved uneventful. The Taney farm across the creek appeared deserted, and no one barked a challenge this time. The forty-odd boys who'd come along on foot set about helping Ryan and the older boys fill the huge barrels. By midmorning the work was finished.

"The river's quite deep in places," Ryan warned as the boys gathered around. "Watch the little ones carefully. Keep away from the creek, and see you don't draw Mr. Taney's attention."

"He's crazy," Todd declared.

"He's best left alone," Ryan said firmly. "Now, who's first in the river?"

"Me!" a dozen voices cried out. Boys scrambled out of their sweat-soaked clothes and plunged into the Brazos. The water seemed to wash away the despair as it cleansed the dirt and eased the fatigue. Ryan sat on the bank and laughed at the foolishness. Suddenly twenty orphans raced up the bank and dragged him into the shallows.

Ryan grabbed one or two and wrestled them under the surface in pretended anger. The scrawny boys bobbed to the surface, all smiles and arms and legs. It reminded Ryan of his own childhood, dunking his little brothers and drowning the summer's heat in a refreshing morning swim.

Suddenly everything changed. Roy Taney came racing across Palo Pinto Creek, shouting a muddle of words and waving his arms frantically. Ryan splashed his way to the bank and caught Roy in his arms.

"Mr. Ryan, Pa's comin'," Roy gasped. "He's got his gun, and he's —"

A shotgun blast drowned the rest. Ryan turned toward the boys and waved them toward the cover of the trees.

"Hurry!" Ryan urged as he began pulling the ones in the shallows out of the river. "Run!"

Lawton Taney waded through the shallow remnant of Palo Pinto Creek. In the distance a train rumbled across the Brazos bridge Ryan had helped construct. Taney's eyes were wide and wild. Fear gripped Ryan's gut, knotted his insides so that he had difficulty moving toward the angry farmer.

"Mr. Ryan!" young Todd called as he pulled on his pants and prepared to join Ryan.

"Get the wagons to cover!" Ryan ordered. "See to the others."

Todd reluctantly grabbed Ren Newton, and two fifteen-year-olds ushered the others into the cover of the nearby live oaks.

"I warned you!" Taney cried as he marched toward Ryan with a loaded shotgun. "I told you to leave my water be!"

"Pa, please," Roy said, rushing to his father's side. Taney shoved the boy out of the way and continued. Ryan watched in stunned silence as the shotgun's

200

barrel grew ever nearer. He wanted to say something, calm Taney's crazed mind, but words simply wouldn't come.

"Mr. Ryan!" Paul Drayton called.

Ryan turned and gazed in horror as Jay Belton and a pair of younger boys hurried to help.

"Get back!" Ryan yelled. Young Drayton raced after them. Taney aimed his shotgun, and Ryan exploded into motion.

Why the shotgun failed to discharge when Ryan slammed into Taney would remain a great mystery. Perhaps the hammers weren't cocked. Maybe Ryan's sudden movement caught Taney by surprise. For whatever reason, it provided Paul Drayton a chance to wrestle Jay Belton to the sandy ground. Ryan tried to do the same to Taney, but madness seemed to lend the farmer unnatural strength. Ryan winced with pain as the butt of the shotgun slammed into his jaw.

He rolled over and groaned. Then the shotgun exploded. Powder obscured the scene a moment. It stung Ryan's eyes. He felt moisture on his right cheek, and he spit blood.

"Pa!" Roy Taney cried.

Ryan stared up at the farmer's ashen face. The shotgun fell from Taney's trembling hands. Ryan then turned and gazed at the four bloody bodies on the riverbank behind him.

"No!" Ryan yelled, lunging toward Taney and tearing at the farmer's throat with angry hands. Taney stepped back and tried to free himself, but

201

Ryan was filled with fury. He swung his right hand again and again, bloodying Taney's forehead, closing one eye, jarring him senseless until young arms pried him loose.

"Jay!" Ryan shouted when he saw the thirteen-year-old's horror-filled face at his side. Blood was smeared across the young man's face and chest, but he appeared unhurt. "You're all right?"

"Scared," Jay admitted. His two small companions were there as well, a bit bloody and thoroughly shaken but otherwise whole.

"I don't understand," Ryan mumbled.

"It's Paul," Todd said, leading Ryan aside. Young Drayton had driven the others to the ground, and he'd received the full impact of the shotgun blast for his efforts.

"Paul?" Ryan asked, kneeling beside the shattered fifteen-year-old.

The boy's lifeless eyes stared upward, seemingly asking for an explanation. Ryan had none to offer. Instead he turned back to Taney.

The farmer leaned against his son's shoulder, whimpering as he rubbed his swollen face.

"He hasn't been himself," Roy muttered. "I swear, he never meant to—"

"That was murder," Ryan accused. "Not a one of us was armed, and we weren't even on his land this time! I'll see he hangs for this!"

"Please, no," Roy sobbed. "It's the heat. He hasn't been the same."

"Tell that to Paul," Todd replied angrily.

202

"It's my fault," Jay mumbled, gripping Ryan's arm tightly and fighting back the first of many tears. "If I'd stayed . . ."

"It's not," Ryan objected. "You didn't come down here with a loaded shotgun to shoot a boy who never harmed a soul in all his life! You didn't pull the trigger! No, the fault lies right there!" Ryan yelled, pointing an accusing finger at Lawton Taney's chest. "Right there!"

"What do we do with Paul?" one of the smaller boys asked.

"Take him home," Ryan answered, kneeling beside the torn young body. "Lord, Rachel's going to take this hard."

"It's hard news," Todd said, swallowing with difficulty.

"Yes," Ryan agreed as he lifted Paul Drayton. Paul had stood near six feet tall, but the body seemed as light as a feather. Blood covered most of the young man's chest and stomach, and Ryan decided to bathe the body before taking it home.

"Let me," Todd offered as Ryan eased the corpse into the river. "You better see to your face. It's pretty much a mess."

Ryan thought to object, but Jay was already leading the way to the wagons. Somehow it seemed fitting for the boys to tend their own. Ren Newton placed his own shirt over Paul's shattered flesh, and Todd brushed Paul's hair to one side and closed his eyelids. They then tied him on the seat of the third wagon, and a somber-faced Sime Phipps climbed up alongside.

"I guess we'll have to try the fishing another time," Jay said, forcing half a smile onto his face.

"Guess so," Ryan agreed. "I don't feel in the mood just now."

The boys mumbled their agreement, and Ryan climbed aboard the lead wagon. Tom took the reins and started the horses in motion. Soon they were headed back to Buck Creek.

Rachel was distraught. She wept openly, then busied herself tending to Ryan's bruised and battered face. It had only now begun to throb, but the pain was nothing to the grief he felt over young Paul's premature death.

"I've seen it so many times before," she whispered. "It's why I wanted to bring them here, so they could experience peace for a change. But death has a way of seeking them out, doesn't it?"

"You warned me against going," Ryan mumbled.

"You aren't to blame," she scolded. "One thing I've learned: When death sets out to strike, it isn't put off. I'm just so angry!"

"Me, too. If I'd had a pistol along, I'd shot Taney dead."

"What would that have proven? No, Ry, life happens. We don't craft it with our hands or our minds. We only do our best to struggle on."

"Yes," he agreed.

204

They buried Paul Drayton beneath a small live oak on the hillside overlooking Buck Creek.

"Paul liked to get up early and watch the sun rise over the creek," Todd explained. "He'd look out there and talk about how one day he'd like to go to sea, be a sailor and see China."

"He never got that far," Ryan said, gripping Rachel's hands. "I didn't know him too well. He didn't talk all that much. What I remember best is how he was always looking after the newcomers. He'd make extra slats for their bed or help 'em stuff their mattress. He was good with the horses, too."

"He liked to cook," Rachel whispered. "I used to laugh at the way he'd pepper everything. He never worried much about himself, just how everyone else was getting along."

"We'll miss him," Jay said, and the others echoed the sentiment.

Bret Pruett appeared at the Taney farm two days later. Charlie Justiss had written out a warrant, and angry townfolk spoke of a quick trial and a speedy hanging. Lawton Taney cheated them. He'd gone off alone that morning and hung himself from the limb of a white oak tree just a mile and a quarter from where he'd slain young Paul Drayton.

"He couldn't live with what he did," Amy Taney explained.

"It was the heat turned him crazy," young Roy

added. "He was a good man before."

Yes, the heat, Ryan Justiss thought as he walked the dry creek bed the night Bret had passed on the news. The heat and the madness that comes with it. Lord, help us, Ryan prayed, glancing up at the simple cross made of two white pickets. Protect us from this growing darkness.

Chapter Seven

August baked the land. Creeks by the score vanished, spreading despair across the county like some dreadful plague. Farmers struggled to keep their crops alive until harvest. Most failed. Ranchers scrambled to move their stock to fresh pasture. Billy Justiss oversaw the relocation of the surviving animals from the parched south range to the crowded sections bordering on the Brazos.

"The land itself is dyin'," Jared Dunlap told Billy as they met in the shallows near where Bluff Creek emptied into the river. "Even the buzzards seem to be headin' elsewhere. There's never been such a time."

"Never," Billy agreed. "I don't think it's ever going to rain again."

"It would take Noah's flood to get the creeks flowin' again. It's pure madness, this drought."

"Yes," Billy mumbled. "Madness."

"How else can you figure it?" Jared asked with raised eyebrows. "Marty Steele's given up on the south range, gone to shootin' his own cattle. And how about that Taney fellow? Shoots a fifteen-year-old kid for swimmin' in the Brazos!"

"Ryan, too," Billy added. "He like to beat Taney to death. Ryan! Why, I don't imagine he's raised a fist in anger three times in his whole life."

"Men blastin' dams and their neighbors plumb to hell! People stealin' flour from the mercantile! Farmers sendin' their boys out to rob anybody who's got anything worth havin'. I tell you, Billy, it's enough to set your hair on end."

"Folks're giving up," Billy said, shaking his head. "Some pray the drought'll end. Others figure it won't, and stop caring. I happened upon little Georg Schneider the other day, just wandering around what's left of Wolf Creek. I don't think they're eating any too regular out that way. The little ones are just skin and bone. Breaks my heart."

"I know," Jared said, staring off into the distance. "Ma's been makin' a lot of trips to those farms lately, dosin' fevers and such. She says a good meal or two and a day or two of rain would work miracles."

"Likely would."

But Billy knew, too, that the chances were slim that either would come to pass.

He met Jared again toward nightfall two days afterward. Even then the air was stifling, and perspiration soaked through their shirts.

"I lost my best bull today," Jared lamented. "Three hands quit, too. All that's left is old Lute Mills."

"I could spare a couple of men," Billy said. "Truth is, there's not much work to be done. Half the time the crew is digging out the bottoms of dry wells or other such nonsense. I haven't got the heart to send anybody packing who's stayed through this summer inferno."

"Well, we never had anybody stay through winter anyway 'cept Lute. We don't have near the land or half the stock you run."

"If you need help, let us know."

They paused a minute as a prairie wolf howled off in the distance. Another and another joined in.

"Wolves," Jared grumbled. "Pickin' at the bones of our herd."

"Well, I guess I'd as soon they get a cow as those blamed buzzards."

"I shot two wolves last week, Billy. They're roamin' the range like nothin' I've ever seen."

"Wes shot a big one up on Caddo Creek day before yesterday."

"They know."

"They know what?" Billy asked.

"It's the season of death."

"What?"

"The wolf's always the first to sense a dead thing's

nearby. Comanches always kept clear of the wolf when he howled like that."

"And now our cattle are dying."

"Not the cattle, Billy. The whole world. Little Charlotte Emery passed on last night. There's a lot of sickness about. It comes of bad water, I think. Lots more'll die. Folks're givin' up."

"I know," Billy admitted. "That's the hardest part of all."

Maybe if Billy hadn't spoken with Jared about the wolves, he wouldn't have ridden to the Cassidy farm so early. Of late he'd arrived around twilight to walk with Colleen. Now he came to speak with Pat Cassidy.

"Mind if we talk a bit?" Billy asked the ruddy-cheeked farmer.

"Getting cold feet, are you, son?" Cassidy asked.

"No, sir. But I've heard the Schneiders have run across some hard luck, and my papa says the Epplers' well has gone dry."

"We've still got the springs up on the mountains. Wolf Creek's bone dry, of course."

"And the cornfields?"

"Come see for yourself."

Billy walked with Cassidy the quarter mile to the first of the cornfields. The stalks were stunted and a brittle brownish-yellow. Pat Cassidy snapped off a husk and held it out to Billy.

"Last year we brought in sweet yellow corn a few

weeks from now. This year all we'll have is this."

Cassidy then crushed the husk into powder. There wasn't a hint of moisture or grain — just dry pulp.

"Is it all this way?" Billy asked.

"Most of it. It's the same all over the county. There's no water in the soil. Corn needs water to grow. This field is a graveyard. We won't harvest anything but disappointment."

"It happens that way sometimes."

"We'll starve this winter. We have a note on the land, too. I can't pay it. We'll be as adrift as the day I stepped off the boat from Ireland. I'm old to start anew, Billy. And the children, well, they'll know hunger. I swore I'd never let that happen."

"It won't," Billy promised. "As long as I've got flour and beef, no neighbor will starve. We'll find a solution."

"I won't accept charity," Cassidy declared.

"Nor will any of us!" Sully added, stepping out from between two rows of cornstalks. Patrick, Flynn, and Brian appeared as well. Billy felt their angry gaze and frowned.

"I don't remember offering anything of the sort," Billy told them with cold, solemn eyes. "But I like to think we'll soon be the same family, and that means we're not averse to helping each other some. You didn't raise your fist when Wes and I brought a crew over to help raise your barn!"

"No," Cassidy admitted. "That was help, sure, but you knew we'd be helping you when you needed the same."

211

"It's what I'm saying now, Mr. Cassidy. These are hard times. To get through them, we'll have to work together."

"So?" Sully asked.

"I told you how I'd want my own house. Sully's got the best eye with a square of anyone in the county. Mr. Cassidy, you make fine chairs and tables. I'll need both, and I'd wager you could sell them elsewhere. As for Patrick and Flynn, I'll bet we can find them suitable work."

"I'm a fair carpenter," Patrick boasted.

"I can mend harness," Flynn added.

"That leaves Brian," Billy said, resting a hand on the eight-year-old's slight shoulder. "I suppose we could sell him to the slaughterhouse in Kansas City. Disguise him as a bull calf. No?" Billy asked as Brian turned red-faced. "Too skinny, you say? Then maybe I'll have to show him how to work horses. Think you're too old to learn a respectable trade like cowboying, Brian?"

"Respectable?" the boy asked, shaking his head. "I thought that's how you made your living, Billy?"

They laughed heartily, and Billy lifted the boy onto one shoulder and started back toward the house.

"Tell you one thing for certain," Billy whispered. "Eugenia will fatten you up some. I'd hate for a chicken hawk to mistake you for a rooster with all that red hair. Might swoop down and carry you off."

Brian scowled, but Billy raced off toward the Albany road, and soon the boy howled with delight.

212

"I thank you for what you said to Pa," Colleen told Ryan that evening as they walked the hillside. "Especially for making Brian laugh. It's been a long summer—a season of tears, Ma calls it. More than food or money, people need to feel useful, need to hope for better days. It's a fine gift, hope."

"You'd best know you're marrying into a family with a strong tendency to take on others' troubles," Billy told her. "Papa's always off giving somebody a hand. My brother Ryan's playing papa to fifty or sixty kids at Buck Creek."

"It's one of the things that endears me to you, Billy Justiss," she said, resting her head on his shoulder.

"Then, we're still going to get married in two weeks?"

"Unless lightning strikes you dead. If you don't appear, that better be why. We Irish are rather vengeful where the honor of our females is concerned."

Billy laughed, then led her down toward the house.

Billy had other matters to occupy his mind besides a pending marriage, though. The dwindling streams had cattle battling over the narrow strips of grass along the Brazos, and Billy had asked Ross to wire every buyer in the Midwest hoping to sell off some

213

of the excess stock. Finally a Chicago buyer agreed to purchase six hundred head. Billy set about rounding up the cattle.

Actually, gathering the herd was the easy part. Getting the animals away from the Brazos and across twenty miles of parched, barren countryside was the true ordeal. Even with veterans like Marty Steele, Hector Suarez, and Wes Tyler directing the outfit, it was a constant battle to keep the beeves trampling first toward the road and later in the desired direction.

Six hundred head could be loaded in cattle cars and shipped the same afternoon. But without water, a sizable portion of the animals would arrive dead. Billy planned to water the stock before coaxing them into the waiting cars, but the banks of Palo Pinto Creek east of Justiss Junction were a cracked wasteland, and what was left of the creek would scarcely quench six hundred thirty Herefords.

Ryan came to the rescue. He had a small army of boys digging three parallel trenches alongside the creek. Then the giant barrels arrived from the Brazos and emptied their precious cargo into the ditches. By the time the cattle arrived, three muddy water troughs awaited them.

Most of them, anyway. Twenty or thirty head had strayed from the main body. Four or five others had merely collapsed from the heat and dust. Once the others were watered and loaded in the boxcars, Billy had the derelict steers shot, slaughtered, and the meat distributed to some of the nearby farms. As for the strays, those that could be driven back to the Flying J were. Most, however, simply roamed the hills until they collapsed. Hungry farmers or prowling wolves disposed of them.

The drive rescued the outfit from a choking gloom. They had shown they could still work cattle in spite of the drought. The orphans, too, celebrated their accomplishments. Ryan's water carriers were hailed as the salvation for the farms, and soon others began hauling water from the river to their dying crops.

For most, it was too late. September usually brought harvest time. In 1882, it brought only defeat. Farms accustomed to shipping wagons of corn to market counted their harvest in bushels. Some fields, like the Cassidys', yielded only parched husks. Daily a parade of wagons passed up the Jacksboro road, bound for the Dakotas and a cooler climate.

"I've heard it rains all summer on the Missouri," Ned Gunther shouted. "I've finished with Texas."

Billy frowned as his father and others tried to argue the discouraged planters out of leaving.

"We can help," Charlie promised. "Loans can be arranged. We can delay your taxes."

But still the wagons rolled northward. It was a pitiful sight, starving children huddling in the beds of wagons with tables and trunks and all the small treasures a family could accumulate in a lifetime of sweat and toil. Most of the horses seemed sure to go lame long before reaching the Red River.

215

"It puts me in mind of when we pulled out of the Petersburg line, bound for Appomattox," Wes remarked. "I never thought I'd see such a time again."

Billy avoided town for several days. He couldn't bear to look at such despair at a time when he was about to begin his future with Colleen. Often he rode the river with Jared Dunlap, recalling other, better times. He took his brothers and little Brian Cassidy fishing. But even on the Brazos the ever-engulfing despair threatened to swallow them.

A spiral of smoke rose from the old Weilding barn, and Billy organized a crew to extinguish the flames. The blackened timbers seemed to Billy a perfect testament to the vanquished hopes and murdered dreams of so many families west of town. Bleached bones of cows and horses were scattered across the county.

"The wolves were right," Billy told Jared as they sat together beside the river that same night. "It is a season of death."

"Look up there," Jared said, pointing to a thin, wisplike cloud that suddenly veiled the moon.

"What is it?" Billy asked.

"The moon grieves," Jared explained. "The Comanches had other words for it. It's what I've always called it."

"The moon should mourn, Jared. So many have lost everything."

"It doesn't mourn what's been," Jared said, tossing a rock into the river. "It's an omen. The worst is yet to come."

Billy shook his head. That was impossible. There was nothing worse than death and despair. He would soon be married to Colleen, and if they couldn't build a better world for everyone, they could at least create a good place for themselves.

Chapter Eight

Charlie Justiss had witnessed more than one exodus in his forty-nine years. Somehow, though, the flow of wagons out of Palo Pinto County that September was different. These were not families fleeing an invading army or being driven from their homes by oppressive taxes or raiding Comanches. These folk had been defeated by nature, cheated by circumstance beyond their control.

There was only so much fight in any man, Charlie supposed, but he hated to read the defeat in the eyes of the departing families.

"Stay, folks," Charlie had pleaded. "We can band together, get you through this trouble. Rains come and go. They'll come again. Stay here and wait for 'em."

A few families turned their wagons around and enlisted the aid of their neighbors. Most listened quietly, then headed on down the road.

Billy called it the season of death. Fields withered and livestock died. Small graveyards appeared above the dried creeks, their small, rough crosses marking the resting places of the discouraged and down-hearted. More than people and cattle were dying, though. The county itself seemed in peril.

My county, Charlie thought.

As he rummaged through the piles of papers on his desk at the courthouse — unpaid taxes, accounts owed to Art Stanley's mercantile for everything from buttons to window glass — he couldn't escape the feeling something was slipping through his fingers. The money wasn't important. Art would be patient, and those who had would help those who didn't. It was the spreading hopelessness that had to be fought.

But how could you fight an enemy you couldn't see?

Charlie was still turning the bills over in his hands when someone knocked at the door.

"Papa, are you all right?" Ross asked.

"Yes," Charlie said, setting aside the accounts and rising slowly.

"It's time we got going, Papa. Everyone else is at the church. We've got a wedding, remember?"

Charlie shook himself out of his stupor. Angela was likely vexed already. He got to his feet, straightened his necktie, then followed Ross out of the courthouse and down the street to the church.

Everyone was waiting. Pat Cassidy paced back and forth, muttering to himself that a Methodist church was better than none at all. His wife, Eileen, occupied herself with seeing that the children behaved. Angela and Vicki saw to it little Hope and Cornelia Cassidy understood their duties as flower girls.

Friends, neighbors, and family crowded the small church. It was a fine chance for the ladies to don their Easter bonnets, and if the close confines of the place made collars tight for the two dozen cowboys, it seemed a small price to pay in order to witness Billy Justiss tying the knot.

The reverend Cyrus Franklin presided over the affair. He was only lately arrived, the latest in a string of ministers to come to Palo Pinto. Unlike the pair of young firebrands before him, Franklin was a married, settled sort of man. Charlie welcomed the change. Cyrus Franklin spoke briefly and to the point. Moreover, he'd seen enough of life to be tolerant of sinners and forgiving of wrong. His wife, Rebecca, proved a great help at the school, and their four daughters were a welcome addition in a town oddly given to boys.

Charlie glanced at the front benches occupied by the family. Chris and Joe tugged at their collars and grumbled. Viktor sat as stiff as a statue beside little Jake. Ross and Bret watched the grandchildren, all except baby Edward, who was safely rocking in his mother's arms.

Assured all was in order there, Charlie stepped outside to where Ryan was bolstering Billy's courage.

"He's about talked himself out of this thing," Ryan said, grinning.

"Well, Papa, I woke this morning, got all necktied and strapped down, and I started thinking.

This is a poor time to be starting a marriage, what with times being so bad and all. The whole county's gone to wolves. Maybe I —"

"Trust an old man to know more than you about these things, son," Charlie said, leading Billy aside. "It's when life's turned sour that a man needs his family most of all. When he's flying high, well, he can do fine riding alone. When you're down to your last gasp, cold and hungry and out of luck, when hope's fading away, it's family gets you through. I know. I've been in all the darkest places a man can know, and it was always the memory of your mama's face, of you kids, that stiffened my spine and sent me riding on."

"Papa, there's never been a time like this."

"There's been worse," Charlie said with darkening brow. "Just answer me this. Can you get along without Colleen? Can you stand the notion of not seeing her again?"

Billy frowned and glanced through the doorway of the church. Inside, the restless audience fanned away the stifling air.

"Keep in mind Pat and Sully are apt to hang you by your toes, too," Ryan added.

"Then, I suppose it's best I go on through with it," Billy said, shaking his head. Then he spotted Colleen. A smile flooded his face.

"Now that's over, we can get along with business," Charlie said, leading his son into the church. Patrick Cassidy took up a fiddle and serenaded the congregation, and Reverend Franklin motioned bride and groom to take their places.

It was a brief service. The minister gave no great

speech nor did he wave his arms about. Instead Franklin merely blessed the couple and prayed for their happiness. Vows and rings were exchanged. Billy and Colleen embraced, and the gaggle of youngsters showered the couple with corn kernals.

Following a barbecue down at the river, Ryan and Rachel escorted Billy and Colleen to Justiss Junction. The newlyweds would spend a week in Fort Worth before returning. Charlie and Angela followed. The same train that would carry the honeymooners would take Joe to Agriculture College and conduct Chris to the Baldwin Academy for a year of study.

Charlie held Angela's hands tightly as she bid the boys farewell at the platform. It was against her judgment to send Chris away, but Charlie knew a year's polish wouldn't hurt. Of course, he also suspected Chris would likely have the fancy school turned upside down by Christmas.

The onset of autumn should have brought relief to the sun-baked land. Instead the hills and prairie turned winter brown. Not so much as a hint of rain broke the drought's deadly grip. To Charlie's dismay, even the mighty Brazos began to shrink.

"The river's dying," Ma Dunlap proclaimed. "What's to happen next?"

Charlie wondered, too. Angry, desperate men took to strong drink. Commerce suffered. Art Stanley sadly posted a *no credit* sign atop his door.

"Art?" Charlie asked. "These folks won't make it through winter without flour and coffee."

"I know," the old freighter said, sadly shaking his head. "Charlie, come over here and look at my books. I'm carrying three quarters of the county already! I've got to pay for this stuff myself, you know."

"Sure," Charlie replied. "I can't help feeling things will turn, though."

"Oh? Maybe that's because you were able to sell your cattle before the worst of this hit. I've lost seven mules since August, and you can't travel to Albany without happening upon some poor animal gone down from the heat."

"Maybe we can work something out with the bank."

"The bank?" Art asked, laughing. "They've got all their money tied up in corn loans. They'll never see a dime of that. Joe Nance tried to draw a hundred dollars out of his account, and Ernest Lowery at the bank said they didn't have that much cash in the vault."

"Anybody else know that?"

"Near the whole town," Art said, closing his ledger and walking to the door. "Ernest set off for Fort Worth, hoping to sell some of those railroad bonds. He left his boy watching the bank. There've been quite a few folks in and out of there all morning, but by the look of 'em, nobody's gotten a nickel from the cash box."

"I hope Ernest gets some cash for those bonds, Art. I've got a fair share of my own savings there. I always figured if the worst came, I'd be able to help

223

some, but . . ."

"You can't loan what you can't lay your hands on," Art grumbled. "I know. It eats at me, too, Charlie. There are no maverick cows to round up anymore."

"No," Charlie agreed. "I believe I'll walk down to the telegraph office, send a few wires."

"Good luck, old friend."

"You, too," Charlie answered, forcing a smile onto his face. "We could use a little luck."

Word of the bank's trouble stirred the people to panic. Those with savings on account stormed the place, battered down the door, and demanded their cash. Young Barney Lowery had his coat torn off, his eyes blackened, and his ribs battered by angry depositors. Only Bret Pruett's arrival saved the young man from lynching.

"Look, folks," Bret called to the boisterous crowd. "See here!"

The vault hung open. It was full of loan papers and a few state bonds, but less than sixty dollars cash occupied an iron box.

"Be patient, friends," Barney pleaded. "Pa's gone to Fort Worth. He'll be back with some cash, enough to get us through the next few months. By then, some of the farmers may be able to pay the interest on their notes."

"With what?" Georgia Staves asked. "No one's growing corn this time of year. Those folks are starving. They don't have two bits to pay you."

"Be patient," Barney begged. "We'll do the best we

can."

"Rob us, you mean," J. C. Parnell asserted. "If I don't get my money, I'll see somebody's jailed!"

The others voiced agreement, and Barney Lowery shuddered.

"Folks, calm down," Charlie said, striding through the door and motioning for quiet. "We'll find a way out of this trouble. I've likely got more money in this bank than the lot of you. If it comes down to it, I'll cash out your holdings myself. You don't want the bank foreclosing on your neighbors, do you?"

"No," the crowd muttered.

"Then you're going to have to have some faith."

"It's mighty hard when you're down to your last sack of flour," Roger Ellis argued. "I paid my note. Now I need to draw from my savings."

"I understand," Charlie said, frowning. "Let's wait and see what Ernest is able to manage. Then we'll see what's to be done."

The others reluctantly agreed. And when Ernest returned from Fort Worth the next morning with several thousand dollars in cash, the people sighed in relief. By nine o'clock a long line of townfolk eager to feel the touch of cash in their fingers again stretched from the bank door down Front Street. Barney swung open the door, and the people filed into the bank calmly. Then the front window exploded.

Barney Lowery stumbled into the street, muttered a cry, then fell face first into the dust. Onlookers screamed and scrambled out of the bank. Women walking their children to school dragged them behind wagons or water troughs. In seconds Bret Pruett and Alex Tuttle appeared on the street.

"There are three men in the bank!" Georgia Staves explained. "They've shot Barney, and they're forcing Ernest to open the vault."

"Do you know any of them?" Charlie asked.

"One's Peter Bachman's oldest boy," Parnell explained. "The other two are strangers."

"Get clear," Bret ordered. "This is for us to handle now."

"Not alone," Charlie objected. "Let me get the Winchesters."

"These aren't killers, Charlie," Bret declared. "We can take care of it. If a bunch of men start shooting, anything can happen."

"They killed Barney," Parnell pointed out.

"We don't know that," Bret argued. "And if you folks get out of the way, maybe we'll have a chance to see. For all any of you know, he's lying out there bleeding his life away."

Parnell stepped back, and the others followed suit. Charlie hesitated, but a fierce look from Bret decided the matter. The sheriff then worked his way toward the bank.

"You three hear me!" Bret called. "This is Sheriff Pruett. You come along out with your hands up, and I'll see you come to trial."

"See us hung, you mean!" one of the gunmen responded. "I tell you what. You stand aside, and nobody else'll get hurt. We've got the banker in here and three or four others. I could start sending you bodies if you press things."

"That right, Ernest?" Bret called.

226

"Miz Brewster's in here," the banker answered. "Got her two girls, too."

"Anybody else?" Tut asked.

"Reverend Franklin's eldest."

"Sarah!" the girl cried. "They've got guns on us, Sheriff!"

Bret scowled. "You haven't killed anybody so far's I can tell," Bret told the bank robbers. "Let me get young Barney some help. Then we'll talk this out."

"Better you clear out of our way!" a second gunman yelled, firing his pistol through the shattered window. The hostages shrieked. Charlie, meanwhile, enlisted the aid of Albert Parnell to rescue Barney Lowery from the street. The young man bled freely from the neck and shoulder, but his eyes appeared alert. The Parnells carried Barney down the street to Doc Garnett's small office next door to the livery.

"Barney's all right," Bret called. "No need you boys get yourselves shot, hear?"

"We've still got these fine ladies in here," the first gunman reminded Bret. "I could shoot a couple of 'em for you."

"Let 'em have the money and leave!" Ernest pleaded.

"That's my Sarah they've got," Mrs. Franklin added.

"Can't be that way," Bret explained to the distraught Franklins. "Don't you see? They've got to understand we won't allow this sort of thing."

"But, Bret," Art Stanley complained, "those're women in there."

"Could be women in there next time, too," Charlie

spoke up. "I know Bret's thinking. Some towns get left alone by these sort. Word gets around that men get away with thieving and murder in Palo Pinto, we'll see 'em descend on us like locusts. Sorry, folks, but Bret's right."

No one argued, but many were clearly not in agreement. Mrs. Franklin stared bitterly toward the bank until her husband managed to coax her inside the mercantile. The street was suddenly deserted except for Bret and Tut. Charlie watched from the door of the hotel as a deadly silence settled over the street.

For ten minutes not a cricket stirred. Then a thick-waisted stranger stepped to the doorway. He held Sarah Franklin as a shield. His companions followed, each holding one of the Brewster girls in front.

Ernest Lowery and Thelma Brewster remained in the bank, hidden from view. The terror in the girls' eyes hinted some harm might have been done to the others.

"Sheriff, you hear me?" the heavyset outlaw cried.

"I hear you," Bret answered from behind a wagon across the street.

"You follow, we'll shoot these gals. I promise you that."

"You best let 'em go now," Bret warned. "I'll never get you a fair trial if any harm befalls these girls."

"You worry about your own hide, Sheriff," the second outlaw said, laughing. "I'll worry about mine."

Henry Bachman remained silent. He held ten-year-old Emily Brewster loosely, and the girl suddenly bit his hand and scrambled toward the safety of the bank.

"Jed, no!" young Bachman cried as the first gunman tossed Sarah aside and aimed at the fleeing Emily. Alex Tuttle shot before the outlaw could fire his pistol, though. A second later Bret killed the second gunman even as he held onto Emily's sister Betty. Bachman tossed aside his pistol and pleaded for mercy. An angry crowd mobbed the would-be thief.

"Stop it!" Bret cried as he tried to pull the outraged citizens away. By that time Thelma Brewster had emerged from the bank. Ernest followed.

"Leave him be!" Tut added, firing into the air.

The heat and frustration of six months' drought released itself in an outburst of hatred, though. No matter how loudly Bret and Tut argued, the mob continued to hammer away at young Bachman. Charlie and others tried to pull their frenzied neighbors aside, but another only jumped in. In ten terrible minutes Henry Bachman was beaten to death.

The robbery and its aftermath left the whole town shaken. It was hard to believe that peaceful shopkeepers and tradesmen could have gone berserk. Henry Bachman was only a month older than Joe Justiss, and not quite as tall. It seemed impossible that a simple farmboy should have thrown in with desperados.

"We had nothing to eat," Peter Bachman said when he came to town with Alex Tuttle that afternoon to claim the body of his eldest son. "It is the land that's done this to me. It starves my children and drives them mad."

Yes, Charlie thought. It drinks the river and sets neighbors at each other's throats. Billy was right. It is a season of death.

Chapter Nine

Jared Dunlap was right, too. The worst still lay ahead. For farmers like Martin Schneider, what corn survived to be harvested had to be sold to pay taxes and provide a bit of cash for the family. Meals soon consisted of rabbits, an occasional quail or turkey, plus a kind of flat biscuitlike cake made from cattail flour. Even rattlesnakes and crows provided a dinner or two.

As the shallow wells and muddy creeks grew foul, bad water became a serious problem. Typhoid fever struck the farms along Palo Pinto Creek. Then Dr. Garnett told Charlie of worse tidings.

"I was out at the Schneider place this morning," the doctor said, taking off his spectacles and frowning heavily.

"And?" Charlie asked.

"Little Emma Weidling is down with a fever. I

looked her over, and it's worse than that. The poor thing coughs up most everything, and that which stays down runs through her with a vengeance. I've seen it before. It's cholera."

Charlie sat down and dropped his head in his hands. No disease was more feared along the frontier. Whole towns had been swept away by cholera epidemics.

"Do the Schneiders know?" Charlie asked.

"I couldn't help but tell 'em. It's crucial the other children be separated immediately. That's where the greatest danger lies."

"Will Emma die?"

"We'll know soon," the doctor said somberly. "To be truthful, she's little more than cramps and convulsions. Sophia says she's been that way three days. I'm surprised she's held on that long."

"I took the younger Weidling boys in, you know," Charlie said, staring off out his office window toward the house. "Those boys rarely see their sisters now. The news will hit hard."

"Charlie, you know cholera's got a way of spreading like a grass fire," the doctor said grimly. "I figure it's the water's brought it here, but who can tell for sure?"

"What should be done?"

"Send riders. Suggest everyone dig fresh wells. For a time, keep the children home."

"Close the school you mean?"

"More than that. See to it the youngsters keep to themselves. If nobody else comes down with it in a week, well, we can go back to normal."

"Can't you order some medicines or something to help?" Charlie asked. "They're scratching folks now to keep them from catching smallpox."

"I don't know anything that can be done for cholera except a lot of care, Charlie. Sophia will do her best. Boiling water should lessen the odds as well. And we'll pray a lot."

"You don't think it's spread to town yet, do you?"

"I don't see how. You can't hide a cholera victim for long."

"Thanks for telling me, Doc. I'll see the school's closed. I'll pass the word to Reverend Franklin, too."

"Good," Dr. Garnett said, turning toward the door. "Can you have someone ride to the farms and ranches, let them know what's to be done?"

"I'll have Tut head out first thing tomorrow morning."

"You know the gravest danger is at Buck Creek. Be sure they spread those boys out some, keep 'em clear of the Schneider youngsters, and boil their drinking water for a time."

"I'll ride out and tell Ryan and Rachel myself."

Charlie did more than that. He posted the school closed right away, then suggested Vicki take her children, Viktor, and Jake to Fort Worth for a week or so.

"I already wired Bowie," he explained. "They'd welcome your visit."

"Papa, I can help," Vicki objected. "I know most of these children. I feel like I'm running away on a

233

responsibility."

"You've never seen cholera," Charlie told her. "It sweeps through a town like a cyclone, and mostly it kills the weak and the young."

"You're really worried?"

"Only a fool wouldn't."

"Then I'll go," she said, shrugging her shoulders. "You'll talk to Eliza, too?"

"Next stop," he told her.

Not only did Eliza and tiny Edward go, Charlie even convinced Angela to leave. It wasn't easy. She never got along with her sister-in-law, Emiline, but the thought of visiting Chris and protecting the grandchildren from Em's overbearing attitude coaxed her into making the trip.

Elsewhere, families guarded their children like gold. New wells were dug, and water from the creeks and from the Brazos was boiled before drunk. Great care was taken that dead animals didn't foul a stream. Dr. Garnett urged folks to keep busy, but to limit their activity when the midday sun blazed down.

With Angela and the children off in Fort Worth, Charlie rode out most evenings to visit old friends. He shared dinner with the Dunlaps one night and exchanged recollections with Joe Nance the next. Mostly he rode to the ranch or down to Buck Creek to check on the orphans.

The Flying J seemed to change daily now. Billy's new house was taking shape nicely. With Sully, Patrick, and Flynn laboring with their father, and little Brian chasing cows down at the river, the place was taking on an Irish flavor. Colleen lent a gentle touch to the old stone ranchhouse. Most nights wildflowers or a sprig of cedar or juniper adorned the dinner table. Eugenia still tended most of the cooking, but Colleen helped.

"She'll do fine, that little girl," Eugenia declared more than once. "Soon she will make the tortillas almost as good as my niece Dulcinea."

That was as high as praise ever got where Eugenia was concerned.

Charlie especially enjoyed riding with Billy and Colleen out to the cliffs overlooking the Brazos. He missed the journeys he'd made there in the old days when he'd lived at the ranch. He'd always felt a sense of wonder while standing on the rim of the high canyon wall, staring out over the winding Brazos and recalling a world that had changed a hundred times in the twelve years he'd walked those cliffs.

Sharing that wonderment with Billy and Colleen brought a closeness to them. Ross had the law, and Ryan had Rachel and the orphans, but it was Billy who'd taken into his hands the land—the beloved ranch that so much blood had been shed to build and to keep. Now Colleen would help him nurture it, help it recover from that seemingly endless summer.

"October's closing in, Papa," Billy whispered as they gazed down at the yellowing leaves on the white oaks and willows. "And still we have no rain."

"Was there ever as hard a time?" Charlie asked.

"Stands Tall," Billy said, gazing toward the base of

235

the cliff where the relentless Comanche chief had made his final stand.

"He was a man, to be fought as a man," Charlie said, staring angrily at the setting sun. "Now there's no one to fight. The enemy's unseen, beyond my grasp, and I'm powerless to stop it!"

"You do what you can," Colleen said, taking Charlie's hand a moment and pressing it with her lips. "Billy does, too. You lend others your strength and your wisdom. Take Pa. He was defeated, but building that house has given him purpose again, pride. Mr. Justiss, I heard how you bought up those notes at the bank so folks wouldn't lose their land. This heat can't last forever. Soon it's bound to rain."

"Yes, soon," Billy echoed.

But will it be soon enough? Charlie asked himself.

Charlie also journeyed often to Buck Creek, or at least to the series of puddles and stagnant ponds that had once been Buck Creek. The orphans had managed to harvest most of their vegetables, but there wouldn't be enough corn to provide for their own needs, much less to sell elsewhere. The cattle were sold or slaughtered, and only a few chickens and hogs remained.

Charlie expected to find the youngsters defeated, discouraged. Such was not the case. The younger ones seemed a little thinner than at Christmas, and the pot held a bit less meat, but there was no shortage of noise. The boys were as eager for one of "Grandpapa's" stories as ever, and Charlie devoted one entire morning to treating the smallest ones to rides around the nearby hills on his horse.

Often Charlie brought a wagonload of linens or old clothes out from town. In spite of their own difficulties, or perhaps because of them, the townfolk more than ever took the orphans at Buck Creek to heart. An old fiddle and a drum arrived from a Jack County friend of Celia Cooke, and Charlie brought those out as well.

"Have you had sickness?" Charlie asked somberly each time.

"No, thank the Lord," Rachel responded. "Oh, we have a cough now and then, a scrape or two almost daily, but no one's been down in bed as I've heard elsewhere."

"We dug new wells," Ryan explained. "And we've been boiling most of the water. It's not always possible, what with so many mouths to keep full, but I try to keep water from the river out during the day. We boil anything we bring up from the wells."

"Pretty soon you'll have to boil the river water, too," Charlie declared. "The Brazos is close to dry in places. Once it stops flowing, there'll be the same danger as at the creeks."

"Papa, you really think the cholera will spread?"

"It has before."

It did spread, but not as Charlie feared. Little Emma Weidling lost her fight for life a week after she took to her bed. The day she was buried beside her parents, her sister Anna and Gregor Schneider

237

collapsed.

Charlie supposed every person in Palo Pinto County spoke prayers for the two ten-year-olds. Then Alek and Georg, the other Schneider boys, took sick.

"What have I done to deserve such a judgment?" Martin Schneider bellowed when Charlie brought food the townswomen had prepared to ease Sophia's burden. "I fear Job's burden was nothing to that placed on my shoulders."

For a time that burden seemed lighter. Doc Garnett sat most of three nights with little Anna and the boys. Alek's fever broke, and the knots in Gregor's belly loosened and allowed the boy to take solid food. Georg worsened, though, and on the first dark lonely night of October, Anna passed on.

Charlie rode the train to Fort Worth to pass on the news. Little Jake seemed hardly to remember his sisters. Viktor sank to his knees and clutched Charlie's legs.

"I should have gone to them," the boy cried. "Papa would have expected me to help Rolf."

"Wasn't anything Rolf or anybody else could have done that Mrs. Schneider and Doc Garnett didn't do," Charlie told the boy. "I know it seems life is unjustly hard sometimes. Bret Pruett lost his whole family when he was younger than you, Viktor. You go on, though. Cry and scream and find yourself a big oak tree to chop down. Then grab hold of Jake and your mama and let go of the grief."

"I wasn't even there when they were buried," Viktor said, sobbing. "They were all alone."

"Rolf was there, and so were the Schneiders. Reverend Franklin read prayers, too. Later, when the illness passes, I'll take you there so you and Jake can say your good-byes."

"You promise?"

"I do," Charlie said, hugging the boy tightly. "I keep my promises, too, don't I?"

Viktor nodded, then went on crying.

Dr. Garnett expected Georg Schneider to die as well, but Fate must have softened her heart at the grief poured out for the Weidling girls. Dark clouds formed over the river, and rain poured down. Thunder shook the ground, and lightning lit the heavens. It rained for three days and three nights.

The storm seemed at once to chase away the gloom and restore the sick. Perhaps it was the cool breeze that flowed through the Schneider cabin or the untainted rainwater that revived little Georg. Whatever, the boy brightened like a new moon, and by the time a rainbow spread its colors across the horizon, Georg was back on his feet.

Charlie tried to find comfort in Georg's smile. Up and down Palo Pinto Creek the sick healed. Creeks began to reappear, and the river rolled along. With the cholera threat gone, Angela and the others returned. As promised, Charlie drove a wagon out to the Schneider place. In back with food and clothing were Viktor and Jake.

Rolf met them at the little graveyard he'd fenced above Caddo Creek, just past the scarred remnant of the Weidling home. The three brothers spoke for a time while Charlie busied himself delivering supplies to the Schneiders a quarter mile away.

"Papa, Rolf is leaving," Viktor explained when Charlie returned.

"Oh?" Charlie asked. "Rolf?"

"There is only death in this place," Rolf said, pointing to the graveyard. "Death and hard work. I plow the fields and pick the corn, but it is for nothing. I am a good farmer, Mr. Justiss, but this is not good land for corn. I go somewhere better."

There were tears in Rolf's eyes, and Charlie gripped the fifteen-year-old's hands.

"I've got a big house in town," Charlie said. "You could come live there, look after your brothers, go to school."

"Viktor, he has the head for school," Rolf said, smiling with pride. "Jakob, too, maybe. I am a farmer. So I was born. So I will die. But not in this place."

"But —"

"It is my choice," Rolf said, squaring his shoulders and nodding to his brothers. "I stayed because I was needed by Anna and Emma. They are gone now. Viktor and Jakob have taken your name. They are your sons. You will be a good father to them. This I know, Judge. Viktor says to me Mrs. Justiss is much like Mama, so I do not worry for them."

"Winter's coming. It won't be easy to find work this time of year. Billy could find a place for you on the ranch, or maybe you could —"

"I must go," Rolf interrupted. "I am strong. I will find work."

Charlie shook the young man's hand. There was iron in Rolf's grip, and grit in his backbone. He had his bearings. It would work out.

"Good-bye, Rolf," Viktor said, embracing his brother. Jake did the same. Then Rolf turned back toward the Schneider place, and Charlie led the boys along to the wagon.

"He'll be all right," Charlie assured them.

"Yes," Viktor declared.

On the long ride back to Palo Pinto Viktor wept openly, yet said nothing. Jake merely nestled his small body between Viktor and Charlie.

It's hard saying farewell to your family, Charlie told himself. And he was glad he and Angela had taken Viktor and Jake into their home and their hearts.

October's shower raised everyone's hopes, but a week went by without so much as a hint of more rain. Charlie managed to contract a few hundred cattle, and again Billy organized a crew and drove stock to the junction. Charlie supposed that was why Randolph Nance sent word that his father wished the Palo Pinto Stockraisers' Association to meet the following Monday at the Brazos Hotel.

Charlie and most of the smaller ranchers arrived early. Georgia Staves put on quite a feed for the event, and even the Kemps rode in. By the time everyone had eaten, though, Joe Nance hadn't appeared.

"Let's start anyway," Ike Kemp suggested.

"Start?" Billy asked. "We don't even know why Joe wanted to meet. You know, Randolph?"

The younger Nance slowly shook his head, then rose to his feet.

"It's unlike Pa to show up late," Randolph declared. "I think I'd better go have a look."

By the time Randolph Nance reached the door of the hotel, a crowd had collected outside. Alex Tuttle stood in the center, his right hand holding the reins of a riderless horse.

"It's Pa's roan!" Randolph shouted. "Where's my horse?"

Charlie accompanied Randolph and Tut as they traced the roan's trail. Less than a mile from the edge of town they came upon Joe Nance. The white-haired old cattleman sat beside the road, his eyes fixed on the distant river where he'd made his home and built his ranch. Randolph slid off his horse and knelt beside his father. Charlie removed his hat.

Joe Nance was dead.

Most likely sunstroke had struck down Joe Nance. Or maybe, Charlie thought, the sight of the range dried up and desolate had finally overcome the old man's heart. Whatever the cause, near every soul in the county gathered the day Joe Nance was laid to rest in the Methodist churchyard.

Randolph and his mother stood quietly as Reverend Franklin read prayers and spoke comforting words. Then Charlie Justiss recounted the many triumphs of Joe Nance's life.

"I proudly called Joe my friend," Charlie said in concluding the eulogy. "I'm glad he came my way. And as we sprinkle lightly the soil of this, his beloved county, over his casket, I can't help feeling we are marking the passing of a time as well as the loss of a friend."

"Amen," the others whispered as one.

III. The Dispute

Chapter One

Old Joe Nance was dead and buried, struck down by the same drought that seemed to sap the strength of Palo Pinto County. Or so it seemed to Charlie Justiss. As October gave way to November, he couldn't escape the sense that a terrifying shadow had fallen across his world. Too many had died already, and now winter was on the way.

Charlie read the traces everywhere. The leaves of the oaks and willows had shed their October cloaks of scarlet and yellow. Bare branches lent a stark emptiness to the landscape. Yellow-brown oceans of brittle buffalo grass covered the hills and ravines above the Brazos. In truth, the bony Herefords cluttering the banks of the river were the sole signs of life.

It ate at Charlie's insides. In the southern part of the county the bones of dozens of cattle littered the range, providing a reminder of that season of death which had come to Texas. Riding along the river, he noticed the new crosses that huddled together in family graveyards. Each represented some neighbor, an old friend or a small child. Cholera and starvation had kept the spades of Palo Pinto busy that autumn. Cyrus Franklin, the Methodist preacher, had furrows carved in his brow for each one of them.

"I pray God gives us the strength to endure this trial," the reverend had told Charlie the previous Sunday afternoon. "I've known desperate times before, but none so great as these."

"Yes," Charlie had said, nodding grimly.

Perhaps that was what had sent Charlie riding. He'd always found peace in the loneliness of the isolated hillsides, in the harsh beauty of the Texas plain. For twelve years, the best years of his life, that plain had been home. And whenever pain or death had visited Charlie Justiss, he'd climbed the high bluffs above the Brazos and sought the quiet solitude of the place.

He urged his big black stallion along past the prowling cattle and on toward the narrow footpath leading to the heights. He dismounted, then began the steep ascent. It seemed the climb grew more difficult each time. Rain and wind had eroded the path. Or perhaps it was only years of trailing cattle and riding the range that made it seem so.

I've grown old here, Charlie thought as he struggled to catch his breath halfway to the top. War wounds ached as the November wind whined across the steep face of the cliff. And when he reached the summit, the desolation there struck him with rare force.

Once the Comanches had set their dead on scaffolds amidst the rock-strewn heights. Now the wood had rotted away, and the bones had given way to the dust that eventually consumed all things. Old Stands Tall and his followers had made a last defiant stand at the river below. Perhaps the Comanche, too, had sought peace there.

Charlie paced back and forth atop the cliff, letting the fierce wind knife its way through him. He wondered if Joe Nance had felt the cold, tasted the despair that seemed to flood the valley they both loved. Nance had tried to fend off the hands of change, to keep life as it had been before. Charlie had always accepted change as a part of growing. Now he wondered if old Joe might not have been right.

Charlie gazed down at the river below. The Brazos continued to flow, but the thin blue line was but a shadow of the normally robust stream that cut through the canyon in late autumn. Beyond, the fan-shaped peninsula formed the Dunlap Ranch, certainly the oldest cattle operation in the county. The Dunlaps had lost sons to Comanches, had a daughter married to one, and lost a boy, Jamie, to rustlers in the lawless Cimarron country south of the Kansas line.

They've known all the hardships and the heartaches a man can experience, Charlie reminded himself. And yet Joe and Irene never surrendered hope or sought an easier path. Their son Jared now ran the ranch just as Charlie's son Billy operated the Flying J. The two young men often rode the river together, sometimes meeting where the mouth of what was left of Bluff Creek joined the river.

Good neighbors were hard to come by. Charlie was glad to bound the Dunlaps on the north. Just east of there, at Fortune Bend, Angela's cousin Luis Morales raised horses. On the east and south, the Flying J bordered market roads. There was rarely much cause for concern there, especially now that the ranch was fenced ten feet from the roads. On the west, though, along Caddo Creek, Ike Kemp had taken up residence.

Kemp was a strange one. Charlie couldn't figure him out. The heavyset rancher had made no secret of his dislike of the Justiss family. More than once the scoundrel had been suspected of raids on neighboring farmers. Kemp had pronounced loudly his disdain for neighbors, especially farmers. Lately there'd come a change, though. Kemp never missed a meeting of the Palo Pinto County Stockraisers. Once or twice he'd even been spotted at Sunday meeting. True, he never contributed to the collection plate, but he had invited Cyrus Franklin out to dinner.

"Maybe Kemp'll come to feel at home here," Charlie muttered, turning to the west. From the heights he could see the box canyon carved by Caddo Creek where it flowed into the Brazos. Upstream, little more than a trickle of the creek remained. Farmer Schneider had diverted most of the headwaters to his fields, choking off the creek from its bed. Elsewhere farmers drove wagons to the Brazos and filled barrels.

No one crossed Kemp's land to do so, though. A pair of farmers from Stephens County tried that in October, much to their regret. One man had died,

250

and the other had returned with his son, both of them stripped to their drawers. Worse, the soles of their feet were scorched and blistered. It seemed Kermit Kemp had set them in a fire and likely would have burned them alive had not a pair of cowboys freed the unfortunate farmers.

"That Kemp's got a vicious streak to him," Bret Pruett had told Charlie afterward. "I wish that had happened in my county. I'd called him to account."

"Be patient," Billy had suggested. "Kemp's far from through here. I remember seeing eyes like his before, on the trail to Kansas. We'll have to deal with him."

Charlie deemed it likely, though in his heart he hoped it wouldn't come to pass. The drought and the approach of winter would provide enough challenges. Maybe Kemp would mellow.

Charlie gazed northward again. Good land, rolling prairie cut by a dozen creeks, stretched toward Jacksboro. The creeks were largely dry now, but the rains would come again. That was good country for cattle, and much of that acreage had been abandoned by bankrupt farmers and defeated ranchers. It might prove a good time to buy. He made a note to speak with Ross and Billy about it. The time might come when Chris or Joe wanted to have his own place, and a considerable stretch along the Brazos had been abandoned.

Land. Joe Nance had once said it was the only true legacy a man ever passed along to his children. Not so, Charlie thought. It's just as important they should know who they are, who their people were, what brought them up the Brazos to Palo Pinto and what price was paid to win the land.

It's time I brought the grandkids up here, Charlie thought. Little Jake and Viktor, too. They're Justisses as well now. Come spring maybe.

The wind whined fiercely through the scrub junipers atop the cliff, piercing the light fabric of Charlie's trousers and making itself felt in each and every weary joint. Charlie said a silent farewell to the place, then started the long journey back down the slope.

It was well past noon when Charlie remounted his horse and headed out toward Caddo Creek. He hadn't paid a visit to Wes Tyler and the line camp in half a month, and Alice had complained the children would scarce recognize him.

"More likely the other way around," Charlie had replied, for after all, how many grizzled oldtimers were left in Palo Pinto County? Besides, young Jeff and little Jake had taken to each other's company since the school had reopened, and rarely the day passed when Charlie didn't learn the details of life at the Tyler place.

Nevertheless, Charlie felt a visit was in order. The line camp had once overseen a few thousand head. Now, with the cattle mostly herded along the Brazos, Wes had to watch the far range with his brother-in-law, young Toby Hart, and a pair of teenage drovers, Tucker Spears and Barret Jenkins.

As Charlie splashed across Bluff Creek and headed south toward the camp, he found himself confronted by Billy and young Brian Cassidy. The two set aside their fishing poles long enough to show off three fat perch and a considerable-sized catfish.

Then Billy turned to more serious matters.

"Headed west?" he asked.

"Planned to," Charlie answered. "Thought I'd stop by and speak to Wes."

"Wait up and I'll go with you, Papa."

"Afraid I'll lose my way?" Charlie asked, laughing.

"No," Billy said, his eyes growing serious. "We've had a bit of trouble out that way. I sent Marlin Silsbee and young Lew Oldham out yesterday to round out Wes's outfit. Though I doubt he found little Lew much comfort, I imagine he appreciates having Silsbee around."

"What kind of trouble?"

"I'll tell you on the way," Billy said, nodding to young Brian. Clearly he didn't wish the boy to pass on the news to Colleen.

"Can I come along?" Brian asked as Billy headed to where a pair of horses were tethered.

"No, you've got to take the fish to Enuncia, little brother. I'll expect them for supper, you know."

"I could do that and catch up with you," Brian said, raising an eyebrow like a question mark.

"Might could, but you'd only be bored," Billy explained, turning back and giving the eight-year-old an affectionate tap on the top of his strawberry-crowned head. "We won't be long."

Brian kicked up a cloud of dust with his boot and grumbled. Billy only laughed. Then he mounted his horse and joined his father. Once they were a mile upstream, Billy explained the problem.

"It's Kemp, of course," Billy began. "You know we've had nothing but trouble ever since he got here.

I don't know how many acres he has to his name, but he rarely seems to take interest in any of it save the land along our west boundary."

"He had his dealings with those Stephens County farmers, Billy."

"Dealings?" Billy asked, shaking his head. "Was pure murder the way I heard it. You know that farmer's boy lost a foot from his burns."

"And now Kemp's turned to us, has he?"

"Papa, you know we've never had a straight accounting of strays from him. For our part, we've chased fifty or sixty head back across Caddo Creek. He's never returned so much as a spring calf. Now we've got most all our stock east of Bluff Creek on account of the creek being so low."

"And?"

"Kemp sent his boys and a pair of hands over yesterday, firing pistols in the air and accusing us of having some of their strays."

"Did we?"

"Of course not," Billy said, spitting at the ground. "That Kermit called Wes a liar, and, well, you know Wes never has had much use for those Kemps. He exchanged a few words you'd never hear in church, and Kermit started to answer with his pistol. Toby lassoed the fool and sent him sprawling. Then that snip of a youngster Barret Jenkins pops up with a loaded shotgun and chases the rest of 'em off."

"They'll be back."

"I figure so. That's why I sent Wes the help."

"Better we go have a talk with the Kemps, smother this fire before it spreads."

"Papa, we've spoken to them before. It does no

254

good."

"Never hurts to try."

"So, you're taking this on yourself, are you?"

Charlie halted his horse and gazed at his son. Billy's face was slightly crimson, and Charlie frowned. He was interfering. And yet he couldn't very well let things get out of hand.

"Would you rather I send Bret out to have a talk with Kemp?" Charlie asked. "Son, this could prove to be more than a boundary squabble. Men could get themselves killed. I hoped all that was past the day Rame Polk was killed."

"I've hardly started this, Papa," Billy complained. "We'll send no riders across the creek. But I swear that if those Kemps ride onto my land shooting guns, I'll see their fire's answered. We've swallowed too much by half, and I'm not sure Wes wasn't right in the first place when he wanted to have it out that first time the Kemps tested us."

"I imagine we'll get a chance to find out," Charlie said grimly. "So, do we ride out and talk to the fool or let Bret do it?"

"If it's up to me, I say we wire Lafe and Malachi, let *them* bring up the matter."

"Do that and we'll be at war, Billy."

"We already are," Billy grumbled. "You just don't see it."

"Well, it's old age, son. I've buried too many friends on too many battlefields. I'd like to bring this misunderstanding to a rapid end."

"It won't work, Papa."

"Probably not," Charlie said, shrugging his shoulders. "Thing is, Billy, I have to try."

"Then, I guess you'd better, but I won't have you riding to the creek without some of our outfit along."

"It's probably be best if everyone was along," Charlie declared. "First, though, we'll talk to Wes."

If Billy Justiss harbored bad feelings toward Ike Kemp, they were grains of sand compared to the fury Wes unleashed at the mention of Kemp's name.

"That boy of his would've shot me, Charlie!" Wes cried. "If Toby hadn't roped him, the fool would've shot anybody in sight. Shoot, little Rose Anne and Alice weren't ten feet away! What would you have done if somebody started firin' a pistol at Angela?"

"You know my answer 'cause you've been with me when it happened," Charlie replied. "Even so, Wes, a range war's bound to be ugly. Which one of our crew would you watch die? Little Barret? Toby? And even then there's scant guarantee you'd settle matters with Kemp. By the look of him, I'd say he's had experience in this sort of thing, too."

"You ask me, he was behind that raid on the Weidling place," Wes muttered.

"I've got my suspicions, too," Charlie confessed. "But we've got law here now, and without proof . . ."

"You give me a half hour with that Kermit, I'll get your proof," Wes promised. "Charlie, Alice and the kids are here. I'm not goin' to let those Kemps ride through here at will."

"Neither am I," Charlie promised. "All I'm saying is that we ought to talk it out first."

"Fine, you just make sure you've got a pistol handy. I'll gather the men. And the peewees, too. I never thought we'd come to this, Charlie Justiss turnin' away from a clear-cut slap in the face!"

Charlie ignored the comment and waited for Wes to collect the cowboys. Then, with Billy alongside, he led the way to Caddo Creek.

All along the way Charlie Justiss rehearsed his words. They must be carefully chosen, harsh enough to exact compliance and yet soft enough to prevent bloodshed. By the time he reached the creek, a dozen phrases had come to mind. In the event, none were of any use, for Ike Kemp himself sat a horse fifty feet east of the boundary creek. With him were five riders. Three others coaxed reluctant Herefords westward across the creek. There was no need to read brands. All of Palo Pinto County knew Ike Kemp ran longhorns.

"Papa!" Billy exclaimed.

"Get the cattle!" Wes Tyler called to Marlin Silsbee, and Silsbee immediately motioned young Oldham to follow and headed toward the creek.

Charlie drank it all in, but somehow his mind refused to believe his eyes. How could anyone so blatantly steal another man's stock?

"Kemp!" Charlie screamed so that a man two miles away might have heard.

Ike Kemp responded by nodding to his companion. One of the riders set off to block Silsbee while Kermit Kemp produced a shotgun and fired it hurriedly in Charlie's direction. The blast was ineffective, Charlie being a good hundred yards distant, but the concussion startled the horses. Charlie gripped his reins tightly and settled the big black, but young Barret Jenkins was flung to the ground. Billy and Toby had difficulty as well. Wes sat a veteran cow pony all too familiar with gunshots. The spry mustang paid the noise no heed, and Wes drew out his revolver and took aim.

"Hold on!" Charlie shouted as he regained his composure. "Kemp, you're a thief and a fool! Get off my land!"

"Your land?" Kemp called, laughing. "You see any creek? No, it's all dried up. Far as I'm concerned, this is my land."

"Your stock, too?" Billy asked.

"I warned you about returnin' my strays," Kemp responded. "I'm takin' these as compensation."

"You're a dead man then," Wes declared.

Charlie waved for calm, but when Kermit Kemp reloaded his shotgun, Wes raced forward and knocked the would-be assassin to the ground.

"He's dead, Charlie!" Wes shouted. "Just say the word."

"I wouldn't be so sure," Ike Kemp warned, reaching for his own pistol. Toby Hart fired a warning shot, and Ike drew his hand back.

"You have to be crazy," Charlie barked. "This is my land, my stock. Did you think we'd just turn away and let you rob us?"

"Sure," Kemp said, smiling. "You're playin' the peacemaker, aren't you, Judge? You don't want to start yourself a range war, do you?"

Charlie's face flashed scarlet, and Wes's eyes begged for the signal to open fire. The Kemp hands at the creek had turned away, and Silsbee was already directing the purloined stock back onto Justiss range.

"Get out of my sight, Kemp," Charlie growled. "You once warned me about crossing onto your land. Know this. You come across that creek again, you or your boys either one, I'll give less thought to shooting 'em than I would to stepping on a ant. You may be able to shoot farmers and burn kids in Stephens County, but you're on *my* land now, in *my* county, and here we have laws."

"Still makin' speeches, huh?" Kemp asked. "This won't be settled with words, Justiss. No, there's just one way to deal with me, and in the end, it'll come to that. It'll be a pleasure listenin' to that reverend read words over your buryin'. A real pleasure, right, boys?"

The others laughed, and Wes's hand shook so that only a miracle kept the Colt from discharging. Kemp then waved his crew back across the parched creek. Charlie gazed bitterly at the departing horsemen.

Chapter Two

Billy Justiss viewed it like a nightmare. What manner of fool stole a neighbor's cattle so blatantly? And how could his father, that tall, proud man who more than anyone had built Palo Pinto County, stand by and watch?

"Papa, we should've shot 'em," Billy grumbled when they rode back to the ranchhouse together.

"No, son, there's a better way," Charlie had argued.

"You're wrong," Billy said, stopping to face his father. "I know you hate to start a war, but it's come. Wasn't us that fired. There's just one way to answer raiders, and that's to shoot 'em. You taught me that."

"It's a different day now."

"Laws and trials didn't stop Rame Polk, Papa. They won't help where Kemp's concerned, either. Did you see his eyes? There's no reasoning with a crazy man. Let me send for Lafe."

"Not till Bret's had his turn."

"Papa, if Bret rides over there, he'd better have a dozen armed men with him. Elsewise Ike Kemp'll kill him."

"I think that's a good idea. Meanwhile, see if you can shift some more men over to Wes. Best let the Dunlaps know what's afoot, too."

"I'll spread the word."

"Watch yourself, son. I haven't figured this thing out, but somehow it's gotten personal. I get the notion those Kemps bear us a grudge. Till we get it all sorted out, best keep your eyes and ears open. And carry a gun."

"You, too," Billy warned.

Billy followed his father's advice. No sooner had he set foot back at the ranch than he dispatched riders, one to the Dunlaps and a second westward down the Albany road to warn the Epplers, Schneiders, Cassidys, and the other small farms that might fall under Ike Kemp's angry gaze. He also sent the Cook brothers, Mitch and Ben, out to help Wes. Logan Thompson, the veteran cowboy sent to warn the Dunlaps, would also join the line camp after delivering his message.

All that activity drew a concerned look from Colleen.

"What's happened?" she asked as Billy finally stormed inside the house.

"Trouble," he told her.

"I guessed that. Brian came in with the fish and said you'd gone off with your papa. And here he didn't so much as drop in to say good day?"

"We had a run-in with Ike Kemp out at Caddo Creek. His boys were helping themselves to some of our stock."

"What? You caught them?"

"Red-handed. That Kermit fired a shotgun at us."

"Anyone hurt?"

"No, thank God. Little Barret Jenkins got himself thrown, sprained an ankle, but he'll be fine."

"Then, why are you so upset? If no one was hurt, and the Kemps were caught, then it's all over."

"No chance of that," Billy grumbled as he paced back and forth. "If it'd been just Wes and me, we'd put a stop to it all today. Papa still hopes for some kind of miracle peace. It won't come. Kemp's crazy. I don't understand exactly what's happening, but we're going to come to blows before all this is finished."

"Maybe you should talk to Bret."

"Papa's going to do that. It won't help. It's like with the Comanches, Colleen. People may think there's a way out, but there isn't. Somebody's going to wind up dying."

"Pa should know."

"I sent a rider. I figure the Schneiders are in danger, too. Later on I'll ride out and talk to everyone. I'm sending for help, too."

"Help?"

"Men who know how to handle themselves in a fight. I know Papa's against it, and so long as Kemp keeps to his side of the creek, I'll keep to my side. Sooner or later it'll be war, though, and when that happens, we'll have need of help."

"Billy, I can't believe what I'm hearing," she said,

resting her head on his chest. "I admit this Kemp seems a strange man, but sure he can't want to bring on violence."

"Wes thinks maybe he already has. Could be he planned the Weidlings' deaths. I wouldn't be surprised."

"But why?"

"Madmen don't always have reasons, Colleen. Anyway, while all this trouble's afoot, I've been thinking maybe your family ought to come out and stay here. Sully and Patrick would be a help if it comes to a fight, and I'd hate to think of any harm befalling little Brian or Cornelia."

"Brian's here more than he's not as is. Cornelia would be welcome, too. I might coax Pa to permit Mary Eileen and Flynn to stay for a time, but it's a long ride from here to school. Ma will not hear of their dodging lessons, you know. I don't think Pa himself will leave the farm, dry as it is, and Sully will stay as well. Patrick's fond of horses, so you might tempt him to come."

"I'm worried Kemp may strike at me through them."

"Don't fret," she said, stroking his hair. "We Cassidys have fought our own battles a long time now. What's more, the farm's on the main road, and it'll be little trouble to send for help."

"The Weidlings were on that road, too," Billy whispered. "It didn't do much for them."

Billy couldn't erase those words from his mind. He barely touched his dinner. Instead he stared across the table at little Brian. His freckled face and bright blue eyes seemed a world away from the fiery hatred that had flashed across Ike Kemp's countenance that afternoon. It would be just like Kemp to strike out at the young.

"Didn't you like my fish?" Brian asked as he finished his supper. "Hard as they were to catch, I thought sure you'd eat your share."

"I've got a lot on my mind," Billy explained.

"Well, that's no excuse for turning up your nose to good food," Colleen declared. "Enuncia will have words for you as well."

"Sure," Billy said, forcing a smile to his lips.

"It's time I was off home," Brian declared, rising from his chair and giving his sister a quick farewell kiss. "Pa will worry."

"I think it's best you stay tonight," Billy said, slipping out of his chair and drawing Brian aside. "There's been trouble on the road."

"So much the worse," Brian explained. "Ma will fret. I have to tell her I've come to no harm."

"I'll tend to that," Billy explained. "Danny Seavers can ride out and tell them."

"Why, I'm not but six years short of Danny's age myself," Brian urged. "You treat me like I'm a baby."

"I care," Billy said, leading the boy back to Colleen. "I'll lend you an old nightshirt, and you can have the guest room all to yourself. Tomorrow I'll have a talk with your father."

"He won't much like it, me not coming home, you know."

"He'll understand," Colleen assured her brother.

"Now get along with you, Brian Cassidy. Find some mischief to keep you busy."

Billy grinned a moment as the boy scampered off toward the kitchen. Enuncia was likely to have help with the dishes, and an Irish yarn or two to boot. The smile fell, though, when Billy gazed out the front window toward the west.

"Billy?" Colleen whispered.

"I was thinking now the old house is all empty, maybe Alice ought to bring the children over here. That cabin of hers is sure to draw Kemp's attention."

"A fine notion. Enuncia and I would welcome the attention. Besides, I ought to have a bit of practice with young ones. We may want to have one of our own someday."

"Practice?" he asked, laughing. "Between us, we've got a dozen younger brothers and sisters, nieces and nephews. I doubt we either one need much practice on that account."

"No," she said, laughing as well.

It was the brightest moment of the evening, and for the shortest of times the gloom left the ranch. It returned with nightfall, and twice Billy awoke that night in a sweat, relieved to discover his nightmare encounter with the Kemps had been but a dream.

Billy rose early that next morning. He devoted the morning to riding the Albany road, visiting with neighbors and family.

"Keep a careful watch," he warned Pat Cassidy. "I wouldn't wander about much after dark, and I'd eye any riders from the west most cautiously."

"Aye," Cassidy replied. "I've done so before."

"You'd all of you be most welcome at the ranch, you know. There'd be a good deal less danger."

"They'd be sure to burn us out," Cassidy objected. "Sully and I would prove a fair match for 'em, I'm thinkin', and Patrick's a fair shot himself. Mary Eileen shot a pair of rabbits just last week herself, and Flynn's got hawk eyes."

"You'll let us look after Brian and Cornelia at least?"

"Aye, so long as you see they keep at their studies. My Eileen's quite firm on that account, you know."

"I spoke to Patrick about working stock."

"So he told me. He's seventeen, and I'd say that's as good an age as any to make up your own mind. See he does a good job and gets a fair wage."

"I will."

"You might have a care for the Schneider youngsters, too," Cassidy suggested. "Wee Georg was sickly not so long past, and he's none too stout even now."

"I'll invite them to stay, too. Brian would welcome the company, I'm sure."

"You've a good heart, Billy Justiss, but it seems to me you're takin' it that the worst is apt to happen. Things mayn't be so dark as you think."

"I pray not," Billy said, shifting his feet nervously. "But I'd never forgive myself for not doing what I could to protect the young ones."

"Aye, just so long as you don't close your eyes to your own well-being."

"Believe me," Billy said, frowning. "I value my hide quite highly."

Enough so, in fact, that he took Patrick Cassidy along to the Schneider farm. The two found Martin Schneider busy diverting water from the dammed remnant of Caddo Creek to his meager vegetable garden. Schneider responded to the sound of approaching horses by calling out a warning to his wife and scrambling toward a loaded shotgun.

"Not much of a greeting," Billy observed.

"No," Schneider admitted, lowering the shotgun. "Since you sent word to us, we have seen riders three, four times. They call to us to leave. Once they shoot at Sophia."

"Maybe it'd be better if you stayed closer to your house," Patrick suggested. "You make it awful easy for Kemp, the two of you way out here all by yourselves."

"I buy this land from Rolf before he leave," Schneider explained. "It is mine, too. There is no water for vegetables back there. Only here, where I can build dam."

"I understand," Billy said, nodding. "People have died here before, though, remember?"

"I never forget," Schneider cried. "I see them. They are my friends, the Weidlings. I bury their girls here with my own hands, me and Rolf."

"I know," Billy said, sighing. "I've been thinking maybe you'd like Colleen and I to keep an eye on little Georg while all this trouble brews. We've got plenty of room. The others would be welcome, too."

"No," Sophia cried. "We are a family. We stick together, *ja?*"

"*Ja,*" Schneider agreed. "Besides, I need the boys to help with the work. It is hard when they are away at school. There is not so much light now when they get home. We must all work very hard."

"Sure, I understand," Billy muttered. "I've sent some extra men out to the line camp. You have trouble, get word to Wes. And don't be afraid to run and hide. Anything that gets burned can be rebuilt."

"We will send word," Schneider promised. *"Danke* . . . thank you, Mr. Justiss. You and your father have been very good to us. But if riders come to our home, we will not run. We fight. It is our land."

Billy nodded grimly, then turned his horse away.

He left Patrick to continue on to the ranch alone. Billy headed to town. He found his father and Ross in the courthouse, staring at the deed registry.

"I warned the neighbors," Billy told them. "I hoped maybe the children might stay at the ranch for a time, but the Schneiders refused, and Pat Cassidy would only let Cornelia and Brian come."

"Well, I wouldn't worry about any raids for a while," Ross declared. "Kemp's chosen different ground for our battle."

"Oh?" Billy asked.

"We had a lawyer named Peters in here this morning," Charlie explained. "He was checking up on the sections along Caddo Creek, especially those parcels of land upstream. You know the old Weidling place belongs to Martin Schneider now. Rolf sold the land before leaving."

"I don't see what sending a lawyer to gaze at the records means," Billy said, shaking his head.

"Maybe nothing," Charlie said, "but if Kemp

could get hold of the upper stream and divert it, change the channel, he could cause us to lose quite a chunk of acreage."

"You can't reroute a creek that easily," Billy argued.

"You can when it's dried up," Ross pointed out. "It's been done down south. Most of the county's newer deeds have surveyor's measurements, but our old deed just mentions the creeks. Our ranch begins wherever Caddo Creek begins."

"So? Papa, I don't see where all this gets Kemp," Billy grumbled. "It's way too much trouble to go through for a bit of acreage. Land is cheap right now."

"Sure, but it's not the value of the land, son," Charlie declared. "It's a matter of taking from us. I still don't know who this Ike Kemp is, but somewhere along the way he's nurtured a considerable grudge against our family. This business of the creek boundary is just another try to provoke us."

"He's succeeding," Billy said angrily. "I'd shot him the other day."

"Maybe we should have," Charlie admitted, "but keep in mind we could wind up facing trial for murder. I'd hate to see any of our outfit hang. Bret rode out there and talked with Kemp. Seems Ike claims *we* took *his* stock, shot at his riders, threatened his son, and tried to start a war. I got a telegram from Austin, too. Seems Kemp wired the Texas Rangers accusing me and Bret of using our authority to persecute the Kemps."

"Everybody knows who's telling the truth," Billy grumbled.

"Not everyone," Ross pointed out. "Kemp's got some powerful friends. This is a whale of a lot more complicated than it seems, Billy. For now, we'd best move with a great deal of caution."

"Yes," Charlie agreed.

Billy nodded. He then walked out the courthouse door and set off for the telegraph office. He sent a brief wire to Lafe Freeman.

NEED YOUR HELP. WILL PAY TOP WAGES. B. JUSTISS.

The moment the telegram was dispatched, Billy breathed easier. Whether the war started in the county deed records or was fought in the courtroom, it was bound sooner or later to wind up being fought in the hills and ravines along Caddo Creek. And when that time came, Billy wanted Lafe Freeman and Malachi Johnson at his side.

Chapter Three

Wes Tyler knew war. Sometimes he felt as if he'd been born to it. As a small boy he and his father had driven off Comanche raiders from the family farm south of San Antonio. He was barely fifteen when his father and two brothers fell in a cornfield outside Sharpsburg, a mile or so away from a little stream called Antietam Creek. When the news reached home, Wes had walked silently past the graves of his mother and younger brother, then saddled a horse and started for Houston. Months later he'd stood in line of battle at Fredericksburg and killed Yankees.

"Sometimes you have to fight awful hard just to survive," Charlie Justiss had told a skeleton-thin Wes that long winter when the winds at Petersburg had cut through him like the icy blades of cavalry sabers.

It was as true now as ever. Drought had parched the land, and the vast herd that had accumulated over the years in the hills above the Brazos had dwindled through large sales and scant grass. There were times that sweltering summer when it seemed that God had turned his wrath upon the land. But through it all Wes Tyler never abandoned hope. How could he? There at his side through it all were Alice and the little ones. Each time he feared the darkness of despair would engulf them, little Jeff would crawl up his knee and hum a tune, or else Rose Anne would appear with some fragile wildflower plucked from the hillside. Tim and Hart, the youngest, chased each other about like a pair of jackrabbits.

And to think he'd once worried over raising a family!

He and Alice had enjoyed seven years above Caddo Creek, and most of the time had been spent in rare peace. Sure, there'd been rustlers and a few raiders during the railroad boom, but before Ike Kemp arrived, Wes had always considered the cabin as a refuge, the final haven in a storm-swept universe. Now that had changed.

He hated Kemp for that, and he wished Charlie would just give him leave to settle things once and for all. Wes would grab Marty Steele and a pair of others, cross the creek, and put an end to those Kemps.

"We'll deal with Kemp in court," young Billy had explained two days before. "We have the law on our side."

Laws? Wes wondered. He'd known the law to be as fickle as a newly-roped mustang, gentle one minute and wild as summer lightning the next. What's more, Wes had a personal stake in seeing Ike Kemp dealt with.

Yes, Wes thought, recalling the dark night when

little Viktor Weidling had scrambled down the creek to warn of raiders. Wasn't long afterward those same horsemen unloaded pistols and rifles into the side of the cabin. On moonless nights Wes could still hear the children screaming, and he remembered young Jeff's gaze—those big round eyes that asked his father if it would ever happen again.

Sure, most of the county thought those raiders had been caught and shot to pieces down south of the Eppler place. Wes knew otherwise. Their leader had been a foul-mouthed man who'd sat close to three hundred pounds on a roan horse. No such man had been among the dead raiders, but one rode back and forth along the west bank of Caddo Creek. His name was Isaac Kemp!

Well, Kemp would never have another chance to bring harm to Alice and the little ones. Wes had long ago promised himself that. And while Billy hadn't given the word to cross the creek, he had invited Alice and the children over to the ranch-house.

"Our place is with you," Alice had argued.

"No, it's best you take to safer quarters," he told her. "The younger Cassidys are there, too. It'll be kind of like a holiday for Jeff and Rose Anne."

"Wes, you be careful."

"Don't you know?" he asked a he held her tightly. "No Kemp's got the bullet to kill me. Shoot, it's been tried. The Yanks put three balls in me at Gettysburg, and Kiowas slashed me back in '71. Truth is, once Charlie gets a gulletful of that Kemp, we'll put a quick finish to things."

"Promise you won't take risks?"

273

"I promise you I'll be around to see little Hart's grandkids," Wes told her with a broad smile. "Now get along with you."

But though Alice had left, the memory of her fearful eyes had remained with Wes. She was gifted with rare intuition and was often prophetic. If she was worried, there might well be cause. Wes, as a result, kept alert.

At first, though, the Kemps kept their distance. Oh, there was no missing the pair of riders patrolling the west side of Caddo Creek, nor was there any question whether their rifles were loaded. Occasionally a shot was fired.

"Just shootin' at some ducks!" the rider would call as the Flying J cowhands scrambled to safety. "This time," the rider would add.

If it had been up to Wes, he'd have returned those shots, maybe even plucked the shooter from his saddle. But Billy warned to avoid trouble.

It just wasn't possible, though.

Midweek, Martin Schneider and his eldest boy Alek drove their wagon along the creek toward the Brazos.

"We have water for the garden," Schneider explained to Wes, "but the well is dry. The children grow thirsty."

Wes waved them along as he would anybody. After all, most everyone who had been around Palo Pinto long considered the Brazos open to anyone. Ike Kemp thought otherwise. The Schneider wagon wasn't a hundred yards from Wes when a rifle shot sliced through a barrel in the bed. The horses whined in terror, and Schneider fought to control

274

the team.

"You're on my land, farmer!" Kemp bellowed. "Get along home before I fill you full of holes."

"This is not your land!" Schneider objected. "I ask the cowboys. They say to come."

"It *is* my land, and you didn't ask *my* cowboys. Now get along!"

Schneider motioned for little Alek to take cover, then climbed down from the wagon and pointed a finger at Kemp.

"You cannot frighten me! I am here by right!" Schneider yelled.

Kemp waved his hands, and a half-dozen riflemen peppered the wagon, splintering the barrels and sending the horses stampeding down the stream. The wagon banged along behind.

Wes had witnessed the whole thing, but there hadn't been much he could do. Only young Barret Jenkins was along, and the dwarfish boy would prove little use in a showdown with Ike Kemp's whole outfit. Wes had sent the youngster to collect the others. Barret hadn't returned when Kermit Kemp marched toward the dry streambed and began firing wildly in Schneider's direction.

"You cannot do this!" Schneider cried.

"I can't?" Kermit asked. "Who's to stop me?"

"I am!" Wes finally shouted, raised a Winchester to his shoulder and neatly slicing a limb from a willow five feet from Kermit's ear.

"Kermit?" Ike called. "Son."

"I'm all right, Pa," Kermit answered angrily. "Just one of those Justiss people tryin' to scare us off."

"We don't scare!" Kemp shouted, laughing as he

275

stepped out toward where Kermit prepared to fire again at Martin Schneider. Wes fired instead, splitting a dirt clod in two no more than a foot from Kermit's boot. Instinctively Kermit danced away.

"Next time somebody's dyin'!" Wes yelled.

"Let's get him, Pa!" Kermit urged.

Schneider, meanwhile, trotted downstream in the direction of his wagon. Young Alek raced after his father. Kermit raised his pistol and fired a shot toward the boy. Alek screamed out in pain and dropped to his knees.

"That's enough!" Wes warned.

The Kemps gathered at the creekbed and began taunting Schneider and his bleeding son. Wes felt his blood boil. He aimed and prepared to fire. There was little a single man could do, he kept telling himself. But the grin on Ike Kemp's face was like a red flag waving under the nose of a Hereford bull.

"Move back!" Wes finally shouted as he started toward the Schneiders, the Winchester cocked and ready to fire.

"Ah, he's got no stomach for a fight," Kermit said, laughing. "These Justiss cowboys like to shoot at the air and trim trees."

"Try me," Wes said, leveling the barrel at Kermit. Kermit swung his own pistol around, but a shot from the trees clipped his boot, slicing into his foot and sending him hobbling off in agony.

"Who's next?" Wes called. He could now spot Hector Suarez, Marlin Silsbee, and a dozen others on the hillside. Ike Kemp noted them as well. Without so much as a nod, Ike stepped back, and his companions retreated rapidly. Wes hurried down to examine young Alek Schneider, and Hector organized the men in a short skirmish line.

"He shot my boy," Schneider sobbed when Wes examined the boy's leg. A bullet had passed through the meaty portion of Alek's left calf, and the wound was bleeding profusely. Wes tore the youngster's shirt into strips and bound the wound. Then Tucker Spears appeared with a horse, and Wes helped the boy onto the animal.

"Tuck, you see this youngster to the ranchhouse," Wes ordered. "See the wound gets dressed."

"I'm on my way," Tucker agreed, leading the horse into the trees.

"Jenk," Wes said, turning to little Barret Jenkins, "find a horse and ride into town. Tell Dr. Garnett Alek's gotten himself shot. Tell Bret, too."

"Yes, sir," Barret replied, racing off after Tucker. Then Wes instructed Logan Thompson to help Schneider recover his wagon and head home.

"I'll see a couple of barrels of fresh water get to your place, too, Mr. Schneider," Wes promised.

"And Kemp?" Schneider asked with wild eyes.

"We'll leave that to Bret."

In the end, though, nothing much came of the shooting. A warrant was sworn, but Ike Kemp and his hands swore it was Kermit who shot in reply to an ambush staged by the Flying J crew. John Peters, the Austin lawyer Ike Kemp had combing the land titles, got a writ from a judge in Jacksboro, and Kermit was released before Bret could even make an arrest.

"So much for the law," Wes told Billy. "Worse trouble will come of this. Wait and see."

Wes didn't have long to wait for that trouble, either. Early the next morning Barret Jenkins roused him with a loud banging on the door.

"Wes, best get up!" the young cowboy called. "Somethin' is stirrin' down at the creek."

Wes scrambled out of bed, pulled on his trousers, and rushed to the door. Outside, Marlin Silsbee had the rest of the crew assembled. Wes couldn't help smiling. Tucker Spears held a rifle taller than he was, and the whole bunch of them were far too young to be taken altogether seriously.

"Listen," Silsbee suggested.

Wes motioned for the others to be silent. From the direction of the creek came a steady hammering. It sounded to all the world as if somebody was raising a barn. But why there?

"Mitch and Ben," Wes said to the Cook brothers, "you two stay here and watch the cabin . . . and the horses. Jenk, you stay with 'em."

Young Jenkins was disappointed, but trudged over to the Cooks without comment.

"Silsbee, you and Thompson take young Lew there," Wes went on, pointing to Lew Oldham. "Find yourselves a good spot in the junipers and keep your rifles ready."

"That mean I come with you, huh?" Tucker Spears called.

"Bring your horse, Tuck," Wes instructed. "May be that you need to ride back to the main ranch for help."

Young Spears nodded, then trotted over to the horses and picked out a spotted mustang. Wes returned inside as the others set off on their assigned

278

tasks. He stuffed handfuls of cartridges into his pockets, strapped on his pistol and then loaded a Winchester. By the time he'd returned outside, Tucker Spears was sitting atop the mustang.

"Ready?" Tucker asked.

"As much so as I'm apt to manage," Wes said, waving the boy along toward the creek. "You keep yourself handy. If there's need to send you for help, I won't have much time to waste handin' out instructions, and you won't have much chance to think. So, do you understand?"

"I was with Hector when we tracked down the rustlers, remember? You can count on me."

Wes grinned. He recognized the boy's solemn gaze. Wes hadn't been too much different back in '62 when he'd appeared before Charlie Justiss, a rawboned young recruit who'd sported hardly a whisker on his chin. Yes, they were much of a kind. The story of the frontier was carved on their faces, illustrated by Wes's battle scars and by the missing ring finger on Tucker Spears's right hand.

Wes waved the young rider along and started for Caddo Creek. The hammering grew even louder. When Wes emerged from the junipers on the hillside overlooking the creek, he discovered a line of fenceposts following the far bank of the creek. But then the fenceline suddenly swung across the dry streambed and onto Flying J range.

Wes felt the anger inside him boil over. Ike Kemp stood with his son Kermit not fifty yards away, urging his crew on.

"Fences," Wes muttered in disgust. Kemp was building fences! Wasn't this the same man who months earlier was ready to murder to keep the range open?

"Go fetch Billy," Wes told Tucker. "Hurry."

The boy turned his horse and galloped off eastward. Tucker was gone less than an hour, and all that time Wes stared down at Kemp and his men.

This is crazy, Wes thought. This Kemp's going to slice the southwest corner off the ranch, steal twenty or thirty acres. Charlie and Billy might be for peace, but they'd never stand for such a thing! This was war.

But when Billy arrived, he seemed oddly reluctant to send his men charging into the Kemp outfit.

"No cattleman would stand for havin' his land stolen!" Wes argued. "Can't you see what's happenin'? It's a challenge, Billy. We got to answer it."

"How many would die!" Billy asked, glancing around at the eager but inexperienced cowboys. "Maybe Papa's right. He's got Ross and Ben Green working on all kinds of charges."

"Kermit wriggled out of those charges easy enough," Wes grumbled. "Billy, give me Hector and Marty, and I'll ride over there tonight and put an end to our troubles."

"And what would we be then, Wes? Wouldn't it be murder?"

"No less than when Kemp sent his riders after the Wieldings."

"We don't know that for sure."

"I know," Wes declared. "Deep down, you and Charlie do, too."

"Maybe," Billy confessed. "And I'd be lying to tell you I'm not half of a mind to send you. But Papa

280

told me something this morning. He said that if you settle everything with bullets and night riders, then it's the Kemps of this world who'll wind up winning. And we'll be as lost as old Stands Tall and his Comanche ghosts."

"I wish that's how it could be," Wes said, sighing. "But I've seen how smart lawyers can twist the law around, how rich men can buy judges, how it all unravels so that there's no real justice at all. I've heard talk about this Peters fellow. He owns a couple of judges, people say. You wait and see if it's not true!"

"I pray it's not," Billy said, turning to stare with fiery eyes at Ike Kemp. "Because then there really will be a war, and none of us is apt to escape being singed a bit in that case."

Wes nodded his agreement to that at least. Then he set about organizing the crew in watches.

Chapter Four

An uncertain peace settled over the farms and ranches bounding Caddo Creek as mid-November arrived. Autumn had been mild, hot even, but now, as winter approached, the winds carried a chill, and the riders Wes Tyler assigned to ride the fenceline erected by Ike Kemp were bundled in woolen coats or buffalo robes. Nights were punctuated by howling wolves and the eerie cries of great-horned owls, but rifles remained in the saddle scabbards or on gun racks.

Rather, the conflict moved to the courts. Ordinarily a Palo Pinto County boundary dispute would have been settled in Charlie Justiss's courtroom, but lawyer Peters quickly saw to it the case was transferred elsewhere. Charlie did his best to see the suit moved to Austin. He even enlisted the aid of Senator Lawrence Rogers, Ross Justiss's father-in-law. Even so, the case was moved instead to Jack County where it was left in the hands of a state circuit judge, Crawford Warren.

Warren's selection apparently pleased no one. Peters almost immediately filed motions to move the case again. Ross called Crawford Warren the last of the prewar graybeards, a one-time Missouri lawyer of doubtful intellect who rarely bothered to read the law, preferring to mete out justice in Solomon-like fashion, often adding personal observations as he passed judgment.

"He's as old as Adam, and about as sensible," declared Ben Green, the hard-hearted attorney whose help Ross had enlisted to prepare the Flying J arguments. "It won't help much your serving with Lee in Virginia, either," Green told Charlie. "Old Crawford fought in the West with Sterling Price, and it's been a source of bitterness to the old fool that Price is rarely regarded as well in Texas as other Southern generals."

"Kemp's man doesn't care much for him, either," Charlie pointed out.

"Peters would prefer Zach Streeter," Green explained. "I've heard talk that Streeter ought to wear a bridle. He's clearly Peters's mule to whip."

"I'd say, all things considered, we might just get a fair hearing," Charlie declared. "Doesn't sound like either side's got much leverage. Let the arguments decide the case."

"You don't understand, Papa," Ross grumbled. "It's a clear matter of Grandpapa's deed. There was even a map with the papers, one you drew yourself, showing the boundaries. Creek or no creek, the bed's the same, and so is the boundary. There've been cases settled before on that very point. Anybody else would rule for us. Warren, well, he's as

283

like as not to get some crazy notion and rule for Kemp."

"Then Kemp keeps the twenty acres," Charlie said, rubbing his palms together as if to wash his hands of the matter. "We'll survive."

"It'll never stop there," Ross remarked grimly. "Kemp will move his fences again and again, change the river itself. He's not after that acreage, Papa, not with hundreds of miles of abandoned range in Stephens County his for paying the back taxes. No, it's personal."

"I get the feeling, too, Mr. Justiss," Green agreed.

"I know it would appear so," Charlie said, shaking his head, "but there's no sense to it. I never saw Ike Kemp before he came here. He's no Yank, so we couldn't have wronged him in the war, and I'm hanged if I can see how he could be related to the Comanches. Raymond Polk had no kin survive him, and besides, if it was a blood grudge, they'd hired a gunman to do the job quick and easy."

"Papa, maybe it's not you he's after. Could be it's Billy or even Wes."

"Makes no sense," Charlie muttered. "There's an element of greed to the way Kemp's gone about things. I think he's simply gone after the top dog, and he's been mighty clever. He uses Stephens County as a base, and he shifts tactics like the devil. One minute he's ready to square off with rifles. The next he's maneuvering in court."

"Well, Crawford Warren or no, we've got the weight of the law behind us and a fair volume of testimony," Green pointed out. "I'd be sorely surprised if we don't win. The very fact that Kemp's

284

fenced the land works for us. Warren's liable to take offense, seeing Kemp's decided the case in his own mind before awaiting any ruling."

"Maybe," Ross admitted. "It's been awful peaceful down at that creek, though, and I've always found that's a sure sign of trouble."

Charlie laughed.

"Son, you wouldn't rather have Kemp raiding the farms, would you? I swear! Lawyers never can see a good side to anything, can they?"

"It's against our credo," Ben Green added with a grin. "Prepare for the worst. It avoids surprises."

Charlie laughed again. Then he sat down between the two lawyers and began examining the bulky documents supporting the Justiss claim on the disputed acreage.

Chapter Five

The week before the trial was to begin, dark clouds appeared on the northern horizon, and for the first time in what seemed an eternity, rain began to fall on Palo Pinto County. Storms were not often considered a good omen, but Billy Justiss judged it so this time. A good downpour would restore Caddo Creek within its sun-cracked banks, and the case would be settled.

Meanwhile, Billy faced a storm of a different sort at home.

"Billy, who's going to arrive next?" Colleen asked as they gazed at the crowded breakfast table at their new house. Alice Tyler was off to town that morning, and Enuncia had ushered the Tyler children over a half hour before. Now Timothy and Hart were sandwiched between Jeff and Rose Anne. Across the table sat little Brian Cassidy and his sister Cornelia.

Alek Schneider, not yet fully recovered from his wound, sat at a sideboard a few feet away.

Billy grinned. It did seem as if they'd taken in half the county.

"I never banked on running a boardinghouse," Colleen went on. "All my life I dreamed of my wedding day as a chance to escape little brothers and sisters. Now it appears you've brought me back to it."

"It's not as bad as Ryan and Rachel have down at Buck Creek," Billy said, laughing. "There are what, sixty, seventy of them? Can you imagine twenty or thirty Brians waking you each morning?"

"I can," she said, resting her hands on her hips. "I won't have it, Billy!"

There wasn't a trace of good humor in her words, and Billy felt his grin fade. She was deathly serious. Well, they'd been married less than three full months, and lately he'd been so occupied with Ike Kemp down at Caddo Creek that they'd scarcely spent an hour together without interruption.

"I was wrong not to've asked you," he admitted. "Mama and Papa have room in town. Would you rather the Tylers went there. Alek's able to go along home, and your papa was none too pleased by the notion of Brian and Cornelia leaving in the first place."

"You know they have to stay," she grumbled. "It would be the worst kind of bad manners to send anyone home now. It's simply that we never have a moment's peace."

"It will be worse when the trial begins, Colleen. I'll be up in Jacksboro, and you'll—"

287

"You want me to stay here. It's not necessary. Enuncia can look after Brian and Cornelia. You'll need someone."

"Yes, I will. I'd be more than happy if you came. Even so, we won't have much time."

"More than if I stay here."

He smiled and drew her closer. It did seem like an eternity since they'd shared so much as an afternoon alone. He touched her cheek with his fingers, and her frown fell away. Then a spoon fell to the floor, followed by an outcry. Enuncia rushed in to quell the disturbance, but Brian raced over and pulled Colleen's hand.

"Cornelia says she's going to drown Jeff," the boy complained. "Tell her to behave, Sissy. You know how bossy she gets when you leave."

Billy started to intervene, but Colleen only sighed and shook her head.

"Let's go talk to Cornelia, Brian. You are sure that you said nothing to her?"

"By the Saints, I didn't," the boy swore, pressing his hand upon his heart. "Would I lie?"

"I've lost track of the times, Brian Cassidy," his sister replied. "Now let's put an end to this quarreling."

That afternoon Pat Cassidy arrived at the ranch with worse news.

"I passed Solomon Kemp on the Albany road," Cassidy explained. "He wasn't alone, Billy boy."

"Well, he's not as stupid as his papa, huh?"

"Were no ordinary pair of cowboys at his side,

lad. One was tall, with long dark hair and a scar across his cheek. The second was dark, too, with a heavy mustache, though. Something peculiar about one of his ears, too. Had a bit of it cut or shot away."

"You think Kemp's hired some shooters?"

"They weren't there to dance with the girls at the church social, lad. It doesn't bode well for your future."

"We're just beginning the trial."

"That'd be a sham, son. What we called in the war a diversion. This Kemp's a sly one, all right. He gets your attention in Jacksboro and then sends raiders against your ranch. It's likely to work, too."

"Wes will still be here."

"He won't have much chance if you keep his feet tied to that creek, Billy. Why not give Sully and myself a half-dozen riders? We could slip in on those Kemps under cover from the west, let them know they are up against more than they might think."

"You know my papa's dead set against that."

"Billy, are you ten years old? Use your head. You know I'm right. Do it and argue with Charlie afterward."

"Kemp's not altogether stupid. He could be waiting for you."

"Ah, he's given up on you doing a blamed thing."

"It's little better than murder, Mr. Cassidy."

"Murder?" Cassidy cried with raised eyebrows. "Murder? You want to talk about murder, speak to Eric Weidling!"

"There's never been any proof that was Kemp's

doing."

"Have a talk with Wes sometime, lad. He knows. And what of Alek Schneider?"

"The trial won't last but a few days. Afterward . . ."

"We could all be dead. Billy, if you're set on your path, well, I'll pray you can live with what comes of it. I believe I'll be sending Cornelia to her aunt, though, and bringing Brian back home where I can keep watch over him."

"You're pretty vulnerable down there."

"At least I'll have my eyes open. No one's apt to slip in and murder me in my bed. Give another thought to what I said, son. Sully and I know the way."

Billy nodded his understanding, but he knew it was out of the question. The Flying J had its traditions, and one was that it didn't start wars or commit murder, no matter how provoked. Billy did make it a point to speak with Wes, though, and he was more than a little glad when Lafe Freeman and Malachi Johnson appeared.

"Who is it we go after?" Lafe asked.

"No one yet," Billy explained. "Just watch the fenceline at Caddo Creek and deal with anyone who threatens the stock or our crew."

"There's talk your neighbor, Ike Kemp, went and hired himself a pair of New Mexico shooters."

"Could be," Billy admitted. "Watch them especially."

"Be best to call 'em out, have done with it," Malachi declared. "I never fancy this waitin' 'round."

"Nor do I," Billy told them, "but Papa doesn't

want anything done that will put the trial in jeopardy."

Lafe shook his head sadly as if to say it was not the way to handle such business, but years in the army and working trail drives had taught the young black man to keep his own counsel. No words were spoken.

Chapter Six

Kemp kept his hands to the west side of the barbed wire fence, though. When the hearing began, the rotund rancher sat between his sons Kermit and Solomon behind their lawyer. Peters wore his poker face, revealing nothing of his feelings.

On the opposite side of the courtroom aisle, Ross Justiss and Ben Green sat behind a pile of documents and several notebooks. Billy and Charlie Justiss sat together on a hard wooden bench behind them. The rest of the courtroom was sprinkled with newspaper correspondents, friends, and interested onlookers.

All rose when Crawford Warren entered the dingy room. The judge nodded to the lawyers, then took a seat behind a long flat table.

"Let's get ourselves started, boys," Warren said. "Who's done the filing here?"

"We have, your honor," Ben Green announced.

"I'd like to draw your attention to the county map included in our exhibits. You'll find the sections in dispute marked."

"Judge Warren," Peters objected, "I believe the map in question was drawn some time ago, and by the plaintiff himself. We argue this map is in serious error. I refer to the fact that Caddo Creek no longer reaches the Albany road, and so that cannot be used as a proper boundary for the properties in dispute."

"In dispute?" Ross cried. "There's no disputing where Caddo Creek is! Come out and see. May not be a lot of water in the stream just now, but there's no mistaking the channel."

"Oh?" Peters asked, raising his eyebrow. "I suppose that's because you Justiss boys map the county as you see it, claim what land you choose, and trample anybody who gets in your way!"

"Your Honor, please," Green pleaded, shaking his head. "You see what we've been up against. This Kemp fellow twists the truth until it looks like pasture hay in November. Let's deal with the facts. Our map was, in truth, drawn by Charlie Justiss, but it's been the accepted chart of Palo Pinto County for close to a decade. What's more, the U.S. Army and the Texas Rangers have used a copy of this same map.

"We all know streams have a way of flooding and drying up in the extremes of our Texas climate, but that doesn't change title to the lands they cross."

"I repeat my objection to this map, Judge," Peters said, stepping around his desk and pacing in front of Judge Warren. "As for young Green there, his argument has no validity. This whole case comes down to whether the State of Texas will allow a single man to rule a county like some European monarch or whether an honest, hard-working rancher like Isaac Kemp can find justice."

Warren listened with amusement, then slammed his gavel on his desk.

"I believe, gentlemen, I'm capable of sifting the truth for myself," the judge declared. "Now, let's have some witnesses called, hear what they have to say, and get this matter settled. I've heard all the charges and countercharges I care to for now. Proceed."

Ben Green then called Charlie to the witness chair, and the testimony began. Green made certain Charlie had a chance to narrate the long history of the Flying J, of winning wild range from Comanches and fending off rustlers on the long treks north to Kansas.

"And you received your original title from the state, didn't you?" Green asked.

"Yes. It was compensation for my father's service at San Jacinto," Charlie explained. "The original grant is at the courthouse in Palo Pinto, your honor," Charlie added, turning to Judge Warren. "We copied the wording, and I also got a letter from the secretary of state in Austin verifying the issuing of title from the state."

"That was fairly standard practice in the case of Republic of Texas veterans," Green explained. "The state, being short on funds, often granted large tracts of land instead."

"I'm aware of the procedure," the judge replied. "I've looked over your copy of the grant, and it seems in keeping with others I've seen."

"And in the twelve years you have occupied this acreage, has anyone before questioned your title?" Green asked.

"Never," Charlie said, gazing at the Kemps. "Why should they? Anyone desiring land has always found plenty."

"And who has paid the county taxes on the disputed acres?"

"I have."

"For twelve years?"

"Yes, for twelve years," Charlie echoed. "Why wouldn't I? I've always met my obligations, and those acres, after all, belong to me."

Ross then questioned Charlie about records and ranch accounts. By the time they'd finished, some of the reporters in back were dozing away, and Judge Warren declared a noon recess.

When court reconvened, Peters had his chance to question Charlie. The lawyer marched back and forth in front of the judge, his hands folded behind his back. Then he eyed Charlie with cold, coyotelike eyes and began.

"Major Justiss, you say you fought for your land," Peters said, smiling slyly. "I understand it's legend in Palo Pinto how you killed Indians. Killing must come easy for you."

"Is that a question?" Charlie asked.

"A statement, I think," Peters said, pacing. "After all, you served in the late war, rose to high rank. It's well known how officers often sacrificed their men to earn glory and promotion. How many men died under your command?"

"Judge Warren," Ross objected, "how does this relate to the subject at hand?"

"I'm merely trying to paint a portrait of the man before you, Your Honor. Are we to believe that a man who is said to have killed hundreds, who has for over a decade taken anything he wanted and stampeded across most of west Texas, would hesitate to carve out his own boundaries?"

Charlie rose angrily. Ross and Ben Green voiced objections.

"Why all the concern for this murderer?" Peters shouted. "Look at the record. Comanches occupied this land, and he teamed up with his bluecoat friends to murder them, man, woman, and child. How did you survive those first years on the range, Major Justiss? How much of your income came from selling horses and cattle to the federal occupation troops? Whatever happened to your neighbors to the east, the Stokelys? Who bought up the notes on their ranch when they fell on hard times? How many acres of land did you and your brother receive from the state when the railroad was built to El Paso? Isn't it true, Major, that you've milked the state of land and livelihood ever since the war?"

"Your Honor, Mr. Justiss isn't on trial here," Green protested. "Does Mr. Peters want to ask questions or assassinate my client's character?"

"I'd guess the latter," the judge said, shaking his head. "Mr. Peters, you won't get many answers when you don't let the witness reply."

"Oh, we know the answers, Your Honor," Peters said, laughing as he walked away. "Soon the entire state will know who Charlie Justiss is."

"Quite a few already do," Ross commented. "And most consider themselves lucky to call him friend. I imagine that's more than you can boast, Peters!"

Judge Warren banged his gavel against the table-top to regain order as the courthouse erupted with a chorus of shouts.

"Do you have any other questions for the witness, Mr. Peters?" Judge Warren asked. "And I'd caution you this time they'd best be phrased so the witness can reply."

"Just one," Peters answered, his fiery eyes boring in on Charlie. "Major, is it true you've hired a pair of darkie bounty hunters to stalk and kill Isaac Kemp?"

"What?" Charlie asked, half falling out of his chair.

"Are you familiar with Lafayette Freeman and Malachi Johnson?"

"I am," Charlie said. "My brother employed them as guards for the railroad work camps. Lafe Freeman rode with my trail herd to Kansas as a youngster. His father cooked for us first time up the trail."

"And are you familiar with his reputation as a hired killer?"

"I'm not at all certain I know what you're talking about," Charlie replied. "To my knowledge, there are no warrants outstanding on Lafe. Truth is, he and Malachi rescued the schoolchildren of Palo Pinto when raiders attacked the town. They've killed, but it's always been within the law and for just cause."

"As you have, eh?" Peters asked, laughing.

"Yes," Charlie answered angrily. "You see, I've never been a man to shirk my duties. I was called to

297

service in '61, signed the muster roll and found myself elected captain of my company. Elected, mind you. As for promotion, I never asked for any gold braid, and I guess they finally made me a major more on account of my habit of surviving getting shot than for any great military training."

"I don't believe this is in answer to any question," Peters said, walking away.

"Oh, it's an answer, all right," Charlie declared. "You asked me a while back about my service to the State of Texas. Well, I'll tell you all about it. I've carried the scars of that service most of my life. My father went to an early grave so we could have our independence from Mexico. I buried good friends in Virginia and left others on fields in Maryland and Pennsylvania. They didn't die to win me promotion, mister! They died for the honor of their state and the people back home.

"You call me a murderer? I never rode down German farmers in the dead of night, and I never shot an eleven-year-old boy because he crossed a neighbor's land to fetch water. You want to talk murder? Ask Ike Kemp there about the Stephens County folks who tried to cross his land, how he stripped 'em, burned a boy's feet so bad he'll walk one-legged all his days.

"I've stayed up nights remembering the faces of men I've fought from Gettysburg to Richmond, at Chickamauga and Antietam. I never fired at a man if I could reach an understanding with him. I'd settle with Kemp if he'd listen to reason, but I won't allow a man to steal my land. Who would?"

The audience hooted their agreement, and Judge

298

Warren hammered for quiet.

"Major, no man serving under the Stars and Bars need apologize for it in my court," the judge added.

"Nor in all of Texas!" a Jacksboro veteran shouted.

Peters drew out a handkerchief and mopped his brow. He then resumed his pacing, seemingly searching for a fresh tack.

"You'd call yourself a hero, I suppose," Peters said at last. "You've held the office of county judge for years now. How have your holdings increased since taking office?"

"The ranch has done quite well," Charlie replied, "though I haven't had too much to do with the day-to-day operations. The last two years the market's been better, and we've had profits."

"How much land have you been able to buy?"

"Ross would have the figures," Charlie said. "He's handled most of that. I guess what you're asking, though, is whether I've gotten rich off my office. Well, sir, Ross also has my pay vouchers among his papers. They'll show you I draw exactly one dollar a year salary. I provide my own horse."

"One dollar?" Peters asked, chuckling.

"Well, Mr. Peters, a man can't give his time away. His neighbors would look on that as charity. Texans won't stand for that."

The courtroom exploded with laughter, and Peters tried to regain the initiative.

"But, Major, everyone knows how you've spent money building bridges and constructing a road to Justiss Junction, a town named for you and situated on land mostly owned by you."

"Yes, sir, a county's got to grow," Charlie declared. "Needs bridges and roads to bring the people close. As for cost, I put up most of the lumber, and the ranch supplied the men. Sometimes I talked Art Stanley into helping out, and when the county had enough funds, we drew on 'em. Mostly, though, folks in Palo Pinto pitch in to build a road or raise a barn. We help each other. Those who've been lucky build a bridge. You help your neighbors, and they'll help you."

"And what exactly have county taxes paid for?" Peters asked, grinning. "Well?"

"Sad to say, Mr. Peters, the State of Texas wants some of it. We have a school in Palo Pinto, and it sometimes needs books."

"Your daughter teaches at that school, doesn't she?"

"That's right."

"And she's paid handsomely, I'm sure."

"Well, not that I've noticed. Her mama still sews for her little ones, and the schoolkids know the day of the week by which dress Vicki wears. I suspect you'll make something of the fact her husband serves the town as sheriff, too. Well, I was against that, but Bret's done a good job. I know you'd like to paint me as a scoundrel who's getting rich off his neighbors, but the truth is that taxes have gone down since I took over. Folks work hard for their money, and they don't like it wasted."

The crowd applauded again.

"So the price of your kind and benevolent oversight of Palo Pinto County hasn't been paid in cash," Peters said, making a quick turn toward the spectators. "It's been paid in other commodities, I fear. Who has bled for your success, Major? Indians? Who else? My client!"

Peters pranced over to his desk and picked up an Austin newspaper. In it a headline declared, SMALL RANCHERS PERSECUTED IN PALO PINTO COUNTY.

Charlie's face flashed red as Peters read how Isaac Kemp was stalked by notorious killers.

"Your Honor!" Ross cried out.

"I don't believe I hear any question," Judge Warren told Peters. "Do you have a question, Mr. Peters?"

"The whole state does, Your Honor. It asks, How long will men like Major Justiss be allowed to use its courts for their personal betterment?"

The crowd grumbled, and some shouted names or issued threats. Judge Warren hammered his gavel again, then asked Peters if he had a question or not.

"No, Your Honor, we know what's happened in Palo Pinto County. It remains to be seen if we can remedy those wrongs."

Charlie was excused, and Green called other witnesses. Billy testified to Kemp's threats and the recent acts of violence. Martin Schneider described Kemp's attack on his wagon, and little Alek appeared, bandaged leg and all, to add force to the testimony. It was late afternoon at that point, and the judge recessed the hearing.

"We did all right," Ben Green told Charlie. "Alek won their hearts, and you won their souls, Charlie. What's more, I could tell that those tax receipts made an impression on Judge Warren."

"Then we're winning?" Billy asked.

"So far. It's early, though."

Indeed it was. By the third day of the hearing, Peters had managed to fill the state's newspapers with all manner of rumor and slander. The more reputable dailies in Houston and Dallas avoided the unsubstantiated charges, and none of the papers in the northern and western sections of the state found much fault with shooting Indians, fighting Yankees, or building railroads. The worst slander quoted a man named Boswell saying that Charlie had hired Lafe Freeman to kill the Kemps and burn their house. The fact that Freeman had black skin stirred some resentment.

"It's all my doing," Billy told Charlie. "You warned me against sending for Lafe and Malachi, but I was worried."

"No, son, it's got nothing to do with you or Lafe or anybody else. Ross wired Senator Rogers. Somebody's made a point of sending this Boswell fellow around like a traveling player. We know where it's come from. If it hadn't been about Lafe, they'd chosen something else."

"I don't like it," Billy grumbled.

"I don't much care for it myself," Charlie said, "but there's not much we can do."

Billy thought otherwise. When Peters began parading his own witnesses, most of them Kemp cowhands who swore to every imaginable outrage, Billy called out loudly. "Where's Boswell? He speaks to everybody else. Bring him to court!"

The crowd picked up the chant, and several of the

newspaper correspondents wired their publishers about the call. When Boswell didn't appear, even the least ethical of the papers changed angles.

The final day of testimony featured Kermit Kemp. Solomon had returned to Palo Pinto, and Ike seemed unwilling to subject himself to any degree of examination. Kermit merely repeated his range companions' accusations.

"And just why do you think you're entitled to shift a boundary that's been recognized for over ten years?" Ross asked when Peters had finished his own questioning.

"Not recognized by me," Kermit replied. "Creeks come and go. Land's got to be surveyed."

"And did you survey the land before building your fence?" Ross asked. "Have you got a report for us to read?"

Kermit shifted nervously in his chair, and Ross repeated the question.

"We didn't need to," Kermit finally answered. "Any fool could see the natural lay of the land."

"Have you ever been taught the surveyor's trade?" Ben Green asked.

"No," Kermit mumbled.

"Then, you wouldn't be able to follow a bearing, lay a direct line from the creek, even if you had the degrees listed on a deed, would you?"

"I don't need such fancy figures or schoolbooks doodles," Kermit boasted. "The range ought to be open. Men ought to run longhorns like they used to, not those white-faced hunks of fat who can't last a hard winter."

"Who was it fenced the boundary between yourself and the Flying J, Mr. Kemp?" Ross asked.

Kermit scowled, then looked at his father with pleading eyes.

"Well?" Ross asked.

"Answer, Mr. Kemp," the judge insisted.

"We did," Kermit admitted. "But it was only on account of those darkie-lovin' Justisses. They'd send nightriders to murder Pa in his sleep!"

"Liar!" Billy cried, rising to his feet and starting down the aisle toward Kermit. "You wouldn't know the truth if it bit you."

"Silence!" Judge Warren called. "Return to your seat, young man, or I'll order you removed."

"See," Kermit said, laughing. "I told you how they are. They'll shoot us. Best lock 'em up, Judge."

"You appear remarkably healthy to me, Mr. Kemp," Judge Warren declared. "I don't see any bandages. Tell me, sir, did that little boy who was in here the other day seem menacing, too? You were afraid when you shot him, weren't you?"

"I never been afraid of nobody," Kermit boasted.

"I thought as much," the judge responded. "Maybe you should be afraid of me, young man, because tomorrow morning I'll have a decision to hand down."

"Your Honor, I still have witnesses to call," Peters protested.

"Do they have anything new to add?" the judge asked. "Because unless this mysterious Mr. Boswell appears or you intend to call Mr. Kemp over there, I don't care to listen. Well?"

Peters appeared slightly stunned at the judge's sudden impatience. The lawyer slumped in his chair, and Ike Kemp frowned.

"I do have some closing remarks," Peters announced.

"Make them brief," Judge Warren suggested. "And to the point."

"Yes, sir," Peters agreed, standing in place. There was no more pacing, none of the old animation in the lawyer's movements. Instead Peters repeated his earlier accusations, spoke of Charlie Justiss as the man who grabbed anything and everything he could while trampling those in his path.

"I ask Your Honor to consider the character of the men involved in this case," Peters said in conclusion. "Charlie Justiss and his sons are takers. My client, Isaac Kemp, like his biblical namesake, is a devout father, a struggler who has lost a wife and sons to those who took his lands. He's been hounded by hired gunmen, subjected to every manner of vile slander imaginable. All I ask, Your Honor, is that you allow Isaac Kemp to retain his lands, acres won by blood and toil."

Judge Warren nodded, then adjourned the proceedings. Ross and Ben Green led Charlie and Billy toward the door. They were all smiles.

"Tomorrow we'll be finished with this," Ross said, sighing. "I'll be glad to get home to Eliza and little Edward. Winter's in the air, and my room at the hotel lets every icy breath of wind in at night."

Charlie voiced similar sentiments.

"Tomorrow," Billy added. "Maybe this judge will convince those Kemps to abide by his ruling. I'd sure like to have a peaceful Christmas."

"Yes," Charlie agreed. "I got a letter from Ryan

saying Rachel and the orphans are planning something special this year."

"Right now a good night's sleep would be special," Ben Green said, yawning. "Until tomorrow, gentlemen."

"Till tomorrow," the other echoed.

Chapter Seven

A knock at the hotel room door roused Billy Justiss from a sound sleep. Beside him Colleen stirred as well.

"Billy, you up?" his brother Ross called from the other side of the door. "Billy?"

"I don't suppose this is a dream," Colleen grumbled. "Billy, you better go see what he wants."

Billy yawned, then rolled out of the bed and stumbled to the doorway. He cracked open the door and blinked his eyes until they began to focus.

"Get some clothes on," Ross commanded. "I just ran across Judge Warren. Seems John Peters wants to have breakfast with him. I think we ought to be close at hand. Could be Peters wants to bargain."

"Why now?" Billy asked, yawning once more. "The judge has surely decided things in his head."

"Most likely in our favor, too," Ross added. "I'd hate to think that skunk Kemp's got his old fox of a lawyer worming anything out of the judge, though. Let's go sit in on things."

"Wouldn't it be better to take Papa?"

"No, I don't think so," Ross said, leaning against the door. "Peters isn't going to say anything if Papa's about. He might not view us quite the same way."

"All right. Let me scrub my face and get some clothes on. I'll meet you downstairs."

"Five minutes, Billy."

"Sure," Billy grumbled.

He closed the door and hurried to get washed up and dressed. Colleen sat on the edge of the bed, an amused smile on her face.

"I guess this hasn't been much of an improvement on the ranch, eh?" he asked. "Back there it was your brother waking us at the crack of dawn. Now it's mine."

"At least Brian will grow out of it. He's just eight."

"Little brothers never grow out of being little brothers," Billy complained. "Big ones aren't a lot better, either."

Billy appeared downstairs a little before eight o'clock. He met Ross and Ben Green at the front desk, and the three of them made their way to the small cafe that occupied the rest of the hotel lobby. John Peters and Judge Warren sat at a small table on the left. Ross pointed to an empty table five feet away, and the three young men took their places there.

"Good morning, Judge," Ross said, nodding to Warren.

"Morning, son," the judge answered. "Never knew

so many lawyers to rise so early on the same day."

"Well, the law doesn't operate on banker's hours," Green said. "Got to protect our interests, you know."

"I do know," Judge Warren said, grinning. "But I wouldn't concern myself. I've made my decision, and it will be announced shortly in open court."

"But you haven't heard my offer," Peters objected.

"I'd be happy to listen, but it won't change my mind, Mr. Peters. Why don't you just have a bit of patience?"

"I'd hoped you might be more reasonable," Peters said icily. "I think it's best I leave now."

Peters rose slowly, glared scornfully at Ross Justiss in particular, then walked toward the wide swinging doors of the hotel.

"Guess he didn't like the menu," Warren observed. "Mind if I join you boys? I never did care to eat alone."

"Not at all," Ross answered. "Make yourself welcome."

A young waitress arrived then, and the foursome placed their breakfast orders. As they sipped coffee and devoured plates full of bacon and eggs, they failed to notice the arrival of a dust-covered cowboy with dark, heavy eyebrows and a droopy moustache. The newcomer kept his collar raised more to hide the slice shot from his left earlobe than to fend off the chill morning air. He strode past milling guests in the lobby and marched into the cafe.

"Sir?" a youngster carrying a platter of dirty plates to the kitchen asked. The stranger pushed the boy to the floor and drew out a cold Remington revolver.

"Warren!" the gunman shouted.

The judge turned instinctively. He saw the approaching assassin and raised his right hand as if to fend off the bullet even now waiting for the pistol's hammer to send it toward the defenseless judge.

"No!" Ross called, standing. Billy dove away.

The killer continued his approach, then calmly aimed and fired. The first bullet struck Crawford Warren in the right wrist and continued onward, slicing across the judge's left temple. A second shot slammed into Warren's chest, and a third struck the jaw, leaving the dying jurist's mouth hanging agape.

"Murder!" a waitress cried.

The gunman instinctively fired toward the outcry, and the unfortunate woman was struck in the throat. The murderer then glanced back at the judge, nodded toward the bloody corpse, and started retreating to the door. A terrified young woman and her young son blocked the path, and the killer brutally shoved them out of the way.

"Fetch a doctor!" Ben Green cried. "Get the sheriff!"

The stunned onlookers managed to regain their senses. Outside a shotgun exploded, and a pair of rapid pistol shots followed. Ross bent over the stricken judge, but Billy headed for the door. Warren was clearly finished, and the better course of action was to deal with the assassin.

Outside the hotel a pair of cowboys exchanged fire with the killer and a companion. The faint light and the fog of powder smoke hanging over the scene made locating a target difficult. A boy of fourteen or so appeared in the doorway with a Winchester, and Billy took the rifle.

"I can shoot," the boy objected. "That's my sister he's killed in there."

"Then you show me how I can get around to the right," Billy urged. "Trust the shooting to me, though."

The confidence in Billy's eyes seemed to persuade the boy. He led the way past some barrels and a wagon to where an alley began. Billy followed the youngster down the dark lane a hundred yards before emerging well down the street.

"There they are," the boy said, pointing to the pair of kneeling figures firing toward the hotel. Billy nudged his companion behind the protective wall of the adjacent building, then advanced a shell into the Winchester's firing chamber and took careful aim at the nearest shooter.

"Now," the boy urged.

Billy fired.

In the midst of the wild exchange up the street, the Winchester's shot was scarcely audible. Its effect was more telling. The shot smashed into the gunman's ribs and spun him around like a weathervane in an autumn twister. Billy fired a second time, and the gunman fell.

His companion scrambled down a nearby alley, climbed aboard a saddlehorse, and sped off northward. Billy recognized the assassin by his upturned collar.

"You got the wrong one," the boy grumbled as he snatched the Winchester from Billy's hands.

"Yes," Billy muttered. "But we'll catch him."

"You will?" the boy asked. "People get shot all the

time around here, and I don't see many killers brought to trial."

"I didn't promise you he'd see trial," Billy growled. "Only that he'd be caught."

The people of Jacksboro were outraged by the killings. In truth they were angered more by the senseless shooting of a cafe waitress than by Crawford Warren's death. The Missouri judge had never been any too popular in Jack County.

A posse was sweeping the county by early afternoon, and newspaper correspondents eager to hear Warren's judgment sent reports of the twin murders instead.

"Well, Kemp's had his way again," Billy grumbled when he met with his father and brother for lunch. "All this has been for naught!"

"No," Ross argued. "A record was kept, and I'll see to it personally that it's delivered to Austin. We'll get another judge assigned to read the transcript and render judgment."

"And just when will that be?" Charlie asked.

"It could be as early as next week or as late as January," Ross answered.

"Later even," Ben Green said. "Until the killer's brought in, no judge is apt to jump at the chance to take on the case."

"Anybody ever see that fellow before?" Charlie asked.

"No one in Jacksboro," Billy grumbled. "But I've heard of a man matching his description."

"Oh?" Charlie asked.

"Pat Cassidy spotted him riding the Albany road with Solomon Kemp. I'll bet he's posted somewhere. He went about it like a man who knew the business well."

"Didn't blink at shooting that girl," Ross commented. "I wish the fellow you hit had lasted long enough to talk."

"Someone will," Billy answered. "They always do."

Billy Justiss passed the balance of the day wading through piles of wanted posters in the county sheriff's office. Others were there, too — the hotel desk clerk, a handful of cafe diners, the woman shoved aside by the retreating killer. Billy knew what to look for, though. He remembered Pat Cassidy's description, especially the part about the missing earlobe. Without it the search might have proven difficult. As it was, Billy managed to pluck a hand-drawn poster from among a stack distributed by Wells Fargo.

COKE MERRICK, the name stenciled at the top read. The description fit the killer like a carefully tailored jacket. He was wanted for armed robbery and murder in Georgia, Texas, Colorado, and the New Mexico Territory.

"Sheriff?" Billy called. "Try this one for a fit."

Sheriff Powell Wilcox took the poster, read the description, then shoved it to the others.

"Could be," the desk clerk said.

"It's him," others announced. "Look at those eyebrows. And see here. It says he carries a

Remington."

"You folks certain?" Wilcox asked.

"I'm not likely to forget," one man said grimly. "I wasn't a foot away from that girl he shot. I'll never get the look of those cold, heartless eyes out of my mind."

The others voiced like sentiments, and Wilcox headed down the street to send out word on the telegraph.

"You figure they'll catch up with him, Mr. Justiss?" one of the witnesses asked.

"It says on that poster he's been wanted for seven years," Billy said. "He's eluded the law so far. If he's nearby, though, his chances are poor. It's hard to hide that chunk of missing ear."

With Coke Merrick identified as the slayer of Crawford Warren, Billy prepared to return to the Flying J that next morning. Ross and Ben Green would remain long enough to ensure the transport of the court records. Charlie Justiss had departed for Palo Pinto shortly after daybreak.

"It will be good to get home," Colleen said as she watched Billy load their belongings into a wagon for the long journey to the Flying J. "I could even put up with a houseful of children for a day or two."

"You want to stop by your papa's place and pick up Brian and Cornelia?"

"I didn't say I was crazy, did I?"

Billy laughed loudly, then helped her up onto the wagon seat. He joined her, and soon the wagon began rolling toward the southwest.

Billy supposed journeys home were never all that unpleasant, but riding along with Colleen on that crisp November morning was like strolling along the Brazos in April. The sun drenched the hills with golden light, and even if the trees appeared bare and somehow lonely, the familiarity of the landscape more than made up for that.

When Billy and Colleen reached Palo Pinto, though, all the warm feelings vanished. No sooner had Billy drawn the wagon to a halt in front of the courthouse than Bret Pruett trotted over and led Billy aside.

"What's wrong?" Billy asked. "Kemp hasn't raided the ranch?"

"No, but he hasn't been idle, either," Bret explained. "Come inside and have a look."

"Anything secret about this?" Billy said, nodding toward Colleen.

"I'm afraid not. The whole state's seen it."

Billy waved Colleen to his side, and together they followed Bret inside the courthouse. They headed for the land office. There Bret stopped. On the desk where Ross Justiss usually recorded deeds lay a dozen newspapers. Each one was turned to an account of the death of Judge Crawford Warren.

"Here," Bret said, passing the first to Billy. "Read the bad news."

"What?" Billy cried as he scanned the first paragraph. "It says here that the judge was asked to breakfast by Papa. That's a lie. Why, Papa wasn't even there. It was John Peters who asked the judge to meet him, and they did meet. The judge joined us afterward."

"The Jacksboro *News* said all that, and most of the other papers followed suit. The strange thing is these same papers are the ones that carried those other slanders last week. I guess the thing that rankles me, Billy, is how so much of this got out so fast. It's as if somebody expected it to happen."

"Maybe somebody did," Billy remarked. "I saw Peters leave. He walked straight to the hotel door. Wasn't five, ten minutes after that when this Merrick fellow stormed in and killed the judge."

"Quite a coincidence."

"So I was thinking. I just wonder if somebody in Jacksboro might not've seen the two of 'em talking. That'd be a big help in tying Kemp in with the killing."

"Read the rest, Billy," Bret advised. "According to those accounts, Kemp was going to get the ruling just the way he wanted it."

"That's clearly a lie," Billy said angrily. "You should have seen Peters sweating that morning."

"That'll come out when they get a ruling on the transcript."

"Sure. When will that be, Bret, January? Later? You know what people are going to figure when they read all this? They'll say Charlie Justiss is taking the law in his own hands, that he's taking after the Kemps. And if Kemp decides to strike back, well, who can blame him, right?"

"That's what scares the devil out of me, Billy," Bret said, slamming his fist against the newspaper-strewn desk. "Keep a close watch on Caddo Creek, my friend."

"I will. But what's more important, though, is

locating this Coke Merrick. He can set things straight."

"I thought about that. I had some new posters printed and sent out on the stage. If I was Kemp, though, I'd find him first and do him in."

"Then, I guess we'll have to find him first."

Billy kept that in mind as he drove Colleen back to the ranch. As soon as he got the bags stowed away, he sent Danny Seavers out to Caddo Creek to fetch Wes Tyler and Lafe Freeman. They rode in together at dusk, and Billy explained the problem.

"Merrick, huh?" Lafe asked. "Yeah, I heard of him. He plied his trade down south for a time, mostly shootin' farmers' kids from ambush as I heard it."

"Sounds familiar," Wes commented. "Maybe this Merrick and our friends the Kemps had dealings before."

"Well, if I was Merrick, I'd keep a weather eye out for Kemp now," Billy said, gazing with wary eyes toward the west. "It's surely to Kemp's advantage to have Merrick out of the way. One other thing. Pat Cassidy said he spotted Soloman with somebody else, a tall stranger with a scar on one cheek. You spot anybody like that?"

"No," Wes answered, shaking his head. "Creek's been pretty quiet since the trial."

"Scar?" Lafe asked. "Across the left cheek, long and straight like from a cavalry saber?"

"Sounds like it," Billy told him. "Sounds familiar?"

"Al Samuels," Lafe declared. "He used to hang around down south, too. Army deserter. A good

317

shot with a rifle, friends, and not afraid to show it. He killed a U.S. marshal up in the Nations. Malachi and I chased him close to three weeks, ran him off into Apache country. I heard he was dead."

"Guess not," Billy said, frowning.

"He will be, though," Lafe promised. "He got four of my men killed when he deserted his post out on the Llano. I caught up with him once before, gave him that pretty scar he wears."

"Then, it sounds to me like he's got cause to be interested in you, too," Wes pointed out. "Maybe you and Malachi ought to watch yourselves."

"Can't," Lafe said, his eyes catching fire. "We've got to go find Coke Merrick."

"And Samuels?" Billy asked.

"Him, too," Lafe added. "They'll be in the same place."

Chapter Eight

Bret's posters drew no response, but even in the wilds of west Texas it was difficult to become invisible. A man with an earlobe shot away and another with a scar across half his face made an impression. Posters might help a sheriff identify a killer, but other eyes sought out Samuels and Merrick as well. Teamsters hauling freight for Art Stanley searched the hills and creeks of Jack and Parker counties for the two gunmen. Lafe Freeman and Malachi Johnson combed the windswept grasslands to the northwest. And a small army of former railroad orphans kept watch on the station towns along the Ft. Worth and Western.

In the end, though, it was Luis Morales who stumbled across Coke Merrick. On the first freezing morning in December, Luis delivered a string of ten mustang ponies to the livery at Potter's City, a market town twenty-five miles west of Palo Pinto. The two outlaws paid little attention to Luis and his two young wranglers, but Luis wasted little time in hurrying word to Palo Pinto.

Sixteen-year-old Ramon Hernandez led Bret Pruett and Alex Tuttle to the Flying J Ranch early the next morning.

"I already wired Lafe," Bret explained. "He and Malachi were in Albany. They'll meet us in Breckenridge. Together we'll head south to Potter's City. I thought you'd best come along to make sure we had the right man, though."

"I'll get my rifle," Billy told his brother-in-law.

By the time he bid Colleen farewell and fetched the rifle, the ranch crew had a horse saddled and waiting.

"You can head along home now," Bret told Ramon. "We can find Potter's City just fine."

"And Luis?" the young man asked.

"We'll send him back as well," Billy said, grinning. "With luck, tomorrow or the day after."

Ramon nodded, then turned his horse and headed north toward the river. Bret led his companions westward, swinging below the Albany road so as to avoid any chance sighting by the Kemps.

After picking up Lafe and Malachi, the little band of vengeful riders headed south. Billy couldn't help noticing the varied faces of his companions. Bret appeared confident but cautious. His eyes swept the hillsides and occasionally glanced behind as if he felt someone trailing along. Tut was nervous, a hair reluctant even. The deputy had fought too many battles, Billy supposed, to feel an eagerness for hunting men.

Lafe and Malachi were the most difficult to read. The two old friends sat their horses lightly, and their fierce gaze fixed on the trail ahead. Clothed in buffalo-hide coats, it was easy to tell how they'd gained the name buffalo soldiers while riding in the cavalry after the war. Their steel-cold nerves had earned them the respect of the Comanches. Billy figured Lafe and Malachi were already rehearsing their strategy for bringing down Merrick and Samuels.

Potter's City was scarcely an hour from Breckinridge under ordinary circumstances. That afternoon the five riders from Palo Pinto County arrived in less than fifty minutes. Bret set off immediately to locate Luis. Then the horse trader led Billy to a small ramshackle hut that served as a sheriff's office.

"I never got one of these," the lawman explained when Bret drew out a pair of wanted posters. "Nobody pays much attention to Potter's City, you know."

"Maybe they will from now on," Bret said. "Luis says they're sitting at a bar in the cantina down the street. We can take them in easy enough, but I wanted you to know what we were doing."

"There's almost $8,000 reward on the pair of them," the sheriff declared. "You hold your horses. This is my town and my jurisdiction. I'll do the arresting."

"Keep the reward," Billy grumbled. "Remember, though, we really don't want Merrick shot. It's important we find out who paid him to murder Judge Warren."

321

"He the one did that?" the sheriff asked. "Well, if you ask me, he's pretty dangerous to go askin' to throw his hands up and surrender."

"Thought we might be more persuasive," Bret said. "A pistol in the back encourages respect for the law."

"Does at that," the sheriff agreed. "Let's go."

The sheriff led the way down the street. Outside, Lafe and Malachi fell in.

"What's the plan?" Lafe asked Billy as they closed in on the cantina.

"We're goin' to walk right in and take 'em," the sheriff boasted. "Don't you worry, boys. It's all in good hands."

Lafe frowned, then pulled Billy aside.

"There's a side door to that place," Lafe announced. "Malachi and I'll watch it. You watch yourself, boss. Those two are quick, and they could have help. There's a third one in there."

Billy nodded, then trotted over to pass the news to Bret. The sheriff paid little attention to the warning. Instead he burst through the door with drawn pistol and called for Merrick to raise his hands.

"You others stand awful still," the sheriff warned. "We've got you—"

The sheriff never finished his sentence. Merrick turned quick as a cat and killed the lawman with a single shot through the head. Samuels and a tall, thin companion drew their guns and opened fire as well. Billy dropped to the ground as the door exploded. Bret and Tut huddled behind a poker table and answered the fire.

"Coke, let's go!" Al Samuels called, and the outlaws hurried toward the side door, led by their unknown companion. It was the thin man's misfortune to open the door. Malachi Johnson sent him stumbling back into the cantina, a bullet through the heart.

"Lord, they're all around us!" Samuels shouted. "Window, Coke."

"Give it up, Merrick!" Bret yelled.

Merrick resumed firing, then threw a chair through a rear window and led the way out of the cantina. Billy slid along the wall and located the fleeing killers fifty yards away, racing toward a pair of grazing horses. He managed to fire twice, but the range was too great. Merrick and Samuels mounted the horses and headed west.

As the smoke inside the cantina began to clear, Lafe entered frowning.

"That fool of a sheriff sure did make a mess of this," Lafe declared.

"Well, he paid for his mistake," Bret said, nudging the lawman's corpse with a boot. "We'd better catch our breath and get after them."

"Leave 'em to run a spell," Lafe suggested. "Those horses just finished haulin' in a stage. Bareback on tired mounts, Merrick and Samuels won't get far. We'll close with 'em tonight, take 'em easy in the dark."

"Senor, what do I do with these men?" the bartender asked, peering around the counter.

"Best bury the sheriff," Bret said. "This other one we'll take back to Palo Pinto. Could be he's posted."

"And who will pay for my cantina?"

Billy stared at the shambles that had earlier been

an orderly if somewhat dingy establishment. He plucked a twenty-dollar gold piece from his pocket and placed it on a nearby table.

"That will not pay for my tables," the smallish man complained. "And what of my window?"

"Collect from Merrick," Lafe suggested.

"He is gone, senor."

"He's likely left some horses, maybe some personals here somewhere. Sell 'em."

The cantina owner grinned and motioned to a slender boy in the back of the room. The two of them began sweeping up the splinters and broken glass. Billy moved aside so Lafe and Malachi could carry the corpse of the third gunman outside. Then Billy himself left the place.

They waited a little more than an hour before trailing Merrick and Samuels. In that time they managed to enjoy a meager dinner of tamales and refried beans. Bret also dispatched Luis back to Palo Pinto with the dead outlaw.

"Five of us are plenty to do what's left," Bret declared. "Truth is, Billy, I wish you'd go back, too."

"No, it's personal where I'm concerned," Billy told them. "And I mean to ensure Merrick survives to come to trial."

"You don't need Samuels, though," Lafe declared. "He's mine."

Lafe's eyes caught fire, and Bret shrugged. Al Samuels was posted dead or alive, after all, and Bret lacked the authority to stop Lafe even if it were possible to do so.

"Come on," Bret told his companions. "Let's get mounted and get it over with. Lafe, you lead the way."

The ex-buffalo soldier, ex-bounty killer, and railroad guard kicked his horse into motion, and the hunt was on.

The weary animals didn't carry Samuels and Merrick far. The outlaws made camp just above the railroad tracks in a steep ravine no more than a mile from Potter's City. Billy guessed they hoped to board a train headed west. No train arrived, though, and the ravine was little better than a snare for the killers.

Bret planned the approach carefully. He and Tut would start down from the east while Malachi descended in like manner from the west. Billy and Lafe would remain on top, ready to shoot if either killer tried to fire.

"You watch Merrick," Lafe whispered as the others started down the steep embankment. "Samuels is mine."

"You must want him pretty badly," Billy pointed out.

"Bad as anybody I ever knew. He put a whip to my back, and he killed two boys close to me as brothers."

"Wouldn't it be better to have him hung?"

"He's slippery, Billy Justiss. He's like a snake, that Samuels. He worms his way right out of jailhouses. Last sheriff had him locked up boasted how killin' a colored man ought not to even be a crime. No, I'm all the law that's needed where Al Samuels is concerned."

Billy frowned and concentrated on Coke Merrick. In the fading light it wasn't easy to tell one from the other. The pair sat beside a small fire, shivering as the growing cold penetrated their cotton shirts.

"Hold still!" Bret suddenly shouted. "You're under arrest!"

"Al!" Merrick yelled as he reached for his pistol.

Billy watched Lafe fire twice in rapid order, and Samuels's head snapped back. Billy himself fired his rifle only when Merrick aimed the deadly Remington at Bret.

Alex Tuttle fired, too, and the pair of bullets hit Coke Merrick from opposite directions at the same instant, toppling the killer to his knees.

"Al!" the outlaw screamed as he fell, bleeding, face first into the sandy base of the ravine. Bret and Tut were on top of Merrick the next moment, and Malachi Johnson appeared beside Al Samuels as well.

"Bret?" Billy called down.

"Merrick's still alive," Bret answered. "Won't be doing any more business with his right hand, but he'll survive to stand trial. Samuels is finished."

Billy worked his way to the bottom of the ravine. Merrick was alive. That was good. They'd bind the wounds and return the murderer for trial. As for Samuels . . .

"Why don't you finish the job?" Merrick asked the next morning when Bret and Tut roused him from a restless sleep.

"You know it might go easier on you, Merrick, if you told us why you shot the judge," Bret said. "The tendons in your right hand are smashed. You can't even move the fingers, I'll wager. Besides that, you've got a shattered kneecap. If you own up to everything, some judge might take kindly to giving you an easy sentence."

"Don't make me laugh," Merrick growled. "No judge is goin' to let me off. I shot one of their own. Besides, I've already got a noose waitin' for me in Waco. I'm dead any way you figure it. Why help you out?"

"My father's got a lot of friends in Austin," Billy told the killer. "He returns favors."

"Your pa?" Merrick said, laughing so that his smashed hand ached. "You don't even know what you're up against. You won't find out from me, either. I promise you that."

"So much more's the shame of it," Billy said, sighing. "Well, your hanging will draw a fair crowd, I'll wager. And the newspapers will flock to your trial."

"Sure they will," Merrick boasted. "I could tell 'em it was Charlie Justiss paid me to shoot the old judge, you know. I might just do that if you take me in."

"One or two might even believe it," Bret said. "The rest would wonder why Charlie's own son-in-law and his third son brought you to trial, though. You and Peters were seen, too."

"Nobody'll testify to it," Merrick declared. "People know what happens to witnesses who buck

John Peters."

"Who'll tend to such matters now?" Bret asked. "We pulled Kemp's fangs when we settled with Samuels and brought you in."

"That'll be the day," Merrick said, laughing loudly. "Wait and see, Sheriff. Wait and see."

Chapter Nine

It was two weeks before Coke Merrick was fit for trial. A Houston lawyer named Hulen arrived to handle the defense, but the case was clearly hopeless. Merrick's cold-blooded murder of Judge Warren and the waitress had been witnessed by a room filled with people. Even Hulen's presentation of another man with a similar notch shot from his ear failed to sway any juror. Most of the bystanders hadn't noticed Merrick's disfigured ear. Few forgot his cold, heartless eyes, though.

Despite the parade of witnesses, Merrick showed little concern. He often shouted threats or exchanged comments with the presiding judge.

"They hang a man for shootin' one judge, I hear," Merrick remarked. "They make him governor for shootin' two."

On the final day of the trial Merrick took the witness stand. Armed guards kept watch outside the doors, and Merrick himself was shackled.

"Coke, do you deny killing Judge Warren?" Hulen asked point blank.

"I did the shootin'," Merrick answered. "As for

the killin', I was no more responsible than the gun."

"How is that possible, Coke? You're a thinking, knowing man. You made the decision to fire, didn't you?"

"No, sir. I only do as I'm told. I was hired."

Billy felt his heart flutter when Hulen asked, "Who hired you, Coke? The people want to know."

"I thought everybody knew," Merrick said, pausing to stare coldly at Billy Justiss in particular. "Charlie Justiss."

The courtroom erupted with cries of disbelief, and reporters scribbled in their notebooks.

"Liar!" Billy hollered.

"Who'd know better'n me?" Merrick asked with icy, hateful eyes. "I'm the one due to be hanged just before Christmas, aren't I?"

Merrick hopped to his feet and tried to scramble down the aisle, but his ankle chains tangled, and he fell to the ground, a heap of whimpering criminal. Pain from his shattered knee swept through him, and he stared pathetically at the barred windows. Desperation drove him on, though, and he paused only when he reached Billy's place in the second row of the gallery.

"I warned you," Merrick barked. "I told you I'd do it."

"Nothing can help you now," Billy replied. "The case is cut and dried, and you're certain to hang."

Merrick merely smiled. Billy turned his head as a pair of Jack County deputies dragged Merrick back to the witness chair.

"I've told the whole of it!" Merrick shouted. "Hang Charlie Justiss!"

Some in the courtroom muttered their agreement, but most hooted and shouted questions. Afterward, Parker Ward, the state prosecutor, reminded the jury of testimony pairing Merrick with John Peters, and questioning Merrick's honesty.

The jury responded by finding Merrick guilty of murder, and the judge passed sentence immediately.

"Death by hanging," the newspaper headlines shouted.

Billy noted with little satisfaction that Merrick had been right about one thing. The hanging was scheduled for December 21. Coke Merrick would die four days short of Christmas.

In the intervening days, Billy tried to ignore the taunts and accusations flying around Jack County. In Palo Pinto, Charlie Justiss's detractors were more cautious. Even so, it seemed as if a stain had spattered the family's honor, and all the newspaper retractions and rebuttal essays wouldn't erase the doubt that had been raised in many people's minds about the Justiss family.

Billy rode to Jacksboro the day before the hanging to plead with Merrick to recant his accusation.

"Sure, boy," Merrick said, grinning. "You recant the rope from around my neck, I'll say anything you want."

"Doesn't it bother you to go to the grave with a lie on your lips?" Billy asked.

"Justiss, I'll burn in hell a dozen times over for the things I've done. You think a lie means anything? I've killed twenty people, maybe more. I've

331

got nothin' but hate for you and your family."

"And what about Ike Kemp? We all know he was behind it. He's let you take the full force of the law on your shoulders. Where's he been? He didn't even appear at the trial."

"Boy, you're too stupid to see the end of your nose," Merrick said, laughing loudly. "Come to the hangin' tomorrow. Watch me swing."

Billy wondered if all condemned men lost their senses. There seemed little else to do in those circumstances. Some faced death with a Bible and a prayer. Others spit and bawled like babies. Maybe Merrick found defiance a comfort.

Billy did stay for the hanging. He hoped perhaps the sight of the gallows might encourage a midnight confession. He was sorely disappointed. Merrick wasn't the least bit sorry, and he stepped down the street toward the gallows with a brisk, lively step.

A crowd of fascinated onlookers gathered around, bundled in woolen cloaks to fend off an icy breeze. There was a taste of snow in the air, and children vocally prayed for a Christmas blizzard.

"Mornin', friends!" Merrick called as he climbed atop the first gallows step. "Glad you all could come to see me."

"To see you hanged, you no-account murderin' trash!" someone shouted. Another threw a rock which struck Merrick's forehead, dazing him.

"Leave him be!" Sheriff Wilcox pleaded. "He'll be dead soon enough."

"Not soon enough for us!" the crowd thundered.

Then, so suddenly that the people could scarce believe it, Coke Merrick was swallowed by a surge of bundled onlookers. A single shot split the air, and people began to run for cover. One of the deputies staggered and fell. A second soon followed. Coke Merrick shed his bonds and limped down the street to where a horse waited.

"Stop him!" the crowd demanded, and a pair of shotguns opened fire from the barber shop and a mercantile next door. Merrick aimed a pistol with his left hand and blew to pieces the barber's window.

"You fools!" Merrick cried. "You thought you'd hang me, did you?"

Then, with a sudden explosion of energy, Merrick pulled himself atop the horse and slapped the animal into motion. He rode toward the end of the street, shouting curses as he went. As he passed the hotel, though, Kermit Kemp and two cowboys jumped into the street and fired a staggering volley at the escaping villain.

Merrick had only an instant to see what was happening. It wasn't enough time to halt the horse or fire in response. The bullets slammed into his chest and tore the life from him. He fell like a heavy oak branch and rolled in the dusty street before coming to a halt. His eyes flooded with shock and dismay and, most of all, surprise. Then he died.

"Who got him?" someone called out.

"Let's buy him a drink!" another added.

"Was fortunate you boys were around," someone else announced.

"Well, my pa heard there might be an escape attempt!" Kermit shouted above the din.

"I'll bet," Billy muttered.

"You're a hero, son," John Peters proclaimed.

"Well, unlike some, Ike Kemp believes in seeing justice done," Kermit declared. "Hear that, you Justisses?"

"I hear it," Billy answered, striding through the nervous crowd until he was no more than ten feet from Kermit. "Mighty interesting how you Kemp boys knew just where to wait, huh? I don't suppose dead Merrick could pose much of a problem."

"Problem?" Kermit asked, laughing.

"Might be he planned to make a little speech atop the gallows, tell how you, Peters, sent him inside the hotel to shoot the judge."

"Slander!" Peters screamed.

"You say you believe in truth and justice?" Billy asked. "Let's see how you feel when the judge in Austin rules on the trial transcript. How much of a believer in truth will Ike Kemp be then?"

"You best worry about yourself!" Kermit suggested. "These folks don't take kindly to having their prisoners freed."

"That's right!" someone shouted, and the crowd grew unruly.

"And just who was it brought Coke Merrick in?" Billy asked. "He threatened to accuse my father if we locked him up. If we'd been guilty, why wouldn't we have shot Merrick dead? Instead we doctored him to health and brought him here for trial. Think about that, friends! We're not the ones who twist the truth, who silence killers so they can't speak the truth. You think about all this, and you'll come to the sensible conclusion. It's Ike Kemp mangles the law, shoots judges, and changes property lines. All I do is take up for my family, protect my stock and my property. You'd do the same!"

The crowd began to shift its sentiments, and Kermit backed his way to the hotel. He gazed nervously at Peters, then at the two Kemp hands. One raised his rifle and fired at the sky. The shot sent the angry crowd surging forward, and Kermit Kemp was rapidly engulfed. If the sheriff hadn't intervened, the angry townfolk might have hung someone after all that chill December morning.

Even so, Kermit, Peters, and the two hands were soundly thrashed.

"I'll remember this, Justiss," Kermit called when the crowd finally broke up. "We'll meet again some dark night on the trail."

"Yes, I know," Billy replied. "That's where you do your best work. Only remember, Kermit, I'm not a twelve-year-old farm kid gone to fill water barrels."

Yes, Billy thought as he glared at Kermit Kemp's battered face. We've had the trial. You move your fence again or cross the creek, somebody will die. Billy touched the cold barrel of the Colt revolver on his hip. He was half-ready to start the killing right then. He knew, though, that the chance would come soon enough.

He turned and headed for the livery. It was a long ride back to Palo Pinto, to home. Colleen would be waiting anxiously. And he had news for his father.

IV. War

Chapter One

Christmas provided a very brief interlude of peace. The Justiss family gathered at Buck Creek with Ryan, Rachel, and their small army of orphans in the hope that the youngsters' good cheer might prove contagious. Chris and Joe were home from school, and Vicki and Eliza had the grandchildren there as well. But the warmth and belonging provided by the season passed all too quickly.

Others had also returned home. Alice Tyler and her little ones had gone back to the line cabin above Caddo Creek.

"Families should be together at Christmas," Alice had told Billy Justiss, and he hadn't argued. He had asked Lafe Freeman and Malachi Johnson to make their headquarters out that way, though, and the range crew had hastily built the former buffalo soldiers a small cabin a quarter mile north of Wes's place.

January greeted Texas with a full-blown blizzard. Sleet and snow lashed at the landscape, and for days no human ventured out into the open. Stock suffered, and when the storm finally relented, the range crews had their work cut out for them. The Flying J's cowboys herded the scattered stock back to the Brazos and repaired damaged roofs and broken fenceposts. Across Caddo Creek, Kemp's outfit appeared to be doing much the same thing.

"Well, at least once this stuff melts, we'll have some water back in some of the streams," Wes Tyler told Billy Justiss. "Maybe it'll keep those Kemps busy awhile, too."

"I hope so," Billy mumbled. "Ross says they'll be appointing a judge to look over the trial record next week."

"Then, we won't have peace for long," Wes said, kicking a stone across the snow-covered hillside. "Maybe Alice and the kids ought to go back to the big house."

"I was thinking that myself," Billy admitted. "Truth is, after a day or two at Buck Creek, I can't get used to all the quiet we're having back at the house. Even with Colleen's family there, the house seems empty. I suggested Joe and Chris come out, but Mama won't hear of that."

"Best get busy and have some kids of your own," Wes advised. "You don't watch out, little Jake's goin' to beat you to it."

340

"I wouldn't say things were that bad," Billy said, laughing. "Not everyone waits to get married till he has gray hair, you know, Wes."

The snow quickly faded into memory, and the days grew brighter. Chill winds still tormented the county by night, but the late mornings and early afternoons were quite pleasant. Billy often rode along what remained of Bluff Creek with Colleen and her brothers and sisters. He even managed to escape once or twice from the obligations of running the ranch long enough to take Brian fishing.

In mid-January, Ross left to oversee the review of the court transcripts in Austin. The new judge, one Ruben Truesdale by name, had asked that both parties appear in person to sum up their arguments. Charlie Justiss had decided to go along to learn the final verdict, and his wife, Angela, chose to accompany him. Chris and Joe jumped at the chance to visit the state capital with their parents prior to returning to school the following week.

"We'd be glad for Viktor and Jake to come out to the ranch, Mama," Billy had told his mother when he heard the news. "The Cassidys have headed back to the farm now, and the house seems awful empty."

"Maybe on Saturday," Angela Justiss had replied. "With the weather so unreliable, I hate for them to make the long trip to school. Eliza's all alone, too. Vik and Jake can be a big help to her."

"Well, that would seem to be best," Billy agreed. "I'll bring 'em out Friday night, though. Saturday, if the sun's out, we can dip a line in the river or ride

341

out to the cliffs."

"Have them at Eliza's early enough on Sunday that they get a fair night's rest, though. We should be home Monday ourselves."

Billy nodded, then led his father aside a moment.

"Papa, I know you expect the judgment to go in our favor. How do you think Kemp's going to react?"

"I've thought about that, son," Charlie answered. "He could bide his time till spring, hit us when we're busy with roundup, or he could strike now. With Lafe and Malachi around, we're not nearly as vulnerable as we were, though."

"They won't be with you in Austin," Billy pointed out. "You watch yourself. Don't forget what happened to Judge Warren."

"I won't," Charlie pledged. "Bowie's assigned us a pair of railroad guards while we're on the train, and the governor's given me a pair of Rangers to watch for trouble at the hotel in Austin. Besides, I don't imagine too many gunhands will care to work for Ike Kemp after they hear what happened to Coke Merrick. None too healthy being in his employ."

"Kermit's still about."

"I'll keep a weather eye open."

"Do that, Papa."

"You do the same, Billy," Charlie said, clasping his son's hands. "You're far closer to the storm that we will be."

Billy nodded, but in truth he was far more concerned for his mother and father down south.

The days ahead proved uneventful, though. Friday when Billy drove a wagon into town to fetch his young brothers to the ranch, Bret passed along a telegram.

CASE WON, it read. HOME MONDAY. PAPA

"Does Kemp know?" Billy asked.

"From the look of Kermit and Solomon when they were in town this morning, I'd say so. Tut or I one will ride the Albany road at night for a while. For sure until Charlie gets back."

"I'd appreciate that," Billy said, stuffing the telegram into his coat pocket. "You two would be welcome to pass the night at the line camp if you'd like."

"I would, but that won't work," Bret explained. "It can't appear as if I'm taking sides."

"You could stay with Pat Cassidy."

"I thought it might be better if we passed the wee hours at the Eppler place. It's not much farther, and the captain's not related to anybody involved."

"Fair enough. But we keep a guard up all night at the camp, and there'll always be coffee brewing."

"I don't suppose it'd hurt anything to drop by for a cup of coffee," Bret said, grinning.

Billy then headed toward the schoolhouse to get Viktor and little Jake. The boys met him halfway, their shaggy blond hair dancing in the afternoon breeze.

"Billy, I know we are to go with you tonight," Viktor said, "but Alek Schneider asks us to visit his farm. We have not been there for a long time. Not since . . ."

Viktor drew his younger brother to his side and frowned heavily. Billy understood. They hadn't been out there since Rolf had left. Their sisters were buried there, and powerful memories lurked there-abouts. It seemed like the boys had been Justisses forever, but in truth it had barely been a year.

"You'll at least have supper with us?" Billy asked. "Colleen and Enuncia have been planning something special for you all week."

"Good!" Jake exclaimed.

Viktor placed a hand over Jake's mouth and quickly searched both sides of the street.

"Eliza is most kind," the boy said, "but she cooks not so well. We go after dinner, yes?"

"Sure," Billy said, motioning them along toward the wagon.

Colleen was a little disappointed to learn her little brothers-in-law wouldn't stay the night, but she de-lighted in seeing them both stuffed with pork pie and lemon cake. Billy wondered if the pair would be able to keep from bursting their britches, but Jake pointed out that his had always been a bit too big. To prove the point, he inhaled and placed both hands between belt and belly.

Viktor had reached that stage of life when it seemed he grew an inch for every step he took, and overfeeding him was nigh impossible. A boy not yet fifteen, he'd attained the appetite of a full roundup crew.

"The Schneiders don't eat so well," Viktor explained after Jake had gone to wash his face and hands. "We could maybe take something with us?"

"There's half a cake and some tarts," Colleen said. "Would you take them along, Viktor? Your brother

344

and I'll never eat them, and they're wasted on the horses."

Viktor beamed a smile, then raced over and kissed her cheek. He then hurriedly withdrew, and Colleen laughed.

"Didn't give her much of a chance to return the favor," Billy pointed out.

"Hush, Billy Justiss," Colleen scolded. "It's more than I get from Flynn, and he's *my* brother. You remember, Viktor, that I have a kiss to give you."

When Jake returned, scrubbed to Viktor's satisfaction, Billy led the boys outside. They hopped in the back of the wagon, and Billy turned the team down the time-worn trail south alongside Bluff Creek and on toward the Albany road and the Schneider place.

It wasn't such a long journey, but the twilight chill encouraged Billy to hurry. The sun was fast settling into the hills to the west, and Viktor and Jake huddled together beneath a woolen blanket.

"If you're cold, I can pick up an extra blanket at the line camp," Billy told them. "The trail takes us right past there."

"We're all right," Viktor said. "In Germany sometimes the snows would be as tall as me. We would go sledding then. Rolf and I once took our sleds down a mountain. We went so fast I thought we would never stop."

"Next time it snows, I'll bet I can put together a sled for you," Billy promised. "Ryan and I made one once. We even skated on Bluff Creek a few times when we were younger. Of course, there isn't much creek to freeze this year."

"*Ja,* summer was long this year," Viktor said,

345

sighing.

Billy gazed at the boy. Viktor whispered to Jake in German, and clearly the two were remembering other times. Billy didn't know if it was because of winter or perhaps because their parents had been gone that brought on such recollections. Since coming to live with Charlie Justiss, Billy hadn't heard Viktor speak ten words of German.

Suddenly the words stopped. An armadillo or a skunk scampered through the yellow buffalo grass just ahead. Off toward Caddo Creek a wolf howled. Then Billy heard something else, a faint rattling sound like beans falling on a hard wooden floor. He suddenly froze. Viktor's face paled, and Jake pulled the blanket up over his face and burrowed his way under the wagon seat.

"Billy?" Viktor said nervously.

"I know," Billy answered. "Somebody's shooting up ahead. Vik, you ever drive a wagon?"

"Ja," the youngster answered. "Yes, I can do it."

"I'm going to turn us around. Then I want you to hop up here and get the two of you back to the ranchhouse. Tell the crew to get mounted, get their guns, and head for the line camp. Understand?"

"You must come with us," Viktor declared.

"No, it's best I see what I can do to help," Billy told them, pulling a rifle he hoped wouldn't be needed from its place beside the brake. "Hop up here and get going," Billy added after he'd turned the wagon. "Don't you stop for anything, either. Tell Hector what I said. Then go inside and stay under cover."

Viktor hesitated a moment, but the urgency in

346

Billy's eyes left no room for argument. Viktor took his place on the seat and urged the horses into motion. Quickly the wagon began rolling back toward the house. Jake poked his head out long enough to gaze with concern, and Billy gave the six-year-old a confident nod. Then the wagon sped off over the hillside, and Billy started toward the line camp.

By the time he covered the three quarters of a mile to the camp, the firing had intensified. The line camp stood atop a gentle rise of ground maybe fifty yards across. The buildings were arranged in horseshoe fashion with Wes's cabin on one end, a stable and hay barn in the center, and the long bunkhouse at the far end. A pair of rifles fired steadily from the bunkhouse, and several guns appeared to be blazing away from the cabin. The other buildings were as quiet as death, and Billy hoped that meant there'd been no one there to begin with. Normally the younger hands slept in the stable.

The attackers shielded themselves by creeping through the brush just above Caddo Creek. Tangled ravines and boulders dotted that area. It provided good cover for the night guard Wes posted, and for defense against raiders from the far side of the creek. Somehow the raiders had managed to sweep in and hit the camp by surprise, though.

Well, Billy thought, I've got a surprise of my own. He then slipped through the gnarled junipers and eerie white oaks to the south. He kept low lest some stray shot from the cabin strike before he could circle around behind the bushwhackers. Kemp had likely decided to strike as soon as the verdict came

347

down. Billy boiled over with rage as he thought of the Tyler kids huddling in terror inside the cabin, of young cowboys like Tucker Spears and Barret Jenkins fighting for their lives. But in a sense he was glad all the uncertainty was past them now. Kemp had made things simple. He'd declared war, and the Flying J outfit had fought before. They would again.

Shortly Billy reached a large outcropping of rock. He and Ryan called the place Shiprock because it resembled the prow of a ship pictured in one of their mother's old books. From the top a good marksman could sweep half of Caddo Creek with rifle fire.

Well, there was no hope of doing that in the faint light that remained, but the spot was well-protected, and if he couldn't be certain of shooting anybody, he could certainly fire at the powder flashes and make them more than a little unsettled.

Billy lacked his father's military experience. He had no head for tactics, and he'd rarely led men in a fight of any consequence. He had an instinct for survival, though, and he knew that country like the tip of his nose. Wherever the Kemp crew was, Billy's rifle would soon fix them in a crossfire between Shiprock and the line camp.

He climbed the rock carefully. Then, at the top, he made himself a shooting stand by piling loose rocks in a low wall. Finally he watched for the tongues of yellow flame that marked the discharge of rifles. He fired at the nearest.

"Lord, where did that come from?" a voice cried out.

Billy fired again, and a scream pierced the January night.

"Kermit, they've gotten in behind us!"

A pair of rifles opened up on the cabin, and Billy delivered three quick shots in their direction. He heard someone tear through the brush while a second figure stumbled out into the open, only to be cut down by rifle fire from the cabin.

"Let's get out of here!" one of the raiders called, and his companions apparently shared the sentiment. Billy counted five, maybe six shadowy figures retreating across the creek from the broken ground below him. Others fled from farther down the creek. Winchesters opened up a hot fire from the creek itself, and the raiders turned in desperate flight.

Billy watched them go with a kind of grim satisfaction. He'd turned them away from the south. Somehow Wes had gotten someone around on the north to do the same thing. If there'd been a bit more light, they might have nabbed the whole bunch. Things being as they were, it was too dangerous to pursue.

Billy retraced his steps down the outcropping and approached the cabin with caution.

"Hey, Wes!" Billy called when he reached the fringe of brush. "It's Billy. I'm coming on in, all right?"

"That you up in the rocks, Billy?" Wes asked.

"Noticed me, huh?" Billy asked as he stepped out from cover, then raced along to the house. Little Jeff Tyler swung open the door, and Billy entered upon a scene of confusion and dismay.

"Sure was glad to hear that rifle bangin' away," Wes said, setting his own rifle against the wall and coughing. The whole cabin was choked with powder smoke. Wood splinters and shattered fragments of cups and plates littered the floor. In the far corner Alice held little Hart and Timothy. Rose Anne, only five herself, helped her brother Jeff reload a rifle.

"The verdict came in today," Billy said, wiping the cold sweat from his forehead.

"I guess that's pretty obvious," Toby Hart remarked. "Tuck was down on guard. They got past him somehow. He's got good ears and sharp eyes. I'm afraid they must've killed him, Billy."

Billy rested a weary hand on the young man's shoulder as if to raise his spirits. It failed to work, and Toby dropped to his knees, exhausted.

"It's goin' to be like this till it's settled now," Wes declared. "I told you way back when we should've ridden out and settled things. Be a lot harder now."

"We had to try it the other way," Billy said. "It's time we had law."

"You don't know about this, Billy," Wes said, lighting a lamp. "I know men like Kemp. I've battled 'em all my life. Your kind of law, Charlie's kind, won't do. Kemp's got no use for truth or honor. He's like a rattlesnake. He's goin' to kill till you step out of his way or else deal with him."

"There'll be no more sidestepping."

"Blamed right there won't be!" Wes shouted. "They could've shot Alice and the kids tonight! I'm goin' out there and find Ike Kemp myself. He won't live to see sunrise. I promise you that."

"No, Wes," Alice pleaded. "You're too upset. Sit down and settle your nerves. You're in no shape to do anything."

350

"She's right," Billy added. "We'll finish Kemp, but not tonight. We're all shaken, and we don't know who's hurt."

Those words had an effect. Wes suddenly turned to Toby, and Billy made his way cautiously outside and began collecting the others.

All but three were quickly accounted for. Marlin Silsbee appeared shortly with Barret Jenkins. Barret's left arm was bound tightly, but blood continued to seep through the bandages. The boy uttered not so much as a whimper, but his pale face communicated great pain.

"I'll take him to Alice," Wes said, wrapping an arm around the wounded cowboy and directing him to the cabin.

"That leaves Tucker," Mitch Cook said. "He was on watch."

"Anybody else hit?" Billy asked.

"None of us," Malachi Johnson called as he emerged from the brush dragging the limp figure of a raider behind him. "There's two more back at the creek and one in the bushes. Lafe's comin' along. He's got Tuck with him."

"Alive?" Lew Oldham asked, jumping to his feet. "He hurt bad?"

"Not so's you'd know from the way he's been flappin' that mouth o' his," Malachi told them. "Got a fair-sized knot on his head. Anybody else'd be dead."

"I'm surprised they didn't finish him straight off," Silsbee said, shaking his head. "These aren't the kind to give you a second chance."

"I played dead!" Tucker cried as Lafe Freeman

351

helped him along toward the camp. "I did a fair bit of bleedin', too."

Billy felt a shudder work its way through him. Young Spears was as white as a ghost, and the left side of his forehead was purple and swollen. One eye was near closed, and the boy seemed barely able to keep his feet.

"Sorry I let 'em sneak in on us," Tucker told the others. "I heard a noise, and before I could spit, three of 'em jumped me."

"Best rest up," Malachi suggested. "Get to a bunk. They're apt to come back in the mornin'."

"Or before," Lafe declared. "You come all by yourself, Mr. Billy Justiss, or did you bring some help?"

"Both," Billy told the weary line crew. "I sent Viktor to fetch Hector and the others."

"Good," Lafe said, leaning against the side of the hay barn. "Leave them to watch for a time. Me, I'm worn through."

The others muttered their agreement. Hector arrived shortly, and Billy saddled himself a horse and prepared to ride home. He walked over to the cabin to check on Barret Jenkins. Alice had cut a bullet from the youngster's forearm, and Barrett was sleeping peacefully in Toby's bed.

"Tomorrow I'll send a wagon out to get Alice and the kids," Billy promised as he stepped to the door.

"No, they're stayin'," Wes declared. "Won't get any worse than tonight, and I'd have 'em close-by so I can see they're safe."

"Alice?" Billy asked.

"We feel the same," she told him. "I never wanted

to leave in the first place. I shot a horse thief when I was thirteen, and I fought Comanches from the time I could walk."

"Besides," Wes added, "we'll settle accounts with Kemp soon."

Billy nodded, but he was far from certain.

Chapter Two

Billy had scarcely mounted his horse when the sounds of gunshots carried up the creek.

"They're back!" Lew Oldham cried, rushing to where his rifle rested.

Billy waved for the boy to lower his rifle. Sound carried a long way in the hill country south of the Brazos. The gunfire was three miles, maybe more, to the south.

"It's the Schneider place!" Wes called from the cabin. "Just like before."

"Silsbee, you and Lew stay here," Billy ordered. "Toby, you and the Cooks watch the creek, see they don't double back around on us. Lafe?"

"I'll fetch Hector and the rest," Lafe said. "Malachi, you watch this young general of ours, see he doesn't get himself shot."

"Do my best," Malachi promised, throwing a blanket onto the back of a brown mustang.

"Wes?" Billy asked.

"You know I'm comin'," Wes said, his cold eyes

gazing icily through the darkness. "How do you want to do it?"

"We'll circle around from the southeast," Billy said. "Lafe and Hector can bring the others down from the north."

"That's what you did last time," Malachi objected. "Good plan, but there's a story my grandpa told me about the fox got himself trapped usin' the same hole in the fence too many times."

"He's right," Wes agreed. "How would you go about it?"

"We three go straight for the house," Malachi said. "You leave Lafe to bring the others 'round by and by. Old Schneider, he's got pluck, but he's sure to need help quick. If these Kemps keep on with it, Lafe and the boys'll give 'em a warm greetin'."

"Let's go," Billy said, shaking off the fatigue and blinking the fear from his eyes. "Stay close and maybe we'll make it."

"We'll make it," Malachi said, confidently tossing Billy a box of cartridges and stuffing two others in his own pockets. "We'll be on 'em like a thunderbolt. Done it before, friends. You'll see."

Billy wasn't convinced, but there was no time to argue. Malachi led the way, and Wes followed Billy at a gallop. In fifteen minutes the three riders burst out of the trees and tore across the Albany road. Kermit Kemp stared in stunned disbelief as the trio of riders darted past. Others were less shaken. Bullets whined past Billy's ear. One tore the heel off his left boot, and another nicked his thigh.

Wes was even luckier. A Winchester slug lodged in the account book he'd absently left in his side pocket. Otherwise the bullet might have entered a lung and stopped his life.

All the danger didn't come from Kemp's raiders, either. Three riders racing at full speed toward his house drew Martin Schneider's attention. Twice rifles fired from the Schneiders' front window had Billy ducking. Finally, though, the three would-be saviors jumped from their horses and rushed to the front porch. Marianne Schneider swung open the door, and the Schneiders found themselves reinforced.

"That was not so wise a thing to do," Martin remarked as he resumed firing at a pair of bushwhackers in back of his barn. "I might have shot you."

"Good thing your aim's off," Billy said, tying a kerchief around his thigh to stop it from bleeding. "More help's coming. For now, though, we have to hold 'em off."

Young Alek hobbled over beside Billy and accepted a handful of rifle shells.

"I don't guess Viktor is coming," the twelve-year-old said. "Not so good a night for us here."

"No," Billy said, frowning. Alek's forearm had been torn by splinters, and he still limped from the bullet Kermit Kemp had put in his leg back at Caddo Creek.

For a few moments the firing died down, and Billy almost convinced himself Kemp might have broken off the attack. After all, the Schneiders were firing steadily, even little Gregor. Georg was reloading rifles, and he was only eight. Malachi Johnson had driven the raiders on the east side of the house to cover, and Wes opened up with deadly effect everytime Kemp sent someone forward from the north.

The Kemps weren't finished yet, though. With a sudden shout a half-dozen men rushed the front door. Martin Schneider killed the first one, but Alek froze, and Marianne dragged Georg into the safety of the parlor. Billy left his own post and headed for the door. Alek scrambled over behind a large chest, but his father continued to fire until a pistol-toting raider fired a shot into Martin's hip, knocking the farmer to the floor.

"Wes!" Billy managed to shout as he fired point-blank at the first raider to leap through the door. A second and third surged in afterward, and Billy did his best to club them with his rifle. Alek shrieked as a fourth man rushed in. Billy had no time to look to the boy's welfare, though. He flung one raider aside, then grappled with another. The two of them rolled across the floor, each jabbing elbows into the other's chest. Billy gripped his opponent's belt and tried to shake him off. A fist slammed down, closing Billy's right eye.

Shots exploded through the room, and a high-pitched scream split the air. Suddenly an image of the Schneider youngsters blasted through Billy's mind. But instead of seeing Alek bloody and lifeless, Billy envisioned Viktor and little Jake. A memory of small eyes gazing sadly at their sisters' graves, of boys bounding across the range behind their older brother, of warm hearts and worshipping eyes, sent new strength surging through Billy's wrists. He threw off his heavier enemy, then lashed out with sudden fury. Bone crunched bone, and a wave of pain raced up Billy's arm, only to be swallowed by anger.

Billy scrambled away as he finally escaped the grasp of the other man. He had only a moment to see a pair of sewing scissors resting beside him on the floor. Then, as the raider drew a pistol from its holster, Billy grabbed the scissors and plunged them into the bushwhacker's dark heart.

The raider didn't die quickly. It wasn't swift and sudden like in one of Marty Steele's war stories. The scissors cut deeply, piercing a lung, and the dying man coughed blood and moaned horribly.

"Lord, you've killed me," he muttered through bloody lips.

"You earned it a dozen times over," Billy barked in reply. He then struggled to his feet and groped for his rifle. He'd expected a dozen men in the small front room, each holding a pistol cocked and ready. Instead he saw only Alek Schneider. The boy leaned heavily on the chest and held an arm sliced by a knife. At his feet lay a large man, shot in the side at close quarters. Another lay between Billy and the corpse in the doorway. Martin Schneider huddled with his daughter in the parlor doorway.

"It's all over," Lafe Freeman called out. "This bunch is finished. We chased the rest on down the road. You all right, Mr. Billy? That your blood or th'other fellow's?"

Billy looked at himself. The front of his coat was smeared with blood, and the side of his face was warm and sticky.

"Some of both," Billy told Lafe. "I'm alive, though."

"Better'n him," Malachi said, easing Billy over to a nearby chair. "Say, I believe I've seen him before."

"Lord, look who it is, Billy," Wes said, stepping closer. "Look."

Billy forced his good eye open and stared into the dying eyes of Kermit Kemp. Young Alek finally noticed as well. The boy limped over and stared hard at the man who'd lamed him. Then all the pain and resentment boiled to the surface, and Alek kicked Kemp in the side, again and again, before Malachi pulled him away.

"No point to that, boy!" Malachi called, restraining the boy. "Better see that arm tended."

"Let me go," Alek begged, wrestling fiercely.

"No, Alek!" his father called. "He is dead."

Malachi let go, and Alek stumbled to the floor beside the lifeless eyes of Kermit Kemp. The boy stepped back and gave the corpse a final furious kick before limping into the parlor.

"We'd better get you back to the house, Billy," Wes declared. "You look half dead."

I am, Billy thought. But I'll live to see the job finished. He closed his eyes a moment and fought back a wave of pain. He saw Alek Schneider's hateful eyes, the corpses littering the front room, the powder smoke that hung like a shroud over the world that had been home since Billy Justiss was no taller than little Barret Jenkins.

"Hector?" Billy called.

"I'm here," the veteran cowboy answered.

"Send Papa word of what's happened. Then get Bret out here. Help the Schneiders . . ."

"We know what to do," Hector said, easing a powerful arm around Billy's back and helping him toward a waiting horse. You go back to the ranch now with Danny. Get some rest. We will talk tomorrow."

"But there's so much to do," Billy objected. "You've got to hurry and—"

"We'll tend to everything," Lafe promised. "You're bleedin', and you'd best get that head tended fast else it'll ache like mine does after a three-bottle night at the junction."

Billy finally surrendered. Danny Seavers and Logan Thompson got their boss mounted and conducted him homeward. Billy remembered almost nothing of it. His mind held but a single image, the sight of the wide, hollow, lifeless eyes of Kermit Kemp.

And somewhere, deep behind that image, was the knowledge that Ike Kemp's past fury had been nothing to what would come now.

Chapter Three

Billy slept soundly. Exhaustion had a way of simplifying life, casting aside all the worries and memories and leaving a perfect sort of blissful rest. He awoke a little before noon. An aching head brought immediate recollection of the violence that had rent the previous night.

"Lie still," Colleen ordered. "You're fortunate to still have your head on that foolish neck, Billy Justiss, and it's best you rest today."

"Can't," he declared, sitting up in his bed. "I need to talk to Bret, get the men organized."

"Bret and Tut have been here since ten o'clock," she told him. "As for the men, Lafe Freeman and Wes have been assigning pairs to watch the road and the creek."

"Then they've done their job," Billy said, staggering to his feet. "It's time I do mine."

He hurriedly dressed and stumbled into the parlor. Bret Pruett sat on the couch with Alex Tuttle. They were sipping coffee from china cups when Billy entered.

"Lord, Billy, what did they do to your head?" Bret asked.

"Got into a bit of a fight last night," Billy told them. "Kemp had his boys on the prowl, or haven't you heard?"

"We heard all right," the sheriff said, frowning. "Was Kermit you killed, Billy. There were others, too. People in town are talking of the massacre at Caddo Creek."

"Newspapers will love that," Billy grumbled.

"Even the worst of them know Schneider didn't invite those fellows into his house," Tut pointed out. "Farm folks will be on your side."

"And what does that mean?" Billy asked. "Are people choosing sides? Am I under arrest? What's going on, Bret?"

"I know no law that punishes a man for saving a neighbor's life," Bret remarked. "I don't think even that old fox Peters could argue a man has no right to defend himself and his family! The problem at hand is what to do now."

"You know what Kemp'll do," Billy told them. "He'll mount up everyone on his place and ride on us."

"He's been a lot more clever than that in the past," Bret argued. "He could call for an investigation, or he could bring somebody in like Merrick."

"Doesn't matter," Wes announced from the doorway. "We won't give him the chance."

"You're not thinking of doing something stupid, are you?" Bret asked. "It's best we wait for Charlie

362

to get back tomorrow, gather together and make plans."

"I thought that's what we were doing now," Billy objected. "By tomorrow Kemp will have had another night to get ready. Worse, he could go riding again tonight."

"No, I figure last night was Kermit's doing," Bret said, rising to his feet and pacing with folded hands between the couch and the door. "Ike's never struck me as the type to go off half-cocked."

"He's not apt to take Kermit's death too well, though," Tut added. "I don't see him standing around waiting for us."

"And we won't wait for him!" Wes shouted. "Why all the talk, Bret? We all of us know what's to be done. If you want to come along, fine. Maybe you'd like to try and arrest 'em for shootin' up the Schneider place, lock 'em up. That's fine, too. But I'm not leavin' those Kemps across the creek so they can come back and shoot at Alice and the kids again. Ask Martin Schneider how he feels about it, lyin' at Doc Garnett's with his leg shot to pieces. Nobody's safe till we finish this."

"It's war," Billy muttered.

"Bret, you don't win by mountin' a guard," Wes explained. "You got to hit the other side, quick and hard so they know you mean it."

"Listen to yourselves," Bret pleaded. "You know what you're saying? Palo Pinto County's been a good place to live, to build a home. One of the reasons for that is that we've had no range wars. Now you're talking about starting one."

"It's already started," Billy objected. "Last night,

363

if not before. I won't say I like the idea much myself, but Wes is right. Give Kemp time, and he can bring in people, send riders out by night to shoot up our homes and families. We can't guard everybody. Nobody's safe."

"At least let me try to bring 'em in for trial," Bret said, stopping long enough to gaze hopefully at his old friends. "The law deserves a chance, doesn't it?"

"It won't work," Wes grumbled.

"But we try anyway, right?" Bret asked.

Billy shook his head, but, in the end, he relented and agreed to let Bret try.

Billy passed the next hour sipping broth and readying himself for the ride to the Kemp place. His head still ached, and his teeth were so sore he hadn't even been able to eat a single one of Enuncia's fluffy biscuits. As the recollection of the melee flooded his mind, Billy tried to find something, anything, to distract him. In desperation, he opened up the ranch ledgers and glanced over the neatly-recorded figures his brother Ross had entered for December.

"You are feeling better, Billy?" Viktor called from the door of the small office Billy had included on the side of the new house.

"It's not so bad as it looks," Billy said, waving the fourteen-year-old to his side. "You did a good job last night, getting home on your own and sending help."

"I should have come back," Viktor said, sitting beside Billy on the floor. "Alek fought beside his father."

"Alek close to got killed," Billy added. "His arm's cut up some, and he's hardly gotten that leg mended."

"His father is badly hurt. Gregor, too."

"Oh? I didn't know that."

"Was shot in the side, Gregor. They have left their house."

"Well, they're still alive," Billy said, patting his brother's back. "Time will mend all that."

"You are going after the others, yes?"

"This afternoon," Billy explained. "They won't have a chance to do this again."

"People said that when my papa and mama got killed," Viktor reminded Billy. "These are bad men. You must be careful."

"I will be."

"I will stay and watch the house. I can shoot a rifle."

"Just see you don't shoot it at anybody who's on our side," Billy remarked with a smile. It was a mistake. Viktor was serious, and the comment struck the thin-faced boy like a knife.

"I will soon be fifteen," Viktor said, frowning heavily. "I am not so good at riding a horse as Chris and Joe, but I am not afraid."

"Never once thought you were," Billy said, resting a hand on the sullen young man's shoulder. "If it was up to me, no boy your age would ever shoulder a rifle in this county. Shoot, Barret Jenkins was shot last night, and he's scarce your size, Vik. We close to had to bury Tucker Spears. Now you tell me Greg Schneider's taken a bullet. He's what, eleven? It's gotten so it's not safe to be young or small or . . .

Vik, this killing business is a terrible thing. It's fine you want to defend your home, stand up for your family, but I pray to high heaven you won't have to. Don't hurry yourself into a man's boots. There are too many sunny summer days, too many creeks to fish and horses to ride and pretty girls to chase."

Viktor gazed up with wide, confused eyes, and Billy laughed.

"Here I am, only just turned twenty-five, talking like I was eighty," Billy said, shaking his head and drawing a grin from Viktor. "That's what all this fighting does, you know. Papa was like that after the war."

"He doesn't say very much about that."

"I know. I understand why now. It's an ugly, messy business, and talking about it just brings it all back."

"Like the night my mama and papa die," Viktor said, sliding closer to Billy and looking up with dark, mist-covered eyes. "I will never forget, not even now when I have a new family."

"Some things you never forget, Vik. Look here," Billy said, rolling up his trouser leg to expose the thin scars left by his father's knife when it had sliced the flesh to drain a rattlesnake's venom. "There's a hole in my left thigh left by a bullet back in '75, too."

"I saw it last summer when we swam in the river."

"There are other scars, too," Billy explained. "The ones left on your heart when friends . . . or family . . . die. And there are worse ones, put there when you kill."

"This Ike Kemp must have many," Viktor grumbled. "Wes says it was he that killed my papa."

"Might've been."

"I will pray you come back safe," Viktor declared. "But I am hoping you will kill this man. He hurts too many people."

"I'm afraid you're right, little brother. But I hope it's not me has to kill him."

Viktor nodded, and Billy set aside the ledger long enough to lift the boy's saddened chin.

Yes, Billy thought, let it be somebody else. But if it has to be me, I'll do it.

Billy was as ready to deal with Ike Kemp as ever when he saddled his horse and prepared to follow Bret to the Kemp ranch a little after four o'clock that afternoon.

"You know this won't solve anything," Wes argued. "Waste of time. I wish there were more of us goin', too."

Billy glanced around him. The whole county had been invited along, but only Henry Eppler and Albert Parnell had appeared. Lafe and Malachi were there, of course, as were Hector Suarez and the Cook brothers. Most of the remaining Flying J hands were spread out along the ranch's boundaries in case the Kemps decided to strike in the meantime.

"Keep yourselves ready," Bret warned. "I'd like to bring this off peacefully, but there's no assurance Kemp won't have an ambush planned."

"More likely so than not," Lafe declared, swinging out to the right. "Sheriff, you go along on. Malachi and I'll head out on the flanks, keep an eye on the trail up ahead."

Billy felt better knowing the pair were scouting. Even though Bret departed the Albany road and swung north across Caddo Creek, there was still a real threat of ambush. The nature of the terrain, all those boulders and ravines, provided ideal shelter for sharpshooters. But as he followed Bret across the broken ground, he found no sign of anyone at all.

"I don't much like this," Tut grumbled. "There are no cattle, not even horse tracks. Where's Kemp got his men? What're they up to?"

"Maybe gone to Mexico," Parnell suggested. "Good riddance!"

"We couldn't be that lucky," Wes told them. "Anyway, I see a house up ahead."

"Billy, you and Wes circle around to the right," Bret instructed. "Hector, you and the Cooks watch the left. Lafe and Malachi will cover the back. Ready, Tut?"

The deputy nodded, and the two lawmen rode toward the porch. They stopped a hundred feet short of the door and ordered Kemp outside.

"Ike's not here!" a slender cowboy said, hobbling out onto the porch. "What you want?"

"To ask some questions," Bret explained. "That leg doesn't look too good. Wound's still bleeding. Get it last night?"

The thin cowboy exchanged a nervous glance with a second man sitting beside the door. A third appeared at the front window of the house holding a shotgun.

"This is Kemp land!" the latter announced. "Now get clear."

"This is Sheriff Pruett of Palo Pinto County," Bret responded. "I'm here officially. Have Ike Kemp come out."

"He ain't here," the thin one repeated. "Now git!"

"No, I think we'll stay a bit," Bret said, nervously eyeing the shotgun. "Maybe you boys can tell me what you were up to last night."

"Playin' cards and dreamin' of women," the third one said, laughing heartily. "What'd you think, Sheriff? Figure we were shootin' up little kids or burnin' farms?"

"Something like that," Bret said, pulling his rifle from its saddle scabbard. "Now raise your hands and come along nice and easy."

"Not a chance," the thin one answered. "I done nothin' wrong. I'll go nowhere."

"Leave him to me!" Wes called from cover. "You give 'em their chance, Bret. We'll take it from there."

Billy glanced at his companions. Bret and Tut appeared nervous, concerned. Malachi and Lafe stood poised to enter the rear door of the house. Their eyes betrayed none of their feelings. Albert Parnell and Henry Eppler were worried. Hector and the Cooks were out of sight, and Wes was ready to shoot.

"I'll give you five seconds," Bret warned.

"Eat your seconds!" the shotgun-wielding cowboy at the window yelled. "Choke on 'em. We stay. You want us, come ahead on!"

Billy dismounted and held his rifle ready. Bret and Tut retreated to cover. Then the afternoon simply exploded.

For close to half an hour Bret's posse peppered

the house with shot. The large man with the shotgun made a try at escape, but Hector cut him down. Then Lafe and Malachi rushed the house, blasting away so that it seemed the place was slowly coming apart inside out. In the end, only the two on the porch escaped the methodical killing of the ex-buffalo soldiers.

"I've had enough!" the thin cowboy finally screamed, throwing his rifle aside. "Me, too," his companion called.

"Just in time, too," Lafe declared as he popped out of the shattered doorway and herded the captives along.

"Any sign of Ike inside?" Bret asked.

"Only a couple of dead hands," Lafe answered. "I'd say from the looks of things, somebody pulled out early this mornin' without botherin' to tidy things. There's an empty safe in there, and breakfast plates still on the kitchen table. Another thing, too," he added, tossing a used rail ticket to Bret. "I'd say that's the one Ike used to come home from Austin. We'd best find him, friends, 'fore he finds one of us."

Billy nodded. His insides grew cold and hollow at the thought of Ike Kemp leading riders up Bluff Creek to the house. Or toward the Cassidy farm, into town where Eliza and little Edward remained defenseless, or to Vicki's.

"What now, Bret?" Wes asked as Hector tied the captives and led them to a pair of waiting horses.

"I guess we have a look around," the sheriff declared.

"Wrong," Billy objected. "You and Tut get these

370

two back to town and watch Palo Pinto. The rest of us go home and look after our families. Wes, you and the Cooks ride down the Albany road and warn everybody to keep an eye out for trouble."

"And what about us?" Lafe asked sourly.

"You and Malachi get the hard part," Billy said, biting his lip. "See if you can pick up Kemp's trail. Then get word to us so we can deal with him."

"Good plan," Bret commented, "only it seems like we're awful spread out."

"I know," Billy admitted. "But I can't think of anything better."

"No, it's the thing to do," Lafe agreed. "You send some wires down to the junction, too, Sheriff. Have 'em stay on the lookout for strangers arrivin' on the train, especially from the west, New Mexico way."

"Done," Bret promised.

"Billy, you get word around to pair up travelin' the road, too. I recognize this fellow's style. He'll try to catch us off guard, shoot one or two at a time from ambush."

"How's that?" Wes asked.

"We been talkin' 'bout it some amongst ourselves," Malachi explained. "Ever since Samuels joined up. We tangled with this bunch before, I'll bet. Heavy man, liked to talk. Only he didn't call himself Kemp."

"No, not then," Lafe added. "Was Ike Keeling back then."

"Keeling?" Billy asked.

"That strikes a chord," Wes added.

"Ought to," Lafe said sourly. "Back when your daddy was still crossin' the Nations, we tangled with

371

another one by that name. Remember, Billy? You was young, but he wasn't an easy one to forget. Wore a patch over one eye, and he'd steal anything wasn't nailed down."

"I remember," Billy mumbled. "I've got good cause. I think I'd better head across to the Dunlaps and let Jared know. Could be we're not the only ones on Ike's mind."

"What's all this about?" Henry Eppler asked. "Who's this Keeling?"

"A face out of a nightmare," Billy said, turning toward the Brazos. "A shadow from the past."

Chapter Four

"I knew this wasn't about any twenty acres of creek bottom," Charlie Justiss said when Billy passed on the news Monday morning at the depot in Justiss Junction. "Keeling!"

"We should've looked at the posters in Bret's back file," Billy said, spreading out one each for Ike, Kermit, and Solomon Keeling. There was a fourth, too. In its center was the face of a wild-eyed redhead with a patch over his left eye. Neatly stenciled below was the name JONAS KEELING.

"He told me the whole thing," Charlie lamented. "Said how he lost a boy while he was off settling his brother's affairs. Wife died of grief afterward. It's a powerful hate drives a man to the steps this one's taken to have his revenge. You tell Jared yet?"

"Soon as we put the pieces together. Ike's not likely to know for sure it was Jared did the killing, of course."

"That tale's been spun a hundred times," Charlie grumbled. "Word gets around, son."

"He's got a score to settle with me, too," Billy declared. "I killed Kermit at the Schneider place."

"Maybe it'd be best if you stayed in Fort Worth for a time," Charlie said.

"Papa, I'll carry a scar on my leg my whole life. You haven't forgotten how it was Keeling put it there, have you?"

"No, son, but once we get word out on the telegraph, there won't be a place in the whole Southwest Ike Keeling can show his face and feel safe."

"He's done all right in the past. No, I don't want to be looking over my shoulder from now on. I'd rather have done with it."

"Well, I don't suppose I can blame you," Charlie admitted. "You look to've been through a war, though, and I'd spare you the rest of this."

"I can't hide, Papa," Billy told him. "It's just not in me. I don't like the killing any better than you, but somebody's got to take a stand someplace."

"What precautions have you taken?"

"I talked Pat Cassidy into moving onto the ranch till this is over. I know the Cassidys are only kin by marriage, but their farm is pretty exposed, lying just this side of the ridge and all. Wes sent the Cooks out to Jared's place. Eliza's moved in with Vicki, and Bret's deputized a dozen men to watch the town at night."

"And what about looking for Keeling?"

"Well, you know about the wires already. Lafe and Malachi are tracking ten riders who left Ike's place yesterday morning."

"Then, I guess it's wait. I hate that!" Charlie said, stomping his boot. "Your mama sure had her sights set on having supper at Buck Creek, too."

"I don't think that's too good an idea just now," Billy told his father. "Viktor and Jake are kind of nervous as is, and not knowing where the raiders are, heading home on the trail tonight isn't too wise."

"Do Marty and Ryan know what's going on?"

"Bret sent word yesterday."

"Best send somebody down to give him a hand watching the south range. Get word to Ryan and Rachel we won't be around for supper."

"I'll go myself."

"Not alone," Charlie warned.

"Logan Thompson's with me. And Tuck Spears. He like to twist my arm off to come. I think Ry better watch that one close or he'll run off with Rachel."

"That would be a sight, Tucker running off with anybody."

Billy laughed for the first time in what seemed like a year. Tucker was but a hair over the size of a fencepost, but the boy had a way with the farmgirls. Mary Eileen Cassidy had been following him around since arriving at the ranch the previous afternoon. She resembled some awe-struck slave, content to follow him around and heed his every word.

"Well, you take care, son," Charlie said in conclusion. "These back roads sure invite an ambush."

"Yes, sir," Billy agreed. "I'll be back well before dusk, though. Kemp—or Keeling, or whoever he is— prefers the night for his kind of business."

Charlie nodded, but the look in his eyes betrayed concern. Billy kept it in mind when he and his companions set off for the orphanage a quarter hour later.

Melting snow upstream had brought a bit of water back to Buck Creek. Billy observed it was hardly more than ankle deep in midchannel, but even so, it brought hope that the worst of the drought might finally be finished.

"We get some healthy rains this spring, we'll have the range ready to run beeves on it again," Marty Steele told Billy. "If nothin' else, those kids up there with Ryan and Rachel ought to be able to swim come April."

"That's a fine thought," Billy commented. "It's about time life got back to normal around here. Kids ought to be fishing instead of carrying rifles and getting shot."

"How come you came out here yourself, Billy?" Marty said, scratching his chin. "Logan's gone on along with your news to Ryan anyhow. Shoot, Tucker could've brought it."

"I guess I needed to ride some," Billy confessed. "And I wanted you to know how serious this is. This Kemp, or Keeling, spent a lot of time figuring this out. I'd guess he knows everybody who was on that cattle drive. He could come after you, Marty. And Ry."

"Ry maybe," Marty said, shaking his head and grinning. "Nobody ever paid any attention to an ordinary cowboy like me."

"Don't bet your life on it. Anyway, I'd feel better if you'd stay up at Buck Creek the next few nights.

There are an awful lot of targets in those bunk-houses."

Marty's smile faded, and he gazed angrily to the west.

"Not even a buzzard would try to get even that way," Marty grumbled. "You're right to worry, though. There's only an empty cabin down here now. Makes sense with the stock gone for me to pass some time up there anyway."

"Thanks."

"Shoot, it's me that's gettin' the best end of this bargain, Billy. Rachel's twice the cook I am, and those boys are fair company. Tuck and Logan stayin'?"

"Logan is. If Tucker's any use, keep him, too."

"He's a good shot, Billy. I taught him myself. Boy's not afraid of anything."

"Maybe he should be," Billy muttered. "I haven't shied away from much myself in this life, but I admit to being nervous right now. Each time I think of how Viktor and Jake might've been with the Schneiders, how Lafe and Malachi could've been ten minutes later . . ."

"Does no good, thinkin' like that," Marty declared. "Come on. If we hurry, Rachel might have some supper left for us."

Billy mounted his horse, and Marty climbed atop a chestnut mare. The two of them then rode along Buck Creek toward the orphanage. There was a refreshing breeze sweeping up from the south, and the sun sprinkled a golden tint on the hills. Billy could almost taste the first trace of spring, even though winter had yet to start its real run.

"Look there," Marty said. "I'd never thought junipers to creep up that fool ravine."

Marty'd scarcely spoken it when he froze.

"Get clear!" he called to Billy, then turned his horse and charged into a nearby sea of cattails. Two rifles fired from the ravine, and the second shot sent Billy's horse galloping after Marty. They rode furiously through briars and brush until they reached a collection of boulders that had tumbled down a hillside. Marty rolled off his saddle and slapped his horse into a gallop toward the creek. Billy grabbed his rifle from its scabbard and jumped down beside the anxious cowboy.

"You were right to worry," Marty said as a rifle sent a bullet whining over their heads. "Neat little ambush. Except I know this road better'n anybody."

"Just about got us all the same," Billy said, fighting to recover his breath. "And we're not out of this by a long shot."

"Oh, I'm not much worried now," Marty said, crawling along the side of a boulder and scanning the ground ahead. "This is an old game with me, playin' cat and mouse with rustlers and bushwhackers. I danced around the Devil's Den at Gettysburg, don't forget. Got myself five or six bluecoats."

"That was a long time ago," Billy reminded him. "These fellows are good at shooting from cover, too."

"So'm I," Marty declared. "Give me that pistol you're carryin', Billy. Then watch that willow up ahead."

"The one overhanging the road?"

"That's the one. One of our friends is in the

second fork. When I stir things up over on the right, you shoot him. I wouldn't care to get a bullet for my trouble."

"I'll see if I can't otherwise entertain the gentleman," Billy promised.

Marty then crept through the high grass, taking pains to give the sharpshooters just enough of a glimpse to entice a shot. The marksman eased his rifle over, and Billy got a fair view of one shoulder and most of the scoundrel's body.

"You've shot your last man, mister," Billy whispered, firing three times rapidly. At under a hundred yards the Winchester was deadly. Bullets slammed into the rifleman and tore him from his perch. The rifle fell to the ground. The would-be killer hung limply in the willow branches.

"They got French!" a voice called from the ravine.

"Watch the one in the grass, fool!" another replied.

By that time Marty had woven his way through the rocks and into the ravine itself. Armed with a pistol in each hand, he surprised the bushwhackers from the rear and opened fire with a vengeance. Billy then charged from the opposite direction, and three hirelings who had moments before waited in ambush now raced toward the creek in hopes of saving their lives. Marty shot the first, and Billy killed another as he splashed into the shallows.

"I got one more in the ravine," Marty called as he popped the empty shell casings from his pistols and hurriedly reloaded.

Billy nodded, then made his way past each corpse, ensuring himself they were dead while at the same time searching for a familiar face. He didn't recognize any of them.

"I've seen the one in the tree before," Marty said, frowning. "He was at the junction the other day. These others aren't from around here. Look at their boots. Red clay's caked on the toes. They've been out on the Llano or up in the Nations."

"This was too close for my liking," Billy said, letting a long breath escape his lips. "We'd best get along to the orphans."

"It'll take some time to fetch the horses."

"They know where to go. So do we. It's not but a mile or so. Besides, a man on foot makes a smaller target."

Marty nodded grimly, then fell into step as Billy led the way past the road and along a low ridge. It wasn't necessary to add staying clear of trails and roads might lengthen one's life.

They were about a half mile from the buildings that made up the Buck Creek Ranch, as the orphans preferred to call their home, when Billy saw Ryan. He and four of the older boys were fishing at a small bend in the creek. A deep pool formed there, and in summer it was a favorite swimming hole. Now it offered some hope of nabbing a perch or a small catfish.

"Good afternoon," Billy called to his brother.

Ryan Justiss jumped a foot in the air and turned nervously.

"Billy, that's a fair way to get yourself shot," Ryan grumbled. "Or scare me into an early grave."

"That pole shoot well, does it?" Marty asked. "We just left some of Keeling's friends up the way."

"I told you I heard shots, Mr. Ryan," little Jay Belton called.

"You all right?" Ryan asked, passing the pole to Jay.

"Better'n they are," Marty said. "But there could be some others about. We'd do better to get back to the house."

Ryan motioned the boys to do just that, and they reluctantly pulled their lines from the water and prepared to follow. A single rifle bullet shattered the calm, though, and Ryan herded his charges toward a nearby live oak. Two others rifles barked, and the youngest of the orphans, a frail twelve-year-old named Benny Gardiner, tumbled to the ground.

"You go right," Marty told Billy. "I've got the left."

But Billy had hardly taken a step when the ground ahead exploded. Two gunmen, maybe more, were making a point of pinning Billy to the ground. Marty, meanwhile, managed to reach cover on the left.

"Did it a bit better this time!" Solomon Keeling bellowed out from across the creek. "I've got men all around you, and three more up the way. They're sure goin' to enjoy havin' supper with that wife of yours, Justiss! Yes, sir."

A brief volley of gunfire from the east punctuated his statement. Then all grew quiet.

Billy took deep breaths and fought off images of slaughtered children . . . of Rachel . . .

Instead he slowly counted to twenty. The numbers

381

occupied his mind, and he was determined to make a run toward Ryan and the boys when he reached fifty.

Meanwhile, Solomon continued explaining his masterly ambush, how proud Ike would be for his settling accounts with part of the crew that had killed his uncle. No mention was made of Kermit, and Billy wondered if it were possible that the Keelings didn't yet know. He reached fifty, though, and discarded the notion as he sprang into motion. His feet carried him like a spring antelope through the brush and brambles as rifles peppered the tall buffalo grass all around him. Billy heard the *swish-swish* of bullets cutting through the live oak leaves overhead. He managed to reach Ryan unhurt, though.

"Lord, Billy, that was crazy," Ryan said, gripping his brother's shoulder. "Give me some cover, eh? I want to get Benny to cover."

Billy nodded, then popped to his feet and sprayed the far bank of the creek with rifle fire. One of the raiders emerged from cover, and Marty shot the fool dead. Ryan, meanwhile, dragged Benny behind the trees. The boy's soft blue eyes stared blankly at the sky, though.

"Jay," Ryan said as he closed little Benny's eyelids, "I want you to get down in that gully back there and keep the others out of sight."

"I can shoot, Mr. Ryan," Jay protested.

"Yeah, I know, son. But right now it's more important to keep everybody safe. Understand?"

Jay gazed at his lifeless friend and nodded without emotion. Billy, though, felt a great rage building up inside him, and he reloaded the Winchester.

Sadly he discovered he had but two spare bullets after filling the fifteen-shot magazine.

"I never thought we'd wind up like this, little brother," Billy told Ryan. "Used to be we could always talk our way out of fixes like this."

"Used to be," Ryan mumbled. "Who would've imagined the two of us holed up at Buck Creek, guarding three railroad orphans from a gang of bushwhackers. Lord, Billy, I feel like I'm back in Kansas, that the last twelve and a half years never happened."

"Kind of wish that was how it was," Billy said, looking at the shattered body beneath them. "But it's not."

"No, I'm afraid not. What now? You always were the one with the notions."

"You got a gun?"

"A pair of trap-door Springfields in those rocks behind you."

"That's real helpful. Well, you take the Winchester. I'll get the others."

"Billy?"

"Just do it, Ry. I got down here. I can get over there, too."

Keeling seemed to sense something was about to happen. He had his companions closing in, but Marty opened fire, and they scrambled back under cover. Billy took that chance to dart toward the rocks. Rifle fire followed him, but the nearby trees and rocks deflected the bullets that might have smashed bone or torn muscle. Billy got to the rifles, then cracked open a box of shells and loaded the first.

"How 'bout handin' me the other one?" Jay Belton asked as Billy took aim on a shadow atop the far hill.

Billy turned and nearly shot the boy.

"Boy, I thought Ryan told you—"

"I'm not a boy," Jay said, taking the rifle and loading a shell. "I might as well get shot up here as down there."

Billy was none too pleased about it, but then what choice was there? The boy was right. And when a pair of raiders broke for the creek, Billy could only hit the first one with the single-shot rifle. Jay sent the other crawling back to cover dragging a leg.

"Told you I could shoot," Jay boasted as he reloaded the rifle. "Now, how do we get out of this mess?"

Billy shook his head and muttered, "We wait and hope they made a mistake. Or that help comes."

Jay's gloomy response mirrored Billy's feeling. Worse, after a sharp exchange down in the cattails, Marty Steele failed to resume firing.

Solomon Keeling quickly sized up the situation. He had Ryan and Billy holed up with three children. Marty was off somewhere to the left, possibly hurt, maybe even dead. Never was there a better chance.

Billy viewed a more desperate position. Only the Winchester could maintain much rate of fire, and that would only be until the rifle ran out of shells. The Springfields had greater range and accuracy, but that wasn't of much use if the fighting came to close quarters. His first thought was to withdraw, or at least cover the youngsters. But for all any of them knew, the road was crawling with Keeling's men.

They moved like an army of ants of the far hillside.

"We've got to get out of here," Jay whispered. "Help Miz Rachel and the kids."

Billy grinned. It sometimes seemed like Jay was a forty-year-old hiding under a mop of yellow hair. The boy's eyes were cold and serious, and he wasn't bashful about firing his rifle.

"Watch the ones on the left," Billy warned as he crept along the rocks. "How'd you get up here anyway? I didn't notice you getting near the reaction I did."

"I just followed the ravine," Jay explained, pointing at how the gully formed a natural tunnel of sorts through the rocky ground.

"Well, I hope it works that well for me," Billy said, filling his pockets with shells before crawling along into the gully. "Watch the left!"

Jay turned his attention to that direction, and Billy crept down the ravine. He passed the two petrified youngsters and emerged just back of Ryan. As Billy greeted his brother, Jay fired at an approaching raider.

"Who's firing back there?" Ryan asked nervously.

"One of the kids," Billy explained.

"I told him to—"

"Ry, he's doing all right, and we need that rifle. I'm going to see if I can get around behind them, shake 'em up some. Watch the creek."

"Billy, you're crazy!"

"People've been saying that all my life," Billy said, creeping through the high grass. "See you in a bit."

Billy hoped he would be alive in a bit. It seemed pretty doubtful just then, particularly when two or

385

three rifles opened up from the cattails on the near side of Buck Creek. It seemed raiders were all around them now. Ryan fended off one charge, and Jay Belton did his best to counter the riflemen on the left. Billy knew it was up to him. He had to shake the outlaws' nerve. The only way he knew to do that was to rattle their leader.

Solomon Keeling kept to a clump of junipers halfway up the far hillside. He wasn't taking many chances personally, but he was carrying the fight to the enemy. Billy estimated six or seven others fanned out on both sides of the creek. Long odds indeed. But if Marty hadn't noticed those out-of-place junipers, Billy would already be dead. He'd come close a dozen times, and so long as he had a rifle and bullets to fire, he was still in the game, as Marty would say.

As they advanced on Ryan's refuge, Keeling's men passed no more than a few feet from Billy. He let them pass. They were, after all, mere pawns on the Buck Creek chessboard. Billy was after the king. And he was in a desperate hurry.

Solomon Keeling wasn't proving very cooperative, though. He had none of his brother's foolhardy bravado. Worse, the others charged Ryan, and the Winchester shot up most of its ammunition in holding them off. It seemed to Billy that every wave of a limb in the January breeze marked a Keeling raider about to pounce on Ryan or the boys.

The Winchester spit out its final two rounds then, and a high-pitched scream warned Billy that the boys in the gully had been taken. The sounds of Ryan scuffling with an attacker in the rocks signaled the failure of Billy's plan. Jay continued to fire, but then a huge mountain of a man bellowed out, "Hey, Solly, look at this!"

The giant flung Jay's Springfield aside and held the boy up by the straps of his overalls. Jay shrieked and squirmed.

"I'll finish this one," the huge outlaw boasted. "You take those two runnin' down the hill."

Billy gazed at the two terrified youngsters scampering toward Buck Creek. A pair of outlaws chased after them. It was then that Solomon Keeling made his only mistake of the afternoon. Laughing, he rose to his feet and aimed at the fleeing boys. In that fragment of an instant, Billy aimed and fired. The Springfield's bullet splintered Keeling's nose and exploded through his head. The killer fell backward into the rocks while Billy feverishly reloaded his rifle and aimed again before the giant realized what had occurred. The shot shattered the huge raider's massive right arm. His grip broke, and Jay scrambled away.

"Solly?" the giant called.

Billy worked frantically to get a fresh shell into the rifle, but before he finished, a terrific blast felled the giant. Simultaneously Marty rose from the cattails and pulled the escaping boys to the ground. Horses galloped up the road, and their riders fired wildly. The surviving raiders abandoned their attack and fled instead for the safety of the far bank of the creek.

Billy let them go. He was sick of the blood and the killing. He worked his way back to the rocks and searched for his brother. Ryan lay on the ground, his face and neck bloody.

"Ry?" Billy gasped, kneeling alongside.

"Lord, you cut that close, Billy," Ryan said, sitting up and drawing out a kerchief. Except for a thin slice torn from his neck, he appeared unhurt.

"Another inch over, and—"

"Tuck would've had himself a wife," Ryan said, halting the bleeding. "Where are the boys?"

"Safe," a husky voice declared, nudging Jay Belton over toward Ryan. Marty brought the other two along soon afterward.

"I don't know how to thank you," Billy said, rising to shake a tall, buckskin-clad stranger's hand.

"No need," the stranger declared, motioning to three companions. They quickly set about collecting the fallen outlaws.

"I don't understand," Ryan said as Jay helped him to his feet. "Who are you?"

"Amos Parkinson," their rescuer explained. "I've been huntin' that big fellow close to a year. What brought 'em after you folks is beyond me. 'Pears like they started a small war here."

"Blood feud of sorts," Billy said. "Ever hear of Ike Keeling?"

"I'd be a poor bounty man not to. He's papered for close to $10,000. I close to caught up with him once."

"That's his boy up the hill there," Billy said.

"He's yours, son. Clean kill. Got him with that Springfield, did you? I favor this old Sharps myself."

Billy stared at the oldtimer's buffalo rifle. Well, the big-bore rifle had sure enough made short work of that giant.

"We'd like to thank you, Mr. Parkinson," Ryan declared. "Would you stay to supper?"

"Got to deliver these fellows to the sheriff. Besides, with Keeling about, I believe I'll do some lookin' around."

"Solomon's posted, too," Billy said, pointing at the younger Keeling lying on the far hillside. "You saved our lives, and you're welcome to the reward."

"Your shot, friend," Parkinson declared. "Besides, I figure it was a judgment o' sorts, our happenin' by. I done things in my life, but I never shot at kids from ambush."

Billy followed Parkinson's eyes to little Benny Gardiner. In his relief at being rescued, he'd forgotten not everyone had been so lucky.

"I'm Billy Justiss," Billy said, taking Parkinson's hand. "If you ever need a job or a meal, drop in and see me at the Flying J. We owe you."

"I'll keep it in mind," the bounty hunter declared, managing a grin in parting. "Can't ever tell when a man's fortunes'll turn. This bunch sure didn't."

"No," Billy agreed.

Chapter Five

Billy paused only long enough to bind Ryan's wound and wash the powder smoke from his eyes before starting the short journey to the orphanage proper. Marty carried the Gardiner boy along by himself, all the while bemoaning the fact that they'd been careless.

"It wasn't that," Billy objected when they at last saw the long bunkhouses that sheltered the parentless boys. "Who would think a boy like little Benny there could be in danger fishing in Buck Creek?"

"Does seem like the world's gone crazy," Ryan agreed.

Jay Belton wrapped a weary arm around Ryan then, and the exhausted survivors of Keeling's raid staggered up toward the house.

Rachel met them halfway. Her eyes were red and swollen, and she hugged each of the boys in turn before pulling Ryan to her side. The she noticed Marty setting his lifeless bundle on the porch.

"It's Benny," Ryan explained. "Poor kid was dead

before we knew what happened."

"You're hurt," she said, making a brief examination of the wound. "Jay, you're battered as well."

"Just shook some," the boy admitted. "I'll get John and Morgan on inside, then—"

"John and Morgan can mind themselves," she said, waving the two other boys on toward the house. "You go tell Herman to boil some water. You and this partner of yours need a scrubbing."

Jay nodded and trotted off. Billy thought to follow, but instead he froze in his steps. For the first time he noticed the missing panes in the front windows, the slices torn in the oak and willow walls of the house. Brass casings littered the porch.

"They were here, too," he said, gripping his rifle tightly.

"Three or four," Rachel explained. "Tucker and that tall man you sent to the house exchanged shots with them. I have to tell you, I was scared to distraction. Then some riders came up the creek, and the bandits left. I suppose they turned their attentions on you."

"More likely took to the hills," Billy said. "The same bunch that chased your outlaws off surprised the batch about to finish us."

"Was anybody here hurt?" Ryan asked. "Where are the boys?"

"A dozen or so went with Tucker to have a look around," she told him. "I put some to work cleaning things up. It's made a mess out of supper, I fear. What's it all about anyway?"

"Revenge," Billy answered. "I'll fill you both in."

That came later, though. First Rachel got Ryan

scrubbed and dressed his wound. In the meantime, Billy took Marty outside for a look around. They soon found Tucker Spears jabbering away at the other boys.

"Any sign of trouble?" Billy asked.

"They didn't have much stomach for facin' Tuck there," Logan Thompson said, grinning. "Boy has a fair eye for shootin', Billy, but he really put the fear in 'em with that mouth of his. They likely thought he'd talk 'em to death."

"I don't talk so much," Tucker objected.

"Do, too," the other boys complained.

"Anyhow, I'll bet Rachel could use some help getting supper ready," Billy said, waving the boys back to the house.

"You bring me somethin', huh, Billy?" Marty said. "I think I'll keep an eye on the creek for a while."

"Me, too," Tucker added, sitting beside Marty and scanning the opposite shore.

"Once we eat, you'd best get along home," Marty told Billy. "They'll be out to the ranch next, I'd guess."

"Could be," Billy agreed. He started to follow the others back to the house, then stopped. Marty rested his chin in his hands and hummed an old camp song. A huge frown filled his face, and his eyes were red and hollow.

"What's wrong?" Billy asked. "Is there something I should know?"

"No, I was just thinkin'," Marty said, patting Tucker on the back and then turning to face Billy. "I let these kids down. They're my family, Billy, and I let 'em down."

"Wasn't you," Billy declared. "No one could suspect that would happen. Anyway, we got 'em through it."

"No, we were fool lucky, and you know it. Most of us were, that is. Lord, I'd give anything if little Benny had gotten to cover."

"Benny?" Tucker asked. "Benny Gardiner?"

"Got himself shot up the creek a mile," Marty explained. "Ambush. Poor kid. I don't think he ever had a cross word for anybody."

"He sure did," Tucker said. "Why, you should've been here when he got here. Was like puttin' up with a mule-stubborn skunk. He never had a good word for anybody, and we finally had to peel off his clothes and scrub him with a brush just so you could stand to be in the bunkhouse. I always kind of liked him, though. People said we looked alike, and, well, I never had a real brother, you know."

"Sorry it worked out like it did, Tuck," Marty mumbled.

"I'll bet he'd like to be up on the hill with Paul Drayton. Paul had a way of lookin' out for the littlest ones."

"I'll get a spade," Billy said, turning toward the house.

"No," Marty objected. "Leave that to us. You go see how Ry's gettin' on. Tuck and I can manage the grave."

Billy nodded, then left them to the grim task.

He explained about the Keelings' grudge over a

393

meager meal of boiled beef and potatoes. Then the orphans gathered on the hillside above Buck Creek and bid Benny Gardiner a final farewell. Billy expected whimpering and high emotion, but the boys stood tight-lipped and solemn. Each passed the grave in turn, whispering to his dead friend or sharing a joke. They knew it could as easily have been a different name Tucker Spears had etched on the simple oak plank that marked the grave.

"These kids know death as an old friend," Ryan explained as Billy saddled a horse for the ride back to the ranch. "There haven't been any feather beds and warm winters for them. They've scratched out a living in rail camps, scrubbed dishes in saloons, or prowled alleys at night. I can count the ones on one hand that aren't missing fingers or don't have some scar to mark their hardships. They've been dealt a bad hand, but they'll be all right, Billy. If they were the kind to throw in their cards, life would've finished 'em a long time ago."

"Funny how things turn out. I used to think if we could just get the ranch going, just deal with the Comanches, just get one more herd up the trail, we'd have some peace. Doesn't happen that way, does it?"

"Ah, you wouldn't know what to do if there wasn't trouble."

"I'd like to try," Billy said sourly. "I would, Ry. I'm worried, too. We've had no word from Lafe and Malachi, and no sign of Ike Keeling."

"Maybe they're all waiting for you back home," Ryan said, laughing so that the wound on his neck resumed its bleeding.

"Watch yourself, little brother," Billy said as he climbed into the saddle. It was a strange thing to say. Ryan had rarely been a younger brother. The two of them had always been partners, a pair of renegade tricksters to pester friend and foe.

Ryan seemed to notice the difference, too.

"Maybe you should get somebody to ride back with you," he suggested.

"I've got a fresh mount and a clear trail," Billy declared. "There's no one at this place who can keep up with me."

And with that said, he slapped his horse into a gallop and took off homeward.

No warm and cheerful welcome awaited Billy Justiss at the Flying J. In truth, a nervous Flynn Cassidy nearly fired both barrels of a shotgun when Billy crossed the bridge over Justiss Creek.

"Lord, Flynn, I'm not that bad a husband for Colleen," Billy cried. "For God's sake put that gun down."

"I'm sorry," the almost fourteen-year-old gasped. "There've been riders all over the place. Hector took a shot at one a half hour ago down at the river. There's blood on the ground, so I'd judge he hit the snake."

"Everybody's all right, though? No one's been hurt?"

"Not as yet," the young man said nervously.

"Any sign of Lafe?"

"Not a one."

Billy frowned. He was beginning to worry. He

395

excused himself then and headed on to the ranch-house.

Colleen was beside herself. With hands glued to hips, she made it crystal clear now was no time to be riding Palo Pinto County alone.

"You make a good target, Billy Justiss," she scolded. "And you can barely see with that eye nigh shut. So get along inside and let me brew you some coffee. It's winter, or did no one tell you?"

Billy grinned and drew her close. Already it had been a long day, and he feared the night would offer little rest.

Chapter Six

He was right. Rifle shots shattered the quiet a dozen times. First came an exchange down at Caddo Creek. Then riders splashed through the shallows where Bluff Creek empties into the Brazos, and Hector Suarez roused a half-dozen hands to chase the raiders across the river. Later, single shots came from east and west, north and south.

"Farmers shootin' foxes," Pat Cassidy declared. "Nervous cowboys huntin' buffalo ghosts."

Billy was not so sure. He hadn't passed along the news of the raid at Buck Creek. No point to stirring up nightmares, he thought. And yet each time he closed his eyes, Billy relived the terrifying skirmish.

Morning found him bleary-eyed and on edge. The weather had turned cold, and frost coated the buffalo grass. The horses stomping about the corral snorted icy gray clouds, and Billy was reminded of a story his mother had once shared about fire-breath-ing dragons and brave knights on horseback, setting out on noble quests.

Well, he'd found nothing very noble about dying. No one would write a song about little Benny Gardiner or Judge Warren. If anyone was likely to be remembered, it would be the Keelings, or perhaps Coke Merritt. That seemed terribly unfair. It was also very true.

Billy tried to turn his mind to other matters. He sat at the breakfast table, sandwiched between Colleen and her young brother Brian, and listened to Pat Cassidy speak of spring planting. But talk of seeding cornfields or repairing roofs was lost on Billy just then. His mind was miles away, out in the hills searching for Ike Keeling. Even if Pat Cassidy could dismiss the predawn rifle shots as nervous cowboys firing at shadows, Billy knew better.

It's Keeling, he thought.

And when Hector spotted a thin pillar of smoke rising from the far side of the Brazos, he spread the alarm.

"Someone's burnin' the Dunlap place!" Danny Seavers shouted from the corral. "Mr. Justiss!"

Billy bolted from the table and raced out the door, pausing only long enough to throw a buffalo-hide cloak over his shoulders. The other hands were gathering hastily at the corral. Hector had three or four men saddling horses and others loading rifles.

"Hear any·shots?" Billy asked as he reached Hector's side.

"No, but something's burning, Billy," Hector explained. "Could be a barn or even the house."

"Not just a prairie fire?"

"As wet as this grass is?" Hector asked, bending over and snatching a few blades of buffalo grass in his hand. "We heard 'em at the river last night."

"All right," Billy said, scanning the crowd. Most of the veteran cowboys were guarding the far-flung stretches of Flying J range. Mitch and Ben Cook were already over at the Dunlap place, helping Jared guard the ranch from attack. Some others were down south with Marty and Ryan. Way too many of the ones left were too young to have been in a real fight before or else were too old to be a lot of use in the one that lay ahead.

"Who's going?" Hector asked.

"You, me, four or five others," Billy said. "Who would you choose?"

"To take or to leave?"

"Take," Billy said. "Danny can ride down and tell Wes to manage the others. Could be Keeling's trying to draw us off."

"I thought of that, too. You haven't heard from Lafe Freeman?"

"No," Billy grumbled. "So who would you take?"

"Well, Walt Hogan and Kit Foote for certain. The Mackenzie brothers, too. And Tonio Valasquez."

"Tonio's young."

"Seventeen. He does what he's told, though, and he could ride through a hailstorm."

"All right, then. Let's get 'em mounted and head out," Billy said, motioning to the horses. "I'll be along in a minute."

He trotted over to the house where Colleen waited with her family. There wasn't time for a long good-bye, but he gripped her hands and gave her a quick kiss on the forehead.

"You should take Sully and Patrick," Pat Cassidy suggested.

"No, you keep 'em here with you," Billy replied. "Wes should be along to organize everybody. Keep your eyes sharp. I wouldn't be surprised if that fire's a trick to draw us off."

"We'll keep the watch," Cassidy promised.

Billy hugged Colleen tightly, then gazed silently into her sad eyes. No words were needed. They both understood he had to go. And they both hoped i' would be a short trip.

Hector led the way to the shallow crossing of the Brazos. A sharp chill greeted them on the northern bank. Billy pointed to the smoke rising from a hillside a quarter mile or so ahead, and Hector waved the others in that direction. As they approached, Billy sniffed the scent of scorched timber. The Dunlap house was up that way, and he shuddered to think that Jared and his aging parents had been set upon by Keeling's raiders.

A hundred yards from the house Mitch Cook appeared in the center of the trail.

"Glad you happened along, Billy," Mitch said, shaking off the effects of exhaustion. "We've had some trouble."

"Hector saw the smoke," Billy replied. "What sort of trouble?"

"Keeling," Mitch mumbled. "What else?"

Mitch led the way on foot to the smoldering ruin of the Dunlap house. It wasn't the first time Joe and

Irene Dunlap had been burned out. Twice before, Comanche raiders had torched their cabins. This time, though, Billy felt responsible. Perhaps he should have sent others to watch the isolated ranch.

Billy shuddered when he saw Irene Dunlap tending her wounded husband in the shelter of a small grove of live oaks. Jared and Ben Cook stood nearby, keeping watch on the boulder-studded land to the north and west.

Billy rolled off his horse and trotted to where Joe Dunlap lay.

"How is he?" Billy asked anxiously. "Hurt bad?"

"Been worse," Irene answered. Ma Dunlap, as most in the county called her, had tended too many fevers and extracted too many bullets to be easily shaken. And yet the sight of old Joe's suffering painted a heavy frown on her face.

"I'll be all right," Joe grumbled. "Just got a bullet in my hip. It's been broken before."

"Have you got a wagon, Jared?" Billy asked.

"In the barn," Jared answered. "Those snakes ran off most of the horses, but I think there are a couple of mules around back."

"Maybe you should get your papa to town, see Doc Garnett has a look at that hip."

"Ma?" Jared asked.

The old woman nodded, and Jared led the way to the barn. As Billy walked alongside, Jared recounted the morning's events.

"They hit a bit before first light," Jared said, grimly pointing to the open ground just north of the house's smoking timbers. "They were clever about it. Two, maybe three of 'em slipped in and splashed the north wall with coal oil. Then they set it afire. By the time we got everybody clear, the rest of 'em were openin' up a steady rifle fire. Even with the Cook boys along, the best I could manage was to hold 'em off."

"So where are they now?" Billy asked nervously.

"Up in the trees to the northwest, I'd judge."

"How many?"

"A dozen, maybe less. A pair of 'em made a rush at the barn," Jared explained, pointing to the corpse lying fifteen yards short of the big double doors. "Mitch shot that one. He had a bucket o' coal oil in one hand and a torch in the other. Went up like wildfire. Lucky there's no grass over there. Elsewise he'd burned half the ranch."

"And that was the end?"

"Others seemed to lose heart. I figure they'll be back, though."

"They didn't press their attack?"

"Not so I noticed. Billy, they pinned us to the rocks maybe half an hour with rifle fire. Then all of a sudden it stopped. I wouldn't suggest runnin' about in the open just yet. We see somebody stirrin' up there from time to time."

Billy nodded, then accompanied Jared inside the barn. Together they dragged out an old wagon, then cautiously hitched it to a team of reluctant mules.

"This time of year the crossing's pretty tricky. Maybe you'd better take 'em in yourself," Billy suggested as they led the wagon around to where Jared's parents waited.

"Would you leave your place to be defended by somebody else?" Jared asked. "You forded the river

402

all right. Send Tonio."

Billy nodded, then trotted ahead to discuss it with Hector. Shortly a reluctant Tonio Valasquez climbed atop the wagon seat and goaded the mules into action. Ma Dunlap sat in the back with Joe, tending his wound and providing what comfort was possible.

A quarter hour later as Billy was preparing to scout the range to the north, a furious volley of rifle fire erupted from the trees to the left. Bullets whined as they deflected off rocks or splintered trees. Billy quickly sought the shelter of a large sandstone boulder and searched for a target. His companions did likewise.

"We'll finish you this time, Dunlap!" Ike Keeling boasted through the powder smoke. The dampness of the ground held the smoke to the rocky landscape, preventing either side from clearly observing the other.

"Hector, I'm going to swing around to the left," Billy said, reloading his rifle and swallowing the fear now surfacing in his throat. "Spread the others out between here and the barn."

"Wait up," Jared called. "I'm goin' with you."

Billy reluctantly nodded, and Hector began moving the remaining cowboys so as to guard the barn.

"Try not to shoot us," Jared warned as he passed the Mackenzies and slipped past Billy. "As for you, Billy Justiss, follow me. I know this country a lot better'n you do."

Billy had to agree, and so he followed Jared into the swirling haze ahead. Together they crept through the junipers and past snarls of pencil cactus and vicious briars. Thorns tore at their knees, and occa-

403

sionally a wild rifle shot shattered a limb overhead, driving them to cover. Finally, though, they emerged on a hillside two hundred yards from the others. Just ahead and a bit below, Ike Keeling was organizing a charge.

"Well?" Billy whispered, pointing to a pile of boulders ahead and just behind Keeling.

Jared nodded, then wove his way through rocks and trees to the spot. Billy followed silently. Then, rising as one, they emptied their rifles into the unsuspecting raiders.

It took just a few minutes to empty the Winchester's magazine. Jared fired his carbine only slightly slower. The cluster of men below them flew in every direction. Some cried in terror. Others screamed as bullets splintered bone or carved through vital organs. Ike Keeling cursed loudly as he led those who could manage toward the north. Then, as quick as lightning, the boulders became the target for every raider.

"Lord help us now," Billy prayed as he fought to reload his rifle. Shots tore at the fragile sandstone, breaking loose slivers and dislodging corners. There was little chance to return the fire, and no hope of escaping.

Jared knew it, too. Billy read the fierce defiance in his friend's eyes. But desperation often provided new strength, and Billy found himself strangely calm and relaxed. When he heard footsteps racing toward them, he popped up and blasted the first figure to the earth. Jared hit the second, and the third was caught in a wicked crossfire as somebody opened up in Keeling's rear. In seconds, the remaining raiders took off like scared pups.

"Who is it?" Jared asked. "Do you see anybody?"

"No," Billy said, staring through the haze in wonder as another raider toppled to the ground.

"Let's join the party," Jared said, nudging Billy onward. Billy held his friend back, though. There were too many rifles firing in far too many directions. In a few minutes, though, the commotion died down. Billy released Jared's arm, and the two of them made their way cautiously toward the fallen raiders just ahead. Two lay lifeless near the rocks. Another held a bleeding abdomen fifty feet away. A fourth and a fifth were in the trees, shot to pieces by the mysterious gunmen from the far right.

The mystery was soon solved, though. Lafe Freeman and Malachi Johnson appeared, dragging still another corpse from the woods.

"I sure am glad to see you two," Billy said, sighing. "It settles my mind some. I've been worried Keeling caught up with you."

"Did, once or twice," Malachi admitted. "We're too slippery for him."

"You got to be a little crazy, Billy Justiss," Lafe then scolded. "We hadn't happened by, you'd been dead sure. Didn't your daddy ever teach you not to get yourselves cut off?"

Billy shook his head and grinned while Jared disarmed the surviving outlaw.

"We get Keeling?" Jared asked.

"No," Malachi said, frowning. "I saw him get clear. Got some of his friends, though."

"I wouldn't rest too easy," Lafe grumbled. "Keeling had maybe a dozen men with him. We cut that

405

to half — for the minute. He split off Solomon Saturday, sent him off with five or six others. Still leaves him a fair company when they all get back together, and only the Lord know where they've headed."

"He'll have a long wait for Solomon," Billy said. "Marty and I killed him down at Buck Creek. Shot up the rest pretty good, too, and there's a bounty man name of Parkinson chasing 'em."

"Amos Parkinson? Old buffalo hunter?" Lafe asked.

"That's him," Billy answered.

"Don't give those fellows much thought, then," Lafe declared. "They'll get rounded up easy enough."

"Which brings us back to Keeling," Jared said sourly. "When do we go after him?"

"First, we'd better find you a horse," Billy pointed out. "Then we can head out."

"Not for a bit," Lafe advised. "You don't chase after a grizzly right off. He's liable to turn and carve you up some. Besides, I feel a storm comin'. Best store up supplies and get some fresh shot."

"Seems wise," Billy agreed. "We can go back to the ranch or send word for Wes to bring us what we need."

"We got some buryin' to do, too," Malachi muttered. "And this one's best sent to town."

"No point," Lafe said, glancing down at the bleeding raider. "Belly wound. Won't make the trip."

The outlaw gazed up with hateful eyes, but it was true enough. Besides, no Palo Pinto jury would allow a raider to escape the hangman's noose.

"So?" Billy asked.

"I'll get some spades from the barn," Jared told them. "If you don't mind restin' on hay, you're welcome to stable your horses and wait out the storm."

"I'll have Hector tend to the burials," Billy added. "Kit Foote can ride back with word of what's happened. I'd judge Bret might want to join the pursuit."

"I'd welcome him," Lafe said. "Only be sure he understands what we're about. I'll offer Keeling no terms, no chance to get off the first shot."

Only now did Billy notice the awkward way Lafe held his left arm. A bulge under his buffalo hide coat hinted of a bandage. So Keeling hadn't been idle while Solomon was attacking Buck Creek.

"Agreed," Billy said, motioning toward the barn. Jared and Malachi leaned over and brought the wounded raider along. Together they walked down the hill and rejoined Hector and the others.

Chapter Seven

Bret Pruett arrived at the Dunlap place that afternoon with a week's supplies and boxes of fresh rifle ammunition tied to two pack horses. Bret also brought word that news of the Keeling raids at Buck Creek and the Dunlap ranch had stirred the people to anger.

"All this is from Art Stanley," Bret explained. "Others are riding out to watch the railroad stations, and some have wired friends and relatives to be on the lookout."

Luis Morales summed up the feeling of many in the county when he brought a dozen fresh horses out that evening.

"Ma Dunlap brought my babies into the world," Luis reminded everyone. "The Dunlaps help everyone. These killers must be brought to judgment!"

Between dusk and the following morning the skies deposited an inch of snow on the countryside. Brisk winds sent the temperature dropping into the teens.

Even so, some thirty riders appeared at the Dunlap barn to join the posse. J. C. Parnell led a delegation of farmers. Pat Cassidy was there with Sully and Patrick. Even old Art Stanley arrived, bringing along a handful of his teamsters. Tucker Spears rode up with five of the older orphans from Buck Creek. Alex Tuttle did his best to corral the angry riders, but they were obviously in a poor humor.

"We don't need an army," Bret explained as he fought to fend off the bitter cold. "Stay home and guard your families. Watch the roads. This Keeling is a sly character, and he could well cross the river and double back on us."

"He won't cross the river anywhere between here and Albany," Albert Parnell declared. "A man'd freeze in no time, what with this wind and all. We used the bridge on the Jacksboro road. He'd have to wade the Brazos."

"It wasn't this cold, yesterday, though," Billy explained. "Maybe we should send a group south toward Potter's City. That's where Merrick went."

"And why Keeling won't," Lafe declared. "It wouldn't hurt to scout out that area, though, check the depots, then ride on toward Albany."

"Tut, you take ten men," Bret suggested. "This weather turns worse, though, you get to cover. Understand?"

"I know all about cold weather," Alex Tuttle answered. "I was born up north, remember?"

"Maybe," Bret admitted, "but you've been a Texan a long time now. Besides, you'll have others with you. We can probably use ten men ourselves. But the others, especially you men with farms in the southern part of the county, would be a lot more help staying close to home and watching the back trails and creek bottoms."

The others reluctantly agreed, and after Tut selected his ten, most of the others set off homeward. With that much settled, Bret, Billy, Jared, Lafe, and Wes Tyler gathered in a kind of council of war to make plans for stalking Ike Keeling north of the Brazos. The first problem was finding the outlaw.

"There are what, twenty of us?" Wes asked. "If we split into smaller groups, say four or five, we can fan out, find Keeling's trail. No way he could hide it in this snow."

"He could've ridden a long way yesterday, though," Billy reminded Wes. "It's best we have an idea where to look."

"If they're on this side of the river, they pretty much have to break back north," Lafe pointed out. He then sketched a map of sorts in the dirt floor of the barn, showing the river and notable creeks in the vacinity of the Dunlap ranch.

"They could head toward old Fort Belknap, then on toward the Nations," Bret declared. "Or west along the river toward Albany. I can't see 'em headed east, not with them knowing we'll alert the sheriffs up that way."

Wes argued they would double around eastward, then cross the county to Justiss Junction and take the railroad to El Paso. And Jared suspected they might take refuge in the remains of Fort Griffin. Billy closed his eyes a moment and tried to imagine what Keeling would try.

"You're all of you wrong," Billy finally announced. "He won't go far. He's not finished with us."

"What?" Bret cried.

"Look at what he's done!" Billy shouted. "He bought land next to the ranch, hired killers to drive off our friends, to shoot us. He fought us in court, paid newspapers to print lies, and that was because Jared shot his no-account brother up on the Cimarron years back. Now look what's happened. He's had his two boys shot. He might not know about Solomon for certain yet, but he will. Keeling's gone to too much trouble on this to let go now. He won't be headed for El Paso or anywhere else. We ought to go look at his ranch first, then scout out the abandoned farms up on Rock Creek."

"He's right," Lafe agreed. "I've seen this Keeling, and his eyes just don't have runnin' in 'em. There's no fear, friends. He's close-by, all right. Revenge drives a man. Well, it can turn back on him sometimes, too, and it sure has this time."

"So, how do we do it?" Bret asked.

"Split up like Wes says," Lafe advised. "Make sure there's a steady hand or two with each group."

"I'd say Wes ought to have a look on the Keeling place," Billy said, nervously gazing southward. "I don't like the notion they could be so close to my family, and they'd be even closer to Alice and the Tyler kids."

"I'll grab Toby and set off right away," Wes said, starting for the door.

"And if they are?" Bret asked.

"I'll send Toby to the ranch, have him bring help. Parnell's bunch will come, and the Cassidys."

"If not, you stay there and keep watch," Billy instructed. "I'd bet they're up at Rock Creek in that case, and we'll do our best to snag the whole bunch. If they get away, though, they're sure to head for familiar ground."

"Seems likely enough," Wes agreed before leaving.

"Now, the rest of us," Billy said, gazing at his companions. It was quickly decided that Malachi and Lafe would take the Cooks and Walt Hogan up north and scout out the region near old Fort Belknap. Bret, the Mackenzie brothers, Luis Morales and Tonio Valasquez would search the three farms on the west bank of Rock Creek. Billy and Jared, together with two of Art Stanley's veteran teamsters, Frank Newland and Stan Gordon, would search the two farms on the east bank.

Outside the barn, the men were more than eager to set off. The wind had died down some, but the air remained frigid, and inactivity stiffened bones and froze a man's vitals. Bret distributed the extra supplies, and those men lacking good mounts drew one of the horses Luis had brought along for that purpose.

Most of the riders who found themselves not needed were more than eager to return home. Others, however, remained, including young Tucker Spears and his orphan friends.

"This isn't a job for youngsters," Billy told the boys. "We buried one of you day before yesterday. I won't do that again."

"I don't plan to get myself killed, Mr. Justiss," a dark-haired boy with bright chestnut eyes and a determined frown spoke up.

"Mr. Justiss, I been shot at, had my head cracked, and seen my friends shot from ambush," Tucker Spears added. "I figure I got a right to get even."

"Well," Billy said, sighing. "you proved you can fight . . . and think, Tuck. But these others should go home."

"That's fine for those farmboys," the dark-haired boy argued, "but the closest thing I got to a home is that bunkhouse back at Buck Creek. I got a right to defend it, don't I? I liked Benny Gardiner. Don't you think we know who had him killed?"

"I know how you feel," Billy admitted, "but you boys don't know what this'll be like. It's no schoolboy's game, you know. It's going to be mean and fast, and people will get killed. Can you kill a man, son?"

"I can," the youngster declared.

"It's more than that," Jared told the orphans. "When a man rides into a battle, he needs to know the rest of his company can be relied on. Shoot, we don't even know your names."

"I'm Val Masters," the dark-haired boy spoke up. "I'm fifteen years old. Fifteen, going on fifty. That's how Mr. Ryan says it. I've shot deer and rabbits for our table."

"And men?" Billy asked.

"Yes," the boy said grimly. "The first time, I was ten. A deserter from Fort Richardson broke into our house. He took a knife after my sister, and I shot him. I got one of the bandits that hit the work train just south of here back in '81. I know what to do, and I'm not afraid to do it."

Billy looked into the eyes suddenly grown dark

413

and determined, then motioned toward the horses and nodded his head.

"How 'bout us?" the three remaining boys asked.

"You go back to town, wait in the sheriff's office," Billy told them. "That way if we need you, we'll know where to look."

"Can't we —" the first began.

"No!" Billy replied angrily. "Now get along with you before I cut a switch. Go!"

Any resemblance the bands of riders might have had to heroes setting out on some noble quest soon faded. The wind blew icy driplets of spray in their faces, and even Billy, bundled in his heavy cloak, shivered. He tried not to think of the boys riding at the end of the line. But maybe an hour of frostbitten fingers and frozen toes would send them back.

Billy doubted that. Tucker had more grit than sense, and young Masters appeared cut from the same cloth. And as they wound their way through the snow-coated rocks and trees northwestward toward Rock Creek, Billy glanced back once or twice. The same fire filled the two young riders' eyes that danced in Jared's. The teamsters, Newland and Gordon, had no such enthusiasm for the expedition. But Billy somehow trusted their reluctance, knowing they wouldn't rush into an ambush or prematurely betray their position.

Once they passed the hills bordering the Dunlap ranch and passed into the broad flatlands cut by Rock Creek, Billy had his crew fan out so that they could search the snowy grassland for tracks. None appeared to the west or east, so Billy swung due north toward the creek. The first of the abandoned farms lay two miles distant, the old Worrell place. Doug Worrell had given up on his drought-stricken acres and set off for the Dakotas. There were no tracks out that way, though, and the house was boarded shut as securely as ever.

"Check out the barn," Billy told Jared. Billy himself inspected the house. He concentrated on the boarded doors and windows, examining the boards and nails for sign of tampering. None appeared. Jared found no sign of visitors in the barn, either.

"Wish there was somebody still livin' here," Jared lamented. "Good hot cup of coffee would sure taste good about right now."

"Sure would," Tucker agreed.

"Cold?" Billy asked.

"No more'n an icicle," the young cowboy replied, managing a smile through chattering teeth.

"When we get to the North place, we'll stop for a time," Billy told them. "Unless Keeling's there, of course. We can build a fire, brew some coffee, and get you boys warmed up a bit."

"We're all right," Val declared.

"Sure you are," Jared said. "That's why your nose and ears are purple."

Billy just shook his head and waved them along. About a half mile short of the North farm they saw the first sign of riders. Tracks of six, maybe seven horses appeared in the snow. Billy motioned a halt, and Jared bent down to have a closer look.

"They rode out this way, Billy," Jared said, pointing to a trail or tracks circling around from the

415

northeast. "Seems like they were lookin' for something."

"Or somebody," Billy noted. "Might be they were searching for Solomon."

"Well, let's see where they headed," Jared suggested.

Billy nodded, then motioned for the others to spread out. He had no intention of riding into an ambush. After continuing a quarter mile he saw smoke rising from the North house's chimney.

"Well, we know where some of 'em are, anyway," Jared remarked. "What now?"

"Take the boys up into the trees," Billy said sourly. "See if you can find a hollow where a fire won't give us away."

"All this snow's bound to wet the wood," Jared argued. "Smoke's bound to show, Billy, and sound carries for miles in this bottomland."

"I know. Do what you can. I'm going to scout a bit. I'll send one of the teamsters after the others."

"Better to send Tuck," Jared objected. "These fellows aren't used to ridin,' and they don't know the lay of the land. Besides, nobody's goin' to mistake Tuck for one of those raiders."

"Then, I guess Gordon and Newland ought to go with you. I'll take Tucker."

"Got a better idea. Let's you and me scout the trail and leave the others to make a camp."

"They'll give us away," Billy objected.

"Those fellows down in that house aren't lookin' past their own noses, Billy. One of us can keep an eye on the door. Anybody tryin' to escape can get himself shot."

"All right," Billy mumbled. He then drew the others together and passed along the news. Tucker and Val voiced complaints, but the teamsters were eager to get to cover. In the end, the boys went along.

Billy and Jared circled around the North place, cautiously concealing their own tracks within the outlaws' trail or else keeping to the tree-cluttered hillsides.

"See there," Jared said, pointing to tracks merging with the main body from the north. "He's got company."

"Then, we better find out how many of 'em are in there, where they are, and then get some help."

"You plannin' to creep in there and ask 'em, Billy?"

"Watch me," Billy said, grinning as he slid off his horse. "Only keep your rifle handy."

Billy then crept through the trees and slipped around behind the barn. He peered through the dirty side window, saw no sign of life, and decided to slip inside. Keeling had quartered no guards in the place. Ten horses pranced nervously in stalls. No hay or water had been provided for the animals, and Billy angrily cursed the raiders for failing to tend their own mounts. Then, fearing even now someone might be en route to the barn to do just that, he made his way back outside, then crept up to the house.

Carson North hadn't bothered to board his windows. He, too, had set off for greener pastures, but he hadn't paid the taxes on his property and thus didn't care if the house had any value to its next occupants or not. The windows were all on the front and back walls, so Billy was able to approach from the side without being noticed. He then crawled along the back wall and listened. Inside, men were laughing and shouting. Their conversation concerned a card game. No one seemed to be guarding against intruders.

Billy carefully stood up and glimpsed inside. His first impression had been a mistake. A pair of riflemen watched the front from the twin windows. A third paced back and forth along the back wall. By mere chance the guard was looking the other way at the moment Billy glanced inside.

He quickly slipped back along the side, then retraced his steps to the barn and back to the trees.

"I couldn't count 'em all," Billy told Jared, "but there are ten horses in the barn. I'd guess that many men in the house. Let's get Tuck started. I want to have this done with."

"I'll stay and watch the door," Jared said. "If you cook some supper, I wouldn't mind a bit of something hot."

"I'll bring it along," Billy promised, mounting his horse and heading back to where the others were no doubt making camp.

It wasn't hard to locate the camp. Billy merely followed the scent of frying bacon and boiling coffee. Billy accepted a cup and sipped the reviving liquid. He then sketched a brief map and handed it to Tucker Spears.

"Follow the creek along to the Jackson place,"

418

Billy explained. "I'd guess by now Bret'll have his group there. Just follow their trail from there."

"I'll be back fast as I can," Tucker promised. "Don't worry. I've been out there before."

"Be careful," Billy told the boy. "I think Keeling's band is all inside, but there could be a stray or two."

Tucker nodded, then headed for his horse. Billy filled a small bag with slabs of fried bacon and two slices of bread, then poured coffee in a canteen.

"Keep an eye out for trouble," he warned the others, then climbed atop his horse and rode back to where Jared kept watch over the outlaw camp.

"Bless you, Billy Justiss," Jared said, accepting the food.

"Anything stirring?"

"Nary a twig."

"Good," Billy declared, dismounting and joining his old friend behind a pile of rocks. "Maybe we're finally going to settle this."

"Yes," Jared agreed. "Finally."

Chapter Eight

They kept watch nearly two hours on that wind-swept hillside, fending off the cold and staring down at the peaceful house that would soon become a battlefield. A little short of three in the afternoon, Val Masters appeared with word that Lafe Freeman had arrived with his band. He, Malachi, and the others were warming themselves at the fire and would soon be along. A half hour later Tucker brought Bret's group up. The others rode up shortly.

"Listen up," Bret told them all. "I want to do this the easy way. Lafe, you take your men behind the barn, then split up. Half take that rise down by the creek. The rest use the barn as cover."

"Be sure you keep 'em from getting' to their horses," Jared added. "Nobody gets away. Understand?"

The others nodded, but Bret was less than pleased and said so.

"If they'll give up, I'd rather take 'em captive,"

Bret explained. "It's Keeling we want. We needn't kill everybody."

"They didn't bother to give Benny much of a chance," Val grumbled.

"We're not outlaws," Bret reminded the fifteen-year-old. "Besides, I don't have any interest in getting any of us killed."

"We'll watch ourselves, Bret," Billy promised. "You want my bunch to take the side or the back?"

"Luis and I'll circle around the side, try to get in front," Bret explained. "You and Jared take 'em from the rear. Billy, watch these young fools, too. Isn't half-hard to get shot, but it's a hard job patching 'em up, getting 'em well again."

Billy nodded, then paired Tucker with the teamsters and led Val down the hillside with Jared.

At first everything went as planned. Suddenly, though, the back door cracked open, and a raider stepped outside. He stared at the figures creeping toward the house, then raised his rifle and fired.

"Ike, the hill's crawlin' with men!" the guard screamed as he slammed the door shut and cowered behind the window.

Ten feet to Billy's left, Frank Newland had muffled a cry and fallen face first into the snow. Billy never hesitated. He raised his rifle and fired into the house. Seconds later the others cut loose a volley, and the sounds of breaking glass and splintering wood exploded across the valley. In ten minutes the house was shot to pieces, and Bret called a halt to the firing.

"All right, you inside the house!" Bret yelled. "Anybody ready to give up and take his chances in court, step through the back door with your hands up."

A single figure staggered through the door, only to be shot from behind.

"That you out there, Charlie Justiss?" Keeling screamed. "Come on and finish it!"

"We will!" Jared answered, firing his rifle toward the voice.

Bret waved his arms to stop the shooting and repeated his offer to accept Keeling's surrender.

"We'll carry on!" Keeling shouted in answer. "Bound to turn bitter cold out there for you boys, and we'll whittle you down by and by."

Bret shook his head and ordered a resumption of their rifle fire. Again bullets slammed into the walls, tore across the single room, and brought death and destruction. Billy's group on the hillside was especially deadly, for their shots struck down into the house through the open window, undeflected by walls.

For half an hour the house returned a brisk fire. Then it grew sporadic before finally dying out.

Billy looked around him. Nathan Mackenzie lay sprawled in the snow twenty feet from the house. Newland, too, was dead. There was no telling if anyone on the far right or around front was hurt.

"You ready to hit 'em, Billy?" Jared asked.

Billy sadly nodded, then prepared to charge. Val Masters stepped close, eager to follow, but Billy pushed the boy to the ground.

"No, not this time, son," Billy whispered. "Crawl over with Tucker and cover us."

There was no argument from Val. The boy could

see Newland's limp body, could smell the smoke and taste the pain all around him. Or so Billy supposed. He didn't care so long as Val scampered off to safety.

"Ready?" Jared asked.

Billy glanced along the line. Tucker continued firing with calm self-assurance. Gordon huddled behind a boulder and fired off an occasional shot. Val Masters did his best to emulate Tucker, but the battle was taking a toll.

Jared then leaped to his feet and raced toward the house. Billy followed. Two shots met their sudden movement, but both were wide of their target. In answer, Tucker, Val, and Gordon fired from the hillside. Billy slammed against the back door, kicked it open, then blasted away at the two figures crouching behind the front windows. Jared burst through the paneless window and killed the only raider guarding the rear of the house. Two other outlaws made a break for the front door, but were caught in a vicious crossfire.

As the smoke cleared, Billy searched the littered interior of the house for some sign of life. A figure on his left stirred slightly, but the man's back showed evidence of three bullet holes. Surviving such wounds was unlikely, but Billy turned the wounded man over so as to offer what comfort might be managed. The outlaw managed to mumble something, then died.

"Keeling!" Jared shouted, making his way across the room to what appeared to be a pile of blankets. Jared pushed the barrel of his carbine into the center of the pile, then kicked aside the blankets. There lay

Ike Keeling, bleeding from a single wound in the shoulder.

"Bad luck, Keeling," Billy said, stepping over and holding Jared's hands still. "Looks like you'll live to hang."

"Trial's a long way from over," Keeling answered, grinning cruelling. "And I'm not in any jailhouse yet."

"I suppose you could bleed to death," Jared replied. "Or my rifle might go off accidentally."

Bret appeared in the doorway then and took charge. Billy led Jared aside, and the two old friends started up the snowy hillside together. Stan Gordon and Tucker were tying Newland on the back of a horse. Hugh Mackenzie and Luis Morales were doing likewise with Nathan. Lafe Freeman busied himself binding Malachi's wounded left arm. The others appeared unhurt except for a few splinters and a scrape or two.

"So, is it over now?" Billy asked, gazing around him at the war-torn hillside. Blood stained the snow, and the eerie north wind whined a mournful tune.

"Will be soon," Jared said, turning to watch Bret escort a handcuffed Ike Keeling to a waiting horse. "Soon."

Epilogue

No high-priced lawyer appeared to defend Ike Keeling. No sympathetic newspaper reporters stirred up support. The trial was short, and the verdict simple. On the first day of February, Isaac Keeling was sentenced to be hung.

Most of the county turned out for the occasion. School was dismissed, and shops closed. Visitors from as far away as Austin stood beside the scaffold and watched Keeling dragged up the steps. There was nothing dignified about the event. The outlaw cursed his accusers and threatened anyone within earshot. When the trap was finally sprung, though, he fell like a rock and died quickly.

Charlie Justiss wasn't there. There were those who

questioned the absence of the county judge at Palo Pinto's most famous hanging, but Charlie declared there'd been too many deaths, and he found no solace in the hanging of the man who had brought that dark violent hour to his beloved Brazos.

Instead Charlie rode along the river to the high cliffs, to that place where old Stands Tall had made his final stand. The Comanche had fought long and hard, but in spite of it all Charlie had always had a grudging respect for him. No such respect existed where Ike Keeling was concerned.

When Charlie reached the cliffs, he found his son Billy waiting near the steep footpath that led to the heights.

"I thought you might be out this way today," Billy said. "I guess they've hung Keeling, eh?"

"This morning," Charlie said as he dismounted. "Can't say I get much satisfaction from it."

"No. We lost some good friends. And some lost even more."

Charlie frowned as he followed his son's eyes westward. He remembered the Weidlings, too. Ike Keeling had added graves to the cemetery. Jordy Banks lay there. And little Benny Gardiner had been murdered down at Buck Creek!

"Seems like it's been a long winter," Charlie finally said. "I'll be ready for spring."

"Me, too, Papa. Want some company on the climb?"

"Sure, son. Fact is, I thought to bring Viktor and

Jake up here next time. Maybe the weather will warm up, and little Charlie can come, too."

Billy nodded, then led the way up the path. When they reached the top, Charlie took his son's hand. Together they stepped to the edge and let the brisk February wind tear at their coats.

"Papa, what is it about this place that makes it special?" Billy asked.

"I don't know that it's possible to put it into words," Charlie whispered, gazing below at the river that had been so much of his life. "It's a high place. Maybe that's why the Indians put their dead here. It's as close as a man can get around here to touching the clouds."

"When I stand up here, I can look out and see the whole country."

"And more," Charlie said, grasping Billy's shoulder. "I see old Stands Tall, the longhorns, every triumph and sadness that's come my way these last long thirteen years. I see a small boy sweating with fever brought on by a rattlesnake bite. I see him a year or so older setting out for Kansas with a thousand contrary longhorns. More than that, I see the future. I see you and Colleen and the children you'll one day bring up here to tell of how the Justisses came and built and survived."

"I will, too," Billy promised.

"I know that, son. It's the legacy I'd leave you."

And when they started back down the steep path a

half hour later, Charlie felt rare pride—in the ranch he'd carved out of hill and ravine, in the county he had nurtured to maturity, and in the family he and Angela had raised to carry on.

BEST OF THE WEST
from Zebra Books

THOMPSON'S MOUNTAIN   (2042, $3.95)
by G. Clifton Wisler

Jeff Thompson was a boy of fifteen when his pa refused to sell out his mountain to the Union Pacific and got gunned down in return, along with the boy's mother. Jeff fled to Colorado, but he knew he'd even the score with the railroad man who had his parents killed . . . and either death or glory was at the end of the vengeance trail he'd blaze!

BROTHER WOLF   (1728, $2.95)
by Dan Parkinson

Only two men could help Lattimer run down the sheriff's killers—a stranger named Stillwell and an Apache who was as deadly with a Colt as he was with a knife. One of them would see justice done—from the muzzle of a six-gun.

BLOOD ARROW   (1549, $2.50)
by Dan Parkinson

Randall Kerry returned to his camp to find his companion slaughtered and scalped. With a war cry as wild as the savages,' the young scout raced forward with his pistol held high to meet them in battle.

THUNDERLAND   (1991, $3.50)
by Dan Parkinson

Men were suddenly dying all around Jonathan, and he needed to know why—before he became the next bloody victim of the ancient sword that would shape the future of the Texas frontier.

APACHE GOLD   (1899, $2.95)
by Mark K. Roberts & Patrick E. Andrews

Chief Halcon burned with a fierce hatred for the pony soldiers that rode from Fort Dawson, and vowed to take the scalp of every round-eye in the territory. Sergeant O'Callan must ride to glory or death for peace on the new frontier.

Available wherever paperbacks are sold, or order direct from the Publisher. Send cover price plus 50¢ per copy for mailing and handling to Zebra Books, Dept. 2257, 475 Park Avenue South, New York, N.Y. 10016. Residents of New York, New Jersey and Pennsylvania must include sales tax. DO NOT SEND CASH.

THE UNTAMED WEST
brought to you by Zebra Books

ILLINOIS PRESCOTT   (2142, $2.50)
by G. Clifton Wisler
Darby Prescott was just fourteen when he and his family left Illinois and joined the wagon train west. Ahead lay endless miles of
the continent's rawest terrain . . . and as Cheyenne war whoops
split the air, Darby knew the farmboy from Illinois had been left
behind, and whatever lay ahead would be written in hot lead and
blood.

TOMBSTONE LODE   (1915, $2.95)
by Doyle Trent
When the Josey mine caved in on Buckshot Dobbs, he left behind
a rich vein of Colorado gold—but no will. James Alexander,
hired to investigate Buckshot's self-proclaimed blood relations
learns too soon that he has one more chance to solve the mystery
and save his skin or become another victim of TOMBSTONE
LODE.

LONG HENRY   (2155, $2.50)
by Robert Kammen
Long Henry Banner was marshal of Waco and a confirmed bach-
elor—until the day Cassandra stepped off the stagecoach. A week
later they were man and wife. And then Henry got bushwhacked
by a stranger and when he was back on his feet, his new wife was
gone. It would take him seven years to track her down . . . to
learn her secret that was sealed with gunpowder and blood!

GALLOWS RIDERS   (1934, $2.50)
by Mark K. Roberts
When Stark and his killer-dogs reached Colby, all it took was a
little muscle and some well-placed slugs to run roughshod over
the small town—until the avenging stranger stepped out of the
shadows for one last bloody showdown.

DEVIL WIRE   (1937, $2.50)
by Cameron Judd
They came by night, striking terror into the hearts of the settlers.
The message was clear: Get rid of the devil wire or the land would
turn red with fencestringer blood. It was the beginning of a brutal
range war.

*Available wherever paperbacks are sold, or order direct from the
Publisher. Send cover price plus 50¢ per copy for mailing and
handling to Zebra Books, Dept. 2257, 475 Park Avenue South,
New York, N.Y. 10016. Residents of New York, New Jersey and
Pennsylvania must include sales tax. DO NOT SEND CASH.*

WHITE SQUAW
Zebra's Adult Western Series
by E. J. Hunter

Available wherever paperbacks are sold, or order direct from the Publisher. Send cover price plus 50¢ per copy for mailing and handling to Zebra Books, Dept. 2257, 475 Park Avenue South, New York, N.Y. 10016. Residents of New York, New Jersey and Pennsylvania must include sales tax. DO NOT SEND CASH.

SWEET MEDICINE'S PROPHECY
by Karen A. Bale

#1: SUNDANCER'S PASSION   (1778, $3.95)

Stalking Horse was the strongest and most desirable of the tribe, and Sun Dancer surrounded him with her spell-binding radiance. But the innocence of their love gave way to passion—and passion, to betrayal. Would their relationship ever survive the ultimate sin?

#2: LITTLE FLOWER'S DESIRE   (1779, $3.95)

Taken captive by savage Crows, Little Flower fell in love with the enemy, handsome brave Young Eagle. Though their hearts spoke what they could not say, they could only dream of what could never be. . . .

#4: SAVAGE FURY   (1768, $3.95)

Aeneva's rage knew no bounds when her handsome mate Trent commanded her to tend their tepee as he rode into danger. But under cover of night, she stole away to be with Trent and share whatever perils fate dealt them.

#5: SUN DANCER'S LEGACY   (1878, $3.95)

Aeneva's and Trenton's adopted daughter Anna becomes the light of their lives. As she grows into womanhood, she falls in love with blond Steven Randall. Together they discover the secrets of their passion, the bitterness of betrayal—and fight to fulfill the prophecy that is Anna's birthright.

Available wherever paperbacks are sold, or order direct from the Publisher. Send cover price plus 50¢ per copy for mailing and handling to Zebra Books, Dept. 2257, 475 Park Avenue South, New York, N.Y. 10016. Residents of New York, New Jersey and Pennsylvania must include sales tax. DO NOT SEND CASH.